/ ... meshift

st

Aurora Award finalist

Seiun Award winner

"An exciting action-packed medical thriller that grips the audience from the moment readers meet Pierre and never slows down until the final twist. Readers will finish this thriller in one exciting sitting."

—*Alternative-Worlds.com*

"You hardly need me to tell you to buy Robert J. Sawyer's latest novel, ***Frameshift***. You know it's good, interesting, and thought provoking. The issues Sawyer is dealing with are not easy ones, but he builds an effective story from them."

—*Analog Science Fiction and Fact*

"Sawyer uses brief, punchy chapters (like some of the Heinlein novels I recall). You'll find yourself sucked in and unable to put it down until you reach the end. An engaging read."

—*Artemis Magazine*

"An unputdownable thriller."

—*Booklist*

"Exciting and engrossing."

—*Kirkus*

"A finely crafted novel with a riveting plot and complex characters, deftly exploring issues of bio-ethics and moral philosophy. By using the metaphor of a murder investigation, told in parallel to the scientific activities of his main character, Sawyer succeeds in illuminating aspects of science as a human activity. Sawyer's is a rather hopeful vision. Perhaps this is his Canadian upbringing showing, a belief in the potential of civil society to overcome the narrow interests of profit and bigotry to create a better world. Sawyer sees the dark sides of technological change and globalization, yet remains hopeful that we, as a society, can overcome them. After reading ***Frameshift***, so do I."

—The Calgary Herald

"This book should be a major novel for a larger audience than the one which visits the science fiction section: a moving, exciting, touching, suspense-laden wonder. I cannot recommend it more highly. Sawyer has my vote for the next Nebula and Hugo awards."

—Barnes and Noble's *Explorations*

"A gripping medical SF thriller. Highly recommended." (Included on ***Library Journal***'s list of the five best SF novels of the year.)

—Library Journal

"Very thought-provoking, well done characters, great suspense, very believable."

—SF Signal

"Robert J. Sawyer is a writer of boundless confidence. ***Frameshift*** is filled to bursting with ideas, characters, incident, and page after page of bold scientific extrapolation."

—***The New York Times***

"Fine writing, engaging characters, convincing science, and a detailed, if horrific, historical background."

—***Starlog***

Praise for Robert J. Sawyer

"A new Robert J. Sawyer book is always cause for celebration."

—*Analog Science Fiction and Fact*

"Sawyer not only has an irresistibly engaging narrative voice but also a gift for confronting thorny philosophical conundrums. At every opportunity, he forces his readers to think while holding their attention with ingenious premises and superlative craftsmanship."

—*Booklist*

"Can Sawyer write? Yes—with near-Asimovian clarity, with energy and drive, with such grace that his writing becomes invisible as the story comes to life in your mind."

—**Orson Scott Card**, author of *Ender's Game*

"Robert J. Sawyer is by any measure one of the world's leading (and most interesting) science-fiction writers. His fiction is a fascinating blend of intellectually compelling big ideas and humane, enduring characters."

—*The Globe and Mail*

"Sawyer is Canada's answer to Michael Crichton."

—*The Toronto Star*

"Sawyer, an articulate fountain of ideas, is the genre's northern star—in fact, one of the hottest SF writers anywhere. By any reckoning Sawyer is among the most successful Canadian authors ever."

—*Maclean's: Canada's National Magazine*

"Sawyer's books—always rich in science, action, and profound thinking—never fail to surprise, delight, and cause us to transcend our ordinary thinking. I've read Crichton, Asimov, Heinlein, Clarke, King, and Koontz—and Sawyer outdoes them all."

—**Clifford A. Pickover**, author of ***Time: A Traveler's Guide***

"A polished, exciting writer. Sawyer writes with the scientific panache and grandeur of Arthur C. Clarke and the human touch of Isaac Asimov."

—*Quill & Quire*

"Cracking open a new Robert J. Sawyer book is like getting a gift from a friend who visits all the strange and undiscovered places in the world. You can't wait to see what he's going to amaze you with this time."

—**John Scalzi**, author of ***Old Man's War***

"No reader seeking well-written stories that respect, emphasize and depend on modern science should be disappointed by the works of Rob Sawyer."

—***The Washington Post***

"Sawyer is a terrific writer. He can write about the most sophisticated science while giving readers the room to understand what's happening and follow the plot."

—***Winnipeg Free Press***

Novels by Robert J. Sawyer

Golden Fleece
End of an Era
The Terminal Experiment
Starplex
Frameshift
Illegal Alien
Factoring Humanity
FlashForward
Calculating God
Mindscan
Rollback
Triggers
Red Planet Blues
Quantum Night
The Oppenheimer Alternative

The Quintaglio Ascension Trilogy

Far-Seer
Fossil Hunter
Foreigner

The Neanderthal Parallax Trilogy

Hominids
Humans
Hybrids

The WWW Trilogy

Wake
Watch
Wonder

For book-club discussion guides, visit **sfwriter.com**

FRAMESHIFT

ROBERT J. SAWYER

SFWRITER.COM Inc.

FRAMESHIFT

Cover and interior: Bibliofic Designs

SFWRITER.COM Inc.
Mississauga, Ontario, Canada

ISBN (Print): 978-1-988415-25-3
ISBN (Kindle): 978-1-988415-04-5
ISBN (ePub): 978-1-988415-04-8

Frameshift is available as an audiobook from Audible

sfwriter.com

Dedication

For Terence M. Green and Merle Casci,
with thanks and friendship

Acknowledgments

Sincere thanks to my agent, **Ralph Vicinanza**; my editor at Tor, **David G. Hartwell**; **Tad Dembinski**, also of Tor; **Jane Johnson** of HarperCollins UK; **Catherine Brown**, M.D., F.R.C.S.(C), obstetrician and gynecologist; **David E. Gilbert**, Life Sciences Division, Lawrence Berkeley National Laboratory; **David Gotlib**, M.D., Resident, Department of Psychiatry, The Johns Hopkins Hospital, Baltimore, Maryland; **Robert A. Hegele**, M.D., F.R.C.P.(C), Division of Endocrinology and Metabolism, St. Michael's Hospital, University of Toronto; **Isla Horvath**, Director of Communications, Huntington Society of Canada; **Joe S. Mymryk**, Ph.D., London Regional Cancer Centre, London, Ontario; **Ariel Reich**, Ph.D., who was my host during my visit to the University of California, Berkeley, and who tracked down follow-up information after I left; and the late Nobel laureate **Luis W. Alvarez**, Ph.D., who graciously allowed me to visit him at the Lawrence Berkeley Laboratory.

Many thanks also to: **Michael** and **Nomi Burstein**; **Stephen P. Conners**; **Richard Curtis**; **Marina Frants**; **Peter Halasz**; **Howard Miller**; **Amy Victoria Meo**; **Lorraine Pooley**; and **Jean-Louis Trudel**.

And, as always, I'm indebted to my regular group of incisive manuscript readers: **Asbed Bedrossian**, **Ted Bleaney**, **David Livingstone Clink**, **Richard M. Gotlib**, **Terence M. Green**, **Alan B. Sawyer**, **Edo van Belkom**, **Andrew Weiner**, and, most of all, my lovely wife, **Carolyn Clink**.

Prologue

It is better to be hated for what you are than to be loved for what you are not.

—**André Gide,**
winner of the 1947 Nobel Prize in literature

Berkeley, California

The Present Day

It seemed an unlikely place to die.

During the academic year, twenty-three thousand full-time students milled about the well-treed grounds of the University of California, Berkeley. But on this cool June night, the campus was mostly empty.

Pierre Tardivel reached out for the hand of Molly Bond. He was a good-looking, wiry man of thirty-three, with narrow shoulders, a round head, and hair the same chocolate brown as his eyes. Molly, who would turn thirty-three herself in a couple of weeks, was beautiful—stunningly so, even without makeup. She had high cheekbones, full lips, deep blue eyes, and naturally blond hair parted in the center and cut short up front but tumbling to her shoulders in back. Molly squeezed Pierre's hand, and they began walking side by side.

The bells in the Campanile had just chimed 11:00 p.m. Molly had been working late in the psychology department, where she was an assistant professor. Pierre didn't like Molly walking home alone at night, so he'd stayed at the Lawrence Berkeley National Laboratory, poised on a hilltop above the campus, until she'd phoned saying she was ready to leave. It was no hardship for him; on the contrary, Molly's usual problem was getting Pierre to take a break from his research.

Molly had no doubts about Pierre's feelings for her; that was one of the few good things about her gift. She did sometimes wish he would put his arm around her as they walked, but he didn't like doing that. Not that he wasn't affectionate: he was French-Canadian, after all, and had the demonstrative nature that went with the first part of that hyphenate, and the desire to cuddle against the cold that came with the second. But he always said there would be time for helping to hold him up later, with her arm around his waist and his around hers. For now, while he still could, he wanted to walk freely.

As they crossed the bridge over the north fork of Strawberry Creek, Molly said, "How was work today?"

Pierre's voice was richly accented. "Burian Klimus was being a pain," he said.

Molly laughed, a throaty sound. Her speaking voice was high and feminine, but her laugh had an earthy quality that Pierre had said he found very sexy. "When isn't he?" she said.

"Exactly," replied Pierre. "Klimus wants perfection, and I guess he's entitled to it. But the whole point of the Human Genome Project is to find out what makes us human, and humans sometimes make mistakes." Molly was pretty much used to Pierre's accent, but three utterings of "yooman" in one sentence was enough to bring a smile to her lips. "He tore quite a strip off Shari's hide this afternoon."

Molly nodded. "I heard someone do an imitation of Burian at the Faculty Club yesterday." She cleared her throat and affected a German accent. "'I'm not only a member of the *Herr* Club for Men—I'm also its chancellor.'"

Pierre laughed.

Up ahead there was a wrought-iron park bench. A burly man in his late twenties wearing faded jeans and an unzipped leather jacket was sitting on it. The man had a chin like two small fists protruding from the bottom of his face and a half inch of dirty-blond hair. Disrespectful, thought Molly: you come to the very home of the 1960s hippie movement, you should grow your hair a *little* long.

They continued walking. Normally, Pierre and Molly would have swerved away from the bench, giving the resting fellow a generous berth—Molly took pains to keep strangers from entering her zone. But a lighting standard and a low hedge sharply defined the opposite edge of the path here, so they ended up passing within a couple of feet of the man, Molly even closer to him than Pierre—

About fucking time that frog showed up.

Molly's grip tightened, her short unpainted fingernails digging into the back of Pierre's hand.

Too bad he's not alone—but maybe Grozny will like it better this way.

Molly spoke in a quavering whisper so low it was almost lost on the breeze: "Let's get out of here." Pierre's eyebrows went up, but he quickened his pace. Molly stole a glance over her shoulder. "He's up off the bench now," she said softly. "He's walking toward us."

She scanned the landscape ahead. A hundred feet in front of them was the campus's north gate, with the deserted cafés of Euclid Avenue beyond. To the left was a fence separating the university from Hearst Avenue. To the right, more redwoods and Haviland Hall, home of the School of Social Welfare. Most of its windows were dark. A bus rumbled by outside the fence—the last bus for a long time, this late. Pierre chewed his lower lip. Footfalls were approaching softly behind them. He reached into his pocket, and Molly could hear the soft tinkle of him maneuvering his keys between his fingers.

Molly opened the zipper on her white leather purse and extracted her rape whistle. She chanced another glance back, and—Christ, a knife! *"Run!"* she shouted, and veered to the right, bringing the whistle to her lips. The sound split the night.

Pierre surged forward, heading straight for the north gate, but after eating up a few yards of path, he looked back. Perhaps now that the man knew the element of surprise was gone, he'd just hightail it in the opposite direction, but Pierre had to be sure that the guy hadn't taken off after Molly—

—and that was Pierre's mistake. The man had been lagging behind—Pierre had longer legs and had started running sooner—but

Pierre's slowing down to look gave the man a chance to close the distance. From thirty feet away, Molly, who had also stopped running, screamed Pierre's name.

The punk had a bowie knife in his right hand. It was difficult to make out in the darkness except for the reflection of streetlamps off the fifteen-inch blade. He was holding it underhand, as if he'd intended to thrust it up into Pierre's back.

The man lunged. Pierre did what any good Montreal boy who had grown up wanting to play on the Canadiens would do: he deked left, and when the guy moved in that direction, Pierre danced to the right and bodychecked him. The attacker was thrown off balance. Pierre surged forward, his apartment key wedged between his index and middle fingers. He smashed his assailant in the face. The man yowled in pain as the key jabbed into his cheek.

Molly ran toward the man from the rear. She jumped onto his back and began pummeling him with clenched fists. He tried to spin around, as if somehow he could catch the woman on top of him, and, as he did so, Pierre employed another hockey maneuver, tripping him. But instead of dropping the knife, as Pierre apparently thought he would, the man gripped it even tighter. As he fell, his arm twisted and his leather jacket billowed open. The weight of Molly on his back drove the blade's single sharpened edge sideways into his belly.

Suddenly blood was everywhere. Molly got off the man, wincing. He wasn't moving, and his breathing had taken on a liquid, bubbling sound.

Pierre grabbed Molly's hand. He started to back away, but suddenly realized just how severe the attacker's wound was. The man would bleed to death without immediate treatment. "Find a phone," Pierre said to Molly. "Call 9-1-1." She ran off toward Haviland Hall.

Pierre rolled the man onto his back, the knife sliding out as he did so. He picked it up and tossed it as far away as he could, in case he was underestimating the injury. He then tore open the buttons on the attacker's light cotton shirt, which was now sodden with blood, exposing the laceration. The man was in shock: his complexion, hard to make out in the wan light, had turned grayish white. Pierre took off his own shirt—a beige McGill University pullover—and wadded it up to use as a pressure bandage.

Molly returned several minutes later, panting from running. "An ambulance is coming, and so are the police," she said. "How is he?"

Pierre kept pressure on the wadded shirt, but the fabric was *squishing* as he leaned on it. "He's dying," he said, looking up at her, his voice anguished.

Molly moved closer, looming over the assailant. "You don't recognize him?"

Pierre shook his head. "I'd remember that chin."

She kneeled next to the man, then closed her eyes, listening to the voice only she could hear.

Not fair, thought the man. I only killed people Grozny said deserved it. But I *don't deserve to die. I'm not a fucking—*

The unspoken voice stopped abruptly. Molly opened her eyes and then gently took Pierre's blood-covered hands off the drenched shirt. "He's gone," she said.

Pierre, who was still on bended knee, rocked slowly backward. His face was bone white and his mouth hung open slightly. Molly recognized the signs: just as the attacker had been moments ago, Pierre himself was now in shock. She helped him move away from the body and got him to sit down on the grass at the base of a redwood tree.

After what seemed an eternity, they at last heard approaching sirens. The city police arrived first, coming through the north gate, followed a few moments later by a campus police car that arrived from the direction of the Moffit Library. The two vehicles pulled up side by side, near where the stand of redwoods began.

The city cops were a salt-and-pepper team: a wide black man and a taller, skinnier white woman. The black man seemed to be the senior officer. He got a sealed package of latex gloves out of his glove compartment and snapped them onto his beefy hands, then moved in to examine the body. He checked the body's wrist for a pulse, then shifted its head and tried again at the base of the neck. "Christ," he said. "Karen?"

His partner came closer and played a flashlight beam onto the face. "He got a good punch in, that's for sure," the woman said, indicating the wound Pierre's keys had made. Then she blinked. "Say, didn't we bust him a few weeks ago?"

The black man nodded. "Chuck Hanratty. Scum." He shook his head, but it seemed more in wonder than out of sadness. He rose to his feet, snapped off his gloves, and looked briefly at the campus cop, a chubby white-haired Caucasian who was averting his eyes from the body. He then turned to Pierre and Molly. "Either of you hurt?"

"No," said Molly, her voice quavering slightly. "Just shaken up."

The female cop was scanning the area with her flashlight. "That the knife?" she said, looking at Pierre and pointing at the bowie, which had landed at the base of another redwood.

Pierre looked up, but didn't seem to hear.

"The knife," she said again. "The knife that killed him."

Pierre nodded.

"He was trying to kill us," said Molly.

The black man looked at her. "Are you a student here?"

"No, I'm faculty," she said. "Psychology department."

"Name?"

"Molly Bond."

He jerked his head at Pierre, who was still staring into space. "And him?"

"He's Pierre Tardivel. He's with the Human Genome Center, up at the Lawrence Berkeley Lab."

The officer turned to the campus cop. "You know these two?"

The old guy was slowly recovering his composure; this sort of thing was a far cry from getting cars towed from handicapped parking spots. He shook his head.

The male cop turned back to Molly and Pierre. "Let me see your driver's licenses and university IDs," he said.

Molly opened her purse and showed the requested cards to the officer. Pierre, chilled without a shirt on, still shaken by the death of the man, arms covered to the elbows with caking blood, managed to get out his brown wallet, but just stared at it as if he didn't know how to open it. Molly gently took it from him and showed his identification to the policeman.

"Canadian," said the cop, as though that were a very suspicious thing to be. "You got papers to be in this country?"

"Papers ..." repeated Pierre, still dazed.

"He's got a green card," said Molly. She leafed through the wallet, found it, and showed it to the officer. The male cop nodded. The female cop had retrieved a Polaroid camera from the cruiser and was taking photos of the scene.

Finally the ambulance arrived. It came through the north gate, but couldn't get down the path to where they were. All the vehicles had turned off their sirens once parked, but the ambulance left its rotating roof light on, making orange shadows dance around the scene. The air was filled with staticky calls over the police and ambulance radios. Two attendants, both male, hurried to the downed man. A few spectators had arrived as well.

"No pulse," said the male cop. "No signs of respiration."

The attendants did a few checks, then nodded at each other. "He's gone all right," said one. "Still, we gotta take him in."

"Karen?" said the male officer.

The female cop nodded. "I've got enough shots."

"Go ahead," said the man. He turned to Pierre and Molly. "We'll need statements from both of you."

"It was self-defense," said Molly.

For the first time, the cop showed a little warmth. "Of course. Don't worry; it's just routine. That guy who attacked you had quite a record: robbery, assault, cross burning."

"Cross burning?" said Molly, shocked.

The cop nodded. "Nasty fellow, that Chuck Hanratty. He was involved with a neo-Nazi group called the Millennial Reich. They're mostly across the Bay in San Francisco, but they've been recruiting here in Berkeley, too." He looked around at the various buildings. "Is your car here?"

"We were walking," said Molly.

"Well, look, it's after midnight and, frankly, your friend seems a bit out of it. Why don't you let officer Granatstein and me give you a lift? You can come by headquarters tomorrow to make a report." He handed her a card.

"Why," said Pierre, finally rallying a bit, "would a neo-Nazi want to attack me?"

The black man shrugged. "No big mystery. He was after your wallet and her purse."

But Molly knew that wasn't true. She took Pierre's blood-encrusted hand and led him over to the police car.

Pierre stepped into the shower, cleaning the blood from his arms and chest. The water running down the drain was tinged with red. Pierre scrubbed until his skin was raw. After toweling off, he crawled into bed next to Molly, and they held each other.

"Why would a neo-Nazi be after me?" said Pierre, into the darkness. He exhaled noisily. "Hell, why would anyone go to the trouble of trying to kill me? After all ..." He trailed off, the English sentence already formed in his mind, but deciding not to give it voice.

But Molly could tell what he had been about to say, and she drew him closer to her, holding him tightly.

After all, Pierre Tardivel had thought, *I'll probably be dead soon anyway.*

Book One

Let us live in the harness, striving mightily; let us rather run the risk of wearing out than rusting out.

—**Theodore Roosevelt**,
winner of the 1906 Nobel Peace Prize

1

August 1943

The screams came like popcorn popping: at first there were only one or two, then there were hundreds overlapping, then, finally, the quantity diminished, and at last there were none left and you knew it was done.

Jubas Meyer tried not to think about it. Even most of the bastards in charge tried not to think about it. Only forty meters away, a band of Jewish musicians played at gunpoint, their songs meant to drown out the cries of the dying, the rumble of the diesel engine in the *Maschinehaus* insufficient to fully mask the sound.

Finally, while Jubas and the others stood ready, the two Ukrainian operators heaved the massive doors aside. Blue smoke rose from the opening.

As was often the case, the naked corpses were still standing. The people had been packed in so tightly—up to five hundred in the tiny chamber—that there was no room for them to fall down. But now that the doors were open, those closest to the exit toppled over, spilling out into the hot summer sun, their faces mottled and bloated by the carbon-monoxide poisoning. The stench of human sweat and urine and vomit filled the air.

Jubas and his partner, Shlomo Malamud, moved forward, carrying their wooden stretcher. With it, they could remove a single adult or two children in each load; they didn't have the strength to carry more. Jubas could count his own ribs easily through his thin skin, and his scalp itched constantly from the lice.

Jubas and Shlomo started with a woman of about forty. Her left breast had a long gash in it. They carried her body off to the dental station. The man there, an emaciated fellow in his early thirties named Yehiel Reichman, tipped her head back and opened her mouth. He spotted a gold filling, reached in with blood-encrusted pliers, and extracted the tooth.

Shlomo and Jubas took the body off to the pit and dumped it in on top of the other corpses, trying to ignore the buzz of flies and the reek of diseased flesh and postmortem bowel discharges. They returned to the chamber, and—

No—

No!

God, no.

Not Rachel—

But it was. Jubas's own sister, lying there naked among the dead, her green eyes staring up at him, lifeless as emeralds.

He'd prayed that she'd gotten away, prayed that she was safe, prayed—

Jubas staggered back, tripped, fell to the ground, tears welling up and out of his eyes, the drops clearing channels in the filth that covered his face.

Shlomo moved to help his friend. "Quickly," he whispered. "Quickly, before they come ..."

But Jubas was wailing now, unable to control himself.

"It gets to us all," said Shlomo, soothingly.

Jubas shook his head. Shlomo didn't understand. He gulped air, finally forced out the words. "It's Rachel," he said, between shuddering sobs, gesturing at the corpse. Flies were crawling across her face now.

Shlomo placed a hand on Jubas's shoulder. Shlomo had been separated from his own brother Saul, and the one thing that had kept him going all this time was the thought that somewhere Saul might be safe.

"Get up!" shouted a familiar voice. A tall, stocky Ukrainian wearing jackboots came closer. He was carrying a rifle with a bayonet attached—the same bayonet Jubas had often seen him honing with a whetstone to scalpel sharpness.

Jubas looked up. Even through his tears, he could make out the man's features: a round face in its thirties, balding head, protruding ears, thin lips.

Shlomo moved over to the Ukrainian, risking everything. He could smell the cheap liquor on the man's breath. "A moment, Ivan—for pity's sake. It's Jubas's sister."

Ivan's wide mouth split in a terrible grin. He leaned in and used the bayonet to slice off Rachel's right nipple. Then, with a flick of his index finger, he sent it flying off the blade into the air. It spun end over end before landing bloody side down in Jubas Meyer's lap.

"Something to remember her by," said Ivan.

He was a monster.

A devil.

Evil incarnate.

His first name was Ivan. His last name was unknown, and so the Jews dubbed him Ivan the Terrible. He had arrived at the camp a year before, in July 1942. There were some who said he'd been an educated man before the war; he used fancier words than the other guards did. A few even contended he must have been a doctor, since he sliced human flesh with such precision. But whatever he'd been in civilian life had been set aside.

Jubas Meyer had done the math, calculating how many corpses he and Shlomo had removed from the chambers each day, how many other pairs of Jews were being forced to do the same thing, how many trainloads had arrived to date.

The figures were staggering. Here, in this tiny camp, between ten and twelve thousand people were executed every day; on some days, the tally reached as high as fifteen thousand. So far, over half a million people had been exterminated. And there were rumors of other camps: one at Belzac, another at Sobibor, perhaps others still.

There could be no doubt: the Nazis intended to kill every single Jew, to wipe them all off the face of the earth.

And here, at Treblinka, eighty kilometers northeast of Warsaw, Ivan the Terrible was the principal agent of that destruction. True, he had a partner named Nikolai who helped him operate the chambers, but it was Ivan who was sadistic beyond belief, raping women before gassing them, slicing their flesh—especially breasts—as they marched naked into the chambers, forcing Jews to copulate with corpses while he laughed a cold, throaty laugh and beat them with a lead pipe.

Ivan reveled in it all, his naturally nasty disposition only worsened by frequent drinking binges. As a Ukrainian, he'd likely started off a prisoner of war himself, but had volunteered for service as a *Wachmann,* and had demonstrated a remarkable technical facility, leading to him being put in charge of the gas chambers. He was now so trusted that the Germans often let him leave the camp. Jubas had once overheard Ivan bragging to Nikolai about the whore he frequented in the nearby town of Wolga Okralnik. "If you think the Jews scream loudly," Ivan had said, "you should hear my Maria."

A miracle happened.

Ivan and Nikolai pulled back the chamber doors, and—

—God, it was incredible—

—a little blond girl, perhaps twelve years old, barely pubescent, staggered naked out of the chamber, still alive.

Behind her, corpses began falling like dominoes.

But she was alive. The Jewish men and women had been packed in so tightly this time that their very bodies had formed a pocket of air for her, separated from the circulating carbon monoxide.

The girl, her eyes wide in terror, stood under the hot sun, gulping in oxygen. And when she at last had the breath to do so, she screamed, *"Ma-me! Ma-me!"*

But her mother was among the dead.

Jubas Meyer and Shlomo Malamud set about removing the corpses, batting their arms to dispel the flies, breathing shallowly to avoid the smell. Ivan swaggered over to the girl, a whip in his hand. Jubas shot a reproachful glance at him. The Ukrainian must have seen that. He forgot the girl for a moment and came over to Jubas, lashing him repeatedly. Jubas bit his own tongue until he tasted salty blood; he knew that screams would just prolong the torture.

When Ivan had had his fill, he stepped back, and looked at Jubas, hunched over in pain. *"Davay yebatsa!"* he shouted.

Even the little girl knew those obscene words. She started to back away, but Ivan moved toward her, grabbing her naked shoulder roughly and pushing her to the ground.

"Davay yebatsa!" shouted Ivan at Jubas. He dragged the girl across the ground to where he'd left his rifle, leaning against the *Maschinehaus* wall. He aimed the weapon at Jubas. *"Davay yebatsa!"*

Jubas closed his eyes.

It was horrible news, devastating news.

The pace of the executions was slacking off.

It didn't mean the Germans were changing their minds.

It didn't mean they were giving up their insane plot.

It meant they were running out of Jews to kill.

Soon the camp would be of no further use. When they'd started, the Germans had ordered the dead buried. But recently they'd been using earthmoving equipment to exhume the bodies and cremate them. Human ash whirled constantly through the air now; the acrid smell of burning flesh stung the nostrils. The Nazis wanted no proof to exist of what had happened here.

And they'd also want no witnesses. Soon the corpse bearers themselves would be ordered into the gas chambers.

“We’ve got to escape,” said Jubas Meyer. “We’ve got to get out of here.”

Shlomo looked at his friend. “They’ll kill us if we try.”

“They’ll kill us anyway.”

The revolt was planned in whispers, one man passing word to the next. Monday, August 2, 1943, would be the day. Not everyone would escape; they knew that. But some would ... surely *some* would. They would carry word of what had happened here to the world.

The sun burned down fiercely, as if God Himself were helping the Nazis incinerate bodies. But of course God would not do such a thing: the heat turned to an advantage as the deputy camp commander took a group of Ukrainian guards for a cooling swim in the river Bug.

The Jews in the lower camp—the part where prisoners were unloaded and prepared—had gathered some makeshift weapons. One had filled large cans with gasoline. Another had stolen some wire cutters. A third had managed to hide an ax among garbage he’d been ordered to remove. Even some guns had been captured.

A few had long ago hidden gold or money in holes in trees, or buried it in secret spots. Just as the bodies had been exhumed, so now were these treasures.

Everything was set to begin at 4:30 in the afternoon. Tensions were high; everyone was on edge. And then, at just before 4:00—

“Boy!” shouted Kuttner, a fat SS man.

The child, perhaps eleven years old, stopped dead in his tracks. He was shaking from head to toe. The SS officer moved closer, a riding crop in his hand. “Boy!” he said again. “What have you got in your pockets?”

Jubas Meyer and Shlomo Malamud were five meters away, carrying an exhumed corpse to the cremation site. They stopped to watch the scene unfold. The pockets on the youngster’s filthy and tattered overalls were bulging slightly.

The boy said nothing. His eyes were wide and his lips peeled back in fear, showing decaying teeth. Despite the pounding heat, he was shaking as if it were below zero. The guard stepped up to him and slapped the boy's thigh with the riding crop. The unmistakable jangle of coins was heard. The German narrowed his eyes. "Empty your pockets, Jew."

The boy half turned to face the man. His teeth were chattering. He tried to reach into his pocket, but his hand was shaking so badly he couldn't get it into the pocket's mouth. Kuttner whipped the boy's shoulder with his crop, the sound startling birds into flight, their calls counterpointing the child's scream. Kuttner then reached his own fat hand into the pocket and pulled out several German coins. He reached in a second time. The pocket was apparently empty now, but Jubas could see the German fondling the boy's genitals through the fabric. "Where did you get the money?"

The boy shook his head, but pointed past the camouflage of trees and fencing to the upper camp, where the gas chambers and ovens were hidden from view.

The guard grabbed the youngster's shoulder roughly. "Come with me, boy. Stangl will deal with you."

The child wasn't the only one with something concealed on his person. Jubas Meyer had been entrusted with one of the six stolen pistols. If the boy were taken to commander Franz Stangl, he'd doubtless reveal the plans for the revolt, now only thirty minutes from its planned start.

Meyer couldn't allow that to happen. He pulled the gun from the folds of his own overalls, took a bead on the fat German, and—

—it was like ejaculation, the release, the moment, the payback—

—squeezed the trigger, and saw the German's eyes go wide, saw his mouth go round, saw his fat, ugly, hateful form slump to the ground.

The signal for the beginning of the revolt was to have been a grenade detonation, but Meyer's gunshot startled everyone into action. Cries of *"Now!"* went up across the lower camp. The canisters of gas were set ablaze. There were 850 Jews in the camp that day; they all ran for the barbed-wire fences. Some brought blankets, throwing them over the cruel knots of metal; others had wire cutters and furiously snipped through the lines. Those with guns shot as many guards as they could. Fire and smoke were everywhere. The guards who had gone swimming quickly returned and mounted horses or clambered aboard armored cars. Three hundred and fifty Jews made it over the fences and into the surrounding forest. Most were rounded up easily and shot dead, the echoes of overlapping gun reports and the cries of birds and wildlife the last sounds they ever heard.

Still, some did make good their escape. They ran out into the woods, and kept running for their lives. Jubas Meyer was among them. Shlomo Malamud got out, too, and began a lifelong search for his brother Saul. And others Jubas had known or heard of made it to safety as well: Eliahu Rosenberg and Pinhas Epstein; Casimir Landowski and Zalmon Chudzik. And David Solomon, too.

But they, and perhaps forty-five others, were all that survived Treblinka.

2

The early 1980s. Ronald Reagan had recently been sworn in as president, and, moments later, Iran had released the American hostages it had been holding prisoner for 444 days. Here in Canada, Pierre Trudeau was in the middle of his comeback term as prime minister, struggling to bring the Canadian constitution home from Great Britain.

Eighteen-year-old Pierre Tardivel stood in front of the strange house in suburban Toronto, the collar of his red McGill University jacket turned up against the cold, dry wind whipping down the salt-stained street.

Now that he was here, this didn't seem like such a good idea. Maybe he should just turn around, head back to the bus station, back to Montreal. His mother would be delighted if he gave up now, and, well, if what Henry Spade's wife had told Pierre about her husband were true, Pierre wasn't sure that he could face the man. He should just—

No. No, he had come this far. He had to see for himself.

Pierre took a deep breath, inhaling the crisp air, trying to calm the butterflies in his stomach. He walked up the driveway to the front door of the side-split suburban home, pressed the doorbell, and heard the muffled sound of the chimes from within. A few moments later, the door opened, and a handsome, middle-aged woman stood before him.

"Hello, Mrs. Spade. I'm Pierre Tardivel." He was conscious of how out of place his Québecois accent must have sounded here—another reminder that he was intruding.

There was a moment while Mrs. Spade looked Pierre up and down during which Pierre thought he saw a flicker of recognition on her face. Pierre had merely told her on the phone that his parents had been friends of her husband, back when Henry Spade had lived in Montreal in the early sixties. And yet she had to have realized there must be a special reason for Pierre to want to visit. What was it Pierre's mother had said when he'd confronted her with the evidence? "I knew you were Henry's—you're the spitting image of him."

"Hello, Pierre," said Mrs. Spade. The voice was richer than it had sounded over the phone, but there was still a trace of wariness to it. "You can call me Dorothy. Please come in." She stepped aside, and Pierre entered the vestibule. Physically, Dorothy bore a passing resemblance to his mother—dark hair, cool blue-gray eyes, full lips. Perhaps Henry Spade had been attracted to a specific type of woman. Pierre unzipped his jacket, but made no move to take it off.

"Henry is upstairs in his room," said Dorothy. *His room.* Separate bedrooms? How cold. "It's easier for him to be lying down. Do you mind seeing him up there?"

Pierre shook his head.

"Very well," she said. "Come with me."

They walked into the brightly lit living room. Two full walls were covered with bookcases made of dark wood. A staircase led to the second floor. Along one side of it were tracks for a small motorized chair. The chair itself was positioned at the top. Dorothy led Pierre upstairs and into the first door on the left.

Pierre fought to keep his expression neutral.

Lying on the bed was a man who appeared to be dancing on his back. His arms and legs moved constantly, rotating at shoulder and hip, elbow and knee, wrist and ankle. His head lolled left and right across the pillow. His hair was steel gray and, of course, his eyes were brown.

"Bonjour," said Pierre, so startled that he'd begun speaking in French. He began again. "Hello. I'm Pierre Tardivel."

The man's voice was weak and slurred. Speaking was clearly an effort. "Hello, P-Pierre," he said. He paused, but whether composing his thoughts or just waiting for his body to yield a little control, Pierre couldn't say. "How is—is your mother?"

Pierre blinked repeatedly. He would not insult the man by crying in front of him. "She's fine."

Henry's head rolled from side to side, but he kept his eyes on Pierre. He wanted more, Pierre knew, than a platitude.

"She's in good health," he said. "She's a loans officer for a large branch of *Banque de Montréal."*

"She's happy?" asked Henry, with effort.

"She enjoys her work, and money is no problem. There was a lot of insurance when Dad died."

Henry swallowed with what appeared to be considerable difficulty. "I, ah, didn't know that Alain had passed on. Tell her ... tell her I'm sorry."

The words seemed sincere. No sarcasm, no double edge. Alain Tardivel had been his rival, but Henry seemed genuinely saddened by his death. Pierre squeezed his jaw tightly shut for a moment, then nodded. "I'll tell her."

"She's a wonderful woman," said Henry.

"I have a picture of her," said Pierre. He pulled out his wallet and flipped to the small portrait of his mother wearing a white silk blouse. He held the wallet where Henry could see it.

Henry stared at it for a long time, then said, "I guess I changed more than she did."

Pierre forced a weak smile.

"Are ... only child?" A few words had gotten lost in the convulsion that had passed over Henry's body like a wave.

"Yes. There—" No, no point in mentioning his younger sister, Marie-Claire, who had died when she was two. "Yes, I'm the only one."

"You're a fine-looking young man," said Henry.

Pierre smiled—genuinely this time—and Henry seemed to smile back.

Dorothy, perhaps detecting the undercurrent, or perhaps just bored with conversation about people she didn't know, said, "Well, I can see you two have things to talk about. I'll go downstairs. Pierre, can I bring you a drink? Coffee?"

"No, thank you," said Pierre.

"Well, then," she said, and left.

Pierre stood beside Henry's bed. Having his own room made perfect sense now. How could it be any other way? No one could sleep next to him, given the constant jerking of his limbs.

The man on the bed lifted his right arm toward Pierre. It moved slowly from side to side, like the bough of a tree swaying in the wind. Pierre reached out and took the hand, holding it firmly. Henry smiled.

"You look ... just like I did ... when I was your age," said Henry.

A tear did slip down Pierre's cheek. "You know who I am?"

Henry nodded. "I—when your mother got pregnant, I'd thought there was a chance. But she ended our relationship. I'd assumed if I'd ... if I'd been right, I'd have heard something before now." His head was moving, but he managed to keep his eyes mostly on Pierre. "I—I wish I'd known."

Pierre squeezed the hand. "Me, too." A pause. "Do you—do you have any other children?"

"Daughters," said Henry. "Two daughters. Adopted. Dorothy—Dorothy couldn't ..."

Pierre nodded.

"Best, in a way," said Henry, and here, at last, he let his gaze wander away from Pierre. "Huntington's disease is ... is ..."

Pierre swallowed. "Hereditary. I know."

Henry's head moved back and forth more rapidly than normal—a deliberate signal all but lost in the muscular noise. "If I'd known I had it, I ... never would have allowed myself to father a child. I'm sorry. V-very sorry."

Pierre nodded.

"You might have it, too."

Pierre said nothing.

"There's no test," said Henry. "I'm sorry."

Pierre watched Henry move about on the bed, knees jerking, free arm waving. And yet in the middle of it all was a face not unlike his own, round and broad, with deep brown eyes. He realized then that he didn't know how old Henry was. Forty-five? Perhaps as old as fifty. Certainly no more than that. Henry's right arm started jerking rapidly. Pierre, not sure what to do, let go of his hand.

"It's ... it's good to finally meet you," said Pierre; and then, realizing that he would never have another chance, he added a single word: "Dad."

Henry's eyes were wet. "You need anything?" he said. "Money?"

Pierre shook his head. "I'm fine. Really, I am. I just wanted to meet you."

Henry's lower lip was trembling. Pierre couldn't tell at first if it was just part of the chorea or had deeper meaning. But when Henry next spoke, his voice was full of pain. "I—I've forgotten your name," he said.

"Pierre," he said. "Pierre Jacques Tardivel."

"Pierre," repeated Henry. "A good name." He paused for several seconds, then said, "How is your mother? Did you bring a picture?"

Pierre went down to the living room. Dorothy was sitting in a chair, reading a Jackie Collins novel. She looked up and gave him a wan smile.

"Thank you," said Pierre. "Thank you for everything."

She nodded. "He very much wanted to see you."

"I was very glad to see him." He paused. "But I should be going now."

"Wait," said Dorothy. She took an envelope from the coffee table and rose to her feet. "I have something for you."

Pierre looked at it. "I told him I didn't need any money."

Dorothy shook her head. "It's not that. It's photographs—of Henry, from a dozen years ago. From when you would have been a little boy. Photographs of what he was like then—the way I'm sure he'd like you to remember him."

Pierre took the envelope. His eyes were stinging. "Thank you," he said.

She nodded, her face not quite masking her pain.

3

Pierre returned to Montreal. His family doctor referred him to a specialist in genetic disorders. Pierre went to see the specialist, whose office wasn't far from Olympic Stadium.

"Huntington's is carried on a dominant gene," said Dr. Laviolette to Pierre, in French. "You have precisely a fifty-fifty chance of getting it." He paused, and smoothed out his steel gray hair. "Your case is very unusual—discovering as an adult that you're at risk; most at-risks have known for years. How did you find out?"

Pierre was quiet for a moment, thinking. Was there any need to go into the details? That he'd discovered in a first-year genetics class that it was impossible for two blue-eyed parents to have a brown-eyed child? That he'd confronted his mother, Élisabeth, with this fact? That she'd confessed to having had an affair with one Henry Spade during the early years of her marriage to Alain Tardivel, the man Pierre had known as his father, a man who had been dead now for two years? That Élisabeth, a Catholic, had been unable to divorce Alain? That Élisabeth had successfully hidden from Alain the fact that their brown-eyed son was not his biological child? And that Henry Spade had moved to Toronto, never knowing he'd fathered a child?

It was too much, too personal. "I only recently met my real father for the first time," said Pierre simply.

Laviolette nodded. "How old are you, Pierre?"

"I turn nineteen next month."

The doctor frowned. "There isn't any predictive test for Huntington's, I'm afraid. You might not have the disease, but the only way you'll discover that is when you finish middle age without it showing up. On the other hand, you might develop symptoms in as few as ten or fifteen years."

Laviolette looked at him quietly. They'd already gone over the worst of it. Huntington's disease (also known as Huntington's chorea) affects about half a million people worldwide. It selectively destroys two parts of the brain that help control movement. Symptoms, which normally first manifest themselves between the ages of thirty and fifty, include abnormal posture, progressive dementia, and involuntary muscular action—the name "chorea" refers to the dancing movements typical of the disease. The disease itself, or complications arising from it, eventually kills the victim; Huntington's sufferers often choke to death on food because they've lost the muscular control to swallow.

"Have you ever thought about killing yourself, Pierre?" asked Laviolette.

Pierre's eyebrows rose at the unexpected question. "No."

"I don't mean just now over concern about possibly having Huntington's disease. I mean ever. Have you ever thought about killing yourself?"

"No. Not seriously."

"Are you prone to depression?"

"No more than the next guy, I imagine."

"Boredom? Lack of direction?"

Pierre thought about lying, but didn't. "Umm, yes. I have to admit to some of that." He shrugged. "People say I'm unmotivated, that I coast through life."

Laviolette nodded. “Do you know who Woody Guthrie is?”

“Who?”

The doctor made a “kids today” face. “He wrote ‘This Land is Your Land.’”

“Oh, yeah. Sure.”

“He died of Huntington’s in 1967. His son Arlo—you have heard of him, no?”

Pierre shook his head.

Laviolette sighed. “You’re making me feel old. Arlo wrote ‘Alice’s Restaurant.’”

Pierre looked blank.

“Folk music,” said Laviolette.

“In English, no doubt,” said Pierre dismissively.

“Even worse,” said Laviolette, with a twinkle in his eye, “*American* English. Anyway, Arlo is probably the most famous person in your position. He’s got a fifty-fifty chance of having inherited the gene, just like you. He talked about it once in an interview in *People* magazine; I’ll give you a photocopy before you go.”

Pierre, unsure what to say, simply nodded.

Laviolette reached for his pen and prescription pad. “I’m going to write out the number for the local Huntington’s support group; I want you to call them.” He copied a phone number from a small Cerlox-bound Montreal health-services directory, tore the sheet off the pad, and handed it to Pierre. He paused for a moment, as if thinking, then picked a business card from the brass holder on his desk and wrote another phone number beneath the one preprinted on the card. “And I’m also doing something I never do, Pierre. This is my personal number at home. If you can’t get me here, try me there—day or night. Sometimes ... sometimes people take news like this very poorly. Please, if you’re ever thinking of doing something rash, call me. Promise you’ll do that, Pierre.” He proffered the card.

“You mean if I’m thinking about killing myself, don’t you?”

The doctor nodded.

Pierre took the card. To his astonishment, his hand was shaking.

Late at night, alone in his room. Pierre hadn't even managed to finish undressing for bed. He just stared into space, not focusing, not thinking.

It was unfair, dammit. Totally unfair.

What had he done to deserve this?

There was a small crucifix above the door to his room; it had been there since he'd been a little boy. He stared up at the tiny Jesus—but there was no point in praying. The die was cast; what was done was done. Whether or not he had the gene had been determined almost twenty years ago, at the very moment of his conception.

Pierre had bought an Arlo Guthrie LP and listened to it. He'd been unable to find any Woody Guthrie at A&A's, but the Montreal library had an old album by a group called the Almanac Singers that Woody had once been part of. He listened to that, too.

The Almanac Singers' music seemed full of hope; Arlo's music seemed sad. It could go either way.

Pierre had read that most Huntington's patients ended their lives in hospital. The average stay before death was seven years.

Outside, the wind was whistling. A branch of the tree next to the house swept back and forth across the window, like a crooked, bony hand beckoning him to follow.

He didn't want to die. But he didn't want to live through years of suffering.

He thought about his father—his real father, Henry Spade. Thrashing about in bed, his faculties slipping away.

His eyes lit on his desk, a white particleboard thing from Consumers Distributing. On it was his copy of *Les Misérables,* which he'd just finished reading for his French-literature course. Jean Valjean had stolen a loaf of bread and no matter what he did, he could not undo that fact; until his dying day, his record was marked. Pierre's record was marked, too, one way or the other, but there was no way to read it. If he were like Valjean—if he were a convict—

then he had a Javert, too, endlessly pursuing him, eventually fated to catch up.

In the book, the tables had turned, with Inspector Javert ending up being the one incapable of escaping his birthright. Unable to alter what he was, he took the only way out, plunging from a parapet into the icy waters of the Seine below.

The only way out ...

Pierre got up, shuffled over to the desk, turned on a hooded lamp on an articulated bone-white arm, and found Laviolette's card with the doctor's home number written on it. He stared at the card, reading it over and over again.

The only way out ...

He walked back to his bed, sat on the edge of it, and listened to the wind some more. Without ever looking down to see what he was doing, he began drawing the edge of the card back and forth across the inside of his left wrist, again and again, as though it were a blade.

4

When she was eighteen, Molly Bond had been an undergraduate psychology student at the University of Minnesota. She lived in residence even though her family was right here in Minneapolis. Even back then, she couldn't take staying in the same house with them—not with her disapproving mother, not with her vacuous sister Jessica, and not with her mother's new husband, Paul, whose thoughts about her were often anything but paternal.

Still, there were certain family events that forced her to return home. Today was one of those. "Happy birthday, Paul," she said, leaning in to give her stepfather a kiss on the cheek. "I love you."

Should say the same thing back. "Love you, too, hon."

Molly stepped away, trying to keep her sigh from escaping audibly. It wasn't much of a party, but maybe they'd do better next year. This was Paul's forty-ninth birthday; they'd try to commemorate the big five-oh in a more stylish fashion.

If Paul was still around at that point, that is. What Molly had wanted to detect when she leaned in to kiss Paul was *I love you, too,* spontaneous, unplanned, unrehearsed. But no. She'd heard *should say the same thing back,* and then, a moment later, the spoken words, false, manufactured, flat.

Molly's mother came out of the kitchen carrying a cake—a carrot cake, Paul's favorite, crowned with the requisite number of candles, including one for good luck, arranged just like the stars on an American flag. Jessica helped Paul get his presents out of the way.

Molly couldn't resist. While her mother fumbled to get her camera set up, she moved in to stand right beside her stepfather, bringing him into her zone again. Molly's mother said, "Now make a wish and blow out the candles."

Paul closed his eyes. *I wish,* he thought, *that I hadn't gotten married.* He exhaled on the tiny flames, and smoke rose toward the ceiling.

Molly wasn't really surprised. At first she'd thought Paul was having an affair: he often worked late on weeknights, or disappeared all day on Saturdays, saying he was going to the office. But the truth, in some ways, was just as bad. He wasn't going off to be with someone else; rather, he just didn't want to be with them.

They sang "Happy Birthday," and then Paul cut the cake.

The thoughts of Molly's mother were no better. She suspected Molly might be a lesbian, so rarely was she seen with men. She hated her job, but pretended to enjoy it, and although she smiled when she handed over money to help Molly with university expenses, she resented every dollar of it. It reminded her of how hard she'd worked to put her first husband, Molly's dad, through business school.

Molly looked again at Paul and found she couldn't really blame him. She wanted to get away from this family, too—far, far away, so that even birthdays and Christmases could be skipped. Paul handed her a piece of cake. Molly took it and moved down to the far end of the table, sitting alone.

Wrapped up in his personal problems, Pierre failed all of his first-year courses. He went to see the dean of undergraduate studies and explained his situation. The dean gave him a second chance: McGill offered a reduced curriculum over the summer session. Pierre would only manage a couple of credits, but it would get him back on the right track for next September.

And so Pierre found himself back in an introductory genetics course. By coincidence, the same pencil-necked *Anglais* teaching assistant who had originally pointed out the heritability of eye color was teaching this one. Pierre had never been one for paying attention in class; his old notebooks contained mostly doodled hockey-team crests. But today he really *was* trying to listen ... at least with one ear.

"It was the biggest puzzle in science during the early 1950s," said the TA. "What form did the DNA molecule take? It was a race against time, with many luminaries, including Linus Pauling, working on the problem. They all knew that whoever discovered the answer would be remembered forever ..."

Or perhaps with *both* ears ...

"A young biologist—no older than any of you—named James Watson got involved with Francis Crick, and the two of them started looking for the answer. Building on the work of Maurice Wilkins and x-ray crystallography studies done by Rosalind Franklin ..."

Pierre sat rapt.

"... Watson and Crick knew that the four bases used in DNA—adenine, guanine, thymine, and cytosine—were each of a different size. But by using cardboard cutouts of the bases, they were able to show that when adenine and thymine bind together, they form a combined shape that's the same length as the one formed when guanine and cytosine bind together. And they showed that those combined shapes could form rungs on a spiral ladder ..."

Rapt.

"It was an amazing breakthrough—and what was even more amazing was that James Watson was just twenty-five years old when he and Crick proved that the DNA molecule took the form of a double helix ..."

Morning, after a night spent more awake than asleep. Pierre sat on the edge of his bed.

He had turned nineteen in April.

Many of those at risk for Huntington's had full-blown symptoms by the time they were—to select a figure—thirty-eight. Just double his current age.

So little time.

And yet—

And yet, so much had happened in the last nineteen years.

Vague, early memories, of baby-sitters and tricycles and marbles and endless summers and *Batman* in first run on TV.

Kindergarten. God, that seemed so long ago. Mademoiselle Renault's class. Dimly recalled celebrations of Canada's centennial.

Being a *Louveteau*—a Cub Scout, but never managing to finish a merit badge.

Two years of summer camp.

His family moving from Clearpoint to Outremont, and he having to adjust to a new school.

Breaking his arm playing street hockey.

And the FLQ October Crisis in 1970, and his parents trying to explain to a very frightened boy what all the TV news stories meant, and why there were troops in the streets.

Robert Apollinaire, his best friend when he was ten, who had moved all of twenty blocks away, and had never been seen again.

And puberty, and all that *that* entailed.

The hubbub when the 1976 Olympics were held in Montreal.

His first kiss, at a party, playing spin the bottle.

And seeing *Star Wars* for the first time and thinking it was the best movie that ever was.

His first girlfriend, Marie—he wondered where she was now.

Getting his driver's license, and smashing up Dad's car two months later.

Discovering the magic words *Je t'aime,* and how effective they were at getting his hand under a sweater or skirt. Then learning what those words really meant, in the summer of his seventeenth year, with Danielle. And crying alone on a street corner after she had broken up with him.

Learning to drink beer, and then learning to like the taste.

Parties. Summer jobs. A school play for which he did lighting. Winning season's tickets to the Canadiens home games in a CFCF radio giveaway—what a year that had been! Walking, unmotivated, through high school. Doing sports reporting for *L'Informateur,* the school newspaper. That big fight with Roch Laval—fifteen years of friendship, gone in one evening, never to be recovered.

Dad's heart attack. Pierre had thought the pain of losing him would never go away, but it had. Time heals all wounds.

Almost all.

All that, in nineteen years. It *was* a long time, was a substantial period, was ... was, perhaps, all the good time he had left.

The pencil-necked teaching assistant had been talking last class about James D. Watson. Just twenty-five when he'd codiscovered the helical nature of DNA. And by the time he was thirty-four, Watson had won the Nobel Prize.

Pierre knew that he was bright. He walked through school because he *could* walk through school. Whatever the subject, he had no trouble. Study? You must be joking. Carry home a stack of books? Surely you jest.

A life that might be cut short.

A Nobel Prize by age thirty-four.

Pierre began to get dressed, putting on underwear and a shirt.

He felt an emptiness in his heart, a vast feeling of loss. But he came to realize, after a few moments, that it wasn't the potential, future loss that he was mourning. It was the wasted past, the misspent time, the hours frittered away, the days without accomplishment, the coasting through life.

Pierre pulled up his socks.

He would make the most of it—make the most of every minute.
Pierre Jacques Tardivel *would* be remembered.
He looked at his watch.
No time to waste.
None.

5

Six years later

Jerusalem

Avi Meyer's father, Jubas Meyer, had been one of the fifty people to escape from the Treblinka death camp. Jubas had lived for three years after the escape, but had died before Avi was born. As a child growing up in Chicago, where Avi's parents had settled after time in a displaced-persons camp, Avi had resented that his dad wasn't around. But shortly after his bar mitzvah in 1960, Avi's mother said to him, "You're a man now, Avi. You should know what your father went through—what all our people went through."

And she'd told him. All of it.

The Nazis.

Treblinka.

Yes, his father had escaped the camp, but his father's brother and three sisters had all been killed there, as had Avi's grandparents, and countless other people they'd been related to or known.

All dead. Ghosts.

But now, perhaps, the ghosts could rest. They had the man who had tormented them, the man who had tortured them, the man who had gassed them to death.

Ivan the Terrible. They had the bastard. And now he was going to pay.

Avi, a compact, homely man with a face like a bulldog, was an agent with the Office of Special Investigations, the division of the United States Department of Justice devoted to hunting down Nazi war criminals. He and his colleagues at the OSI had identified a Cleveland autoworker named John Demjanjuk as Ivan the Terrible.

Oh, Demjanjuk didn't seem evil now. He was a bald, tubby Ukrainian in his late sixties, with protruding ears and almond-shaped eyes behind horn-rimmed glasses. And, true, he seemed not nearly as cunning as some reports had made out Ivan the Terrible to be, but, then again, he was hardly the first man to have had his intellect dulled by the passing decades.

The OSI agents had shown photo spreads containing pictures of Demjanjuk and others to Treblinka survivors. Based on their identifications, and an SS identity card recovered from the Soviets, Demjanjuk's U.S. citizenship had been revoked in 1981. He'd been extradited to Israel, and now was standing trial for the one capital crime in all of Israeli law.

The courtroom in Jerusalem's *Binyanei Ha'uma* convention center was large—indeed, it was actually Hall Two, a theater rented for this trial, the most important one since Eichmann's, so that as many spectators as possible could see history being made. Much of the audience consisted of Holocaust survivors and their families. The survivors were an ever dwindling number: since Demjanjuk's denaturalization trial in Cleveland, three of those who had identified him as Ivan the Terrible had passed away.

The judges' bench was on the stage—three high-back leather chairs, with the one in the center even taller than the other two. The bench was flanked on either side by a blue-and-white Israeli flag. To stage left, the prosecution's table and the witness box; to stage right, the table for the defense attorneys and, just behind them, the dock where Demjanjuk, wearing an open-necked shirt and blue sports jacket, sat with his interpreter and guard. All the furnishings were of polished blond wood. The stage was raised a full meter above the general audience seating. Television crews lined the back of the theater; the trial was being broadcast live.

The trial had been under way for a week. Avi Meyer, there as an OSI observer, whiled away the time waiting for the court to be called to order by rereading a paperback of *To Kill a Mockingbird.* Harper Lee's tale had affected him profoundly the first time he'd read it in university. Not that the experiences of Scout—Miss Jean Louise Finch, that is—growing up in the Deep South bore any resemblance to his own upbringing in Chicago. But the story—of the truths we hide, of the search for justice—was timeless.

In fact, maybe that book had as much to do with him joining the OSI as did the ghosts of the family he had never known. Tom Robinson, a black man, was charged with raping a white girl name of Mayella Ewell. The only physical evidence was Mayella's badly bruised face: she'd been punched repeatedly by a man who had led with his left. Her father, a nasty impoverished drunk, was left-handed. Tom Robinson was a cripple; his left arm was twelve inches shorter than his right, and ended in a tiny shriveled hand. Tom testified that Mayella had thrown herself at him, that he'd rejected her advances, and that her father had beaten her for tempting a black man. There was not one shred of evidence to support the rape charge, and Tom Robinson was physically incapable of inflicting the beating.

But in that sleepy Southern town of Maycomb, Alabama, the all-male, all-white jury had found Tom Robinson guilty as charged. A white girl's testimony *had* to be taken over a black man's and, well, even if Robinson wasn't guilty of this particular crime, he was a shiftless nigger and doubtless guilty of something else.

That justice needed righteous guardians there could be no doubt. And there had been one in *To Kill a Mockingbird:* Jean Louise's lawyer father, Atticus Finch, who represented Tom despite the calumny of the townsfolk, who gave a spirited, intelligent, dignified defense.

Back then, in the thirties, the courthouse, like everything else, had been segregated. The blacks had to sit in the balcony. Jean Louise and her brother Jem had snuck into the courthouse and found a place to watch from up there, near the kindly Reverend Sykes.

When the case was over, when Tom Robinson was taken off to jail, when all the whites had ambled out, the blacks waited in silence until Atticus Finch gathered up his law books. As he made his way out, the black men and women, knowing in their bones that Tom was innocent, that this was their lot, that Atticus had done his best, rose to their feet and stood in silent salute. The Reverend Sykes spoke to Atticus's young daughter. "Miss Jean Louise," he said, "stand up. Your father's passin'."

Even in defeat, a righteous man is honored by those who know he did his best in an honorable cause. *Your father's passin'...*

Supreme court justice Dov Levin and Jerusalem district court judges Zvi Tal and Dalia Dorner—the tribunal that would decide John Demjanjuk's fate—came into the theater. As soon as the three were seated, the clerk rose and announced, *"Beit Hamishpat!* State of Israel versus Ivan 'John,' son of Nikolai Demjanjuk, criminal file 373/86 at the Jerusalem District Court, sitting as the Special Court under the Law for the Punishment of Nazis and Their Collaborators. Court session of 24 Shevat 5747, 23 February 1987, morning session."

Avi Meyer folded down a page corner to mark his place.

"My name is Epstein, Pinhas, the son of Dov and Sara. I was born in Czestochowa, Poland, on March third, 1925. I lived there with my parents until the day we were taken to Treblinka."

Avi Meyer, who had just turned forty and so was particularly conscious of the signs of aging, thought Epstein looked ten years younger than sixty-two. He was tall, with a full head of reddish brown hair combed straight back from his forehead.

The panel of three judges listened intently: bearded Zvi Tal, a yarmulke crowning his thick gray hair; Dov Levin, dour, balding, wearing horn-rimmed glasses; and Dalia Dorner, her hair cropped short, wearing a jacket and tie just like her male colleagues. "Your Honors," said Epstein, turning to them, "I remember an incident—I have nightmares about it still. One day, a little girl managed to escape alive from the gas chamber. She was twelve or fourteen. Like Jubas Meyer, Shlomo Malamud, and others, I was forced to be a corpse bearer, removing the dead from the chambers." Avi Meyer sat up straight at the mention of his father's name. "The girl's words still ring in my ears," said Epstein: 'Mother! Mother!'" He paused for a moment and wiped tears from his eyes. "Well, Ivan went after Jubas, and ..."

Avi Meyer felt his heart pounding. Epstein had trailed off, and was now looking again from judge to judge, lingering longest on Dalia Dorner, as if intimidated by the female presence. "I'm sorry," said the witness. "I'm too ashamed to repeat the words Ivan used next."

Dov Levin frowned and removed his glasses. "If it's important that we hear the words, then say them."

Epstein sucked in breath, then: "He beat Jubas, then shouted, *'Davay yebatsa'* ..."

Levin raised his shaggy black eyebrows. "Which means?"

Epstein squirmed in his chair. "'Come fuck,' in Russian. He was saying to Jubas, take off your pants and come fuck. And he pointed at the terrified girl."

Avi Meyer tasted bile at the back of his throat. He'd thought he'd heard all the horrors twenty-seven years ago, after his bar mitzvah. His mother was dead now; he hoped she had never known.

Mickey Shaked, one of the three Israeli prosecutors, had a full head of curly hair and sad, soulful eyes. He placed the cardboard photo spread in front of Epstein. It was a sheet with eight photographs on it: two rows of three pictures and a final row of two. All were of Ukrainian men suspected of war crimes. The first five photos were passport shots; the sixth was clipped from some other document. Only the seventh and eighth were regular snapshots—almost twice as big as the others. Of the eight photos, only the seventh showed an almost totally bald man; only the seventh showed a round-faced man.

"Do you see anyone whose face you recognize among these pictures?" asked Shaked.

Epstein nodded, but at first was unable to give voice to his thoughts. He finally placed a finger on the seventh picture. "I recognize him," he said.

"In what way?"

"The forehead, the round face, the very short neck, the broad shoulders, the ears that stick out. This is Ivan the Terrible as I remember him from Treblinka."

"And do you see this same man anywhere in this court today?" asked Shaked, looking around the vast theater as if he himself had no idea where the monster might be.

Epstein raised his voice as he pointed at Demjanjuk. "Yes, he's sitting right there!"

Spectators actually applauded. Demjanjuk's Israeli lawyer, Yoram Sheftel, spread his arms imploringly at the bench. Judge Levin scowled, as if reluctant to interrupt good theater, but finally called the room to order.

Another witness was on the stand now: Eliahu Rosenberg, a short, stocky man with gray hair and dark bushy eyebrows.

"I ask you to look at the accused," said Prosecutor Mickey Shaked. "Scrutinize him."

Rosenberg turned to the three judges. "Will you ask the accused to take off his glasses?"

Demjanjuk immediately removed his glasses, but as Mark O'Connor, his American lawyer, rose to object, Demjanjuk put them back on.

"Mr. O'Connor," said Judge Levin, frowning, "what is your position?"

O'Connor looked at Demjanjuk, then at Rosenberg, then back again at Judge Levin. Finally, he shrugged. "My client has nothing to hide."

Demjanjuk stood up and took off his glasses again. He then leaned forward and spoke to O'Connor. "It's okay," Demjanjuk said. "Have him come closer." He pointed to the edge of his booth. "Have him come right here."

O'Connor at first shushed Demjanjuk, but then seemed to think that perhaps he did have a good idea. "*Mar* Rosenberg," he said, "why don't you come over for a closer look?"

Rosenberg left the witness stand and, without taking his eyes off Demjanjuk, closed the distance. Spectators whispered to themselves. Rosenberg placed a hand on the edge of Demjanjuk's dock to steady himself. *"Posmotree!"* he shouted. *Look at me!*

Demjanjuk met his eyes and stuck out his hand. *"Shalom,"* he said.

Rosenberg stumbled backward. "Murderer!" he shouted. "How dare you offer me your hand?" Avi Meyer watched as Rosenberg's wife, Adina, who was seated in the third row, fainted. Her daughter caught her in her arms. Rosenberg stormed back to the witness stand.

"You were asked to come closer and have a look," said Judge Dov Levin. "What did you see?"

Rosenberg's voice was shaking. "He is Ivan." He swallowed, trying to gain composure. "I say that without hesitation or the slightest doubt. He is Ivan from Treblinka—Ivan from the gas chambers. I'll never forget those eyes—those murderous eyes."

Demjanjuk shouted something. Avi Meyer hadn't made it out clearly, and O'Connor, his hearing impaired by the translation headset, apparently also missed it. He took off the earphones and turned to face his client.

Avi strained to hear. "What did you say?" asked O'Connor.

Demjanjuk, red-faced, crossed his arms in front of his chest, but said nothing. Demjanjuk's Israeli lawyer, Yoram Sheftel, leaned closer to O'Connor and spoke in English. "He said to Rosenberg, *'Atah shakran'*—'You are a liar.'"

"I'm telling the truth!" shouted Rosenberg. "He is Ivan the Terrible!"

6

Thirteen months later

Minneapolis

Molly Bond felt—well, she wasn't sure *how* she felt. Cheap, but excited; full of fear, but full of hope.

She would turn twenty-six this summer, and was now well on her way to her Ph.D in behavioral psychology. But tonight she wasn't studying. Tonight, she sat in a bar a few blocks from the University of Minnesota campus, the smoky air stinging her eyes. She'd already had a Long Island iced tea, trying to build up her courage. She was wearing a tight-fitting red silk blouse, with no bra underneath. When she looked down at her chest, she could see the points made by her nipples pressing against the material. She'd already undone one button before entering, and now she reached down and undid a second one. She was also wearing a black leather skirt that went less than halfway down her thigh, dark stockings, and spike-heeled black shoes. Her blond hair was hanging loosely around her shoulders, and she had on green eye shadow, and lipstick as bright red as the silk top.

Molly looked up and saw a man enter the bar: a not-bad-looking guy in his mid-twenties, with brown eyes and lots of dark hair. Italian, maybe. He was wearing a UM jacket, with "MED" on one sleeve. Perfect.

She saw him looking her over. Molly's stomach was fluttering. She glanced at him, managed a small smile, then looked away.

It had been enough. The guy came over and took the barstool next to her, well within her zone.

"Can I buy you a drink?" he asked.

Molly nodded. "Long Island iced tea," she said, indicating her empty glass. He motioned for the bartender.

His thoughts were pornographic. When he didn't think she was looking, Molly could see him peering down her front. She crossed her legs on the stool, bouncing her breasts as she did so.

It wasn't long before they were back at his place. Typical student apartment, not far from the campus: empty pizza boxes in the kitchen, textbooks spread out on the furniture. He apologized for the mess and started cleaning off the couch.

"No need for that," said Molly. There were only two doorways off the living room, and both were open; she moved over to stand in the one that led to the bedroom.

He came over to her, his hands finding her breasts through the blouse, then under the blouse, then quickly helping her remove the blouse altogether. Molly undid his belt buckle, and they shed the rest of their clothes on the way to the bed, plenty of light still spilling in from the living room. He opened his night-table drawer, took out a three-pack of condoms, and looked at Molly. "I hate these things," he said, testing the waters, hoping she'd agree. "Kills the sensation."

Molly slid her palm across his hairy chest, down his muscular arm, and onto his hand, taking the condoms from him, and putting them back in the still-open drawer. "Then why bother?" she said, smiling up at him. She moved her hand to his penis and stroked it into full erection.

Five years later

Washington, D.C.

Avi Meyer sat in his apartment, mouth hanging open.

Demjanjuk had been found guilty, of course, and sentenced to death. The outcome had been obvious from the beginning of the trial. Still, there had to be an appeal: it was mandatory under Israeli law. Avi hadn't been sent to Israel for the second trial; his bosses at the OSI were confident nothing would change. Surely all the claims filtering into the press were just clever ploys by Demjanjuk's grandstanding attorneys. Surely the interview aired on CBS's *60 Minutes* with Maria Dudek, a skinny woman now in her seventies, with white hair beneath a kerchief, ragged clothing, and only a few teeth left, a woman who had been a prostitute in the 1940s in Wolga Okralnik near Treblinka, a woman who had had a regular john—a regular *ivan*—who operated the gas chambers there, a woman who had screamed in bought passion for him—surely this old woman was mistaken when she said her client's name had not been Ivan Demjanjuk but rather Ivan *Marchenko.*

But no. Avi Meyer was watching all the OSI's work unravel on CNN. The Israeli Supreme Court, under Chief Justice Meir Shamgar, had just overturned the conviction of John Demjanjuk.

Demjanjuk had now been held prisoner in Israel for five and a half years. His appeal had been delayed three years due to a heart attack suffered by Judge Zvi Tal. And during those three years, the Soviet Union had fallen and formerly secret files had been made public.

Just as Maria Dudek had said, the man who had operated the gas chamber at Treblinka had been Ivan Marchenko, a Ukrainian who *did* bear a resemblance to Demjanjuk. But the resemblance was only passing. Demjanjuk had been born April 3, 1920, while Marchenko had been born February 2, 1911. Demjanjuk had blue eyes while Marchenko's were brown.

Marchenko had been married before the outbreak of World War II. Demjanjuk's son-in-law, Ed Nishnic, had gone to Russia and tracked down Marchenko's family in Seryovka, a village in the district of Dnepropetrovsk. The family had not seen Marchenko since he'd enlisted in the Red Army in July 1941. Marchenko's abandoned wife had died only a month before Nishnic's visit, and his daughter broke down and cried upon learning of the horrors her long-missing father had perpetrated at Treblinka. "It's good," she was reported to have said between sobs, "that mother died not knowing."

When those words had been relayed to him, Avi's heart had jumped. It was the same sentiment he'd felt upon learning that Ivan had forced his own father to rape a little girl.

The KGB files contained a sworn statement from Nikolai Shelaiev, the other gas-chamber operator at Treblinka, the one who had been, quite literally, the lesser of two evils. Shelaiev had been captured by the Soviets in 1950, and tried and executed as a war criminal in 1952. His deposition contained the last recorded sighting by anyone anywhere of Ivan Marchenko, coming out of a brothel in Fiume in March 1945. He had told Nikolai he had no intention of returning home to his family.

Even before Maria Dudek had spoken to Mike Wallace, even before Demjanjuk was stripped of his U.S. citizenship, Avi had known that the last name used by Ivan the Terrible while at Treblinka might indeed have been Marchenko. But that was of no significance, Avi had assured himself: the name Marchenko was intimately linked to Demjanjuk, anyway. In a form Demjanjuk had filled out in 1948 to claim refugee status, he had given it as his mother's maiden name.

But before the first trial, the marriage license of Demjanjuk's parents, dated 24 January 1910, had come to light. It proved his mother's maiden name wasn't Marchenko at all; rather, it was Tabachuk. When Avi had questioned Demjanjuk about why he'd put "Marchenko" on the form, Demjanjuk had claimed he'd forgotten his mother's real maiden name and, considering the matter of no consequence, had simply inserted a common Ukrainian surname to complete the paperwork.

Right, Avi had thought. Sure.

But now it seemed it had been the truth. John Demjanjuk was not Ivan ...

... and Avi Meyer and the rest of the OSI had come within inches of being responsible for the execution of an innocent man.

Avi needed to relax, to get his mind off all this.

He walked across his living room to the cabinet in which he kept his videotapes. *Brighton Beach Memoirs* always cheered him up, and *A Funny Thing Happened on the Way to the Forum,* and ...

Without thinking it through, he pulled out a two-tape set.

Judgment at Nuremberg.

Hardly lightweight but, at three hours, it would keep his mind occupied until it was time to go to bed.

Avi put the first tape in his VCR and, while the stirring overture played, popped some Orville Redenbacher's in the microwave.

The movie played on. He drank three beers.

The tables had been turned at Nuremberg: Burt Lancaster played Ernst Janning, one of four German judges on trial. It seemed like a small, supporting role, until Janning took the stand in the movie's final half hour ...

The case against Janning hinged on the matter of Feldenstein, a Jew he'd ordered executed on trumped-up indecency charges. Janning demanded the right to speak, over the objections of his own lawyer. When he took the stand, Avi felt his stomach knotting. Janning told of the lies Hitler had sold German society: "'There are devils among us: Communists, liberals, Jews, Gypsies. Once these devils will be destroyed, your misery will be destroyed.'" Janning shook his head slightly. "It was the old, old story of the sacrificial lamb."

Lancaster spoke forcefully, bringing every bit of his craft to the soliloquy. "It is not easy to tell the truth," he said, "but if there is to be any salvation for Germany, we who know our guilt must admit it, whatever the pain and humiliation." He paused. "I had reached my verdict on the Feldenstein case before I ever came into the courtroom. I would have found him guilty whatever the evidence. It was not a trial at all. It was a sacrificial ritual in which Feldenstein the Jew was the helpless victim."

Avi stopped the tape, deciding not to watch the rest even though it was almost over. He went to the bathroom and brushed his teeth.

But he'd accidentally pushed PAUSE instead of STOP. After five minutes, the tape disengaged and the TV blared at him—more of CNN. He returned to the living room, fumbled for the remote—

—and decided to continue on to the end. Something in him needed to see the finale again.

After the trial, after Janning and the other three Nazi jurists were sentenced to life imprisonment, Spencer Tracy—playing the American judge, Judge Haywood—went at Janning's request to visit Janning in jail. Janning had been writing up memoirs of the cases he was still proud of, the righteous ones, the ones he wanted to be remembered for. He gave the sheaf of papers to Haywood for safekeeping.

And then, his voice containing just the slightest note of pleading, Lancaster again in full control of his art, he said, "Judge Haywood—the reason I asked you to come. Those people, those millions of people ... I never knew it would come to that. You must believe it. You must believe it."

There was a moment of silence, and then Spencer Tracy said, sadly, softly, "*Herr* Janning, it came to that the first time you sentenced a man to death you knew to be innocent."

Avi Meyer turned off the TV and sat in the darkness, slumped on the couch.

"Devils among us." Hitler's phrase, according to Janning. Back in his wooden storage cabinet, next to the blank spot for *Judgment at Nuremberg* was *Murderers Among Us: The Simon Wiesenthal Story*.

Echoes, there. Uncomfortable ones, but echoes still.

Once these devils will be destroyed, your misery will be destroyed.

Avi had wanted to believe that. Destroy the misery, let the ghosts rest.

And Demjanjuk—Demjanjuk—

It was the old, old story of the sacrificial lamb.

No. No, it had been a righteous case, a just case, a—

I had reached my verdict before I ever came into the courtroom. I would have found him guilty whatever the evidence. It was not a trial at all. It was a sacrificial ritual.

Yes, down deep, Avi Meyer had known. Doubtless the Israeli judges—Dov Levin, Zvi Tal, and Dalia Dorner—had known, too.

Herr *Janning, it came to that the first time you sentenced a man to death you knew to be innocent.*

Mar Levin, it came to that the first time you sentenced a man to death you knew to be innocent.

Mar Tal, it came to that ...

Giveret Dorner, it came to that ...

Avi felt his intestines shifting.

Agent Meyer, it came to that the first time you sentenced a man to death you knew to be innocent.

Avi got up and stared out his window, looking out on D Street. His vision was blurry. We'd wanted justice. We'd wanted someone to pay. He placed his hand against the cold glass. What had he done? What had he done?

Now the Israeli prosecutors were saying, well, if Demjanjuk wasn't Ivan the Terrible, maybe he'd been a guard at Sobibor or some other Nazi facility.

Avi thought of Tom Robinson, with his crippled black hand. Shiftless nigger—if he wasn't guilty of raping Mayella Ewell, well, he was probably guilty of something else.

CNN had shown the theater that had been turned into a courthouse, the same theater Avi had sat in five years previously, watching the case unfold. Demjanjuk, even now not freed, was taken away to the jail cell where he'd spent the last two thousand nights.

Avi walked out of his living room, into the darkness.

Miss Jean Louise, stand up. Your father's passin'.

But not even the ghosts stood to mark Avi Meyer's exit.

7

Pierre Tardivel became a driven man, committed to his studies. He decided to specialize in genetics—the field that, after all, had turned his life upside down. He distinguished himself at once, and began a brilliant research career in Canada.

In March 1993, he read about the breakthrough: the gene for Huntington's disease had been discovered, making possible a simple, inexpensive DNA test to determine if one had the gene, and therefore would eventually get the disease. Still, Pierre didn't take the test. He was almost afraid to now. If he didn't have the disease, would he slack off? Begin wasting his life again? Coast out the decades?

At the age of thirty-two, Pierre was appointed a distinguished postdoctoral fellow at the Lawrence Berkeley Laboratory, situated on a hilltop above the University of California, Berkeley. He was assigned to the Human Genome Project, the international attempt to map and sequence all the DNA that makes up a human being.

The Berkeley campus was exactly what a university campus should be: sunny and green and full of open spaces, precisely the kind of place one could imagine the free-love movement having been born at.

What was less wonderful was Pierre's new boss, crusty Burian Klimus, who had won a Nobel Prize for his breakthrough in DNA sequencing—the so-called "Klimus Technique," now widely used in labs around the world.

If Professor Kingsfield from *The Paper Chase* had been a wrestler, he'd have looked like Klimus, a thickset, completely bald man of eighty-one, with a neck half a meter in circumference. His eyes were brown, and his face, though wrinkled, showed only the wrinkles that went with a contracting body; there were no laugh lines—indeed, Pierre saw no signs that Klimus *ever* laughed.

"Don't worry about Dr. Klimus," Joan Dawson, the Human Genome Center's general secretary, had said on Pierre's first day at his new job. Although Klimus's full title was William M. Stanley Professor of Biochemistry—about a quarter of LBL's eleven hundred scientists and engineers had teaching duties at either the Berkeley or San Francisco campuses of UC—Pierre had been told up front that the old man preferred to be called "Doctor," not "Professor." He was a thinker, not a mere teacher.

Pierre had immediately taken a liking to Joan—although it felt strange to be calling a woman twice his own age by her first name. She was kind and gentle and sweet: the gray-haired and bespectacled den mother to all the absent-minded professors as well as the UCB students who did scutwork on the Human Genome Project. Joan often brought in homemade cookies or brownies and left them for everyone to enjoy by the ever-present pot of Peet's coffee.

Indeed, shortly after he'd begun, Pierre found himself seated opposite Joan's desk, munching on a giant butter cookie with M&M's baked into it, while he waited for an appointment with Dr. Klimus. Joan was squinting at a sheet of paper. "This is delicious," Pierre said. He gestured at the plate, which still had five big cookies on it. "I don't know how you can resist them. It must be quite a temptation to keep eating them."

Joan looked up and smiled. "Oh, I don't eat any myself. I'm a diabetic, you see. Have been for about twenty years. But I love to bake, and people seem to like the goodies I bring in so much. It gives me a lot of pleasure seeing people enjoy them."

Pierre nodded, impressed by the self-sacrifice. He had seen earlier that Joan wore a Medic Alert bracelet; now he understood why. Joan went back to squinting at the page on her desk, but then sighed and proffered it to Pierre. "Would you be a dear, and read that bottom line for me? I can't make it out."

Pierre took the sheet. "It says, 'All Q4 staffing reports are due in the director's office no later than 15 Sep.'"

"Thank you." She sighed. "I'm starting to get cataracts, I'm afraid. I guess I'll have to have surgery at some point." Pierre nodded sympathetically—cataracts were common among elderly diabetics.

He looked at his watch; his appointment was supposed to have begun four minutes ago. Damn, but he hated wasting time.

Although Molly had toyed with trying to get a job at Duke University, which was famous for its research into putative psychic phenomena, she instead accepted an associate professorship at the University of California, Berkeley. She'd chosen UCB because it was far enough away from her mother and Paul (who was hanging in, much to Molly's surprise) and her sister Jessica (who had now been through a brief marriage and divorce) that they were unlikely to ever visit.

A new life, a new town—but still, dammit all, she kept making the same stupid mistakes, kept thinking that, somehow, this time things would be different, that she could take spending an evening sitting across from a guy thinking piggish thoughts about her.

Rudy hadn't been any worse than her previous sporadic dates, until he'd gotten a couple of drinks into him—and then his surface thoughts devolved into nothing more than a constant stream of pornography. *Boy, I'd like to fuck her. Eat her pussy. Split 'em wide, baby, split 'em wide ...*

She'd tried changing the topic of conversation, but no matter what they were talking about, the thoughts on the surface of Rudy's mind were like washroom-stall graffiti. Molly observed that the Oakland A's were doing well this season. *Fucking want to hit a home run with you, babe.* She asked Rudy about his work. *Work on* this, *babe! Suck it down all the way ...* She mentioned that it looked like rain. *Gonna shower you, babe, shower you with cum ...*

Finally, she could take no more of it. It was only 8:40—awfully early to end a date that had begun at 7:30—but she had to get out of there.

"Excuse me," said Molly. "I've—I think the pesto sauce is disagreeing with me. I don't feel very well. I think I should go home."

Rudy looked concerned. "I'm sorry," he said. He signaled for the waiter. "Here, we'll get going; I'll take you back to your place."

"No," said Molly. "No, thank you. I—I'll walk home. I'm sure a little walk will help my digestion."

"I'll come with you."

"No, really, I'll be fine. You're sweet to offer, though." She took her wallet out of her little purse. "With tax and tip, my share should be about fifteen dollars," she said, putting that amount on the tablecloth.

Rudy looked disappointed, but at least his concern for her health was genuine enough to have banished the *Penthouse Forum* commentary from his mind. "I'm sorry," he said again.

Molly forced a smile. "Me, too," she said.

"I'll call you," said Rudy.

Molly nodded and hurried out of the restaurant.

The night air was warm and pleasant. She started walking without really thinking about where she was heading. All she knew was that she didn't want to go back to her apartment. Not on a Friday night; it was too lonely, too empty.

She was on University Avenue, which, not surprisingly, ended up taking her to the campus. She passed many couples (some straight, some gay) going the other way, and picked up clearly sexual thoughts from those who unavoidably entered her zone—but that was fine, since the thoughts weren't about her. She came to Doe Library and decided to go in. The pesto sauce was in fact making her intestines grumble a bit, so a trip to the washroom might indeed be in order.

After she finished, she went up to the main floor. The library was mostly empty. Who wanted to be studying on a Friday night, after all, especially this early in the academic year?

"'Evening, Professor Bond," said a librarian sitting at an information desk. He was a lanky, middle-aged man.

"Hi, Pablo. Not many people here tonight."

Pablo nodded and smiled. "True. Still, we've got our regulars. The night watchman is here, as usual." He jerked a thumb at an oak table some distance away. A handsome man in his early thirties with a round face and chocolate hair sat hunched over a book.

"Night watchman?" said Molly.

"Doc Tardivel," said Pablo, "from LBL. Been coming in here most nights lately and stays right up to closing. Keeps sending me back to the stacks for various journals."

Molly glanced at the fellow again. She didn't know the name and didn't recall ever seeing him around the campus. She left Pablo and ambled into the main reading room. The copies of many current journals were stored in a wooden shelving unit that happened to be close to the table this Tardivel fellow was using. Molly made her way over to the unit and began looking for a recent issue of *Developmental Psychology* or *Cognition* to while away an hour or two with. She crouched down to go through the piles of journals on the bottommost shelf, her slacks pulling tight as she did so.

A thought impinged upon her consciousness, like the lighting of a feather on naked skin—but it was unintelligible.

The journals were out of chronological order. She worked her way through the pile, reshuffling them so that the most recent issues were on top.

Another thought fluttered against her consciousness. And suddenly she realized the cause for her difficulty in reading it. The thought was in French; Molly recognized the mental sound of the language.

She found last month's copy of *DP,* straightened up, and scanned the room for a place to sit. There were plenty of empty chairs, of course, but, well ...

French.

The guy thought in French.

And a foxy guy he was, too.

Molly sat down next to him and opened her journal. He looked up, a slightly surprised expression on his face. She smiled at him and then, without really thinking about it, said, "Nice night."

He smiled back. "It sure is."

Molly's heart pounded. He was still thinking in French. She'd known foreigners before, but all of them had switched to thinking in English when speaking that language. "Oooh, what a lovely accent!" said Molly. "Are you French?"

"French-Canadian," said Pierre. "From Montreal."

"Are you an exchange student?" asked Molly, knowing full well from what Pablo had said that he was not.

"No, no," he said. "I'm a postdoc at LBL."

"Oh, so you must know Burian Klimus." Molly feigned a shudder. "There's a cold character."

Pierre laughed. "That he is."

"I'm Molly Bond," said Molly. "I'm an associate professor in the psych department."

"Enchanté," said Pierre. "I'm Pierre Tardivel." He paused. "Psychology, eh? I've always been interested in that."

"Wow," said Molly softly.

"Wow?"

"You really do that. Canadians, I mean. You really say 'eh.'"

Pierre seemed to blush a little. "We also say 'You're welcome.'"

"What?"

"Out here, if you say 'Thank you' to someone, they all seem to reply 'Uh-huh.' We say 'You're welcome.'"

Molly laughed. *"Touché,"* she said. And then she touched her hand to her mouth. "Hey—I guess I know some French after all."

Pierre smiled. It was a very nice smile indeed.

"So," said Molly, looking around at the musty shelves of books, "you come here often?"

Pierre nodded. There were lots of thoughts on the surface of his mind, but to Molly's delight she could make sense out of none of them. And French—French was such a beautiful language, it was almost like soft background music rather than the irritating noise of most people's articulated thoughts.

Before she had really considered it all the way through, the words were out. "Would you like to get a cup of coffee?" she said. And then, as if the suggestion needed some justification, added, "There's a great cappuccino place on Bancroft."

Pierre had an odd look on his face, a mixture of disbelief and pleasant surprise at his unexpected good fortune. "That would be nice," he said.

Yes, thought Molly. It would indeed.

They talked for hours, the background accompaniment of Pierre's French thoughts never intrusive. He might be as big a pig as most other men, but Molly doubted that. Pierre seemed genuinely interested in what she had to say, listening attentively. And he had a wonderful sense of humor; Molly couldn't remember the last time she'd enjoyed anyone's company so much.

Molly had heard it said that French men—both Canadian and European French—had a different attitude toward women than American men did. They were more relaxed around them, less likely to be *on* all the time, less inclined to be constantly trying to prove themselves. Molly had only half believed it. She harbored a suspicion that their apparently blasé attitude toward female nudity was some vast conspiracy: "Keep a poker face, and they'll wave their tits right in front of you!" But Pierre really did seem to be interested in her mind and her work—and that was a bigger turn-on for Molly than any macho display.

Suddenly it was midnight and the café was closing.

"My God," she said. "Where did the time go?"

"It went," said Pierre, "into the past—and I enjoyed every moment of it." He shook his head. "I haven't taken a break like this for weeks."

His eyes met hers. *"Merci beaucoup."*

Molly smiled.

"At this time of night, surely you should be escorted safely to your car or home," said Pierre. "May I walk you there?"

Molly smiled again. "That would be nice. I live just a few blocks from here." They left the café. Pierre walked with his hands clasped behind his back. Molly wondered if he was going to try to hold her hand, but he didn't.

"I really need to see more of this area," said Pierre. "I've been thinking about going over to San Francisco tomorrow, do a little sight-seeing."

"Would you like company?"

They had arrived at the entrance to her apartment building. "I'd love that," said Pierre. "Thank you."

There was a moment of silence. Molly was thinking, well, of course, we'd have to meet up again in the morning, unless—the thought, or maybe just the nighttime breeze, made her shiver—unless he spent the night. But what Pierre was thinking was a complete mystery. "Perhaps we could meet for brunch at eleven," he said.

"Sure. That place right across the street is great," Molly said, pointing.

She wondered if he was going to kiss her. It was exciting not knowing what he was thinking of doing. The moment stretched. He didn't make his move—and that was exciting, too.

"Till tomorrow, then," he said. *"Au revoir."*

Molly went inside. She was grinning from ear to ear.

8

Pierre and Molly's relationship had been building nicely. He had been to Molly's apartment three times now, but she had yet to see his place. Tonight was the night, though: A&E was showing another *Cracker* made-for-TV movie with Robbie Coltrane, and they both loved that series. But Molly only had a thirteen-inch TV, and Pierre had a twenty-seven-inch set—you needed a decent size to properly follow a hockey game.

He'd cleaned up some, gathering the socks and underwear from the living-room floor, getting the newspapers off his green-and-orange couch, and doing what he considered to be a decent job of dusting—wiping the sleeve of the Montreal Canadiens jersey he was wearing across the top of the TV and stereo cabinet.

They ordered a La Val's pizza during the final commercial break, and, after the movie was over, they chatted about it while waiting for the pizza to arrive. Molly loved the use of psychology in *Cracker*; Coltrane's character, Fitz, was a forensic psychologist who worked with the Manchester police.

"He *is* an amazing fellow," agreed Pierre.

"And," said Molly, "he's sexy."

"Who?" asked Pierre, puzzled. "Not Fitz?"

"Yes."

"But he's a hundred pounds overweight, an alcoholic, a compulsive gambler, and he smokes like a chimney."

"But that *mind,*" said Molly. "That intensity."

"He's going to end up in a hospital with a heart attack."

"I know," sighed Molly. "I hope he has decent health insurance."

"Britain is like Canada—socialized medicine."

"'Socialized' is kind of an ugly word here," said Molly. "But I must say the idea of universal health care *is* appealing. It's too bad Hillary didn't get her way." A pause. "I guess it was a shock for you to have to start paying for your health insurance."

"I'm sure it will be. I haven't got around to it yet."

Molly's jaw dropped. "You don't have any health insurance?"

"Well ... no."

"Are you covered under the faculty-association group plan?"

"No. I'm not faculty, after all; I'm just a postdoc."

"Gee, Pierre, you really should have some medical insurance. What would you do if you were in an accident?"

"I hadn't thought about that, I guess. I'm so used to the Canadian system, which covered me automatically, that I hadn't thought about having to actually *do* something to get insurance."

"Are you still covered under the Canadian plan?"

"It's actually a provincial plan—the Québec plan. But I won't meet the residency requirements this year, which means, no, I'm not really covered."

"You better do something soon. You could be wiped out financially if you had an accident."

"Can you recommend somebody?"

"Me? I have no idea. I'm under the faculty-association plan. That's with Sequoia Health, I think. But for individual insurance, I haven't a clue who's got the best rates. I've seen ads for a company called Bay Area Health, and another called—oh, what is it?—Condor, I think."

"I'll call them up."

"Tomorrow. Do it tomorrow. I had an uncle who broke his leg once and had to be put in traction. He didn't have any insurance, and the total bill was thirty-five thousand dollars. He had to sell his house to pay for it."

Pierre patted her hand. "All right already. I'll do it first thing."

Their pizza arrived. Pierre carried the box to the dining-room table and opened it up. Molly ate her pieces directly from the box, but Pierre liked his to be burn-the-roof-of-your-mouth hot, so he nuked each of his slices for thirty seconds before eating them. The kitchen smelled of cheese and pepperoni, plus an aroma of slightly moist cardboard coming from the box.

After she'd finished her third slice, Molly asked, out of the blue, "What do you think about kids?"

Pierre helped himself to a fourth piece. "I like them."

"Me, too," said Molly. "I've always wanted to be a mother."

Pierre nodded, not knowing exactly what he was supposed to say.

"I mean," continued Molly, "getting my Ph.D. took a lot of time and, well, I never met the right person."

"That happens sometimes," said Pierre, smiling.

Molly nibbled at her pizza. "Oh, yes. 'Course, it's hardly an insurmountable problem—not having a husband, I mean. I have lots of friends who are single moms. Sure, for most of them that wasn't the way they planned it, but they're doing fine. In fact, I ..."

"What?"

She looked away. "No, nothing."

Pierre's curiosity was aroused. "Tell me."

Molly considered for a time, then: "I did something pretty stupid—oh, six years ago now, I guess it was."

Pierre raised his eyebrows.

"I was twenty-five, and, well, frankly, I'd given up any hope of finding a man I could have a long-term relationship with." She raised a hand. "I know twenty-five sounds young, but I was already six years older than my mom was when she'd had me, and—well, I don't want to go into the reasons right now, but I'd been having a terrible time with guys, and I didn't see that that was likely to ever change. But I *did* want to have a child, and so I ... well, I picked up some men—four or five different one-night stands." She held up a hand again, as if feeling a need to make it all seem somewhat less sordid. "They were all medical students; I was trying to choose carefully. Each time I did it was at the right point in my cycle; I was hoping to get pregnant off one of them. I wasn't looking for a husband, you understand—just for, well, just for some sperm."

Pierre had his head tilted to one side. He clearly didn't know how to respond.

Molly shrugged. "Anyway, it didn't work; I didn't get pregnant." She looked at the ceiling for a few moments, and drew in breath. "What I got instead was gonorrhea." She exhaled noisily. "I suppose I'm lucky I didn't get AIDS. God, it was a stupid thing to do."

Pierre's face must have shown his shock; they'd slept together several times now.

"Don't worry," said Molly, seeing his expression. "I'm completely over it, thank God. I had all the follow-up tests after the penicillin treatment. I'm totally clean. Like I said, it was a stupid thing to do, but—well, I *did* want a baby."

"Why'd you stop?"

Molly looked at the floor. Her voice was small. "The gonorrhea scarred my fallopian tubes. I *can't* get pregnant the normal way anymore; if I'm ever going to do it, it'll have to be via in vitro fertilization, and, well, that costs money. Around ten grand per attempt, last time I looked. My health insurance doesn't cover it, since the blocked tubes weren't a congenital condition. But I've been saving up."

"Oh," said Pierre.

"I—ah, I thought you should know ..." She trailed off, and then shrugged again. "I *am* sorry."

Pierre looked at his slice of pizza, now growing cold. He absently picked a green pepper off it; they were only supposed to be on half, but a stray one had ended up on one of his slices. "I would never say it's for the best," said Pierre, "but I guess I'm old-fashioned enough to think a child should have both a mother and a father."

Molly did meet his eyes, and held them. "My thought exactly," she said.

At two o'clock in the afternoon, Pierre entered the Human Genome Center office—and found to his surprise that a party was going on. Joan Dawson's usual supply of home-baked goodies hadn't been enough; someone had gone out and bought bags of nachos and cheesies, and several bottles of champagne.

As soon as Pierre entered, one of the other geneticists—Donna Yamashita, it was—handed him a glass. "What's all the excitement about?" asked Pierre over the noise.

"They finally got what they wanted from Hapless Hannah," said Yamashita, grinning.

"Who's Hapless Hannah?" asked Pierre, but Yamashita had already moved away to greet someone else. Pierre walked over to Joan's desk. She had a dark liquid in her champagne glass. Probably diet cola; as a diabetic, she wasn't supposed to drink alcohol. "What's happening?" said Pierre. "Who is Hapless Hannah?"

Joan smiled her kindly smile. "That's the Neanderthal skeleton on loan from the Hebrew University at Givat Ram. Dr. Klimus has been trying to extract DNA from the bone for months, and today he finally finished getting a complete set."

The old man himself had moved nearer—and for once there was a smile on his broad, liver-spotted face. "That's right," he said, his voice cold and dry. He glanced sideways at a chubby man Pierre recognized as a UCB paleontologist. "Now that we have Neanderthal DNA, we can do some real science about human origins, instead of just making wild guesses."

"That's wonderful," replied Pierre above the din of people milling about the small office. "How old was the bone?"

"Sixty-two thousand years," said Klimus triumphantly.

"But surely the DNA would have degraded over all that time," said Pierre.

"That's the beauty of the site where Hapless Hannah was found," said Klimus. "She died in a cave-in that completely sealed her in—she was an actual, honest-to-goodness cavewoman. Aerobic bacteria in the cave used up all the oxygen, so she'd spent the last sixty thousand years in an oxygen-free environment, meaning her pyrimidines didn't oxidize. We've recovered all twenty-three pairs of chromosomes."

"What a lucky break," said Pierre.

"It sure is," said Donna Yamashita, who had suddenly appeared again at Pierre's elbow. "Hannah will answer a lot of questions, including the big one about whether Neanderthal was a separate species—*Homo neanderthalensis*—or just a sub-species of modern humanity—*Homo sapiens neanderthalensis,* and—"

Klimus spoke over top of her. "—And we should be able to tell whether Neanderthals died out without leaving any descendants, or whether they crossbred with Cro-Magnon, and therefore mixed their genes with ours."

"That's terrific," said Pierre.

"Of course," said Klimus, "there'll still be many questions unanswered about Neanderthals—fine details of physical appearance, culture, and so on. But, still, this is a remarkable day." He turned his back on Pierre, and in an unexpected display of exuberance, tapped the side of his champagne glass with his Mont Blanc pen. "Everybody—everybody! Your attention, please! I'd like to propose a toast—to Hapless Hannah! Soon to become the best-known Neanderthal in history!"

9

Pierre's lab looked like just about every other lab he'd ever seen: a poster of the periodic table on one wall; a well-used copy of the *Rubber Bible* lying open on a desk; lots of glass labware set up on retort stands; a small centrifuge; a UNIX workstation with Post-it notes stuck to the bezel around the monitor; an emergency shower station, in case of chemical spills; a glass-enclosed work area under a fume hood. The walls were that sickly yellow-beige that seems so common in university environments. The lighting was fluorescent; the floor, tiled.

Pierre was working at one of the counters that lined all four walls of the room, staring at DNA autorads positioned over an illuminated panel built into the countertop. He was wearing a stained white lab coat, but it wasn't buttoned up, so his Quebec Winter Carnival T-shirt was visible underneath. He'd never been more shocked than when an American student had mistaken the *Bonhomme* on the shirt for the giant Stay-Puft marshmallow man from *Ghostbusters*—something akin to confusing Uncle Sam with Colonel Sanders.

Burian Klimus appeared in the doorway, looking most put out. Standing next to the old man was an attractive Asian-American woman with black hair that had been teased into a frizzy halo around her face. "That's him," said Klimus.

"Mr. Tardivel," said the woman. "I'm Tiffany Feng, from Condor Health Insurance."

Pierre nodded at Klimus. "Thanks for bringing her up, sir," he said. The ancient geneticist scowled, then shambled away.

Tiffany was in her late twenties. She was carrying a black attaché case, and was dressed in a blue jacket and matching pants. Her white blouse was open more than one might expect at the top. Pierre was amused; he suspected Tiffany dressed differently when going to see a prospective male customer than she did when the customer was female.

"I'm sorry I'm late," said Tiffany. "Traffic was murder coming across the bridge." She handed him a yellow-and-black business card, then looked appreciatively around the lab. "You're obviously a scientist."

Pierre nodded. "I'm a molecular biologist, working on the Human Genome Project."

"Really?" said Tiffany. "What a fascinating area!"

"You know about it?"

"Sure. We've had some great lectures on it at work." She smiled. "Anyway, I understand you're interested in talking about insurance options."

Pierre motioned for Tiffany to take a seat. "That's right," he said. "I'm from Canada, so I've never bought health insurance before. For a little while longer I'll still meet the Québec residency test, but—"

Tiffany shook her head. "I've helped several Canadians over the years. Your provincial health plans cover you only to the dollar value that the same services would cost in Canada, where prices for medical services are set by the government. Here, there are no price controls. You'll find that most procedures are more expensive, and your Quebec plan won't cover the extra. Plus, the provincial plans provide for medical treatments, but not such things as private hospital rooms." She paused. "Do you have any insurance under the faculty-association plan?"

Pierre shook his head. "I'm not faculty. I'm just a visiting researcher."

She moved her attaché case up onto the lab bench and opened it. "Well, then you'll need a comprehensive package. We offer what we call our Gold Plan, which provides for one hundred percent of all your emergency hospital bills, including ambulance transfers, and anything else you might need, such as wheelchairs or crutches. Plus, it also covers all your routine medical needs, such as annual physical checkups, prescriptions, and so on." She handed him a gold-embossed trifold brochure.

Pierre took it and browsed through it. Huntington's patients usually ended their lives with a protracted hospital stay. If it turned out he had the disease, he'd certainly want a private room for that, and—ah, good. This package also covered at-home nursing services and even experimental drug treatments. "Looks good," said Pierre. "How much are the premiums?"

"They're on a sliding scale." She pulled a yellow-and-black binder out of her attaché case. "May I ask how old you are?"

"Thirty-two."

"Do you smoke?"

"No."

"And you don't currently have any medical condition, like diabetes, AIDS, or a heart murmur?"

"Right."

"Are your parents still alive?"

"My mother is."

"What did your father die of?"

"Umm, you mean my biological father, right?"

Tiffany blinked. "Yes."

Henry Spade had passed away four years ago; Pierre had gone to Toronto for the funeral. "Complications from Huntington's disease."

Tiffany closed the binder. "Oh." She looked at Pierre for a moment. "That makes things rather complex. Do *you* have Huntington's?"

"I have no idea."

"You have no symptoms?"

"None."

"Huntington's is carried on a dominant gene, right? So you've got a fifty-fifty chance of having inherited the gene."

"That's right."

"But you haven't taken the genetic test for it?"

"No."

She sighed. "This is very awkward, Pierre. I don't make the decisions about who gets covered and who doesn't, but I can tell you what's going to happen if we put your application in now: you'll be rejected on the basis of family history."

"Really? I guess I should have kept my mouth shut."

"That wouldn't have done you any good in the long run; if you ever submitted a claim related to your Huntington's, we'd investigate. If we found that you'd been aware of your family history at the time you applied for insurance, we would disallow the claim. No, you did the right thing telling me, but ..."

"But what?"

"Well, as I said, this *is* awkward." She opened the binder again, going to one of the tabbed sections at the back. "I don't usually show this chart to clients, but ... well, it explains it pretty clearly. As you can see, we have three basic levels of premiums in each age/sex group. Internally, we refer to them as the H, M, and L levels—for high, medium, and low. If you had a family history that showed a predisposition to, oh, say, to having a heart attack in your forties, something like that, we'd still issue you a policy, but at the H premium level—the highest level. If, on the other hand, you had a favorable family history, we'd offer you the M level. Now, M is still pretty high—"

"I'll say!" said Pierre, looking at the figure in the column labeled "Males, 30 to 34."

"Right, it is. But that's because we're not allowed to require genetic testing of applicants. Because of that, we have to assume that you might indeed have a serious genetic disorder. Now, what I'm supposed to do after showing you that premium level is say, 'Well, you know, I can't ask you to have a genetic test, but if you *choose* to, and the results are favorable, then I'd be able to offer you *this* premium here'—the L premium."

"That's only half as much as the M premium."

"Exactly. It's an incentive to have the test, see? We don't *make* you take a genetic test, but if you decide to do so voluntarily, you can save a lot of money."

"That hardly seems fair."

Tiffany shrugged. "Lots of insurance companies do it this way now."

"But you're saying I can't get *any* health insurance because of my family history?"

"Right. Huntington's is just too costly, and your risk level, at fifty percent, is too high, to consider covering you at all. But if you take a test that proves you don't have the gene—"

"But I don't want to take the test."

"Well, this gets even more complicated." She sighed, trying to think of how best to explain it. "Last month, Governor Wilson signed a Senate bill into law. It comes into effect on January first—ten weeks from now. The new law says California health insurers will no longer be able to use genetic testing to discriminate against people who carry the gene for a disease, but have no symptoms of it. In other words, we will no longer be able to consider merely *having* the gene for Huntington's or ALS or any other late-onset illnesses to be a preexisting condition in otherwise healthy people."

"Well, it *isn't* a preexisting condition."

"Politely, Mr. Tardivel, that's a matter of interpretation. The new California law is the first of its kind in the nation; in every other state, having bad genes *does* amount to a preexisting condition, even if you're asymptomatic. Even those few states that *do* have anti-genetic-discrimination laws—Florida, Ohio, Iowa, a couple of others—even they make exceptions for insurance companies, allowing them to use actuarial or claims experience in deciding whom to insure and what premiums to charge."

Pierre frowned. "But what you're saying is, because we're in California, if I wait until January first, you won't be able to reject me on the basis of my family history?"

"No, we'll still be able to do that—that's valid information that you're a high-risk candidate, and we're not obligated to give policies to high-risk people."

"Then what's the difference?"

"The difference is that genetic information *supersedes* family-history information. Do you see? If we have concrete genetic info, it takes precedence over anything we might infer from the medical histories of your parents or siblings. If you take the genetic test, then, under the new state law, we *have* to give you a policy regardless of its results related to Huntington's disease. Even if the test proves that you *do* have the Huntington's gene, we still have to insure you as long as you apply before you have any symptoms; we *can't* reject you or charge you a higher premium based on actual genetic information."

"Wait a minute—that's crazy. If I don't take the test, you've got a fifty-fifty shot that I'll end up making a lot of claims due to my Huntington's, and so you reject me because of my family history. But if I do take the test, and even if it's a hundred percent definite that I *will* get Huntington's and therefore make a lot of claims, you *will* insure me?"

"That's right, or at least it will be, after January first, because of the new law."

"But I don't want to take the Huntington's test."

"Really? I'd have thought you'd like to know."

"No. No, I don't. Hardly any Huntington's at-risks have taken the test. Most of us don't want to know for sure."

Tiffany shrugged a little. "Well, if you want to be insured, it's your only option. Look, why don't you fill out the forms today, but date them January—well, January second; the first business day in the new year. I'll call you up then, and you can let me know what you want to do. If you've already taken the test by that point, or are prepared to take it, I'll put the policy application in; if not, I'll just tear it up."

It was obvious that Tiffany simply didn't want to risk losing a sale, but, dammit, this had already taken far too much time; Pierre certainly didn't want to go through the same rigmarole again with somebody else. "I'd like to see some other plans before I make my decision," he said.

"Of course." She showed Pierre a variety of policies: the predictable Silver and Bronze Plans, with progressively fewer benefits; a hospital-only plan; a drug-only plan; and so on. But Tiffany pressed hard for the Gold Plan, and Pierre finally agreed, telling himself he would have made exactly the same decision even if her blouse had been done up all the way.

"You won't regret your choice," said Tiffany. "You're not just buying health insurance—you're buying peace of mind." She got a form from her briefcase and handed it to Pierre. "If you could just fill this out—and don't forget to date it January second." She opened the left side of her jacket. There was a pocket inside the jacket, with a row of identical retractable ballpoint pens clipped to it. She extracted one, closed her jacket, and handed the pen to Pierre.

He pressed down on the pen's button with his thumb, extending the point, and filled out the forms. When he was done, he handed the form back to her, and absently went to put the pen in his own breast pocket.

Tiffany pointed at it. "My pen ... ?" she said.

Pierre smiled sheepishly and handed it back to her. "Sorry."

"So, I'll call you at the beginning of the year," she said. "But be careful between now and then—we wouldn't want anything to happen to you before you're insured."

"I still don't know if I'm going to take the test," he said.

She nodded. "It's up to you."

Pierre thought, *It hardly seems that way,* but decided not to argue the point further.

10

Pierre had searched long and hard for an area to specialize in. His first instinct had been to do research directly into Huntington's disease, but ever since the Huntington's gene had been discovered, many scientists were concentrating on that. Naturally, Pierre hoped they would find a cure—and soon enough to help him, of course, if it turned out that he himself did have the disease. But Pierre also knew of the need for objectivity in science: he couldn't afford to piss away what time he might have left chasing slim leads that would probably amount to nothing—leads that someone without Huntington's would know enough to abandon, but that he, out of desperation, might devote far too much time to.

Pierre decided instead to concentrate on an area most other geneticists were by and large ignoring, in hopes that such territory would be more likely to yield a breakthrough that might indeed get him a Nobel Prize. He centered his research on the so-called junk DNA, or *introns:* the 90 percent of the human genome that did not code for protein synthesis.

Exactly what all that DNA *did* do no one was quite sure. Some parts seemed to be foreign sequences from viruses that had invaded the genome in the past; others were endlessly stuttering repeats—ironically, similar in structure to the very unusual gene that caused Huntington's; others still were deactivated leftovers from our evolutionary past. Most geneticists felt the Human Genome Project could be completed much more quickly if the junk nine-tenths were simply ignored. But Pierre harbored the suspicion that there was something significant coded in some as yet undeciphered way into that mess of nucleotides.

His new research assistant, a UCB grad student named Shari Cohen, did not agree.

Shari was tiny and always immaculately dressed, a porcelain doll with pale skin and lustrous black hair—and a giant diamond engagement ring. "Any luck at the library?" asked Pierre.

She shook her head. "No, and I've got to say this seems like a long shot, Pierre." She spoke with a Brooklyn accent. "After all, the genetic code is simple and well understood."

And so, indeed, it seemed to be. Four bases made up the rungs of the DNA ladder: adenine, cytosine, guanine, and thymine. Each of those was a letter in the genetic alphabet. In fact, they were usually referred to simply by their initial letters: A, C, G, and T. Those letters combined together to form the three-letter words of the genetic language.

"Well," said Pierre, "consider this: the genetic alphabet has four letters, and all its words are three letters long. So, how many possible words does the genetic language have?"

"Four to the third," said Shari, "which is sixty-four."

"Right," said Pierre. "Now, what do these sixty-four words actually do?"

"They specify the amino acids to be used in protein synthesis," replied Shari. "The word AAA specifies lysine, AAC specifies asparagine, and so on."

Pierre nodded. "And how many different amino acids are used in making proteins?"

"Twenty."

"But you said there are sixty-four words in the genetic vocabulary."

"Well, three of the words are punctuation marks."

"But even taking those into account, that still leaves sixty-one words to express only twenty concepts." He moved across the room and pointed to a wall chart labeled "The Genetic Code."

Shari came over to stand next to him. "Well, just as in English, the genetic language has synonyms." She pointed at the first box on the chart. "GCA, GCC, GCG, and GCT all specify the same amino acid, alanine."

"Right. But *why* do these synonyms exist? Why not just use twenty words, one for each amino?"

Shari shrugged. "It's probably a safety mechanism, to reduce the likelihood of transcription errors garbling the message."

Pierre waved at the chart. "But some aminos can be specified by as many as six different words, and others by only one. If synonyms protected against transcription errors, surely you'd want some for every word. Indeed, if you were designing a sixty-four-word code simply for redundancy, you might devote three words apiece to each of the twenty amino acids, and use the four remaining words for punctuation marks."

THE GENETIC CODE

Alanine	Arginine	Aspartic acid	Asparagine	Cysteine	Glutamic acid	Glutamine
GCA GCC GCG GCT	AGA AGG CGA CGC CGG CGT	GAC GAT	AAC AAT	TGC TGT	GAA GAG	CAA CAG

Glycine	Histidine	Isoleucine	Leucine	Lysine	Methionine [START]	Phenylalanine
GGA GGC GGG GGT	CAC CAT	ATA ATC ATT	CTA CTC CTG CTT TTA TTG	AAA AAG	ATG	TTC TTT

Proline	Serine	Threonine	Tryptophan	Tyrosine	Valine	STOP
CCA CCC CCG CCT	AGC AGT TCA TCC TCG TCT	ACA ACC ACG ACT	TGG	TAC TAT	GTA GTC GTG GTT	TAA TAG TGA

Shari shrugged. "I guess. But the DNA system wasn't designed; it evolved."

"True, true. Still, nature tends to come up with optimized solutions through trial and error. Like the double helix itself—remember how Crick and Watson knew they'd found the answer to how DNA was put together? It wasn't because their version was the only possible one. Rather, it was because it was the most *beautiful* one. Why would some aspects of DNA be absolutely elegant, while others, including something as important as the actual genetic code, be sloppy? My bet is that God or nature, or whatever it was that put DNA together, is *not* sloppy."

"Meaning?" said Shari.

"Meaning maybe the choice of which synonym is used when specifying an amino acid actually encodes additional information."

Shari's delicate eyebrows went up. "Like, if we're an embryo, insert this amino, but if we've already been born, don't insert it!" She clapped her hands together. The mystery of how cells differentiated throughout the development of a fetus still hadn't been solved.

Pierre held up his hand. "It can't be anything as direct as that, or geneticists would have noticed it long ago. But the choices of synonyms over a long stretch of DNA—be it in the active portions, or in the introns—might indeed be significant."

"Or," said Shari, now pouting slightly at having her idea rejected, "it might not."

Pierre smiled. "Sure. But let's find out, one way or the other."

A Sunday morning.

Molly Bond loved going over to San Francisco—loved its seafood restaurants, its neighborhoods, its hills, its cable cars, its architecture.

The street Molly was on was deserted; not surprising, given how early it was. Molly had come to San Francisco to attend the Unitarian fellowship there; she wasn't particularly religious, and had found the hypocrisy of most of the clergy she'd met in her life unbearable, but she did enjoy the Unitarian approach, and today's guest speaker—an expert on artificial intelligence—sounded fascinating.

Molly had parked a few blocks from the fellowship hall. The meeting didn't start until nine o'clock; she thought she might go into McDonald's for an Egg McMuffin beforehand—her one vice that she periodically but only halfheartedly tried to break was her fondness for fast food. As she headed along a steeply angled sidewalk approaching the restaurant, she noticed an old man up ahead at the side of the road in a black trench coat. The man was bent over, poking with a walking stick at something lying at the base of a tree.

Molly continued along, enjoying the crisp early-morning air. The sky was cloudless, a pristine bowl of blue arching over the stuccoed buildings.

She was now only a dozen paces or so from the man in black. His trench coat was an expensive London Fog model, and his black shoes had recently been polished. The man was eighty if he were a day, but tall for a man that age. He was wearing a navy blue watch cap that pressed his ears against his head. He also had the collar of his trench coat turned up, but his neck was thick, with loose folds of skin hanging from it. The old guy was too absorbed in what he was doing to notice her approach. Molly heard a small whimpering sound. She looked down and her mouth dropped in horror. The black-clad man was poking at a cat with his stick.

The cat had obviously been hit by a car and left to die. Its coat, mottled white, black, orange, and cream, was smeared down the entire left side with blood. It had clearly been hit some time ago—much of the blood had dried to a brown crust—but it was still oozing thick red liquid from one long cut. One of the cat's eyes had popped partway from its skull and was clouded over in tones of bluish gray.

"Hey!" Molly shouted at the man in black. "Are you crazy? Leave that poor thing alone!"

The man must have stumbled on the cat by accident, and had apparently been enjoying the pathetic cries it made each time he jabbed it with his stick. He turned to face Molly. She was disgusted to see that his ancient bone-white penis, erect, was protruding from his unzipped trousers, and that his other hand had been on it.

"Blyat!" cried the man in an accented voice, his dark eyes narrowing to slits. *"Blyat!"*

"Get out of here!" Molly yelled. "I'm going to call the police!"

The man snapped *"Blyat"* at her once more, then hobbled away. Molly thought about going after him and detaining him until the police could arrive, but the very last thing in the world she wanted to do was touch the vile character. She loomed in to look at the cat. It was in terrible shape; she wished she knew a way to put it quickly out of its misery, but anything she might try would probably just torture the poor creature more. "There, there," she said in soothing tones. "He's gone. He won't bother you anymore." The cat moved slightly. Its breathing was ragged.

Molly looked around; there was a pay phone at the end of the block. She hurried over to it, called directory assistance, and asked for the SPCA emergency number. She then dialed that. "There's a cat dying at the side of the road," she said. She craned her neck to see the street signs. "It's just off the sidewalk on Portola Drive, a half block up from the corner of Swanson. I think it was hit by a car, perhaps an hour or two ago ... No, I'll stay with the animal, thanks. Thanks ever so—and please hurry."

She sat cross-legged on the sidewalk next to the cat, wishing she could find it in her heart to stroke the poor animal's fur, but it was too disgusting to touch. She looked down the street, furious and distraught. The black-clad old man was gone.

11

Three weeks later.

Pierre sat in his lab, looking at his watch. Shari had said she might be late getting back from lunch, but it was now 14:45, and a three-hour lunch seemed excessive even by West Coast standards. Perhaps he'd been crazy hiring someone who was just about to get married. She'd have a million things to do before the wedding, after all, and ...

The door to the lab opened, and Shari walked in. Her eyes were bloodshot and although she'd obviously taken a moment to attempt to fix her makeup, she'd clearly been crying a lot.

"Shari!" said Pierre, rising to his feet and moving over to her. "What's wrong?"

She glanced at Pierre, her lower lip trembling. Pierre couldn't remember the last time he'd seen someone look so sad. Her voice was low and quavering. "Howard and I broke up." Tears were welling again at the corners of her eyes.

"Oh, Shari," said Pierre. "I'm so sorry." He hadn't known her that long and wasn't sure if he should pry—and yet, she probably needed somebody to talk to. Everything had been fine before she left for lunch; Pierre's might very well be the only friendly face she'd seen since whatever had happened.

"Did you—did you have a fight?"

Tears rolled slowly down Shari's cheeks. She shook her head.

Pierre was at a loss. He thought about drawing her close to him, trying to comfort her, but he was her employer—he couldn't do that. Finally he settled on, "It must hurt."

She nodded almost imperceptibly. Pierre led her over to a lab stool. She sat on it, placing her hands in her lap. Pierre noticed the engagement ring was gone. "Everything was going so well," she said, her voice full of anguish. She was quiet for a long time. Again, Pierre thought about reaching out to her—a hand on her shoulder, say. He hated to see anyone in such pain. "But—but my parents came over from Poland after World War II, and Howard's parents are from the Balkans."

Pierre looked at her, not understanding.

"Don't you see?" she said, sniffing. "We're both Ashkenazi."

Pierre lifted his shoulders slightly, helpless.

"Eastern European Jews," said Shari. "We had to go for counseling."

Pierre didn't really know much about Judaism, although there were lots of English-speaking Jews in Montreal. "Yes?"

"For Tay-Sachs," said Shari, sounding almost angry that it had to be spelled out.

"Oh," said Pierre, very softly, understanding at last. Tay-Sachs was a genetic disease that resulted in a failure to produce the enzyme hexosaminidase-A, which, in turn, caused a fatty substance to accumulate in the nerve cells of the brain. Unlike Huntington's, Tay-Sachs manifested itself in infancy, causing blindness, dementia, convulsions, extensive paralysis, and death—usually by the age of four. It was almost exclusively found among Jews of Eastern European extraction. Four percent of American Jews descended from there carried the gene—but, again unlike Huntington's, the Tay-Sachs gene was recessive, meaning a child had to receive genes from both parents to get the disease. If both the father and the mother carried the gene, any child of theirs had a 25-percent chance of having Tay-Sachs.

Still—maybe Shari had misunderstood. Yes, she was a genetics student, but ... "So you both have the gene?" asked Pierre, gently.

Shari nodded and wiped her cheeks. "I had no idea that I carried it. But Howard—he suspected he carried the gene, and never said a word to me." She sounded bitter. "His sister discovered she had it when she got married, but it was okay, because her fiancé didn't have it. But Howard knew that since his sister had it, he himself had to have a 50-percent chance of being a carrier—and he never told me." She looked briefly at Pierre, then dropped her gaze down to the floor. "You shouldn't keep secrets from someone you love."

Pierre thought about himself and Molly, but said nothing. There was quiet between them for perhaps half a minute.

"Still," said Pierre at last, "there are options. Amniocentesis can determine if a fetus has received two Tay-Sachs genes. If you found that it had, you could have an ..." Pierre couldn't quite bring himself to say "abortion" out loud.

But Shari simply nodded. "I know." She sniffed a few times. She was quiet for a moment, as if considering whether to go on. "But I've got endometriosis; my gynecologist warned me years ago that I'm going to have a very hard time conceiving. I told Howard that when we got serious. I really, really want to have children, but it's going to be an uphill battle, and ..."

Pierre nodded. And there was no way she could afford to have pregnancies terminated.

"I'm so sorry, Shari, but ..." He paused, not sure if it was his place to say anything more.

She looked at him, her face a question.

"You could adopt," said Pierre. "It's not so bad. I was raised by someone who wasn't my biological father."

Shari blew her nose, but then laughed a cold laugh. "You're not Jewish." It was a statement, not a question.

Pierre shook his head.

She exhaled noisily, as if daunted by the prospect of trying to explain so much. Finally, she said, "Six million Jews were killed during World War II—including most of my parents' relatives. Ever since I was a little girl, I've been brought up to believe that I've got to have children of my own, that I have to do my part to help restore my people." She looked away. "You don't understand."

Pierre was quiet for a while. Then, at last, he said softly, "I am sorry, Shari." He did, finally, touch her shoulder. She responded at once, collapsing against his chest, and sobbed softly for a very long time.

12

Pierre and Molly were sitting side by side on his green-and-orange living-room couch, his arm around her. It had reached the point where they were spending almost every night together, as often at his place as hers. Molly snuggled her back into the crook of his shoulder. Shafts of amber from the setting sun streamed in through the windows. Pierre had actually vacuumed today, the second time since he'd moved in. The low angle of the sunlight highlighted the paths his Hoover had made.

"Pierre," Molly said, but then fell silent.

"Hmm?"

"Oh, nothing. I—no, nothing."

"No, go ahead," Pierre said, eyebrows raised. "What's on your mind?"

"The question," said Molly, slowly, "is more what's on *your* mind?"

Pierre frowned. "Eh?"

Molly seemed to be wrestling with whether to go on. Then, all at once, she sat up straight on the couch, took Pierre's arm from her shoulder, and brought it into her lap, intertwining her fingers with his. "Let's try a little game. Think of a word—any English word—and I'll try to guess it."

Pierre smiled. "Anything at all?"

"Yes."

"Okay."

"Now concentrate on the word. Con—it's 'aardvark.'"

"C'est vrai," said Pierre, shocked. "How'd you do that?"

"Try again," said Molly.

"Okay—I've got one."

"What's pie—pie-rim-ih-deen? Is that French?"

"How did you do that?"

"What's that word mean?"

"Pyrimidine. It's a type of organic base. How did you do that?"

"Let's try it again."

Pierre disengaged his hand from hers. "No. Tell me how you did that."

Molly looked at him. They were sitting so close together that her gaze kept shifting from his left eye to his right. She opened her mouth as if to say something, closed it, then tried again. "I can ..." She shut her eyes. "God, I thought telling you about my stupid bout with gonorrhea was hard. I've *never* told *anyone* this before." She paused and took a deep breath. "I can read minds, Pierre."

Pierre tipped his head to one side. His mouth hung slightly open. He clearly didn't know what to say.

"It's true," said Molly. "I've been able to do it since I was thirteen."

"Okay," Pierre said, his tone betraying that he felt this was all some trick that could be exposed if enough thought were given to it. "Okay, what am I thinking now?"

"It's in French; I don't understand French. Voo—lay—voo ... coo, something ... The word *moi*—I know that one."

"What's my Canadian Social Insurance Number?"

"You're not thinking about the actual number. I can't read it unless you're actually thinking of it." A pause. "You're saying the numbers in French. *Cinq*—that's five, right? *Huit*—eight. *Deux*—two. Um, you're repeating it to yourself; it's hard to keep track. Just run through it once. *Cinq huit deux ... six un neuf, huit trois neuf.*"

"Reading minds is ..." He stopped.

"'Not possible' is what you were about to say."

"But how?"

"I don't know."

Pierre was quiet for a long time, sitting absolutely still. "Do you have to be in physical contact with the person?" he said at last.

"No. But I do have to be close—the person has to be within what I call my 'zone,' no more than about three feet away. It's been very difficult to do any empirical studies, being both the experimenter and the experimental subject, and without revealing to those I'm with what I'm trying to do, but I'd say the—the *effect*—is governed by the inverse-square law. If I move twice as far away from you, I only hear—if 'hear' is the correct word—your thoughts a quarter as ... as 'loudly,' so to speak."

"You say 'hear.' You don't see my thoughts? Don't pick up mental pictures?"

"That's right. If all you'd done was conjure up an image of an aardvark, I couldn't have detected it. But when you concentrated on the word 'aardvark' I—well, 'heard' *is* as good a word as any—I heard it as clearly as if you'd whispered it in my ear."

"That's—incredible."

"You thought about saying 'amazing,' but changed your mind as the words were coming out."

Pierre leaned back into the couch, stunned.

"I can detect what I call 'articulated thoughts'—words your brain is using," said Molly. "I can't detect images. And emotions—thank God, I can't pick up emotions."

Pierre was looking at her with a mixture of astonishment and fascination. "It must be overwhelming."

Molly nodded. "It can be. But I make a conscious effort not to invade people's privacy. I've been called 'standoffish' more than a few times in my life, but it's quite literally true. I *do* tend to stand off—to not be too close to people physically, keeping them out of my zone."

"Reading minds," said Pierre again, as if repetition would somehow make the idea more palatable. *"Incroyable."* He shook his head. "Do other members of your family have this—this ability?"

"No. I questioned my sister Jessica about it once, and she thought I was crazy. And my mom—well, there are nights my mom never would have let me go out if she could have read my mind."

"Why keep it a secret?"

Molly looked at him for a moment, as if she couldn't believe the question. "I want to live a normal life—as normal as possible, anyway. I don't want to be studied, or turned into a sideshow attraction, or God forbid, asked to work for the CIA or anything like that."

"And you say you've never told anyone before?"

She shook her head. "Never."

"But you're telling me?"

She sought out his eyes. "Yes."

Pierre understood the significance. "Thank you," he said. He smiled at her—but the smile soon faded, and he looked away. "I don't know," he said. "I don't know if I could live with the idea that my thoughts aren't private."

She shifted on the couch, tucking one bent leg under her body and taking his other hand. "But that's just it," Molly said earnestly. "I can't read your thoughts—*because you think them in French.*"

"I do?" said Pierre, surprised. "I didn't really know that I thought in any language. I mean, thoughts are, well, *thoughts.*"

"Most complex thought *is* articulated," said Molly. "It *is* formulated in words. Trust me on this; this is my field. You think in French exclusively."

"So you can hear the words of my thoughts, but not understand them?"

"Yes. I mean, I know a few French words—everyone does. *Bonjour, au revoir, oui, non,* stuff like that. But as long as you continue thinking in French, I won't be able to read your mind."

"I don't know. It's *such* an invasion of privacy."

Molly squeezed his hands tightly. "Look, you'll always know that your thoughts are private when you're outside my zone—more than three or so feet away."

Pierre was shaking his head. "It's like—*mon Dieu,* I don't know; it's like discovering your girlfriend is really Wonder Woman."

Molly laughed. "She has much bigger boobs than me."

Pierre smiled, then leaned in and gave her a kiss. But after a few seconds, he pulled away. "Did you know I was going to do that?"

She shook her head. "Not really. Maybe a half second before it was obvious."

Pierre leaned back against the couch again. "It changes things," he said.

"It doesn't have to, Pierre. It only changes them if you let it."

Pierre nodded. "I—"

And Molly heard the words in his mind, the words she had been longing to hear but that had yet to be spoken aloud, the words that meant so much.

She snuggled against Pierre. "I love you, too," she said.

Pierre held her tight.

After several moments, he said, "So what happens now?"

"We go on," said Molly. "We try to build a future together."

Pierre exhaled noisily.

"I'm sorry," said Molly at once, sitting up again and looking at Pierre. "I'm pushing again, aren't I?"

"No," said Pierre. "It's not that. It's just ..." He fell silent, but then thought about what Shari Cohen had said to him that afternoon. *Howard never told me. You shouldn't keep secrets from someone you love.* Pierre took a deep breath, then let it out slowly. "Damn," he said at last, "this is a night for great revelations, isn't it? You're not pushing, Molly. I do want to build a future with you. But, well, it's just that I may not have much of a future."

Molly looked at him and blinked. "Pardon?"

Pierre kept his eyes on hers, watching for her reaction. "I may have Huntington's disease."

Molly sagged backward a bit. "Really?"

"You know it?"

"Sort of. A man who lived down the street from my mother's house had it. My God, Pierre. I'm so sorry."

Pierre bristled slightly. Molly, although dazed, had enough presence of mind to recognize the reaction. Pierre wanted no pity. She squeezed his hand. "I saw what happened to Mr. DeWitt—my mother's neighbor. But I don't really know the details. Huntington's is inherited, right? One of your parents must have had it, too, no?"

Pierre nodded. "My father."

"I know it causes muscular difficulties."

"It's more than that. It also causes mental deterioration."

Molly looked away. "Oh."

"Symptoms can appear anytime—in one's thirties, or forties, or even later. I could have another twenty good years, or I might start to show signs tomorrow. Or, if I'm lucky, I don't have the gene and won't get the disease at all."

Molly felt a stinging in her eyes. The polite thing to do might have been to turn away, to not let Pierre know that she was crying—but it would not have been the honest thing. It wasn't pity, after all. She looked him full in the face, then leaned in and kissed him.

Once she'd pulled away, there was an extended silence between them. Finally, Molly reached a hand up to wipe her own cheek, and then used the back of her hand to gently wipe Pierre's cheek, which was also damp. "My parents," said Molly slowly, "divorced when I was five." She blew air out, as if ancient pain were being expelled with it. "These days, five or ten good years together is as much as most people get."

"You deserve more," said Pierre. "You deserve better."

Molly shook her head. "I've never had better than this. I—I haven't had much success with men. Being able to read their thoughts ... You're different."

"You don't know that," said Pierre. "I could be just as bad as the rest of them."

Molly smiled. "No, you're not. I've seen the way you listen to me, the way you care about my opinions. You're not a macho ape."

Pierre smiled slightly. "That's the nicest thing anyone has ever said to me."

Molly laughed, but then immediately sobered. "Look, I know this sounds like I'm full of myself, but I know I'm pretty—"

"In point of fact, you are drop-dead gorgeous."

"I'm not fishing for compliments here. Let me finish. I know I'm pretty—people have told me that ever since I was a little girl. My sister Jessica has done a lot of modeling; my mother still turns heads, too. She used to say the biggest problem with her first marriage was that her husband had only been interested in her looks. Dad is an executive; he'd wanted a trophy wife—and Mom was not content to be just that. You're the only man I've ever known who has looked beyond my outer appearance to what's inside. You like me for my mind, for ... for ..."

"For the content of your character," said Pierre.

"What?"

"Martin Luther King. Nobel laureates are a hobby of mine, and I've always had a fondness for great oratory—even when it's in English." Pierre closed his eyes, remembering. "'I have a dream that one day this nation will rise up and live out the true meaning of its creed: We hold these truths to be self-evident, that all men are created equal. I have a dream that my four little children will one day live in a nation where they will not be judged by the color of their skin but by the content of their character.'" He looked at Molly, then shrugged slightly. "Maybe it's because I might have Huntington's, but I do try to look beyond simple genetic traits, such as beauty." He smiled. "Not to say that your beauty doesn't move me."

Molly smiled back at him. "I have to ask. What does *'joli petit cul'* mean?"

Pierre cleared his throat. "It's, ah, a bit crude. 'Nice ass' is a close approximation. Where did you hear that?"

"In Doe Library, the night we met. It was the first thought of yours I picked up."

"Oh."

Molly laughed. "Don't worry." She smiled mischievously. "I'm glad you find me physically attractive, so long as it's not the *only* thing you care about."

Pierre smiled. "It's not." But then his face grew sad. "But I still don't see what kind of future we can have."

"I have no idea, either," said Molly. "But let's find out together. I do love you, Pierre Tardivel." She hugged him.

"I love you, too," he said, at last giving the words voice.

Still embracing each other, with her head resting on his shoulder, Molly said, "I think we should get married."

"What? Molly, we've only known each other a few months."

"I know that. But I love you, and you love me. And we may not have a lot of time to waste."

"I can't marry you," said Pierre.

"Why not? Is it because I'm not Catholic?"

Pierre laughed out loud. "No, sweetheart, no." He hugged her again. "God, I do love you. But I can't ask you to get into a relationship with me."

"You're not asking me. I'm asking you."

"But—"

"But nothing. I'm going into this with my eyes wide open."

"But surely—"

"That argument won't work."

"What about—"

"I don't care about that, either."

"Still, I'd—"

"Oh, come on! You don't believe that yourself."

Pierre laughed. "Are all our arguments going to be like this?"

"Of course. We don't have time to waste on fighting."

He was silent for several moments, chewing on his lower lip. "There is a test," he said at last.

"Whatever it is, I'll try," said Molly.

Pierre laughed. "No, no, no. I mean, there's a test for Huntington's disease. There's been one for a while now; they discovered the Huntington's gene in March 1993."

"And you haven't taken the test?"

"No ... I—no."

"Why not?" Her tone was one of curiosity, not confrontation.

Pierre exhaled and looked at the ceiling. "There's no cure for Huntington's. It's not like anything could be done to help me if I knew. And—and—" He sighed. "I don't know how to explain this. My assistant Shari said something to me today—she said, 'You're not Jewish,' meaning there were parts of her that I could never understand because I hadn't walked in her shoes. Most people at risk for Huntington's haven't had the test."

"Why? Is it painful?"

"No. All that's needed is a drop of blood."

"Is it expensive?"

"No. Hell, I could do it myself, using the equipment in my lab."

"Then why?"

"Do you know who Arlo Guthrie is?"

"Sure."

Pierre lifted his eyebrows; he'd expected her ignorance to be the same as his had been all those years ago. "Well," he went on, "his father Woody died of Huntington's, but Arlo still hasn't had the test." A pause. "Do you know who Nancy Wexler is?"

"No."

"Everyone with Huntington's knows her name. She's the president of the Hereditary Disease Foundation, which spearheaded the search for the Huntington's gene. Like Arlo, she's got a fifty-fifty chance of having Huntington's—her mother died of the disease—and she's never taken the test, either."

"I don't understand why people don't take it. I'd want to know."

Pierre sighed, thinking again of what Shari had said to him. "That's what everyone who *isn't* at risk says. But it's not that simple.

If you find out you've got the disease, you lose all hope. It's inescapable. At least now, I have some hope ..."

Molly nodded slightly.

"And—and, well, I sometimes have trouble getting through the night, Molly. I've ... contemplated suicide. Lots of Huntington's at-risks have. I've ... come close a couple of times. What's kept me from doing it is the chance that maybe I don't have the disease." He sighed, trying to decide what to say next. "One study showed that twenty-five percent of those who do take the test and are found to have the defective gene actually attempt suicide—and one in four of those succeeds. I'm ... I'm not sure I could make it through all the dark nights if I knew for sure I had it."

"But the flip side is that if you found you didn't have it, you could relax."

"Flip side is almost exactly right. It *is* a flip of the coin; the chances are exactly fifty-fifty. But I'm afraid you're wrong when you say I could relax. Fully ten percent of those who take the test and find they don't have the disease still end up with severe emotional problems."

"Why on earth would that be true?"

Pierre looked away. "Those of us who are at risk for Huntington's live our lives based on the presumption that they might be cut short. We often give up things because of that. I—before you, I hadn't been involved with a woman for nine years, and, to be honest, I didn't think I ever would be again."

Molly nodded, as if a mystery had finally been explained. "This is why you're so driven," she said, her blue eyes wide. "Why you work so hard."

Pierre returned the nod. "But when you've made sacrifices and then discover they were unnecessary, the regret can be too much to bear. That's why even some of those who discover they don't have the disease end up killing themselves." He was quiet for a long time. "But now—now, it isn't just me. I guess I should have the test."

Molly reached out and stroked his cheek. "No," she said. "No. Don't do it for me. If you ever want to take it, do it for yourself. I was serious: I want to marry you and, if you do turn out to have the disease, we'll deal with that at the time. My proposal wasn't contingent on your taking the test."

Pierre blinked. He was close to tears. "I'm so lucky to have found you."

She smiled. "I feel the same way about you."

They held each other tightly. When their embrace ended, Pierre said, "But I don't know—maybe I *should* take the test anyway. I did do what you asked, you know: I met with someone from Condor Health a couple of weeks ago. But I couldn't get a policy."

"You *still* don't have health insurance?"

Pierre shook his head. "See, right now, they'd reject me based on my family history. But in two months, on New Year's Day, a new California law comes into effect. It doesn't bar the use by insurance companies of family-history information, but it does bar the use of genetic info, and the latter takes precedence over the former. If I take the test for Huntington's, regardless of the results, then they have to insure me; they can't even charge me a higher premium, so long as I have no symptoms."

Molly was quiet for a moment, digesting this. "I meant what I said: I don't want you to take the test for me, and, well—if you can't get insurance down here, we could move to Canada, no?"

"I—I suppose. But I don't want to leave LBL; being here is the opportunity of a lifetime."

"Well, there are thirty million Americans without health insurance. But they mostly manage—"

"No. No, it's one thing to let you risk being married to someone who might become very sick; it's quite another to ask you to additionally risk financial ruin. I should have the test."

"If you think it's best," said Molly. "But I'll marry you either way."

"Don't say that now. Wait till we have the test results."

"How long will that take?"

"Well, normally a lab requires you to go through months of counseling before they'll administer the test, to make sure you really want to take it and are going to be able to deal with the results. But ..."

"Yes?"

Pierre shrugged. "It's not a hard test—no harder than any other genetic test. As I said, I could do it myself in my lab at LBL."

"I don't want you to feel pressured into doing this."

Pierre shrugged. "It's not you doing the pressuring; it's the insurance company." He was quiet for a while. "It's all right," he said finally. "It's time I found out."

13

"Explain what's going on to me," said Molly, sitting on a stool in Pierre's lab. It was ten o'clock on a Saturday morning. "I want to understand exactly what's happening."

Pierre nodded. "Okay," he said. "On Thursday, I extracted samples of my DNA from a drop of my own blood. I separated out my two copies of chromosome four, snipped off particular segments using special enzymes, and set about making radioactive images of those segments. It takes a while to develop those images, but they should be ready now, so we can actually check what my genetic code says in the specific gene associated with Huntington's disease. That gene contains an area called IT15—'interesting transcript number fifteen,' a name given to it back when people didn't know what it was for."

"And if you've got IT15, you've got Huntington's?"

"It's not as simple as that. Everybody has IT15. Like all genes, IT15's job is to code for the synthesis of a protein molecule. The protein IT15 makes has recently been dubbed 'huntingtin.'"

"So if everyone has IT15," said Molly, "and everybody's body produces huntingtin, then what determines whether you have Huntington's disease?"

"People with Huntington's have a mutant form of IT15, which causes them to produce too much huntingtin. Huntingtin is crucial to organizing the nervous system in the first few weeks of an embryo's development. It should cease to be produced at a certain point, but in those with Huntington's disease it isn't, and that causes damage to the developing brain. In both the normal and mutant versions of IT15, there's a run of repeating nucleotide triplets: cytosine-adenine-guanine, or CAG, over and over again. Well, in the genetic code, each nucleotide triplet specifies the production of one specific amino acid, and amino acids are the building blocks of proteins. CAG happens to be one of the codes for making an amino acid called glutamine. In healthy individuals, IT15 contains between eleven repeats and thirty-eight repeats of this CAG triplet. But those who have Huntington's disease have between forty-two and a hundred or so CAG repeats."

"Okay," said Molly, "so we look at each of your chromosome fours, find the beginning of the run of CAG triplets, then simply count the number of repeats of that triplet. Right?"

"Right."

"You're sure you want to go through with this?"

Pierre nodded. "I'm sure."

"Then let's do it."

And they did. It was painstaking work, carefully examining the autoradiograph film. Faint lines represented each nucleotide. Pierre used a felt-tipped marker to write in the letters beneath each triplet: CAG, CAG. Molly, meanwhile, tallied the number of repeats on a sheet of paper.

Without blood samples from Élisabeth Tardivel and Henry Spade, there was no easy way to tell which of his chromosome fours had come from his father, so he had to check them both. On the first one, the string of CAG triplets ended after seventeen repeats.

Pierre breathed a sigh of relief. "One down, one to go," he said.

He began checking the sequence on the second chromosome. No reaction when they reached the tally of eleven; that was the normal minimum. When they got to twenty-five, though, Pierre found his hand shaking.

Molly touched his arm. "Don't worry," she said. "You said you could have as many as thirty-eight and still be normal."

Pierre nodded. "But what I didn't say was that seventy percent of all normal people have twenty-four or fewer repeats."

Molly bit her lower lip.

Pierre continued sequencing. Twenty-six, twenty-seven, twenty-eight.

His eyes were blurring.

Thirty-five. Thirty-six. Thirty-seven. Thirty-eight.

Damn. God damn.

Thirty-nine.

God fucking damn it.

"Still," said Molly, trying to sound brave, "thirty-eight may be the normal limit, but you have to have at least forty-two ..."

Forty.

Forty-one.

Forty-two.

"I'm sorry, honey," said Molly. "I'm so sorry."

Pierre put down his marker. His whole body was shaking.

"God, I am so sorry," said Molly.

A fifty-fifty shot.

A flip of a coin.

Heads or tails.

Call it!

Pierre said nothing. His heart was pounding.

"Let's go home," said Molly, stroking the back of his hand.

"No," said Pierre. "Not yet."

"There's nothing more to be done here."

"Yes, there is. I want to finish the sequencing. I want to know how many repeats I have."

"What difference does that make?"

"It makes all the difference," said Pierre, his voice shaking. "It makes all the difference in the world."

Molly looked perplexed.

"I didn't tell you everything. *Merde. Merde. Merde.* I didn't tell you everything."

"What?"

"There's an inverse correlation between the number of repeats and the age of onset of the disease."

Molly didn't seem to understand, or didn't want to. "What?" she said again.

"The more repeats, the sooner symptoms are likely to appear. Some patients get Huntington's as children; others don't get it until their eighties. I—I have to finish the sequencing; I have to know how many repeats I've got."

Molly looked at him. There was nothing to say.

Pierre rubbed his eyes, blew his nose, and bent back to the autorad film. The tally kept growing. Forty-five.

Fifty.

Fifty-five.

Sixty.

Time continued to pass. Pierre felt faint, but he pressed on, marking letters over and over again on the film: CAG, CAG, CAG ...

Molly got up and walked across the room. She found a box of Kimwipes—expensive, lab-quality tissues. She used them to dry her eyes. She tried to hide from Pierre the fact that she was crying.

Finally, Pierre hit a codon that wasn't CAG. The total count: seventy-nine repeats.

There was silence between them for a time. Somewhere in the distance, a fire-truck siren was wailing.

"How long?" asked Molly at last.

"Seventy-nine is a very high number," said Pierre softly. "Very high." He sucked in air, thinking. "I'm thirty-two now. The correlation is inexact. I can't be sure. But ... I don't know, I guess I'd expect to see symptoms very soon. Certainly by the time I'm thirty-five or thirty-six."

"Well, then, you—"

"At the outside." He raised a hand. "The disease can take years or decades to run its course. First symptoms might just be a reduction in coordination, or facial tics. It might be years before things got serious. Or ..."

"Or?"

Pierre shrugged. "Well," he said, his voice full of sadness, "I guess that's it."

Molly reached for his hand, but Pierre pulled it away. "Please," he said. "It's over."

"What's over?" said Molly.

"Please. Let's not make this difficult."

"I love you," said Molly, softly.

"Please don't ..."

"And I know you love me."

"Molly, I'm dying."

Molly moved over to him, draped her arms around his neck, and rested her head against his chest. His thoughts were all in French.

"I still want to marry you," Molly said.

"Molly, I only want what's best for you. I don't want to be a burden on you."

Molly held him tighter. "I want to marry you, and I want to have a child."

"No," said Pierre. "No, I can't become a father. The number of CAG repeats tends to increase from generation to generation—it's a phenomenon called 'anticipation.' I have seventy-nine; any child of mine who got the gene from me might very likely have even more—meaning he or she might come down with the disease as a teenager, or even earlier."

"But—"

"No buts. I'm sorry; this was crazy. It can never work." He saw her face, saw the hurt, felt his own heart breaking. "Please, don't make it harder for both of us. Just go home, would you? It's over."

"Pierre—"

"It's over. *I've wasted too much time on this already.*"

He could see that the words had cut her. She headed for the laboratory door, but looked back at him once more. He didn't meet her eyes.

She left the room. Pierre sat down on a lab stool, his hands still shaking.

14

Pierre called Tiffany Feng and told her to go ahead and put in his health-insurance application at the first of the year. Condor might have disputed the informal testing if the result had been negative, but there was no conceivable advantage to lying about having Huntington's. Tiffany said Pierre's statement on Human Genome Center letterhead, notarized by the campus archivist, would be acceptable proof that the test had indeed been conducted.

Pierre went back to spending his evenings in Doe Library. Periodically he'd look up, look around, look for a familiar face.

She never appeared.

He spent each evening reading, searching the literature for information on junk DNA—now, more than ever, he knew he was in a race against time. He was already seven years older than James D. Watson had been when he'd made his great breakthrough—and only two years younger than Watson had been when he'd accepted his Nobel Prize.

A wall clock above Pierre's chair was ticking audibly. He got up and moved to another table.

He'd started with current material and was working his way backward. A reference in a magazine index caught his eye. "A Different Kind of Inheritance."

Different kind of inheritance ...

Could it be?

He asked Pablo to dig up the June 1989 *Scientific American.*

There it was—exactly what he'd been looking for. A whole different level of information potentially coded into DNA, and a plausible scheme for the reliable inheritance of that information from generation to generation.

The genetic code consisted of four letters: A, C, G, and T. The C stood for cytosine, and cytosine's chemical formula was $C_4H_5N_3O$—four carbons, five hydrogens, three nitrogens, and an oxygen.

But not all cytosine was the same. It had long been known that sometimes one of those five hydrogens could be replaced by a methyl group, CH_3—a carbon atom attached to three hydrogens. The process was called, logically enough, cytosine methylation.

So when one wrote out a genetic formula—say, the CAG that repeated on and on in Pierre's own diseased genes—the C might be either regular cytosine or the methylated form, called 5-methylcytosine. Geneticists paid no attention to which one it was; both forms resulted in exactly the same proteins being synthesized.

But this article in *Scientific American,* by Robin Holliday, described an intriguing finding: almost always when cytosine undergoes methylation, the base next to the cytosine on the DNA strand is guanine: a CG doublet.

But C and G side by side on one side of a DNA strand meant that G and C would be found on the opposite side. After all, cytosine always bonds with guanine, and guanine with cytosine.

In the article, Holliday proposed a hypothetical enzyme he dubbed "maintenance methylase." It would bind a methyl group to a cytosine that was adjacent to a guanine *if and only if* the corresponding doublet on the other side was already methylated.

It was all hypothetical. Maintenance methylase might not exist.

But if it did—

Pierre looked at his watch; it was almost closing time. He photocopied the article, returned the magazine to Pablo, and went home.

That night he dreamed of Stockholm.

"Good morning, Shari," said Pierre, coming into the lab.

Shari was dressed in a beige blouse under a wine-colored two-piece suit. She'd cut her long, dark hair recently and was now wearing it fashionably short, parted on the left, and curving in toward her neck at the bottom. Like Pierre, Shari was burying herself in her work, trying to get over the loss of Howard.

"What's this?" she said, holding up an autorad she'd found while tidying up. The lab would have been a pigsty if it weren't for Shari's periodic attempts to restore order.

Pierre glanced at the piece of x-ray film. He tried to sound nonchalant. "Nothing. Just garbage."

"Whoever this DNA belongs to has Huntington's disease," said Shari matter-of-factly.

"It's just an old sheet."

"It's yours, isn't it?" asked Shari.

Pierre thought about continuing to lie, but then shrugged. "I thought I'd thrown it out."

"I'm sorry, Pierre. I'm so sorry."

"Don't tell anyone."

"No, of course not. How long have you known?"

"Few weeks."

"How is Molly taking it?"

"We—we've broken up."

Shari put the film in a Rubbermaid garbage pail. "Oh."

Pierre shrugged a little.

They looked at each other for a moment. Pierre's mind did what he supposed every male's did in moments like these. He thought for an instant about him and Shari, about the possibilities there. Both of them carried diseased genes. He was thirty-two and she was twenty-six—not an outrageous difference. But—but there were other gulfs between them. And he saw on her face no indication, no suggestion, no inkling. The thought had not occurred to her.

Some gulfs are not easily crossed.

"Let's not talk about it," said Pierre. "I—I've got some research I want to share with you. Something I found in the library last night."

Shari looked as though she wanted to pursue the subject of Pierre's Huntington's further, but then she nodded and took a seat on a lab stool.

Pierre told her about the article in *Scientific American*; about the two forms of cytosine, the regular one and the 5-methylcytosine variant; and about the hypothetical enzyme that could turn the former into the latter but would do so only if the cytosine in the CG doublet on the opposite side of the strand was already methylated.

"Hypothetically," said Shari, stressing the word. "If this enzyme exists."

"Right, right," said Pierre. "But suppose it does. What happens when DNA reproduces? Well, of course, the ladder unzips down the middle, forming two strands. One strand contains all the left-hand components of the base pairs, maybe something like this ..." He wrote on the blackboard that covered most of one wall:

Left side: T-C-A-C-G-T

"See that CG doublet? Okay, let's say its cytosine is methylated." He went over the pair again with his chalk, making it heavier:

Left side: T-C-A-**C**-**G**-T

"Now, in DNA reproduction, free-floating nucleotides are plugged into the appropriate spots on each strand, meaning the right-hand side of this one will end up looking like this ..." His chalk flew across the blackboard, writing in the complementary sequence:

Left side: T-C-A-**C**-**G**-T
Right side: A-G-T-G-C-A

"See? Directly opposite the left-hand CG pair is the right-hand GC pair." He paused, waiting for Shari to nod acknowledgment of this. "Now the maintenance methylase comes along, and sees that there isn't parity between the two sides of the strand, so it adds a methyl group to the right-hand side." He went over the GC pair, making it darker, too:

Left side: T-C-A-**C**-**G**-T
Right side: A-G-T-**G**-**C**-A

"At the same time, the other half of the original strand is being filled in with free-floating nucleotides. But maintenance methylase would do exactly the same thing to it, duplicating cytosine methylation on both sides, if originally present on one side."

Pierre clapped his hands together to shake off chalk dust. "*Voilà!* By postulating that one enzyme, you end up with a mechanism for preserving cytosine-methylation state from cell generation to cell generation."

"And?"

"And think about our work on codon synonyms." He waved vaguely at the wall chart labeled "The Genetic Code."

"Yes?"

"That's one possible additional level of coding hidden in DNA, if the choice of which synonym used is significant. Now we've got a second possible type of additional coding in DNA: the code made by whether cytosine is methylated or not. I'm willing to bet that one or both of those additional codes is the key to what the so-called junk DNA is really for."

"So what do we do now?" asked Shari.

"Well, as Einstein is supposed to have said, 'God is subtle, but malicious he is not.'" He smiled at Shari. "No matter how complex the codes are, we should be able to crack them."

Pierre went home. His apartment seemed vast. He sat on the living-room couch, pulling idly at an orange thread coming unraveled from one of the cushions.

They were making progress, he and Shari. They were getting close to a breakthrough. Of that he felt sure.

But he wasn't elated. He wasn't excited.

God, what an idiot I am.

He watched Letterman, watched Conan O'Brien.

He didn't laugh.

He started getting ready for bed, dumping his socks and underwear on the living-room floor—there wasn't any reason not to anymore.

He'd been reading Camus again. His fat copy of the *Collected Works* was facedown on one of the couch's orange-and-green cushions. Camus, who had taken the Literature Nobel in '57; Camus, who commented on the absurdity of the human condition. "I don't want to be a genius," he had said. "I have enough problems just trying to be a man."

Pierre sat down on the couch and exhaled into the darkness. The absurdity of the human condition. The absurdity of it all. The absurdity of being a man.

Bertrand Russell ran through his mind, too—a Nobel laureate in 1950.

"To fear love," he'd said, "is to fear life—and those who fear life are already three parts dead."

Three parts dead—just about right for a Huntington's sufferer at thirty-two.

Pierre crawled into bed, lying in a fetal position.

He slept hardly at all—but when he did, he dreamt not of Stockholm, but of Molly.

15

"I can't let you redo the exam," said Molly to the male student sitting opposite her, "but if you undertake another research project, I can give you up to ten marks in extra credit for that. If you get eight or above, you'll pass—just barely. It's your choice."

The student was looking at his hands, which were resting in his lap. "I'll do the project. Thank you, Professor Bond."

"That's all right, Alex. Everyone deserves a second chance."

The student got to his feet and left the cramped office. Pierre, who had been standing just outside the door waiting for Molly to be alone, stepped into the doorway, holding a dozen red roses in front of him.

"I'm so sorry," he said.

Molly looked up, eyes wide.

"I feel like a complete heel." He actually said "eel," but Molly assumed he meant the former, although she thought the latter was just as applicable. Still, she said nothing.

"May I come in?" he said.

She nodded, but did not speak.

Pierre stepped inside and closed the door behind him. "You are the very best thing that ever happened to me," he said, "and I am an idiot."

There was silence for a time. "Nice flowers," said Molly, at last.

Pierre looked at her, as if trying to read her thoughts in her eyes. "If you will still have me as your husband, I would be honored."

Molly was quiet for a time. "I want to have a child."

Pierre had given this much thought. "I understand that. If you wanted to adopt a child, I'd be glad to help raise it for as long as I'm able."

"Adopt? I—no, I want to have a child of my own. I want to undergo in vitro fertilization."

"Oh," said Pierre.

"Don't worry about passing on bad genes," said Molly. "I was reading an article about this in *Cosmo.* They could culture the embryos outside my body, then test them for whether they'd inherited Huntington's. Then they could implant only healthy ones."

Pierre was a lapsed Catholic; the whole idea of such a procedure still left him uncomfortable—tossing out viable embryos because they didn't pass genetic muster. But that wasn't his main objection. "I was serious about what I said before. I think a child should have both a mother and a father—and I probably won't live long enough to see a child grow up." He paused. "I can't in good conscience begin a new life that I know I'm not going to be around to see through its childhood," he said. "Adoption is a special case—we'd still be improving the child's life, even if it wouldn't always have a father."

"I'm going to do it anyway," said Molly firmly. "I'm going to have a baby. I'm going to have in vitro fertilization."

Pierre felt it all slipping away. "I can't be the sperm donor. I—I'm sorry. I just can't."

Molly sat without saying anything. Pierre felt angry with himself. This was supposed to be a reunion, dammit. How did it get so off track?

Finally, Molly spoke. "Could you come to love a child that wasn't biologically yours?"

Pierre had already considered this when contemplating adoption. *"Oui."*

"I was going to have a child without a husband anyway," said Molly. "Millions of children have grown up without fathers; for most of my childhood, I didn't have one myself."

Pierre nodded. "I know."

Molly frowned. "And you still want to marry me, even if I go ahead and have a child using donated sperm?"

Pierre nodded again, not trusting his voice just then.

"And you could come to love such a child?"

He'd been all prepared to love an adopted child. Why did this seem so different? And yet—and yet—

"Yes," said Pierre, at last. "After all, the child would still be partly you." He locked onto her blue eyes. "And I love you completely." He waited while his heart beat a few more times. "So," he said, at last, "will you consent to be Mrs. Tardivel?"

She looked at her lap and shook her head. "No, I can't do that." But when she lifted her face, she was smiling. "But I do want to be Ms. Bond, who happens to be married to Mr. Tardivel."

"Then you will marry me?"

Molly got up and walked toward him. She put her arms around his neck. *"Oui,"* she said.

They kissed for several seconds, but when they pulled apart, Pierre said, "There is one condition. At any time—*any* time—if you feel my disease is too much for you, or you see an opportunity for happiness that will last the rest of your life, rather than the rest of mine, then I want you to leave me."

Molly was silent, her mouth hanging slightly open.

"Promise," said Pierre.

"I promise," she said at last.

That night, Pierre and Molly did what they had often done before they'd broken up: they went for a long walk. They'd stopped at a café on Telegraph Avenue for a light snack, and now were just ambling along, occasionally looking in shop windows. Like many young couples, they were still trying to get to know every facet of each other's personalities and pasts. On one long walk, they had talked about earlier sexual experiences; on another, relations with their parents; on others still, debates about gun control and environmental issues. Nights of probing, of stimulating conversations, of each refining his or her mental image of the other.

And tonight, the biggest question of all came up as they strolled, enjoying the early evening warmth. "Do you believe in God?" asked Molly.

Pierre looked down at the sidewalk. "I don't know."

"Oh?" said Molly, clearly intrigued.

Pierre sounded a bit uncomfortable. "Well, I mean it's hard continuing to believe in God when something like this happens. You know: my Huntington's. I don't mean I started questioning my faith last month, when we finally did the test. I started doing that back when I first met my real father." Pierre had explained all about his discovered paternity on another long walk.

Molly nodded. "But you did believe in God before you found out you might have Huntington's?"

Pierre nodded as they continued along. "I guess. Like most French-Canadians, I was raised Roman Catholic. These days I only go to Mass on Easter and Christmas, but when I was living in Montréal, I went every Sunday. I even sang in the church choir."

Molly winced; she had heard Pierre sing. "But it's hard for you to believe now," she said, "because a beneficent God couldn't do that sort of thing to you."

They'd come to a park bench. Molly gestured for them to sit down, and they did so, Pierre draping his arm over her shoulders. "Something like that," he said.

Molly touched Pierre's arm and seemed to hesitate for a moment before replying. "Forgive me for saying this—I don't want to sound argumentative—but, well, I always find that sort of reasoning a trifle shallow." She held up a hand. "I'm sorry; I don't mean it to sound like a criticism. It's just that the—the *harshness* of our world is apparent to anyone who looks. People starving in Africa, poverty in South America, drive-by shootings here in the States. Earthquakes, tornadoes, wars, diseases." She shook her head. "I just—to me, I'm just saying to me—it always seems strange that one could go along without questioning one's faith until something personally happens. You know what I'm saying? A million people starve to death in Ethiopia, and we say that's too bad. But we—or someone we know—gets cancer or a heart attack or Huntington's or whatever, and we say, Hey, there must be no God." She smiled. "I'm sorry; pet peeve. Forgive me."

Pierre nodded slowly. "No, you're right. You're right. It *is* silly when you put it that way." He paused. "What about you? Do you believe in God?"

Molly shrugged. "Well, I was raised a Unitarian—I still sometimes go to a fellowship over in San Francisco. I don't believe in a personal God, but perhaps in a creator. I'm what they call a theistic evolutionist."

"Qu'est-ce que c'est?"

"That's someone who believes God planned out all the broad strokes in advance—the general direction life would take, the general path for the universe—but, after setting everything in motion, he's content to simply watch it all unfold, to let it grow and develop on its own, following the course he laid down."

Pierre smiled at her. "Well, the course we've been laying down leads back to my apartment—and it *is* getting late."

She smiled at him. "Not too late to know me in the biblical sense, I trust."

Pierre stood up, offered his hand to Molly, and helped her stand up as well. "Yea, verily."

16

It was a small, quiet wedding. Pierre had originally thought they'd get married at UCB's chapel, but it turned out not to have any such thing—California political correctness. Instead, they ended up being married in the living room of Molly's coworker, Professor Ingrid Lagerkvist, with the chaplain from Molly's Unitarian fellowship conducting the service.

Ingrid, a thirty-four-year-old redhead with the palest blue eyes Pierre had ever seen, served as Molly's matron of honor; Ingrid was normally quite slim, but was now five months pregnant. Pierre, who had been in California for less than a year now, enlisted Ingrid's husband, Sven—a great bear of a man with long brown hair, a huge reddish-brown beard, and Ben Franklin glasses—to be his best man. Also in attendance: Pierre's mother, Élisabeth, who had flown down from Montreal; bubbly Joan Dawson and a dour Burian Klimus from the HGC office; and Pierre's research assistant, Shari Cohen (whom Pierre could not help notice looked sad throughout the whole affair; it had perhaps been an error asking her to attend a wedding just three months after her own engagement had broken up). Absent were any members of Molly's family; she hadn't even told her mother she was getting married.

Molly and Pierre had argued a bit about what vows they should exchange. Pierre refused to have Molly pledge to keep the marriage "in sickness and in health," reiterating that she should feel free to leave anytime if he should fall ill. And so:

"Do you, Pierre Jacques," asked the white-haired Unitarian, wearing a secular three-piece suit with a red carnation in the lapel, "take Molly Louise to be your wife, to cherish and honor her, to love and protect her, to respect her and help her fulfill all her potential for so long as you carry each other in your hearts?"

"I do," said Pierre, and then, smiling at his mother, he added, *"Oui."*

"And do you, Molly Louise, take Pierre Jacques to be your husband, to cherish and honor him, to love and protect him, to respect him and help him fulfill all his potential for so long as you carry each other in your hearts?"

"I do," she said, staring into Pierre's eyes.

"By the authority vested in me by the state of California, I take great pride and pleasure in pronouncing you a married couple. Pierre and Molly, you may—"

But they already were. And a long, lingering kiss it was, too.

Their honeymoon—five days in British Columbia—had been wonderful. But soon they were back at work, Pierre keeping his standard long hours at the lab. They'd let their separate apartments go, and had bought a six-room house on Spruce Street with white stucco walls, next to a bungalow done in pink stucco. The final vestiges of Pierre's inheritance from Alain Tardivel's life insurance covered the down payment. Pierre had taken a beating converting the money to U.S. dollars, but was delighted to discover mortgage interest was deductible here, something it hadn't been back in Canada. Pierre enjoyed having a backyard, and plants grew spectacularly in this climate, although the giant snails gave him the willies.

Tonight, a warm evening in June, Pierre sat at the dining-room table, its top littered with little Chinese food containers. Tiffany Feng had long ago sent him a fully executed copy of his Gold Plan policy, but what with the marriage, moving into the house, and his work at the lab, he was only just getting around to looking it over. Molly, meanwhile, had had her fill of Chinese and was now sitting on a couch in the adjacent living room, browsing through *Newsweek.*

"Hey, listen to this!" said Pierre, speaking loudly enough to be heard in the next room. "Under 'Standard Benefits,' it says: 'In cases in which amniocentesis, genetic counseling, or other prenatal testing provides indications that a child will require extensive neonatal or later-life medical treatment, Condor Insurance, Inc., will pay all costs required to terminate the pregnancy at a hospital or government-licensed abortion clinic.'"

Molly looked up. "It's a fairly standard benefit; the university's staff policy has that, too."

"That doesn't seem right, somehow."

"Why not?"

Pierre frowned. "It's just that ... I don't know—it just seems a form of economically forced eugenics. If the baby isn't perfect, you can have it aborted for free. But listen to this other clause—this is the one that really gets me: 'Although our prenatal health benefits normally roll over into covering neonatal care, if amniocentesis, genetic counseling, or other prenatal testing provide indications that a child will be born manifesting symptoms of a genetic disorder, and the mother has not taken advantage of the benefit described under section twenty-two, paragraph six'—that's the free-abortion-of-defective-babies benefit—'neonatal health coverage will be withdrawn.' You see what that means? If you *don't* take the offer of a free abortion once it becomes clear that you're going to have a less-than-perfect baby, and instead go ahead and give birth to the child, your insurance to cover the child's needs is canceled. The insurance company is providing an enormous economic incentive to terminate all but perfect pregnancies."

"I suppose," said Molly, slowly. She had gotten up and was now standing in the entrance to the dining room, leaning against the wall. "Still, didn't I read about a case of the exact opposite? A couple, both of whom were genetically deaf, chose to abort their child because prenatal testing showed that it was *not* going to be deaf, and so they felt they wouldn't be able to relate to it. This sort of thing goes both ways."

"That case was different," said Pierre. "I'm not sure I agree with the morality of it—aborting a normal child simply because he *was* normal—but at least it was the *parents* making the choice on their own, not being coerced by an outside agency. But this—" He shook his head. "Decisions that should be private, family affairs—whether it's to continue a pregnancy, or, as in my case, whether it's to take a genetic test as an adult—are essentially being made for you by insurance companies. You have to terminate the pregnancy, or lose insurance; you have to take the test, or lose insurance." He shook his head. "It stinks."

He picked up the chop suey container, looked inside, but put it back down without taking any more. His appetite was gone.

17

It was Molly's turn to make dinner. Pierre used to try to help her, but had soon learned it was actually easier for her if he just stayed out of the way. She was making spaghetti tonight—about ten minutes' work when Pierre did it, since he relied on Ragú for the sauce and a Kraft shaker for the cheese. But for Molly it was a big production, making the sauce from scratch and grating up fresh Parmesan. Pierre sat in the living room, channel surfing. When Molly called out that dinner was ready, he headed into the dining nook. They had a butcher-block style table with green wicker chairs. Pierre pulled out his chair without looking and tried to sit down, but almost immediately he hopped back onto his feet.

There was a plush toy bee sitting on his chair, with giant Mickey Mouse eyes and a fuzzy yellow-and-black coat. Pierre picked it up. "What's this?" he said.

Molly entered from the kitchen, bearing two plates of steaming spaghetti. She set them down before she spoke. "Well," she said, nodding at the bee, "I think it's time we had my flowers fertilized."

Pierre raised his eyebrows. "You want to go ahead with the IVF?"

Molly nodded. "If it's still okay with you." She held up a hand. "I know it's a lot of money, but, well—frankly, I'm scared by what happened to Ingrid." Molly's friend Ingrid Lagerkvist had given birth to a boy with Down's syndrome; the odds of having a Down's child go up with age.

"We'll find the money," said Pierre. "Don't worry." His face broke into a broad grin. "We're going to have a baby!" He sprinkled cheese on his spaghetti, then did something Molly always found amusing: he cut his spaghetti into little bits. "A baby!" he said again.

Molly laughed. *"Oui, monsieur."*

Pierre's boss, Dr. Burian Klimus, looked up and nodded curtly at each of them in turn. "Tardivel. Molly."

"Thank you for agreeing to see us, sir," said Pierre, sitting down on the far side of the broad desk. "I know how busy you are." Klimus was not one to waste energy acknowledging the obvious. He sat silently behind his cluttered desk, a slightly irritated expression on his broad, ancient face, waiting for Pierre to get to the point. "We need your advice. Molly and I, we'd like to have a child."

"Flowers and a Chianti are an excellent starting point," said Klimus in his dry voice, brown eyes unblinking.

Pierre laughed, more out of nervousness than because of the joke. He looked around the office. There was a second door, leading to some other room. Behind Klimus's desk was a credenza with two globes on it. One was a globe of the Earth, with no political boundaries marked; the other was—Pierre guessed, based on its reddish color—a globe of Mars. There were framed astronomical photos on the walls. Pierre returned his gaze to Klimus. "We've decided we want to undergo in vitro fertilization, and, well, you wrote that big article about new reproductive technologies for *Science* with Professor Sousa, so ..."

"Why IVF?" asked Klimus.

"I have blocked fallopian tubes," said Molly.

Klimus nodded. "I see." He leaned back in his chair, which creaked as he did so, and interlaced his fingers behind his bald head. "Surely you understand the rudiments of the procedure: eggs would be removed from Molly and mixed with Pierre's sperm in a petri dish. Once embryos are created, they're implanted, and you hope for the best."

"Actually," said Pierre, "we weren't planning to use my sperm." He shifted slightly in his seat. "I, ah, I'm not in a position to be the biological father."

"Are you impotent?"

Pierre was surprised by the question. "No."

"Do you have a low sperm count? There are procedures—"

"I have no idea what my sperm count is. I assume it's normal."

"Then why? You have an adequate mind. Why not father a child?"

Pierre swallowed. "I, ah, carry some bad genes."

Klimus nodded. "Voluntary eugenics. I approve." He paused. "But, you know, once the embryo is eight cells in size, we can usually remove a single cell for PCR and then genetic testing, so—"

Pierre saw no reason to debate it with the old man. "We're going to use donated sperm," he said firmly.

Klimus shrugged. "It's up to you."

"But we're looking for recommendations for a clinic. You visited a number of them while doing that article. Is there one you'd suggest?"

"There are several good ones here in the Bay Area," said Klimus.

"Which would be the cheapest?" said Pierre. Klimus looked at him blankly. "We, ah, understand the procedure costs around ten thousand dollars."

"Per attempt," said Klimus. "And IVF has only a twenty percent success rate. The average cost of actually getting a baby through this method is forty thousand dollars."

Pierre's jaw dropped. *Forty* thousand? It was a huge amount of money, and their mortgage was a killer. He doubted they could manage that much.

But Molly pressed on. "Do the clinics choose the sperm donors?"

"Occasionally," said Klimus. "More often, the woman chooses from a catalog, listing the potential fathers' physical, mental, and ethnic characteristics. And—" He stopped in midsentence, completely dead, as though his mind were a million miles away.

Pierre finally leaned a bit closer. "Yes?" he said.

"What about me?" asked Klimus.

"I beg your pardon?" said Pierre.

"Me. As donor."

Molly's jaw dropped a little. Klimus saw that and held up a hand, palm out. "We could do it here at LBL. I can do the fertilization work, and Gwendolyn Bacon—an IVF practitioner who owes me a favor—I'm sure I could get her to do the egg extraction and embryo implantation."

"I don't know," said Pierre.

Klimus looked at him. "I propose a deal: use me as the donor, and I'll pay the costs for the procedure, no matter how many attempts it takes. I've invested my Nobel money well, and have some lucrative consulting contracts."

"But ..." began Molly. She trailed off, not knowing what to say. She wished there wasn't the wide desk between them so she could read his mind, but all she could detect was a barrage of French from Pierre.

"I am old, I know," said Klimus, without humor. "But that makes little difference to my sperm. I'm fully capable of serving as the biological father—and I'll provide full documentation to show myself free of HIV."

Pierre gulped air. "Won't it be awkward, knowing the donor?"

"Oh, it'll be our secret," said Klimus, raising his hand again. "You want good DNA, no? I'm a Nobel Prize winner; I have an IQ of one-six-three. I'm a proven commodity as far as longevity is concerned, and I have excellent eyesight and reflexes. Plus, I don't carry genes for Alzheimer's or diabetes or any other serious disorder." He smiled slightly. "The worst thing programmed into my DNA is baldness, and I do confess I was hit with that at an early age."

During Klimus's long statement, Molly had started out by shaking her head slightly back and forth, back and forth, but that had stopped by the time he reached his conclusion. She looked now at Pierre, as if to gauge his reaction.

Klimus, too, turned his eyes on Pierre. "Come on, young man," he said, and then his face split in a dry, cold grin. "Better the devil you know."

"But why?" asked Pierre. "Why would you be interested?"

"I'm eighty-four," said Klimus, "and have no children. I simply wish for the Klimus genes to not disappear from the gene pool." He looked at each of them in turn. "You're a young couple, just getting started. I know what you make, Tardivel, and can guess what you make, Molly. Tens of thousands of dollars is a lot of money to you."

Pierre looked at Molly and shrugged. "I ... I *suppose* it would be okay," he said slowly, not at all sure of himself.

Klimus brought his hands together in a loud clap that sounded like a gunshot. "Wonderful!" he said. "Molly, we'll make an appointment for you with Dr. Bacon; she'll prescribe hormone treatments to get you to develop multiple eggs." Klimus rose to his feet, cutting off further discussion. "Congratulations, Mother," he said to Molly, and then, in an unexpected display of bonhomie, he came over and laid a bony arm on Pierre's shoulder. "And congratulations to you, too, Father."

"Big trouble," said Shari, coming into Pierre's lab and holding up a photocopy. "I found this note in a back issue of *Physical Review Letters.*" She looked upset.

Pierre was spinning down his centrifuge. He left it whirling under inertia and looked up at her. "What's it say?"

"Some researchers in Boston are contending that although the DNA that codes for protein synthesis is structured like a code—one word wrong and the message is garbled—the junk or intronic DNA is structured like a *language,* with enough redundancy that small mistakes don't matter."

"Like a language?" said Pierre excitedly. "What do they mean?"

"In the active parts of the DNA, they found that the distribution of the various three-letter codons is random. But in the junk DNA, if you look at the distribution of 'words' of three, four, five, six, seven, and eight base pairs in length, you find that it's just like what we have in a human language. If the most common word appears ten thousand times, then the tenth most common appears only one thousand times, and the hundredth most common appears just a hundred times—which is very much like the relative distribution of words in English. 'The' is an order of magnitude more common than 'his,' and 'his' is an order of magnitude more common than, say, 'go.' Statistically, it's a very distinctive pattern, diagnostic of a real language."

"Excellent!" said Pierre. "Excellent."

Vertical frown lines were marring Shari's otherwise porcelain-smooth forehead. "It's terrible. It means other people have been making good progress on this problem, too. That note in *Physical Review Letters* was published in the December fifth, 1994, issue."

Pierre shrugged. "Remember Watson and Crick, hunting for the structure of DNA? You recall who else was working on the same problem?"

"Linus Pauling, among others."

"Pauling, exactly—who'd already won a Nobel for his work on chemical bonding." He looked at Shari. "But even old Linus couldn't see the truth; he came up with a Rube Goldberg three-stranded model." Pierre had learned all about Goldberg since coming to Berkeley; he was a UCB alumnus and an exhibition of his cartoons was on display on campus. "Sure, some others have been working in the same area we're pursuing. But I'd rather you come in here and tell me that there's good reason to think something meaningful *is* coded in the non-protein-synthesizing DNA than to say everyone who ever looked at it before has concluded it really is just junk. I know we're on the right track, Shari. I know it." He paused. "You've done good work. Go home; get a good night's sleep."

"You should go home, too," Shari said.

Pierre smiled. "Actually, tonight the tables are turned. I'm waiting for Molly. She's got a late departmental meeting. I'll stay here till she calls."

"All right. See you tomorrow."

"Good night, Shari. And be careful—it's pretty late already."

Shari left the room and started walking down the corridor. She went outside and waited for the shuttle bus to arrive. It did so, and she rode it down to the campus proper. She wanted to run a few errands on campus before heading home, one of which took her near the psychology building, where Pierre's wife was apparently still working. Just outside it, Shari was unnerved to collide with a rough-looking young man pacing impatiently back and forth as if he were waiting for someone. He was dressed in a leather jacket and faded jeans, and had closely cropped blond hair and a strange chin that looked like two protruding fists.

Nasty customer, Shari thought as she scurried away into the darkness ...

Book Two

The farther back you can look, the farther forward you are likely to see.

—**Sir Winston Churchill,**
winner of the 1953 Nobel Prize in literature

18

Nighttime. Two police officers, one black, one white. A blood-splattered sidewalk. A man named Chuck Hanratty dead, his body taken away by ambulance. Pierre chilled in the nighttime breeze, his shirt lying in a stiffening wad, soaked with blood.

"Look, it's after midnight," said the black cop to Molly, "and, frankly, your friend seems a bit out of it. Why don't you let Officer Granatstein and me give you a lift? You can come by headquarters tomorrow to make a report." He handed his card to her.

"Why," said Pierre, slowly coming out of shock, "would a neo-Nazi want to attack me?"

The cop lifted his broad shoulders. "No big mystery. He was after your wallet and her purse."

But Molly had read the man's mind, and knew that this wasn't a simple mugging—it was a deliberate, premeditated attempt on Pierre's life. She gently grasped her husband's hand and took him over to the police car.

Pierre and Molly lay in bed, Molly holding him tightly.

"Why," said Pierre again, "would a neo-Nazi be after me?" He was still badly shaken. "Hell, why would anyone go to the trouble of trying to kill me? After all ..." His voice trailed off, but Molly could read the already formulated English sentence: *After all, I'll probably be dead soon anyway.*

Molly shook her head as much as her pillow would allow. "I don't know why," she said softly. "But he was after you. You in particular."

"You're sure?" asked Pierre, his voice betraying the faint hope that Molly was mistaken.

"As we passed him, Hanratty was thinking, 'About fucking time that frog showed up.'"

Pierre stiffened slightly. "You can't tell the cops that," he said.

"Of course not." She forced a small laugh. "They wouldn't believe me anyway." She paused. "But he'd been ordered to kill you, ordered by someone named Grozny—and he'd apparently already killed several other people for this Grozny, too."

Pierre was still trying to digest it all. A man had died right in front of him. Yes, it had been self-defense, but one could nonetheless say that Pierre had indeed killed him. Pierre had come across the continent to the home of the free-love, antiwar movement, and he'd ended up with a human being's blood spilling out onto his hands.

A knife slicing into the man's body; Molly on his back, Pierre tripping him.

If only Hanratty had dropped the knife. If only ...

Dead.

Dead.

He couldn't shake the horror, couldn't escape the pain.

Pierre would take the next day off work—something he had never done before except for his honeymoon.

"Maybe you should get some counseling," Molly said. "Ingrid did a study of Desert Storm vets. She could recommend someone who handles posttraumatic stress."

Pierre shook his head. They'd also tried to get him into counseling when he'd first discovered that he was at risk for Huntington's. But counseling seemed a never-ending proposition. He didn't have time for that.

"I'll be all right," he said, but the words sounded flat.

Molly nodded and continued to hold him tight.

Avi Meyer sat hunched over his metal government-issue desk at OSI headquarters in Washington. His window, the vertical blinds angled to block most of the sun, looked out over the gridlock of K Street. It was noon and already his chin felt rough as he supported it with his left hand.

Susan Tuttle, his assistant, came in. "Pasternak just faxed over a report—you might be interested."

"What is it?"

"A neo-Nazi from San Francisco named Chuck Hanratty was killed two days ago."

"How old was he?"

"Hanratty? Twenty-four—"

Avi waved an arm dismissively. "Not old enough to be a war criminal. Except that it means there's one less asshole in the world, why'd Pasternak think I'd care?"

"Hanratty was killed in a fight while trying to mug a French-Canadian named Pierre Tardivel."

Avi scowled. "Yes?"

"And this Tardivel works at Lawrence Berkeley in the Human Genome Center there, so his boss is—"

Avi's shaggy eyebrows lifted. "Burian Klimus."

"Exactly."

Avi stabbed the intercom button on his desk. "Pam?"

A woman's voice. "Yes?"

"I need to get a flight to California ..."

When Pierre had gone to Berkeley police headquarters to file his report, he'd asked the black man—Officer Munroe, his name turned out to be—for more information about Chuck Hanratty. Munroe really didn't have much to add. Hanratty had lived, and was most frequently arrested, in San Francisco. After mulling it over for a day, Pierre decided to drive across the Oakland Bay Bridge and try his luck at SFPD headquarters.

It was raining. The bridge turned into the 101, and headquarters was just south of that at 850 Bryant, between Sixth and Seventh Streets. Pierre furled up his umbrella, entered the building, and made his way down the short corridor that led to the desk sergeant, a burly white man with curly black hair atop a loaf-shaped head. He had a computer screen mounted at an angle beneath his desk, visible through a glass window on the desktop. He was reading something on it, but looked up when Pierre cleared his throat. "Yes, sir, what can I do for you?"

Pierre wasn't sure where to begin. "I was mugged a few nights ago."

"Oh, yeah? You want to fill out a report?"

"No, no. I've already done that, over in Berkeley. I was just looking for more information. The guy who mugged me lived here, and, well, he died during the attempt. Fell on his own knife."

"What'd you say your name was?"

"Tardivel. T-A-R-D-I-V-E-L."

The sergeant typed on his keyboard. "Can I see some ID?"

Pierre opened his wallet and found his Quebec driver's license. The sergeant looked at it, nodded, and turned back to his monitor. "Well, sir, I don't know what kind of info you're looking for. If he died in the attempt, it's not like we're still looking for suspects in the mugging."

"I understand that," said Pierre, nodding. "I was just interested in other cases this same guy was involved in."

The sergeant eyed Pierre suspiciously. "Why?"

Pierre figured the truth was the simplest approach. "The officers over in Berkeley said Hanratty had been a member of a neo-Nazi group. I've been racking my brain trying to figure out what such a person would have against me."

"You Jewish?"

Pierre shook his head.

"But you *are* a foreigner. The skinheads aren't keen on immigrants."

"I suppose, but ... well, I was wondering if I could see the file on him."

The cop looked at Pierre for a time. "Hardly," he said at last.

"But—"

"We're not running a library here. Your case is closed. If your insurance company needs some paperwork to substantiate a claim, they can contact us or the Berkeley PD through normal channels. But otherwise, forget it."

Pierre thought briefly about trying to push the point but realized it was hopeless. He laid a sarcastic *"Merci beaucoup"* on the man and headed back to the lobby. It was still raining, so he stopped just inside the front doors to get his umbrella ready. As he was doing so, his eyes happened to glance over the building directory, made of little white plastic letters slid into a black board with slots in it, covered by glass.

FORENSICS, 314.

Pierre's eyebrows went up. He looked back. The sergeant had his head tilted down, reading. Pierre turned around, walked past him, and entered the elevator.

He got off on the third floor and found room 314. There was a sign on the door that said FORENSICS. Beneath it were two names in smaller letters: H. Kawabata and J. Howells. He pushed the door open and stuck his head in. "Hello?"

A tall, fortyish Asian woman appeared from behind a room divider. She had frosted blond hair cut in a pageboy style, three rings on her right hand, a chain-link bracelet on her right wrist, a matching choker, and two small studs in her left ear. She wore a white lab coat, unbuttoned, over a pink pantsuit. Her lipstick matched the suit. "Can I help you?" she said in a rapid-fire voice.

Pierre didn't like to make assumptions, but this one seemed a safe bet. "Ms. Kawabata?" he said.

"That's me."

Pierre smiled and entered the room. "Forgive me. I was in the building on other business and I couldn't resist stopping by. I know I should have made an appointment, but—"

The Asian woman's voice hardened slightly. "All purchasing is done through the office on the fourth floor."

Pierre shook his head. Maybe he needed to acquire better taste in sports jackets. "I'm not a salesman," he said. "I'm a geneticist. I'm with the Human Genome Center at Lawrence Berkeley."

She touched a hand to her lips. "Oh, I'm sorry! Come in, come in, Mister ... ?"

"Tardivel. Dr. Pierre Tardivel."

"I'm Helen," said the woman, extending her hand. "I did my graduate work at UCB. Say, I hear you got that Nobel winner running things now, what's his name ..."

"Burian Klimus," said Pierre.

Helen nodded. "The Klimus Technique, right—wonderful method; we're starting to use it here. How is he to work for?"

Pierre decided to be honest. "He's a bear. Fortunately, he's spending a lot of time at the Institute of Human Origins these days; he's gotten interested in Neanderthal DNA."

Helen smiled. "I saw him on TV once—he looks old enough to have firsthand knowledge of that."

Pierre laughed and looked around the room. Like just about every lab he'd ever been in, this one had some *Far Side* cartoons taped to the filing cabinets. "Nice equipment you've got here," he said.

Helen looked at the centrifuges, microscopes, and other hardware, as if appraising them herself. "It does the trick. We don't get to do nearly as much DNA work in-house as I'd like, but it's quite exciting when I get to testify in court. We nailed a serial rapist last week. Doesn't get much better than that."

Pierre nodded. "I read about that case in the *Chronicle*. Congratulations."

"Thanks."

"You know, I'm wondering if you can help me out. I—I was assaulted last week; that's why I'm down here. I'm trying to find out why that particular person might have gone after me and, well ..."

"And they told you to take a hike downstairs, right?"

Pierre smiled. "Exactly."

"What do you want to know?"

"One of the officers who came to investigate said the guy who attacked me was a neo-Nazi, and he had a long record. I was wondering if there was any other info I could see about him."

Helen frowned. "Are you really with the Human Genome Center?"

Pierre was about to reach for his wallet, but then decided against it. Instead, he smiled. "Try me."

Helen's eyes twinkled. "Let's see ... What's a riflip?"

"Restriction-fragment-length polymorphism," said Pierre at once. "The variation from person to person in the sizes of DNA pieces snipped out by a specific restriction enzyme."

Helen smiled. "I'd love a tour of your lab, Pierre."

This time Pierre did pull out his wallet. He removed a business card—he'd gotten new ones the previous month, when the lab had changed its name from Lawrence Berkeley Laboratory to Lawrence Berkeley *National* Laboratory—and handed it to her. "Anytime."

She walked over to her desk and slipped the card into a little metal card box. She then moved over to her computer terminal. "What would you like to know?"

"The man who attacked me was named Chuck Hanratty. I'm still trying to figure out *why* he went after me in particular. It's a bit unnerving, having somebody try to kill you."

Helen tapped at the keyboard with two fingers. Her delicate eyebrows went up. "You offed him."

"He fell on his own knife, actually. Does it really say I killed him?"

"No, no. Sorry. It says he was killed in a struggle with his intended victim. What do you want to know?"

"Anything at all. Anybody else he'd ever attacked, for instance."

"I'll print you out a copy of his rap sheet; just don't ever tell anyone where you got it. And—that's interesting. After he died, some of our people went over his rooming house. Guy lived in the Tenderloin—rough neighborhood. Anyway, among the things they found was a wallet containing credit cards belonging to a fellow named Bryan—that's with a Y—Proctor. Cross-reference in the file says that Proctor was shot to death here in SF by an unknown intruder two days before the attack on you. They found a gun at Hanratty's place, too. Ballistics confirmed it was the murder weapon in the Proctor case."

"Did this Proctor leave any family behind?"

Helen touched some more keys. "A wife."

"Is there any way I could speak to her?"

Helen shrugged. "That'd be up to her."

19

"Pierre Tardivel?"

Pierre was bent over his lab countertop. He looked up. "Yes?"

A short man with a bulldog face and blue-gray stubble entered the room. "My name is Avi Meyer." He snapped open an ID case, flashed a photo card. "I'm a federal agent, Department of Justice. I'd like to have a word with you."

Pierre straightened up. "Ah—sure. Sure. Have a seat." Pierre indicated a lab stool.

Avi continued to stand. "You're not an American—"

"No, I'm—"

"From Canada, right?"

"Yes, I was born—"

"In Quebec."

"Québec, yes. Montréal. What's this all—?"

"What brings you to the States?"

Pierre thought about saying "Air Canada," but decided against it. "I'm on a postdoctoral fellowship."

"You're a geneticist?"

"Yes. Well, my Ph.D. is in molecular biology, but—"

"What is your association with the other geneticists here?"

"I'm not sure what you mean. They're my colleagues; some are my friends—"

"Professor Sinclair—what's your association with him?"

"With Toby? I like him well enough, but I hardly know him."

"What about Donna Yamasaki?"

Pierre raised his eyebrows. "She's nice, but her name—"

"Did you know her before coming to Berkeley?"

"Not at all."

"You work under Burian Klimus."

"Yes. I mean, there are several layers between him and me, but, sure, he's the top person here."

"When did you first meet him?"

"About three days after I started here."

"You didn't know him beforehand?"

"Well, his reputation, of course, but—"

"You're not related to him, are you?"

"To Klimus? He's Czech, isn't he? No, I'm not—"

"Ukrainian, actually. You had no contact with him prior to coming to Berkeley?"

"None."

"Do you belong to any of the same groups as any of the other geneticists here?"

"Most of us are in some of the same professional associations. Triple-A-S, stuff like that, but—"

"No. *Outside* your profession."

"I don't belong to any outside groups."

"None?"

Pierre shook his head.

"You were attacked a short time ago."

"Is that what this is about? Because—"

"Did you know—"

"—I gave the police a full report. It was self-defense."

"—the man who attacked you?"

"Know him? Personally, you mean? No, I'd never seen him before in my life."

"Then why did he attack you? You of all people?"

"That's what *I* want to know."

"So you don't think it was just a random attack?"

"The police certainly believe so, but ..."

"But what?"

"Nothing, really. It just—"

"Do you have reason to think it *wasn't* a random attack?"

"—seemed to me ... what? No, no, not really. Just—no."

"And you'd never seen the attacker around this lab before?"

"I'd never seen him *anywhere* before."

"Never seen him with, say, Professor Klimus?"

"No."

"Ever see him with Dr. Yamasaki? Dr. Sinclair?"

"No. Look, what's this all about?"

"The man who attacked you belonged to a neo-Nazi organization."

"The Millennial Reich, yes."

"You know the group?" said Avi, eyes narrowing.

"No, no, no. But one of the police officers mentioned it."

"You have any connection with the Millennial Reich?"

"What? No, of course not."

"What are your politics, Mr. Tardivel?"

"NDP. What diff—"

"What the hell is 'NDP'?"

"A Canadian democratic-socialist party. What possible difference—"

"Socialist? As in *National* Socialist?"

"No, no. The NDP is—"

"What do you feel about, say, immigration?"

"I *am* an immigrant. I came here less than a year ago."

"Yes, and you've already killed an American citizen."

"It was self-defense, dammit. Ask the police."

"I've seen the report," said Avi. "Why would a neo-Nazi want to attack you, Mr. Tardivel?"

"I have no idea."

"You have no connection to neo-Nazi organizations?"

"Certainly not."

"There are a lot of anti-Semites among the Montreal French."

Pierre sighed. "You've been reading too much Mordecai Richler; I'm not anti-Semitic."

"What about the other geneticists here?"

"What kind of question is that?"

"Do any of the geneticists here at Lawrence Berkeley—or down at the university—have connections that you know of to Nazi organizations?"

"Of course not. I mean, well—"

"Yes?"

"No, nothing."

"Mr. Tardivel, your evasiveness is trying my patience. You're not yet a citizen here; you wouldn't want any special annotations in your immigration record. I could have you back in Canada faster than you can say Anne Murray."

"Christ, I—look, the only guy who even comes close to being a Nazi is ..."

"Yes?"

"I don't want to get him in any trouble, but ... well, Felix Sousa is a professor at UCB."

"Sousa? Anyone else?"

"No. You know Sousa?"

Avi grimaced. "The whites-are-superior-to-blacks guy."

Pierre nodded. "Tenured prof. Nothing they can do to shut him up. But if anybody's a Nazi here, it's him."

Avi nodded. "All right, thank you. Don't mention this conversation to anyone."

"I still don't know—"

But Avi Meyer was already out the door.

"Susan? It's Avi. Yeah—yeah. What? *Corrina, Corrina,* with Whoopi Goldberg. Yeah, it was okay; better than the food anyway. Yes, I saw Tardivel this afternoon. He didn't come out and say it, but I think he feels the attack was aimed right at him, which makes the connection even tighter. I'm going to spend tomorrow going over the files at the SFPD and the Alameda County sheriff's office on the Millennial Reich. No, I'm avoiding Klimus, at least for the time being. Don't want to tip our hand ..."

20

"Since we're going to have a baby," said Molly, sitting on their living-room couch, "there's something I want you to do."

Pierre put down the remote control. "Oh?"

"I've never had anyone study my—my gift. But since we *are* going to have a child, I think maybe we should know some more about it. I don't know if I want the child to be telepathic or not; part of me hopes it is, part of me hopes it isn't. But if it does turn out to share my ability, I want to be able to warn him or her before it develops. I went through hell when it started happening to me when I turned thirteen—thought I was losing my mind."

Pierre nodded. "I've certainly been curious about the science behind what you can do, but I didn't want to pry."

"And I love you for that. But we *should* know. There must be something different in my DNA. Can you find what it is?"

Pierre frowned. "It's almost impossible to find the genetic cause of something with only one sample. If we knew of a large group of people who had your ability, we might be able to track down the gene responsible. That's how the Huntington's gene was found, after all. They used blood samples from seventy-five families around the world that had Huntington's sufferers. But with you being the world's only known legitimate telepath, I don't think there's anything we can do in terms of looking for a gene."

"Well," said Molly, "if we can't find it by working from the DNA up, what about reverse engineering? My guess is that there's something chemically different in my brain—a neurotransmitter, say, that no one else has, a chemical that perhaps allows me to use my brain's neuronal wiring as a receiver. If we could isolate it and establish its amino-acid sequence, could you search my DNA for the code that specifies those amino acids?"

Pierre lifted his shoulders. "I suppose that might be possible, if it's a protein-based neurotransmitter. But neither of us has the expertise to do that kind of work. We'd have to get someone else involved, to take the fluid samples and to separate out the neurotransmitters. And even then, it's just a hunch that that's the cause of your telepathy. Still," he said, his voice taking on a faraway tone, "if we could identify the neurotransmitter, maybe someday they could synthesize it. Maybe all anyone needs to read minds is the right chemicals in the brain."

But Molly was shaking her head. "I don't mean to sound sexist," she said, "but I've always suspected the only reason I've survived this long is because I'm a woman. I shudder to think what some testosterone-crazed male would do when he picked up offensive thoughts—probably kill everyone around him." She brought her gaze back to meet Pierre's. "No. Maybe someday far in the future, humanity might be able to handle something like this. But not now; it's not the right time."

Pierre was setting up an electrophoresis gel when the phone in his lab rang for the third time that morning. He sighed, wheeled across the room on his chair, and picked up the handset.

"Tardivel," he snapped into the mouthpiece.

"Hi, Pierre. This is Jasmine Lucarelli, over in endocrinology."

Pierre's tone immediately warmed. "Oh, hi, Jasmine. Thanks so much for getting back to me."

"Uh-huh. Listen—where did you say you got that fluid sample you sent over?"

Pierre hesitated slightly. "Ah, it was from a woman."

"I've never quite seen anything like it. The specimen contained all the usual neurotransmitters—serotonin, acetylcholine, GABA, dopamine, and so on—but there was one protein in there I'd never seen before. Quite complex, too. I'm only assuming it's a neurotransmitter because of its basic structure—choline is one of its chief constituents."

"Have you worked out its full makeup?"

"Not personally," said Dr. Lucarelli. "One of my grad students did it for me."

"Can you send me a copy?"

"Sure. But I'd still like to know where this came from."

Pierre exhaled. "It's—it's a prank, I think. A biochem student cobbled it together, trying to make a monkey out of his prof."

"Shit," said Lucarelli. "Kids today, eh?"

"Yeah. Anyway, thanks for looking at it. If you'd send me your notes on its chemical structure, I'd be grateful—I, ah, want to put a copy in the student's file, in case he tries a stunt like this again."

"Sure thing."

"Thanks very much, Jasmine."

"No problem."

Pierre hung up the phone, his heart pounding.

Pierre had spent the last fourteen days studying the unusual neurotransmitter from Molly's brain. Whether it was the key to her telepathy or just a by-product of it, he didn't know. But the substance, despite its complexity, was just another protein, and like all proteins it was built up from amino acids. Pierre worked out the various sequences of DNA that could code for the creation of the most distinctive chain of aminos in the molecule. There were many possible combinations, because of codon synonyms, but he calculated them all. He then built up segments of RNA that would complement the various sequences of DNA he was searching for.

Pierre took a test tube full of Molly's blood and used liquid nitrogen to freeze it to minus seventy degrees Celsius. That ruptured the cell membranes of the red corpuscles, but left the hardier white corpuscles intact. He then thawed the blood out, the ruptured reds dissolving into lightweight fragments.

Next, he spun the tube in a centrifuge at 1600 rpm. The millions of white corpuscles—the only large objects left in the blood sample now—were forced down to the end of the tube, forming a solid white pellet. He removed the pellet and soaked it for a couple of hours in a solution containing proteinase K, which digested the white corpuscles' cell membranes and other proteins. He then introduced phenol and chloroform, which cleared away the protein debris in twenty minutes, then added ethanol, which over the next two hours precipitated out the delicate fibers of Molly's purified DNA.

Pierre then worked on adding his special RNA segments to Molly's DNA, and looked to see if they clamped on anywhere. It took over a hundred tries before he got lucky. It turned out that the sequence that coded for the production of the telepathy-related neurotransmitter was on the short arm of chromosome thirteen.

Pierre used his terminal to log on to GSDB—the Genome Sequence Database, which contained all the genetic sequences that had been mapped out by the hundreds of labs and universities worldwide working on decoding the human genome. He wanted to see what that part of chromosome thirteen looked like in normal people. Fortunately, the gene that occurred there had been sequenced in detail by the team at Leeds. The normal value was CAT CAG GGT GTC CAT, but Molly's specimen began TCA TCA GGG TGT CCA—completely different, which—

No.

No, *not* completely different. Just shifted one place to the right, one nucleotide—a T, in this case—having been accidentally added in the copying of Molly's DNA.

A *frameshift* mutation. Add or remove one nucleotide, and every genetic word from that point on is altered. Molly's TCA TCA GGG TGT CCA coded for the amino acids serine, serine, glycine, cysteine, and proline, whereas the standard CAT CAG GGT GTC CAT coded for histidine, glutamine, glycine, valine, and arginine; both chains had glycine in the middle because GGG and GGT were synonyms.

Frameshifts usually garbled everything, turning the genetic code into gibberish. Many human embryos spontaneously abort very early on, before their mothers even know they're pregnant; frameshifts were a likely reason for many of those failures. But this one—

A frameshift mutation that might cause telepathy.

Pierre sagged back in his chair, stunned.

21

Although the ground had recently been broken for a dedicated genome facility to be built at LBNL, at the moment the Human Genome Center was shoehorned onto the third floor of Building 74, which was part of the Life Sciences Division. Medical research was also done in this building, meaning they didn't even have to go outside to find a small operating theater.

It was the Friday night of the Labor Day long weekend, the last holiday of the summer. Most everybody was out of town or at home enjoying the time off. Molly and Pierre met Burian Klimus, Dr. Gwendolyn Bacon, and her two assistants in Klimus's office, and the six of them headed downstairs.

Pierre kept Klimus company outside as Molly lay on a table in the theater. Dr. Bacon—a gaunt, tanned woman of about fifty, with hair as white as snow—stood by as one of her assistants administered an intravenous sedative to Molly, and then Bacon herself inserted a long, hollow needle into Molly's vagina. Monitoring her progress with ultrasound equipment, Bacon used suction to draw out sample material. The hormones she'd been treating Molly with should have caused her to develop multiple oocytes to maturity this cycle, instead of the usual one. The material was quickly transferred to a petri dish containing a growth medium, and Bacon's other assistant checked it under a microscope to make sure it did indeed include eggs.

Finally, Molly got dressed, and Pierre and Klimus came into the theater. "We got fifteen eggs," Bacon said, with a slight Tennessee accent. "Good work, Molly!"

Molly nodded but then backed away from everyone in the room, rubbing her right temple a bit. Pierre recognized the signs: she clearly had a headache, and wanted to put some distance between herself and others to get some mental peace and quiet. The headache was no doubt brought about by the uncomfortable procedure and bright lights, and had probably been exacerbated by having had to listen to Dr. Bacon's doubtlessly intense and clinical thoughts while performing the extraction.

"All right," said Klimus from across the room. "Now, if you people will leave me alone, I'll take care of ... of the rest of the procedure."

Pierre looked at the man. He seemed slightly ... well, embarrassed was probably the right word. After all, the old guy was now about to whack off into a beaker. Pierre wondered for a moment what he was going to use to help him along. *Playboy? Penthouse? Proceedings of the National Academy?* The semen could have been collected weeks before, but fresh sperm had a 90 percent chance of fertilizing the eggs, versus only 60 percent for the frozen variety.

"Don't fertilize all the eggs," said Dr. Bacon to Klimus. "Save half for later." That was good advice. It was possible that Klimus's sperm had low motility (not unusual in elderly men) and would fail to fertilize the eggs. This way, if need be, some eggs would be in storage to try again later with a different donor, saving Molly from another round of needle aspiration.

Once Klimus's sperm was added, the mixture would be placed in an incubator. Klimus would return tomorrow night at this time to check on what was happening: fertilization should take place pretty quickly in the dish, but it would be a day before it could be detected. He'd phone Pierre, Molly, and Dr. Bacon with the results, and assuming they did have fertilized eggs, they would all return the following night, Sunday evening, by which time the embryos would be at the four-cell stage, ready for implantation. Dr. Bacon would then insert four or five directly into Molly's uterus through her cervical canal.

If none implanted, they'd try again later. If one or two did implant, a standard pregnancy test should reveal positive results in ten to fourteen days. If more than that implanted, well, Pierre had read about a procedure called "selective reduction"—another reason he hadn't been keen on having his own sperm generate embryos for IVF. Selective reduction was done many weeks into the pregnancy by using ultrasound to target the most accessible fetuses, then injecting poison directly into their hearts.

"Well," said Bacon, after scrubbing down and removing her gown, "I'm going home. Keep your fingers crossed."

"Thank you *so* much," said Molly, sitting on a chair across the room.

"Yes, thank you," said Pierre. "We really appreciate it."

"My pleasure," said Bacon. She and her assistants left.

"You two should get going, as well," said Klimus to Pierre and Molly. "Go out to dinner; keep yourselves occupied. I'll call you tomorrow night."

The phone rang in Pierre and Molly's living room at 8:52 the following evening. They looked at each other anxiously, not sure for half a second who should answer it.

Pierre nodded at Molly, and she dived for it, bringing the handset to her face. "Hello?" she said. "Yes? Really? Oh, that's wonderful! That's marvelous! Thank you, Burian. Thank you so much! Yes, yes, tomorrow. We'll be there at eight. Thanks a million! See you then."

Pierre was already on his feet, his arms around his wife's waist from behind. She put down the handset. "We've got seven fertilized eggs!" she said.

Pierre turned her around and kissed her passionately. Their tongues danced for a while, and his hands fondled her breasts. They collapsed back down on the couch, making wild, hot love, first licking and kissing each other, she taking him into her mouth, he lapping at her, and then, of course, the most important of all, driving his penis into her, pounding, pounding, as if to propel his own sperm through her blocked fallopian tubes, and at last exploding in orgasm, after which the two of them lay spent, cuddling together.

Pierre knew that for the rest of his life, he would think of that spectacular lovemaking session as the real moment his child had been conceived.

Craig Bullen came into the ultramodern office on the thirty-seventh floor of the Condor Health Insurance Tower in San Francisco. Sitting at his desk as he had every weekday for the past four decades was Abraham Danielson, the founder of the company. Bullen had mixed feelings about the old man. He was a crusty bastard, to be sure, but he had handpicked Bullen fifteen years ago, when Bullen had graduated from the Harvard Business School. "You're the most rapacious kid I've seen in years," Danielson, who was old even back then, had said—and he'd meant it as a compliment. Danielson had brought Bullen up through the ranks, and now Bullen was CEO. Danielson still kept his hand in, though, and Bullen often turned to the old man for reality checks. But today Danielson's ancient face was creased more than usual, a frown deepening his myriad wrinkles.

"What's wrong?" asked Bullen.

Danielson gestured at the spreadsheet printout covering his desk. "Projections for the next fiscal year," he said in a gruff, dry voice. "We'll still be doing fine in Oregon and Washington, but this new anti-genetic-discrimination law will be killing us here in Northern Cal. We got a raft of new policies this year from people we'd never have insured before, so that's pushed the bottom line up a bit for the time being. But next year and in each subsequent year, many of those people will start showing overt symptoms, and begin filing claims." He sighed, a rough, papery sound. "I thought that we were in the clear after Hillary Clinton fell flat on her face—the smug bitch—but if Oregon or Washington State adopt a California-style law, well, hell, we might as well close up shop and go home."

Bullen shook his head slightly. He'd heard Danielson go on like this before, but it was getting worse as the years went by. "We're lobbying like mad in Salem and Olympia," Bullen said, trying to calm the old man. "And the HIAA is fighting hard in D.C. against any similar federal regulation. The California law is an aberration, I'm sure."

But Danielson shook his head. "Where's that steely-eyed realism, Craig? The days of profits in the health-insurance industry are numbered. Christ, if we could get the bottom line up enough, I'd sell my thirty-three percent and get the hell out." Danielson sighed again, and looked up. "Was there something you wanted to see me about?"

"Yeah," said Bullen, "and it's apropos in a way, too. We got a letter from a geneticist at"—he consulted the sheet he was holding—"the Ernest Orlando Lawrence Berkeley National Laboratory. He objects to our clause that encourages terminating genetically flawed pregnancies."

The old man gestured with a bony hand for the letter. Once he had it, he skimmed its text. "'Bioethics,'" he said contemptuously. "And 'the human side of the equation.'" He harrumphed. "At least he didn't mention *Brave New World.*"

"Yes, he did. That's what the bit about 'Huxleyian nightmare' refers to."

"Tell him to go to hell," said Danielson, passing the letter back to his protégé. "Ivory-tower guy—doesn't know the first thing about the real world."

Pierre had had the copy of Chuck Hanratty's rap sheet that Helen Kawabata had given him for eight weeks now. He'd been eager to talk to Bryan Proctor's widow, but couldn't bring himself to disturb her until a decent period had passed following her husband's murder.

But now he regretted waiting—she seemed to have moved in the interim. He checked the address on the piece of fanfold paper again. No doubt about it: this dingy apartment building, a few blocks south of San Francisco's Chinatown, was the place where Bryan Proctor had lived before Chuck Hanratty had shot him dead. But although there were twenty-one names on the buzzboard in the lobby, not one of them was Proctor. Pierre was about to give up and go home when he decided to try the superintendent. He pressed the button labeled SUPER and waited.

"Yes?" said a female voice through a very staticky intercom.

"Hello. I'm looking for Mrs. Proctor."

"Come on in. Suite 101."

He heard a clunking going on inside the door, followed by an annoying buzz. It dawned on Pierre—of course! Bryan Proctor must have been the super; that's why his buzzer wasn't labeled by name.

He made his way through the lobby. It was a run-down building, with worn and stained carpeting. Suite—if it deserved that term—101 was next to the single elevator. A large woman with one of those golf-ball chins fat people sometimes have was standing in the open doorway. She was wearing old jeans and a tattered white T-shirt. "Yes?" she said, by way of greeting. "The vacancy's on the second floor. We need first and last months' rent, plus references."

Pierre had seen the sign for the two-bedroom apartment when he'd pulled up to the building. "I'm not here about the apartment. Forgive me for coming by without calling first, but you've got an unlisted number, and I ... well, I don't know where to begin. I'm terribly sorry about the loss of your husband."

"Thank you," she said guardedly, her eyes narrowing. "Did you know Bryan?"

"No, no, not at all."

"Then if you're trying to sell something, please leave me alone."

Pierre shook his head in wonder; he must look like Willy Loman. "No—no, it's not that. It's just that—well, see, I'm Pierre Tardivel."

Her face was blank. "Yes?"

"I was the last person Chuck Hanratty attacked. I was there when he died."

"You killed that bastard?"

"Umm, yes."

She stood to one side. "Please, come in. Can I offer you a drink? Coffee? Beer?"

She led the way into the living room. It had only two bookcases, one holding bowling trophies and the other mostly CDs. There *was* a paperback book splayed open facedown on the coffee table—a Harlequin romance. "A beer would be nice," said Pierre.

"Have a seat on the couch and I'll get it." She disappeared for a few moments, and Pierre continued to look around. Copies of *The National Enquirer* and *TV Guide* sat atop a television set that looked about fifteen years old. There were no framed pictures, but there *was* a poster of the Grand Canyon held up with yellowing tape. There was no sign that the Proctors had any kids. Sympathy cards were lined up along the lid of an old record turntable.

Mrs. Proctor returned and handed Pierre a Budweiser can. He pulled the tab, took a swig, and winced. He'd never get used to this cow piss Americans called beer.

"It's better this way," said Mrs. Proctor, sitting in a chair. "Even if they'd caught Hanratty, he'd have been back on the streets in just a couple of years. My husband's dead—but he wasn't anyone important. They wouldn't have given Hanratty the chair for that."

Pierre said nothing for a time, then: "Hanratty attacked me—me in particular. It wasn't just a random mugging."

"Oh? The police told me—"

"No, he was after me. He, ah, he said so."

Her piglike eyes went wide. "That a fact?"

"But I'd never met him before in my life. Heck, I've only been in California for a year now."

"Color me surprised," said the woman.

"Sorry?"

"You got one heck of an accent."

"Oh, well, I'm from Montreal."

"That up in Canada?"

"Yes."

"One of our old tenants moved out, took a job in Vancouver. I wonder if you'd know him?"

Pierre smiled indulgently. "Ma'am, Canada is bigger than the United States. Vancouver's a long way from where I lived."

"Bigger than the States? Get out of here. 'States the biggest country on Earth."

Pierre rolled his eyes, but decided not to pursue the point. "Anyway," he said, "since Hanratty went after me in particular, I was wondering if he also went specifically after your husband."

"Can't see why he would," said the woman. "It was just a break-in, the police said. Guy didn't expect my husband to be home. Probably figured, being super and all, that Bryan had a lot of power tools worth stealing. He did—but he kept them down in the boiler room, not here. Bryan apparently surprised the bastard, and he shot him."

"I suppose. But what if he was after your husband, rather than his tools?"

"What on Earth for?"

"Well, I don't know. I'm just wondering if he and I had anything in common. Hanratty was a member of a neo-Nazi group. It's possible he didn't like me because I'm a foreigner, for instance."

"My Bryan was born right here in the good old U.S. of A. In Lincoln, Nebraska, to be exact."

"What about his politics?"

"Republican—although sometimes he couldn't bother getting off his duff to vote."

"And his religion?"

"Presbyterian."

"Did he go to university?"

"Bryan?" She laughed. "He's an eighth-grade dropout." She held up a hand. "Doesn't mean he was stupid, mind you. He was a good man, and he could fix just about anything. But he didn't have a lot of school."

"And he was older than me, wasn't he?"

"Depends. You as young as you look?"

"I'm thirty-three."

"Well, my Bryan was forty-nine." She grew a bit wistful at the mention of the age. "There's nothing worse than dying young, is there?"

Pierre nodded. Nothing worse.

Pierre looked over the counter in the lab. Ever since he'd been a little boy, he'd hated cleaning up after himself. It just wasn't nearly as much fun putting things away as it was taking them out. But it had to be done. He'd spread beakers and retort stands all across the countertop. And some of the labware had to be carefully washed; a molecular-biology lab was a perfect breeding ground for germs, after all.

He dismantled the retort stand and put it away in one of the cupboards. He then picked up a beaker and took it over to the sink, rinsing it out under cold water, then placing it in a rack to dry. Next, he got his petri dishes and put them in a special bag for disposal. He returned to the table and reached out for a large flask, picked it up, and watched it fall from his trembling hand. Shards of glass went everywhere and the flask's liquid contents made a yellowish splash across the tiled floor.

Pierre swore in French. Just tired, he told himself. Long day. Still a bit distracted from the meeting with Bryan Proctor's widow. Need a good night's sleep.

He went to get the broom and dustpan, and began sweeping up the broken glass.

Tired. Nothing more than that.

And yet—

God, would he have to go through this every time he dropped something? Every time he took a misstep? Every time he bumped into a wall?

Damn it—he—was—just—tired! Tired, that's all.

Unless—

Unless it was fucking goddamn Huntington's disease, at last rearing its monstrous head.

No. It was nothing.

Nothing.

He carried the dustpan over to the garbage pail and emptied it.

Tomorrow, everything would be fine.

Surely, it would be fine.

22

Pierre and Molly stood in their bathroom early in the morning and looked at the test strip together. A blue plus sign blossomed into existence on its white surface.

"Oui!" said Pierre.

"Wow," said Molly. "Wow."

Pierre kissed his wife. "Congratulations."

"We're going to be parents," said Molly, dreamily.

Pierre stroked her hair. "I never thought this could happen. Not for me."

"It's going to be wonderful."

"You'll make a terrific mother."

"And you'll make a great daddy."

Pierre smiled at the thought. "Do you want a boy or a girl?"

"You know, we probably could have asked Burian. He could have sorted his sperm, if we'd told him. There's a difference between male-producing sperm and female-producing, isn't there?" Pierre nodded. Molly paused, considering his question. "I don't know. I suppose a girl, but that's only because of my family life, I'm sure. My mother and sister and I were alone for a long time before Paul showed up. I'm not sure how I'd be with a little boy."

"You'd do fine."

"Do you have a preference?"

"Me? No, I guess not. I mean, I know that every man is supposed to want a son he can play catch with, but ..." He trailed off, deciding not to complete the thought. "Maybe having a girl *would* be simpler," he said.

Molly had missed, or was choosing to ignore, the undercurrent. "I really don't care which it is," she said at last, her voice still dreamy. "Just as long as it's healthy."

After a long day at the Human Genome Center, Joan Dawson was pleased to be approaching home. She was walking from the BART station; the walk was almost a mile, but she did it every night. At her age, she wasn't up to any more-strenuous exercise, but she did spend all day at her secretarial desk, and diabetics had to be particular about their weight.

There was hardly anyone around; she lived in a quiet neighborhood. When she and her husband had bought here in 1959, there had been lots of young families. The neighborhood had grown up with them, but although these had qualified as starter homes all those years ago, they were out of the reach of today's young couples. Now this area was home mostly to elderly people—the lucky ones still husband and wife, but many of the others, like Joan, having lost their spouses over the years. Her Bud had passed on in 1987.

Joan came up the walk to the front of her house, opened the lid on the mailbox, scooped up the bills, smiled when she saw her copy of *Ellery Queen's* had arrived, fumbled for her keys, and let herself in. She turned on the porch light, made her way up to her living room, and—

"Joan Dawson?"

Her heart practically shot out of her chest, it was beating so hard. She turned around. A young white man with a shaven head and tattoos of skulls on his forearms was looking at her with pale blue eyes.

Joan was still holding her purse. She thrust it at him. "Take it! Take it! You can have my money."

The man was wearing a black Megadeath T-shirt with a denim vest over it, jeans with artful slashes in them, and gray Adidas. He shook his head. "It's not your money I'm after."

Joan started backing away, still holding the purse in front of her, but now as if it were a shield. "No," she said. "No—there's jewelry upstairs. Lots of jewelry. You can have it all."

The punk started walking toward her. "I don't want your jewelry, either."

Joan had backed into the glass-topped coffee table. She tumbled backward over it, and the glass cracked with a sound like a rifle going off. She scrambled to her feet. Pain stabbed at her from her ankle; she'd wrenched it badly going down. "Please," she said, whimpering now. "Please, not that."

The skinhead stopped approaching for a moment, a look of revulsion on his face. "Fuck, woman, don't be disgusting. You're old enough to be my grandmother."

Joan felt a surge of hope fighting to the surface against all the terror. "Thank you," she said. "Thank you, thank you, thank you." She'd backed against the rough brick of the fireplace now.

The man pulled his vest open. He had a long single-edged hunting knife with a black handle in a sheath under his arm. He pulled out the weapon and amused himself for a second by sending a glint of light playing down Joan's horrified face.

Joan fumbled for the fireplace poker, found it, raised it in front of her. "Stay back!" she said. "What do you want?"

The man grinned, showing tobacco-stained teeth. "I want," he said, "for you to be dead."

Joan inhaled deeply, prelude to a scream, but before she could get it out, the man flipped the knife out of his hand, and it landed smack-dab in the middle of her chest, burying itself halfway to the hilt. She slumped to the tiled area just in front of the fireplace, her mouth still in the perfect "O" of the stillborn scream.

Pierre sat in front of his UNIX workstation. The monitor was on, but he wasn't reading its display; rather, he was leafing through the *Daily Californian,* the UCB student newspaper. News about the campus football team; big debates about UCB's elimination of racial quotas for students; a letter to the editor complaining about Felix Sousa.

Pierre's mind wandered back to the last time he'd spoken to somebody about Sousa. He'd been talking to that strange bulldoglike fellow who had blustered into this very room over three months ago. Ari something. No, no—not Ari. *Avi.* Avi—Avi *Meyer,* that was it.

Pierre never had figured out what that had all been about. He closed the newspaper and turned to his computer, opening a window on the governmental telephone database CD-ROM, accessible through the LAN.

Avi Meyer had said he worked for the Department of Justice. The database didn't contain individual agent listings, but Pierre did find a general-inquiry number in Washington. He highlighted the number, pressed the key for his telephone program, ticked the personal-call option in the dialogue box that popped up, and let his modem dial the call for him while he held his telephone handset to his ear.

"Justice," said a female voice at the other end. All that was missing, thought Pierre, were Truth and the American Way.

"Hello," he said. "Do you have someone there named Avi Meyer?"

Keyclicks. "Yes. He's out of town right now, but I can put you through to his voice mail, or let you speak to a receptionist at OSI."

"OSI?" said Pierre.

"The Office of Special Investigations," said the voice.

"Oh, of course," said Pierre. "Well, if you say he's not in, I'll just try again another time. Thanks." He hung up, then clicked on his CompuServe icon and logged on to Magazine Database Plus, which had become one of Pierre's favorite research tools since he'd discovered it a couple of months ago. It contained the full text of all the articles in over two hundred general-interest and specialty magazines—including such publications as *Science* and *Nature*—going back as far as 1986. He typed in two search strings, "Special Investigations" and "OSI," and selected whole-words-only, so that the latter wouldn't result in a deluge of matches on "deposits" or "Bela Lugosi."

The first hit was in an article from *People* magazine about Lee Majors. In his 1970s TV series *The Six Million Dollar Man,* he'd worked for a fictitious government agency called the OSI. Pierre continued his search.

The second hit was right on target: an article in *The New Republic* from 1993. The highlighted sentence began: "Then there is the conduct of Demjanjuk's major enemy in this country, the Office of Special Investigations, which set the wheels of injustice moving against him ..."

Pierre read on, fascinated. The OSI was indeed part of the Department of Justice—a division founded in 1979, devoted to exposing Nazi war criminals and collaborators in the United States.

The case against this Demjanjuk fellow—a retired autoworker from Cleveland, a simple man with just a fourth-grade education—had started out as the OSI's first big success. Demjanjuk had been accused of being Ivan the Terrible, a guard at the Treblinka death camp. He'd been extradited to Israel, where he was found guilty in 1988, the second of two war-crimes trials ever held there. As in the first trial, that of Adolf Eichmann, Demjanjuk was sentenced to death.

But the OSI's reputation was blackened when, on appeal, the Israeli supreme court overturned the conviction of John Demjanjuk. In an inquest into the whole mess, U.S. federal judge Thomas Wiseman found that the OSI had failed to meet even "the bare minimum standards of professional conduct" in its proceedings against Demjanjuk, presuming him to be guilty and ignoring all evidence to the contrary.

Pierre continued reading. The OSI had known that the real name of the man they'd wanted was Marchenko, not Demjanjuk. Now, yes, John Demjanjuk *had* listed his mother's maiden name incorrectly as Marchenko on his application for refugee status, but he'd later claimed he'd simply forgotten her real name, and so had just filled in a common Ukrainian one.

Pierre skimmed other articles about the Demjanjuk affair, from *Time, Maclean's, The Economist, The National Review, People,* and elsewhere. He found part of Demjanjuk's life story interesting because of the rocky marriage of his own parents, Élisabeth and Alain Tardivel. Demjanjuk had married a woman named Vera in a displaced-persons camp on September 1, 1947. Nothing remarkable about that—except that when Vera and Demjanjuk had met, she was already married to another DP, Eugene Sakowski. Sakowski went to Belgium for three weeks, and, while he was gone, John Demjanjuk had taken up with Vera; when Sakowski returned, Vera divorced him and married John.

Pierre let his breath escape in a long sigh. Triangles were everywhere, it seemed. He wondered what his own life would have been like if his mother had ignored the church and divorced Alain Tardivel so that she could have married Pierre's real father, Henry Spade. Things would have been so—

A sentence on the screen caught his eye: a description of Demjanjuk. Magazine Database Plus contained text only—no photographs—but a picture nonetheless formed in Pierre's mind: a Ukrainian, bald, sturdy, thick necked, with thin lips, almond eyes, and protruding ears.

Shit ...

It couldn't be.

It could *not* be.

The man had won a Nobel Prize, after all.

Yeah—and fucking Kurt Waldheim had ended up as United Nations secretary-general.

Bald, protruding ears. Ukrainian.

Demjanjuk had been identified based on those features. But Demjanjuk had not been Ivan the Terrible.

Meaning somebody else had been.

Someone the articles called Ivan Marchenko.

Somebody who might very well still be at large.

Burian Klimus was Ukrainian, and by his own recent statement had been bald since youth. He had large ears—not unusual for a man his age—but Pierre had never thought of them as protruding. Still, a little plastic surgery could have corrected that years ago.

And Avi Meyer was a Nazi hunter.

A Nazi hunter who had been sniffing around the Lawrence Berkeley Lab—

Meyer had asked about several geneticists, but he hadn't really been interested in all of them. He'd consistently referred to Donna Yamashita as Donna Yamasaki, for instance—there's no way he wouldn't have known the correct name of someone he was actually investigating.

And, anyway, neither Yamashita nor Toby Sinclair—the other geneticist Meyer had asked about—was old enough to be a war criminal.

But Burian Klimus was.

Pierre shook his head.

God.

If he was right, if *Meyer* was right—

Then Molly was carrying within her the child of a monster.

23

Pierre knew where to find any biology journal on campus, but he had no idea which of UCB's libraries would have things like *Time* and *The National Review.* He wanted to see the pictures of Demjanjuk, both as he appeared today and, more importantly, the old photos from which he'd been misidentified as Ivan. Joan Dawson seemed to know just about everything there was to know about the university; she'd doubtless know where he could find those magazines. Pierre left his lab and headed down to the HGC general office.

He stopped short on the threshold. Burian Klimus was in there, getting his mail out of the cubbyhole with his name on it just inside the door. From the back, Pierre could see where Klimus's ears joined his head. There were white creases there. Were they scars? Or did every old person have creases like that?

"Good morning, sir," said Pierre, coming into the office.

Klimus turned and looked at Pierre. The dark brown eyes, the thin lips—was this the face of evil? Could this be the man who had killed so many people?

"Tardivel," Klimus said, by way of greeting.

Pierre found himself staring at the man. He shook his head slightly. "Is Joan in?"

"No."

Pierre glanced at the clock above the door and frowned. Then a thought struck him. "By the way, sir, I ran into someone you might know a couple of months ago—a Mr. Meyer."

"Jacob Meyer? That moneygrubbing little prick. He's no friend of mine."

Pierre was taken aback—that sure sounded like an anti-Semitic comment, precisely the kind a Nazi would make without thinking ... unless, of course, this Jacob Meyer fellow really did happen to be a moneygrubbing little prick. "Uh, no, this fellow's name was Avi Meyer."

Klimus shook his head. "Never heard of him."

Pierre blinked. "Guy about this high?" He held his hand at the height of his Adam's apple. "Shaggy eyebrows? Looks like a bulldog?"

"No."

Pierre frowned, then looked again at the clock. "Joan should have been in three hours ago."

Klimus opened an envelope with his finger.

"Wouldn't she have told you if she had an appointment?"

Klimus shrugged.

"She's a diabetic. She lives alone."

The old man was reading the letter he'd taken from the envelope. He made no reply.

"Do we have her number?" asked Pierre.

"Somewhere, I suppose," said Klimus, "but I have no idea where."

Pierre looked around for a phone book. He found one on the bottom shelf of a low-rise bookcase behind Joan's desk and began flipping through it. "There's no J. Dawson listed."

"Maybe it is still under her late husband's name," said Klimus.

"Which was ... ?"

Klimus waved the letter he was holding. "Bud, I think."

"There's no B. Dawson, either."

Klimus's old throat made a rough noise. "No one's first name is really Bud."

"A nickname, eh? What for?"

"William, usually."

"There's a W. P. Dawson on Delbert."

Klimus made no reply. Pierre dialed the phone. An answering machine came on. "It's a machine," said Pierre, "but it's Joan's voice, and—Hello, Joan. This is Pierre Tardivel at LBNL. I'm just calling to see if you're all right. It's now almost one, and we're just a bit worried about you. If you're in, could you pick up the phone?" He waited for about thirty seconds, then hung up. Pierre chewed his lower lip. "Delbert. That's not too far, is it?"

Klimus shook his head. "About five miles." Pierre looked at the clock again. An elderly diabetic, living alone. If she was having an insulin reaction ...

"I think I'm going to take a swing by her place."

Klimus said nothing.

Pierre pulled up Joan's driveway. Something amiss about the house, though: the porch light was still on, even though it was now well into the afternoon. He walked up to the front door. A morning paper, the *San Francisco Chronicle,* was still on the stoop. Pierre rang the doorbell and waited for a response, tapping his foot. Nothing. He tried again. Still no answer.

Pierre exhaled noisily, unsure what to do. He looked around. There were several large stones in the small flower bed in front of the house. He lifted each of them up, looking for a hidden key—but all he found was a large slate gray salamander, another thing about Berkeley he'd yet to get used to. He hefted the largest stone, thought about using it to break the frosted entryway window, but didn't want to go to extremes ...

He walked down the wide stretch of lawn between this houseand the one adjacent to it, feeling enormously self-conscious. There was a picket fence, mostly covered with peeling white paint, between the front yard and the back. Part of the fence was a gate, and Pierre lifted the rusting catch, swung it open, and made his way into the backyard, most of which was given over to well-tended vegetable gardens. The rear part of the house had small windows and a sliding glass door overlooking the backyard. Pierre moved up to the first window and pressed his face against the glass, boxing his eyes against the reflected sky with his hands. Nothing. Just a small wallpapered room with a TV and a corduroy-upholstered La-Z-Boy in it.

He tried the second window. The kitchen. Joan had every conceivable gadget: food processor, juicer, blenders, bread maker, two microwaves, and more.

He moved over to the glass door, moved his face up to it, and—

Jesus God—

Joan was on her side, facing him, eyes still open. A pool of dark crusted blood more than a meter in diameter had spilled out of her; its shape was irregular on the low-pile carpet, but had neatly filled the tiled area in front of the fireplace. Pierre felt his breakfast climbing his throat. He hurried back to his car, drove till he found a pay phone at a 7-Eleven, and dialed 9-1-1.

Pierre sat on Joan's front stoop, arms supporting his chin, waiting. A Berkeley police car pulled up at the curb. Pierre looked up, held a hand to his brow to shield his eyes, and squinted to make out the uniformed figures approaching against the glare of the afternoon sun: a beefy black man and a slim white woman.

"Mr. Tardivel, isn't it?" said the black man, taking off a pair of sunglasses and putting them in the breast pocket of his jacket.

Pierre rose to his feet. "Officer—?"

"Munroe," said the man. He nodded at his partner. "And Granatstein."

"Of course," said Pierre, nodding at each of them. "Hello."

"Let's see it," said Munroe. Pierre led them down the path between this house and the adjacent one, through the gate, which he'd left open, and into the backyard. Munroe had his billy club out, in case he needed to use it to smash in a window, but when he got to the glass door, he saw the lock had been jimmied. "You haven't been inside?" asked Munroe.

"No."

Munroe entered and made a cursory examination of the body. Granatstein, meanwhile, started looking around the yard for anything the assailant might have dropped during his escape. Munroe came back outside and took out a small notebook, bound with a wire spiral along its top. He flipped to a blank page. "What time did you arrive?"

"At 13:15," said Pierre. "I mean, at 1:15."

"You're sure of that?"

"I look at my watch a lot."

"And she was dead when you got here?"

"Of course—"

"You ever been out here before?"

"No."

"Then what brought you here today?"

"She was late for work. I thought I'd check on her."

"Why? What business is it of yours?"

"She's a friend. And she's a diabetic. I thought she might have been having an insulin reaction."

"What were you doing around the back of the house?"

"Well, she didn't answer the doorbell, so—"

"So you went snooping around?"

"Well, I—"

"The knife that did it is gone, but judging by the cut it made, it was very similar to the one that killed Chuck Hanratty."

"Wait a minute—" said Pierre.

"And you just happen to be at the scene of both killings."

"Wait a goddamn minute—"

"I think you should come downtown with us, make another statement."

"I didn't do it. She was dead when I found her. Look at her; she's been dead for hours."

Munroe's one long eyebrow knotted together in the middle. "How would you know that?"

"I'm a Ph.D. in molecular biology; I know how long it takes for blood to turn that dark."

"All just coincidence, is that right?"

"Yes. Yes."

"You say you worked together?"

"That's right. At the Human Genome Center, Lawrence Berkeley National Laboratory."

"Someone tried to kill you, and now, four months later, someone *does* kill her. Is that it?"

"I guess."

Munroe looked unconvinced. "You'll have to hold tight until the coroner arrives, then we'll head downtown."

Pierre was sitting on a wooden chair in a small interrogation room at Berkeley police headquarters. The room smelled of sweat; Pierre could also smell Officer Munroe's coffee. The lights overhead were fluorescents, and one of the tubes was strobing a bit, giving Pierre a headache.

The metal door had a small window in it. Pierre saw a flash of blond hair through it, then the door opened, and—

"Molly!"

"Pierre, I—"

"Hello, Mrs. Tardivel," said Officer Munroe, moving between them. "Thank you for coming down." He nodded at the sergeant who had escorted Molly to the room.

It was a sign of how upset she was that Molly didn't reflexively correct Munroe about her name. "What's going on?" she asked.

"Were you with your husband last night between five and seven?" The coroner's initial analysis suggested that Joan Dawson's death had occurred between those hours.

Molly was wearing an orange sweatshirt and blue jeans. "Yes," she said. "We'd gone out to dinner together."

"Where?"

"Chez Panisse."

Munroe's eyebrow climbed his forehead at the mention of the expensive restaurant. "What was the occasion?"

"We'd just found out that we're going to have a baby. Look, what's—"

"And you were there from five o'clock on?"

"Yes. We had to go that early to get in without a reservation. Dozens of people saw us there."

Munroe pursed his lips, thinking. "All right, all right. Let me make a phone call." He stepped out of the room.

Molly surged toward Pierre, hugging him. "What the hell's going on?" she said.

"I went by Joan Dawson's house this morning. She'd been murdered—"

"Murdered!" Molly's eyes were wide.

Pierre nodded.

"Murdered ..." repeated Molly, as if the word were as foreign as the occasional French phrases that passed Pierre's lips. "And they suspect you? That's crazy."

"I know, but ..." Pierre shrugged.

"What were you doing at Joan's place, anyway?"

He told her the story.

"God, that's horrible," said Molly. "She was—"

Just then, Munroe reentered the room. "Okay," he said. "Good thing you got that accent, Mr. Tardivel. *Everybody* at Chez Panisse remembered you. You're free to go, but ..."

Pierre made an exasperated sound. "But what? If I'm free—"

Munroe held up his beefy hand. "No, no. You're cleared. But, well, I was going to say watch your back. Maybe it is all coincidence, but ..."

Pierre nodded grimly. "Yeah. Thanks."

Molly and Pierre left the station; Molly had taken a taxi over. They got into Pierre's Toyota, which was stiflingly hot, having sat for two hours now in direct sunlight in the police parking lot. As they drove back to the university, Pierre asked her which of the campus's libraries might have *People* or *Time.*

"Doe, probably—on the fourth floor. Why?"

"You'll see."

They headed there. Pierre refused to tell Molly what he was looking for, and he was careful to keep thinking in French, lest she pluck it from his mind. A librarian got the back issues Pierre wanted. He quickly leafed through them, nodded at what he found, then spread a copy of *People* out on a worktable and took some pieces of paper—flyers about the library's overdue-fines policy—and used them to mask everything except a small photograph: a 1942 picture of John Demjanjuk.

"All right," said Pierre, pointing at the table. "Go have a look at that photo and tell me if you recognize the person in it."

Molly leaned in and stared at the photo. "I don't—"

"It's an old photo, from 1942. Is it anyone you know?"

"That's a long time ago, and—oh, I see. Sure, it's Burian Klimus, isn't it? Gee, he must have had his ears fixed."

Pierre sighed. "Let's go for a walk. There's something we have to talk about."

"Shouldn't you go tell them at the lab about Joan's murder?"

"Later. This can't wait."

"That photo wasn't of Burian Klimus," said Pierre as they walked out of Doe Library and headed south. It was a beautiful early autumn afternoon, the sun sliding down toward the horizon. "It's of a man called John Demjanjuk."

They passed by a group of students heading the other way. "That name's vaguely familiar," said Molly.

Pierre nodded. "He's been in the news a fair bit over the years. The Israelis tried him for being Ivan the Terrible, the gas chamber operator at the Treblinka death camp in Poland."

"Right, right. But he was innocent, wasn't he?"

"That's right. It was a case of mistaken identity. Someone else who looked a lot like Demjanjuk was the real Ivan the Terrible. And he's still at large."

"Oh," said Molly. And then, *"Oh."*

"Exactly: Burian Klimus looks like Demjanjuk—at least somewhat."

"Still, that's hardly reason enough to suspect him of being a war criminal."

Pierre looked up. An airplane contrail had split the cloudless sky into two equal halves. "Remember I told you a federal agent came to see me after Chuck Hanratty attacked me? Well, I found out today that he's with the part of the Department of Justice that's devoted to tracking down Nazis."

"I find it hard to believe that a man who won a Nobel Prize could be that evil."

"Well, Klimus didn't win the Nobel *Peace* Prize, after all. Anyway, the man who operated the gas chambers—Ivan Marchenko—he'd been a prisoner of war himself before volunteering for service to the Nazis. Who knows what he did before or after the war? Who knows what level of education he had?"

"But a Nobel laureate—"

"You know who William Shockley was?" asked Pierre.

"Umm, the *inventeur* of the transistor?"

Pierre smiled. "You're cheating."

Molly blushed a little.

"But, anyway, yeah, Shockley invented the transistor, and he won a Nobel Prize for that in 1956. He was also a raving, out-and-out racist. He claimed that blacks were genetically inferior to whites, and that the only smart blacks were smart because they had some white blood in them. He advocated sterilization of the poor, as well as anyone with a below-average IQ. Believe me, I've read enough biographies of Nobel laureates to know that not all of them were good people."

"But even if Burian is this Ivan Marchenko—"

"If he's Marchenko, then, well—" He looked down at Molly's stomach. "Then the baby is Marchenko's, too."

"Oh, shit—I hadn't even thought about that." She lowered her eyes. "I keep thinking of it as *your* baby ..."

Pierre smiled. "Me, too. But, well, if it *is* the child of Ivan the Terrible, then ... then maybe we don't want to continue with the pregnancy."

They'd come to the plaza just inside Sather Gate. Pierre motioned for them to rest on one of the benches placed against the low retaining wall. Molly sat down, and Pierre sat next to her, placing an arm over her shoulders.

She looked at him. "I know we've only known for sure that I'm pregnant for a day, but, well, I've *felt* pregnant ever since the implantation was done. And I've wanted this so long ..."

Pierre stroked her arm. "We could try again. Go to a regular clinic."

Molly closed her eyes. "It's *so* much money. And we were so lucky to get an implantation on the first attempt this time."

"But if it *is* Marchenko's child ..."

Molly looked around the plaza. People were walking in all directions. Some pigeons were waddling by a few feet away from them. She turned back to Pierre. "You know I love you, Pierre, and I admire the work you do as a geneticist. And I know geneticists believe in 'like father, like son.' But, well, you know *my* speciality: behavioral psychology, just like good old B. F. Skinner taught. I honestly believe it doesn't matter who the biological parents are, so long as the child is brought up by a caring mother and a loving father."

Pierre thought about this. They'd argued nature-versus-nurture once or twice before on their long evening walks, but he'd never expected it to be anything more than an academic debate. But now ...

"You could find out for sure," said Pierre. "You could read Klimus's mind."

Molly shrugged. "I'll try, but you know I can't dig into his mind. He has to be thinking—in English, in articulated thoughts—directly about the topic. That's all I can read, remember. We can try to maneuver the conversation in such a way that his thoughts might turn to his Nazi past, but unless he actually formulates a sentence on that topic, I won't be able to read it." She took Pierre's hand and placed it on her flat stomach. "But, regardless, even if he is a monster, the child in here is *ours.*"

It was late afternoon on the West Coast, and therefore early evening in Washington. Pierre struggled through the DOJ voice-mail system to get to the appropriate mailbox: "This is Agent Avi Meyer. I'm in Lexington, Kentucky, until Monday, October eighth, but am checking my voice mail frequently. Please leave a message at the tone."

Beep!

"Mr. Meyer, this is Dr. Pierre Tardivel at the Lawrence Berkeley National Laboratory—remember me? Look, one of our staff members was killed last night. I need to talk to you. Call me either here or at home. The number here is ..."

24

Joan Dawson's funeral was held two days later in an Episcopalian church. Pierre and Molly both attended. While waiting for the service to begin, Pierre found himself fighting back tears; Joan had been so kind, so friendly, so helpful ...

Burian Klimus arrived. It seemed wrong to take advantage of such a solemn occasion, but opportunities for Molly to actually see Klimus were few and far between. When the old man sat down in a pew at the back, Molly and Pierre got up and moved over to sit next to him, Molly right beside him.

"It's such a shame," said Molly, in a low voice.

Klimus nodded.

"Still," said Molly, "what a lifetime to have lived through. Somebody said Joan had been born in 1929. I can't imagine how frightening it must have been for a ten-year-old girl to see the world go to war."

"It was no easier for a twenty-eight-year-old man," said Klimus dryly.

"I'm sorry," said Molly. "Where were you during the war?"

"The Ukraine, mostly." *And Poland.*

"Spend any time in Poland?" said Molly. Klimus looked at her. "My, ah, father's family was there."

"Yes, for a short time."

"There was a camp there—Treblinka."

"There were several camps," said Klimus.

"Terrible places," said Molly. She tried a different tack. "'Burian'—is that the Ukrainian equivalent of 'John'? Every language seems to have its own version of John: Jean in French, Ivan in Russian."

"No, it's not. In Ukrainian, 'John' is also 'Ivan.'" He looked embarrassed for a moment. "'Burian' actually means 'dwells near the weeds.'"

"Oh. Still, I love Ukrainian names. They're so musical. Klimus, Marcynuk, Toronchuk, Mymryk ... *Marchenko.*"

Ivan Marchenko, thought Klimus, the names falling together naturally in his mind. "Yes, I suppose they are," he said.

"The war must have been terrible, and—"

"I don't like to think of it," Klimus said, "and—oh, excuse me. There's Dean Cowles; I should really say hello." Klimus rose and walked away from them.

As Pierre drove himself and Molly to the cemetery, he turned to look at his wife. "Well? Any luck?"

Molly shrugged. "It's hard to tell. He certainly didn't think anything along the lines of, Gee, my secret identity is Ivan the Terrible and I killed hundreds of thousands of people. Of course, that's not surprising—most people who have done terrible things in their pasts have built up psychological defense mechanisms to keep the memories from coming to mind. Still, he *does* know the name 'Ivan Marchenko'—he put those two names together at once in his head."

Pierre frowned. "Well, I'm seeing Avi Meyer this afternoon. Maybe he'll have concrete answers about Klimus's past."

Avi Meyer flew directly to San Francisco from Kentucky, where he'd been investigating some octogenarian KKK members. He and Pierre had arranged to meet privately at Skates, on Berkeley's Seawall Drive at the Marina. The restaurant jutted out over the Bay, supported by pillars that didn't seem nearly strong enough to hold it up. Seagulls perched on the edge of its gently sloping roof, trying to hold on in a rising wind. It was midafternoon, with a leaden sky. They got a table by one of the huge windows, looking out across the water to San Francisco.

"All right, Agent Meyer," said Pierre as soon as he sat down, "I know you're some kind of Nazi hunter. I also know that I was attacked, and my friend Joan Dawson is dead. Tell me the connection—tell me why you are poking around LBNL."

Avi sipped his coffee. He looked past the hanging plants and out the window. An aircraft carrier was moving along the Bay, heading for Alameda. "We routinely monitor university and corporate genetics labs."

Pierre tilted his head. "What?"

"We also keep an eye on physics departments, political science, and several other areas."

"What on Earth for?"

"They're natural places for Nazis to end up. I don't need to tell you that there's always been a whiff of controversy about genetics research. Creating a master race, discrimination based on genetic makeup—"

"Oh, come on!"

"You yourself mentioned Felix Sousa—"

"He's not part of HGC; he's just a biochem prof at the university, and besides—"

"—and there's Philippe Rushton, up in your native Canada, giving a whole new meaning to 'Great White North'—"

"—Rushton and Sousa are too young to be Nazis."

"The universities are lousy with people hiding from one thing or another; in Canada, half your profs are Vietnam draft dodgers."

"So's your president, for Pete's sake."

Avi shrugged. "You ever see *The Stranger?* Orson Welles film? It's about a Nazi who takes a job as an American college professor. I can name over one hundred actual cases of the same thing."

"Which is why you think Burian Klimus is Ivan Marchenko."

Avi's small mouth dropped open. "You're good," he said at last.

"I need to know if it's true."

"Why should you care? I've gone over your files from McGill and U of T—"

"You've what?"

"You weren't a campus activist. Didn't belong to any social-justice groups. Why should you care what Klimus might have done half a century ago? A French speaker from Montreal—why should someone like you care?"

"Dammit, I told you before I'm not an anti-Semite. Maybe there is a problem with that in Québec, but I'm not part of it." Pierre tried to calm himself. "Look, I've seen pictures of Demjanjuk. I know what he looked like as a young man, know he bore a resemblance to Klimus."

A waitress appeared. "Sprite," said Pierre. She nodded and left.

"Klimus looks even more like Marchenko than Demjanjuk did," said Avi.

Pierre blinked. "You've got photos of Marchenko?" None of the Magazine Database Plus articles mentioned the existence of such things.

Avi nodded. "The Israelis have had Marchenko's SS file since 1991." He opened his briefcase, pulled out a manila envelope, and took two sheets from it. The first was a photostat of an old-looking form, with a small head-and-shoulders photograph attached to its upper-left corner. The second was a blowup of that photo. It showed a man of thirty, with a broad face (twisted here in a cruel frown), incipient baldness, and protruding ears.

Pierre's eyebrows went up. "You can certainly see the resemblance to Demjanjuk."

Avi frowned ruefully. "Tell me about it."

Pierre looked at the photostats.

"So," said Avi, tapping the enlarged photo, "is that Burian Klimus?"

Pierre exhaled. "The ears are different—"

"Klimus's don't protrude. But that's an easy enough thing to have fixed."

Pierre nodded, and looked at the blowup again. "Yeah. Yeah, it could be Klimus."

"That's what I thought when I saw Klimus's picture in *Time* when he was named director of the Human Genome Center. If he *is* Marchenko, you have no idea what a monster that man was. He didn't just gas people, he tortured them, raped them. He used to love to slice nipples off women's breasts."

Pierre winced at that. "But do you have any proof, besides his appearance, that Klimus might be Marchenko?"

"He's a geneticist."

Pierre's tone was sharp. "That's not a crime."

"And he was born in the same Ukrainian town as Ivan Marchenko, and in the same year—1911."

"Really?"

"Uh-huh. And then there's what happened to you. The attack on you was the first direct connection between the Nazi movement and the genetics work going on at Lawrence Berkeley."

"But Chuck Hanratty was a *neo*-Nazi."

"Sure. But a lot of neo-Nazi groups were started by real World War II Nazis. Do you know the name of the leader of the Millennial Reich?"

"No."

"In documents the SFPD has captured, he's referred to by the code name Grozny."

Pierre's stomach fluttered. *He'd been ordered to kill you,* Molly had said, having read Chuck Hanratty's mind as he died, *by someone named Grozny.*

"Grozny," repeated Pierre. "What does that mean?"

"Ivan Grozny is Russian for Ivan the Terrible. It's what the people at Treblinka called Ivan Marchenko."

Pierre's head was swimming. "But this is crazy. What could Klimus have against me?" The waitress appeared and deposited Pierre's Sprite.

"That's a very good question."

"And what about Joan Dawson? What could Klimus have against her?"

Avi shook his head. "I have no idea. But if I were you, I'd watch my back."

Pierre frowned and looked out at the roiling waters of the Bay. "You're the second person to say that to me recently." He took a sip of his drink. "So what do we do now?"

"There's nothing we can do, until some proof materializes. These cases don't break overnight, after all; if Klimus is Marchenko, he's eluded detection for fifty years now. But keep your eyes and ears open, and report anything you find to me."

25

Seven months later

"Thanks for letting me come," said Pierre, keeping his hand steady by holding firmly onto the edge of a desk. Although he still felt as though he didn't really belong here, Pierre could no longer deny the truth: he was clearly manifesting symptoms of Huntington's disease. The support-group meeting was held in a high-school classroom in San Francisco's Richmond district, halfway between the Presidio and Golden Gate Park.

Carl Berringer's head jerked back and forth, and it was a few moments before he was able to reply. But when he did, his words were full of warmth. "We're glad to have you. What'd you think of the speaker?" Berringer was a white-haired man of about forty-five with pale skin and blue eyes. The guest speaker had spoken on coping with the juvenile form of Huntington's.

"She was fine," said Pierre, who had tuned out the talk and simply spent the meeting surreptitiously watching the others, most of whom were in much later stages of the disease. After all, besides his father, Henry Spade, Pierre had never really seen anyone else with advanced Huntington's up close. He watched their pain, their suffering, the contorted faces, the inability to speak clearly, the torture of something as simple as trying to swallow, and the thought came to him that perhaps some of them would be better off dead. It was a horrible thing to think, he knew, but ...

... but there, because there is no grace of God, go I. Pierre's condition was getting steadily worse; he'd broken dozens of pieces of labware and drinking glasses by now. Still, only those who knew him well yet suspected anything serious was amiss. Just a tendency toward dancing hands, occasional facial tics, a slight slurring of speech ...

"You work at LBL, don't you?" asked Carl, his head still moving constantly.

Pierre nodded. "Actually, it's L-B-*N*-L now. They added the word 'National' to the lab's name almost a year ago."

"Well, we had a guy from your lab give a talk a couple of years ago. Big old bald guy. Can't remember his name, but he won a Nobel Prize."

Pierre's eyebrows went up. "Not Burian Klimus?"

"That's the guy. Boy, were we lucky to get him. All we can offer speakers is a Huntington's Society coffee mug. But he had just been appointed to Lawrence Berkeley, and the university was sending him out to speaking engagements." Carl's hands had started moving, as if he were doing finger-flexing exercises. Pierre tried not to stare at him. "Anyway," said Carl, "I'm glad you came. Hope you'll become a regular. We can all use some support."

Pierre nodded. He wasn't sure he was any happier now that he'd finally relented and come here. It seemed an unnecessarily graphic reminder of what his future held. He looked around the room. Molly, hugely pregnant, was off in one corner sipping mineral water with a middle-aged white woman, apparently a caregiver. She was doubtless hearing what was in store for her.

The really bad cases weren't even here; they would be bedridden at home or in a hospital. He looked around, counted eighteen people: seven obvious Huntington's patients, seven more who were clearly their caregivers, and four whose status wasn't easy to determine. They could have been recently diagnosed as having the Huntington's gene, or they could have been caregivers for patients too ill to attend the meeting themselves. "Is this the normal turnout?" asked Pierre.

Berringer's head was still jerking, and his right arm had started moving back and forth a bit, the way one's arm does when walking. "These days, yes. We've lost five members in the last year."

Pierre looked at the tiled floor. Huntington's *was* terminal; that was the one unshakable reality. "I'm sorry," he said.

"We'd expected some of them. Sally Banas, for instance. In fact, she'd held on longer than any of us had thought she would." Berringer's head movements were distracting; Pierre fought the irritation growing within him. "Another one was a suicide. Young man, only been to a couple of meetings. Recently diagnosed." Berringer shook his head. "You know how it is."

Pierre nodded. Only too well.

"But the other three ..." Berringer had reached his left arm over to help steady his right. "World's a crazy place, Pierre. Maybe it's not so bad up in Canada, but down here ..."

"What happened?"

"Well, they were all pretty new members—only recently manifesting the disease. They should have had years left. One of them—Peter Mansbridge—was shot. Two others were knifed to death, six months apart. Muggings, it seems."

"God," said Pierre. What had he done, coming to the States? He'd been assaulted, Joan Dawson had been murdered, and every time he turned around he heard about more violent crime.

Berringer tried to shake his head, but the gesture was obscured by the jerking motion. "I don't ask for pity," he said slowly, "but you'd think anyone who saw one of us moving the way we do would leave us in peace, instead of killing us for the few bucks we might have in our wallets."

26

At last, the long-awaited day came. Pierre drove Molly to Alta Bates Hospital on Colby Street. In the Toyota's trunk, as there had been for the last two weeks, were Molly's suitcase and a video camcorder—an unexpected gift from Burian Klimus, who had insisted to Pierre and Molly that videotaping the birth was all the rage now.

Alta Bates had beautiful delivery rooms, more like hotel suites than hospital facilities. Pierre had to admit that one thing missing from Canada's government-run hospitals was any touch of luxury, but here—well, he was just thankful that Molly's faculty-association health plan was covering the expenses ...

Pierre sat on a softly padded chair, beaming at his wife and newborn daughter.

A middle-aged black nurse came in to check on them. "Have the two of you decided on a name yet?" she asked.

Molly looked at Pierre, making sure he was still happy with the choice. Pierre nodded. "Amanda," she said. "Amanda Hélène."

"One English name and one French," said Pierre, smiling at the nurse.

"They're both pretty names," said the nurse.

"'Amanda' means 'worthy of being loved,'" said Molly.

There was a knock at the door, and then, a moment later, the door swung open. "May I come in?"

"Burian!" said Molly.

"Dr. Klimus," said Pierre, a bit surprised. "How good of you to come."

"Not at all, not at all," said the old man, making his way across the room.

"I'll leave you alone," said the nurse, smiling and exiting.

"The birth went well?" asked Klimus. "No complications?"

"Everything was fine," said Molly. "Exhausting, but fine."

"You recorded it all on videotape?"

Pierre nodded.

"And the baby is normal?"

"Just fine."

"A boy or a girl?" Klimus asked. Pierre felt his eyebrows lifting; that was usually the first question, not the fourth.

"A girl," said Molly.

Klimus moved closer to see for himself. "Good head of hair," he said, touching a gnarled hand to his own billiard-ball pate, but making no other comment about the child's paternity. "How much does she weigh?"

"Seven pounds, twelve ounces," said Molly.

"And her length?"

"Seventeen inches."

He nodded. "Very good."

Molly discreetly moved Amanda to her breast, mostly hidden by her hospital robe. Then she looked up. "I want to thank you, Burian. We both do. For everything you've done for us. We can't begin to say how grateful we are."

"Oui," said Pierre, all his fears having dissipated. His daughter was an angel; how could she possibly have a devil's genes? *"Mille fois merci."*

The old man nodded and looked away. "It was nothing."

Je ne suis pas fou, thought Pierre, a month later. *I'm not crazy.*

And yet the frameshift was gone. He'd wanted to do more studies of the DNA sequence that produced the strange neurotransmitter associated with Molly's telepathy. He'd used a restriction enzyme to snip out the bit of chromosome thirteen that coded for its synthesis. So far, so good. Then, to provide himself with an unlimited supply of the genetic material, he set up PCR amplification of it—the polymerase chain reaction, which would keep duplicating that segment of DNA over and over again. Needing nothing more than a test tube containing the specimen, a thermocycler, and a few reagents, PCR could produce a hundred billion copies of a DNA molecule over the course of an afternoon.

And now he had billions of copies—except that, although the copies were all identical to each other, they weren't the same as the original. The thymine base that had wormed its way into Molly's genetic code, causing the frameshift, hadn't been incorporated into the copies. At the key point, the snips of DNA produced through PCR all read CAT CAG GGT GTC CAT. Just like Pierre's own did; just like everybody's did.

Could he have screwed up? Could he have misread the sequence of nucleotides in that original sample of Molly's DNA he'd extracted from her blood all those months ago? He rummaged in his file drawer until he found his original autorad. No mistake: the thymine intruder *was* there.

He went through the long process of making another autorad from another piece of Molly's actual original DNA. Yup, the thymine showed up there, too—the frameshift was present, shifting the normal CAT CAG GGT GTC CAT into TCA TCA GGG TGT CCA.

PCR was a simple chemical procedure. It shouldn't care if the thymine really belonged there or not. It should have just faithfully duplicated the string.

But it had not. It—or something in the DNA reproduction process—had *corrected* the string, putting it back the way it was supposed to be.

Pierre shook his head in wonder.

"Good morning, Dr. Klimus," said Pierre coming into the HGC office to pick up his mail.

"Tardivel," said Klimus. "How is the baby?"

"She's fine, sir. Just fine."

"Still have all that hair?"

"Oh, yes." Pierre smiled. "In fact, she's even got a hairy back—even *I* don't have a hairy back. But the pediatrician says that's not unusual, and it should disappear as her hormones become better balanced."

"Is she a bright girl?"

"She seems to be."

"Well-adjusted?"

"Actually, for someone just a month old she's rather quiet, which is nice, in a way. At least we're managing to get some sleep."

"I'd like to come by the house this weekend. See the girl."

It was a presumptuous request, thought Pierre. But then—dammit, he *was* the child's biological father. Pierre felt his stomach knotting. He cursed himself for thinking anything this complex would end up not being a source of problems. Still, the man was Pierre's boss, and Pierre's fellowship was coming up for renewal.

"Um, sure," said Pierre. He hoped Klimus would detect the lack of enthusiasm and decide not to pursue the matter. He took his mail from its cubbyhole.

"In fact," said the old man, "perhaps I'll come over for dinner Sunday night. At six? Make an evening of it."

Pierre's heart sank. He thought of something Einstein had once said: Sometimes one pays most for the things one gets for nothing. "Sure," Pierre said again, resigning himself to it. "Sure thing."

The old man nodded curtly, then went back to sorting through his mail. Pierre stood still for a few moments, then, realizing he had been dismissed, took his own mail and headed on down the corridor to his lab.

27

Burian Klimus sat in Molly and Pierre's living room. Amanda didn't seem to take to him at all, but, then again, he didn't make any effort to hold her or baby-talk to her. That bothered Pierre. The old man had *wanted* to see the girl, after all. But instead of playing with her, he just kept asking questions about her nursing and sleeping habits, all the while—to Pierre's astonishment—scrawling notes in Cyrillic in a pocket-size spiral-bound notebook.

Finally, it was time for dinner. Pierre and Molly had both agreed that although tonight was Pierre's turn to cook, the evening would probably go better with something more elaborate than hot dogs or Kraft Dinner. Molly prepared chicken Kiev (Klimus *was* Ukrainian, after all), potatoes au gratin, and Brussels sprouts. Pierre opened a bottle of Liebfraumilch to go with it, and the three adults made their way to the table, leaving Amanda—whom Molly had breast-fed earlier—contentedly napping in her bassinet.

Pierre tried all sorts of polite topics for conversation, but Klimus rose to none of them, so he finally decided to ask the old man what he was working on.

"Well," said Klimus, after taking another sip of wine, "you know I'm spending a lot of time at the Institute of Human Origins." The IHO was also in Berkeley; its director was Donald Johanson, discoverer of the famous *Australopithecus afarensis* known as Lucy. "I'm hoping to make progress with Hapless Hannah's DNA in resolving the out-of-Africa debate."

"Great film," said Molly lightly, really not wishing to see the conversation devolve into shoptalk. "Meryl Streep was excellent."

Klimus raised an eyebrow. "I know Pierre knows about Hannah, Molly, but do you?"

She shook her head. He told her about his breakthrough with extracting intact DNA from the Israeli Neanderthal bones, then paused to fortify himself with another sip of wine. Pierre got up to open a second bottle.

"Well," said Klimus, "there are two competing models for the origin of modern humans. One is called the out-of-Africa hypothesis; the other is the multiregional hypothesis. They both agree that *Homo erectus* started spreading out from Africa into Eurasia as much as 1.8 million years ago—Java man, Peking man, Heidelberg man, those are all specimens of *erectus.*

"But the out-of-Africa hypothesis says that modern man, *Homo sapiens*—which may or may not include Neanderthals as a subgroup—evolved in east Africa, but didn't expand out of there until a second migration from Africa just one or two hundred thousand years ago. The out-of-Africa proponents say that when this second wave caught up with various *erectus* groups in Asia and Europe, they defeated them, leaving *Homo sapiens* as the only extant species of humanity."

He paused long enough to let Pierre pour him another glass of wine. "The multiregional hypothesis is quite different. It says all those *erectus* populations went on evolving, and they *each* gave rise independently to modern man. That would explain why *Homo sapiens* seems to appear in the fossil record pretty much simultaneously across all of Eurasia."

"But surely," said Molly, intrigued despite herself, "if you have isolated populations, you'd end up with different species evolving in each area—like on the Galápagos Islands." She rose to start clearing the dishes.

Klimus handed her his dinner plate. "The multiregionalists contend that there was a lot of inbreeding among the various populations, allowing them to evolve in tandem."

"Inbreeding from France all the way to Indonesia?" said Molly, disappearing into the kitchen for a moment. "And I thought my sister got around."

Pierre laughed, but when Molly returned she was shaking her head. "I don't know," she said. "This multiregional stuff seems more like an exercise in political correctness than good science—an attempt to avoid Felix Sousa's which-race-came-first question and say, 'Hey, we all evolved together at once.'"

Klimus nodded. "Ordinarily, I should agree with you, but there are excellent sequences of skulls going all the way from *Homo erectus* through Neanderthal man and into fully modern humans in Java and China. It *does* look like independent evolution toward *Homo sapiens* went on at least in those locations, and possibly elsewhere, too."

"But that's evolutionarily absurd," said Molly. "Surely the classical model of evolution says that, through mutation, one individual in a population spontaneously gains a survival advantage, and then his or her offspring, because of that advantage, outcompete everyone else, eventually creating a new species."

Pierre got up to help Molly serve dessert—a chocolate mousse she had made. "I've always had a problem with that method," he said. "Think about it: it means that a few generations down the road, the entire population is descended from that one lucky mutant. You end up with a very small gene pool that way, and that tends to concentrate recessive genetic disorders." He handed a glass bowl to Klimus, then sat down. "It's like Queen Victoria, who carried the hemophilia gene. Her offspring inbred with the royal houses of Europe, devastating them. To suppose that whole populations are reduced to a single parent every time a major mutation-driven advantage occurs would make life extraordinarily precarious. If an accident didn't kill off the lucky mutant, his or her offspring might die off anyway through genetic diseases." He sampled the mousse, then nodded, impressed. "Now, if evolution *could* somehow occur simultaneously across widely dispersed populations, as the multiregionalists are suggesting, well, I suppose that would avoid that problem—but I can't think of any mechanism that would allow that kind of evolution, although—"

Amanda started crying. Pierre immediately got back on his feet and hurried over to her, picking her up, holding her against his shoulder, and bouncing her up and down gently. "There, there, honey," he cooed. "There, there." He smiled at Klimus, back in the dining room. "Sorry about this," he said.

"Not at all, not at all," said Klimus. He pulled out his notebook and jotted something down.

28

Six weeks later

"Look at Mommy, sweetheart. Come on, look at Mommy. There's a good girl. Now, Daddy's got to prick your arm a little bit. It'll hurt, but not too much, and it'll only last a second. Okay, sweetheart? Here's my finger. Give it a good squeeze. That's right. Okay, here we go. No, no—don't cry, honey. Don't cry. It's over now. Everything's going to be all right, baby ... everything's going to be just fine."

Pierre checked a small sample of Amanda's DNA. His daughter lacked the frameshift mutation on chromosome thirteen, and so presumably wouldn't grow up to be a telepath. Molly seemed to have curiously mixed feelings about this, but Pierre had to admit he was relieved.

Pierre's earlier work had shown that only one of Molly's two chromosome thirteens had the telepathy frameshift, meaning

Amanda had had only a fifty-fifty chance of inheriting it from her mother (Amanda, of course, would have received one of Molly's thirteens and one of Klimus's thirteens). So there was really nothing remarkable about baby Amanda not having inherited her mother's frameshifted gene, and yet—

And yet, during simple PCR amplification of Molly's DNA, the frameshift had been *corrected,* so—

So was this a case of Amanda actually, by the luck of the draw, receiving the non-frameshifted chromosome thirteen from her mother, or—

Or did *none* of Molly's eggs contain the frameshifted DNA? Had it been somehow corrected there, too, just as it had in PCR replication?

Obviously, the frameshift couldn't be corrected every time it appeared, or it would have been fixed when Molly herself was developing as an embryo thirty-odd years ago. But still, somehow, it was being corrected now. Pierre had to know whether the correction was present in Molly's unfertilized eggs, or whether the correction was only made after the egg was fertilized and had started dividing.

Thanks to the pre-IVF hormone treatments, Molly had brought a large number of eggs to maturity in a single cycle. Gwendolyn Bacon had extracted fifteen from her for the IVF attempt, but she had told Klimus to only attempt to fertilize half of them, meaning seven or eight of Molly's unfertilized eggs were presumably still here in Building 74.

After phoning Molly to get her permission, Pierre left his own lab and walked down to the same small surgical theater in which Molly's eggs had been extracted over a year ago. Pierre knew one of the techs there: the guy was a San Jose Sharks fan, and the two of them often argued hockey. Pierre had no trouble getting him to find and hand over Molly's eggs, seven of which were indeed still in cold storage.

Of course, it was possible that a random selection of seven eggs might all have the same maternal chromosome thirteen, but the odds were against it. The chances were as slim as a family having seven children and all of them being boys: 50% x 50% x 50% x 50% x 50% x 50% x 50%, which was 0.078%—a minuscule likelihood.

And yet that apparently had happened. Not one of the eggs had the frameshift.

Unless—

Molly's two chromosome thirteens differed from each other in other ways, of course. Pierre started testing other points on the chromosomes extracted from the eggs, and—

No. The eggs had *not* all gotten the same chromosome thirteen.

Four of them had received one of Molly's chromosome thirteens—the one that, in Molly's body, didn't have the frameshift.

And three had received the other one of Molly's thirteens—the one that, in Molly's body, *did* have the frameshift.

And yet, incredibly, the frameshift had been corrected out of every one of the eggs ...

A month later, Pierre and Molly drove to San Francisco International Airport. Pierre was about to meet his mother-in-law and sister-in-law for the first time. Amanda was going to be baptized the next day; although the Bonds weren't Catholic, Molly's mother had insisted on being on hand for this, at least.

"There they are!" said Molly, pointing through a sea of people, all struggling with their bags and luggage carts.

Pierre scanned the crowd. He'd seen pictures of Barbara and Jessica Bond before, but none of the faces leaped out at him. But now two women were waving at them from the back of the group, wide grins across their faces. They jostled their way through the little exit gate the crowd was funneling out of. Molly rushed over and hugged her mother and then, after a moment of sibling awkwardness, hugged her sister, too.

"Mom, Jess," Molly said, "this is Pierre."

There was another awkward moment, then Mrs. Bond moved in and hugged him. "It's wonderful to meet you at long last," she said, just the barest hint of a dig in her voice. She'd not been pleased when Molly had gotten married without even inviting her.

"It's a pleasure to meet you, too," said Pierre.

"Hey," said Jessica, a note of light teasing in her voice, perhaps trying to defuse the tension her mother's remark had engendered. "You told us he was French-Canadian, but you didn't say he had such a sexy accent."

Molly giggled, something Pierre had never before heard her do. She and Jessica were suddenly teenagers again. "Go find your own immigrant," she said, then turned to Pierre. "Honey, this is Jessica."

Jessica held out her hand, the back of it facing up. *"Enchantée,"* she said.

Pierre adopted the role being requested of him. He bent low and kissed the back of her hand. *"C'est moi, qui est enchanté, mademoiselle."* She giggled. Jessica was a real knockout. Molly had mentioned that Jess had done modeling and he could see why. She was a taller, tartier version of her sister. Her makeup was expertly applied: black eyeliner, a dusting of blush, and pink lipstick. Molly was standing right beside him; Pierre felt momentarily anxious, but relaxed when he realized he was indeed musing about all this in French.

"I'm afraid our car is parked a fair distance away," he said. The women's bags weren't very big. Even a few months ago, Pierre would have picked one up with each hand and simply carried them. But his condition was getting worse in small but noticeable daily increments, and he was now just as likely to drop them. Although his foot had been shaking somewhat, he'd hoped he'd been doing a credible job of making it look like toe tapping, as if he were some jittery type-A personality.

A few feet away, a big man was making a macho show of discarding the baggage cart his female companion had found and carrying a bulging Samsonite case himself. Pierre moved as fast as he could, seizing the cart and placing Jessica's and Barbara's bags on it. At the least, he could certainly push the cart for them. Indeed, it was probably better having it as a sort of discreet walker as they embarked on the long hike to the garage.

"How was the flight?" asked Pierre.

"It was a flight," said Jessica. Pierre smiled, sensing a kindred spirit. What more could one say about spending hours in a tin can?

"Where's Amanda?" asked Barbara, her tone making clear that she was very much the new grandmother, eager to see her first grandchild.

"A neighbor is looking after her," said Molly. "We thought all this"—she rolled her eyes, indicating the hubbub around them—"would be too much for her."

"I would have loved to have been there for you," said Barbara. Pierre allowed himself a slight sigh, lost on the background noise of the cavernous terminal. His mother-in-law wasn't going to easily forgive Molly for cutting her out of so much of Molly's life. Barbara and Jessica were only going to be here for four days, but it was clearly going to seem longer.

They passed through a pair of sliding glass doors into the late-afternoon sunshine. As soon as she was out of the terminal, Jessica fished a pack of Virginia Slims from her purse and lit one. Pierre jockeyed slightly so as not to be downwind from her. Suddenly she looked far less attractive.

Molly opened her mouth as if to reproach her sister, but in the end said nothing. Her mother clearly recognized the expression, though, and shrugged. "It's no use," she said. "I've told her a thousand times to quit."

Jessica took a deep, defiant drag. They continued on toward the parking lot.

"Have either of you been to California before?" asked Pierre, the role of defuser now falling to him.

"Disney World when I was a kid," said Jessica.

"Disneyland," corrected Molly, sounding every bit the big sister. "Disney World is in Florida."

"Well, whichever it was, I'm sure they still remember you throwing up all over the teacup ride," snapped Jessica. She looked to Pierre with wide eyes, as if still stunned by it all. "How anyone could get motion sickness on the teacups is beyond me."

Pierre spotted his car. "We're over there," he said, gesturing with his head as he steered the luggage cart.

Yes, he thought. A long stay indeed.

Pierre managed to carry the bags up the front steps. Molly looked on with compassion. They had worried about those steps when they bought the house, and watching him struggle with the bags gave her a clear foretaste of what was to come for him. The back door opened onto level ground; they knew eventually that it would end up as his principal entrance.

Once the bags were inside, Molly's mother and sister plopped down, exhausted, in the living-room chairs.

"Nice place," said Jessica, looking around.

Molly smiled. It *was* a nice place. Pierre's taste in furnishings was abysmal (Molly shuddered every time she thought of that hideous green-and-orange couch he'd had), but she had a good eye for such things; she'd even taught a course on the psychology of aesthetics one year. They'd furnished the whole room in natural blond wood and green malachite accents.

"I'm going next door to get Amanda," said Molly. "Pierre, maybe you can get Mom and Jess a drink."

Pierre nodded and set about doing just that. Molly went through the front door and out into the twilight, enjoying being alone for a moment. It had been so much easier rebuilding her relationship with her mother and sister through letters and long-distance phone calls. But now that they were here, she had to face their thoughts again: her mother's disapproval of the way Molly had left Minnesota, her dubiousness about her whirlwind romance and marriage to a foreigner, her thousand little criticisms of the way Molly dressed and the five extra pounds she hadn't quite gotten rid of since the pregnancy.

And Jessica, too, with her infuriating vacuousness—not to mention her outrageous flirting with Pierre.

It had been a mistake having them come out here—of that, already, there could be no doubt. She would try to keep them out of her zone during the rest of their stay, try not to hear their thoughts, try to remember that they, as much as baby Amanda, were her flesh and blood.

She walked next door to the pink-stuccoed bungalow and rang the bell.

"Hi, Molly," said Mrs. Bailey as the woman opened the screen door. "Come to take your angel away?"

Molly smiled. Mrs. Bailey was a widow in her mid-sixties who seemed to have a bottomless appetite for baby-sitting Amanda. Her eyesight was poor, but she loved holding the baby and singing to her in an off-key but enthusiastic way. Molly stepped into the entryway, and Mrs. Bailey went over to Amanda, who had been napping on the couch. She picked her up and carried her over to Molly. Amanda blinked her large brown eyes at her mother and allowed herself to be passed from one woman to the other.

"Thanks so much, Mrs. Bailey," said Molly.

"Anytime, my dear."

Molly rocked Amanda in her arms as she carried her back to their house. She walked up the steps and let herself in the front door.

The arrival of the baby was enough to get Barbara and Jessica up off the couch. Pierre, although also wanting to see his daughter, apparently realized he'd have no luck competing against the three women for access. He settled back in his chair, grinning.

"Oooh," said Jessica, leaning in to look at the baby cradled in Molly's arms. "What a little darling!"

Her mother leaned in, too. "She's gorgeous!" She waved a finger in front of the baby's eyes. Amanda cooed at all the attention.

Molly felt her heart pounding, felt anger rising within her. She pulled the baby away and moved across the room.

"What's wrong?" asked her sister.

"Nothing," said Molly, too sharply. She turned around, forced a smile. "Nothing," she said again, more softly. "Amanda was sleeping next door. I don't want to overwhelm her."

She moved toward the staircase and started up. She saw Pierre trying to catch her eye, but continued on.

Dog, Jessica had thought.

My God—what an ugly kid! her mother had thought.

Molly made it to the top floor and into the bedroom before she began to shake with anger. She sat on the edge of the bed, rocking her beautiful daughter back and forth in her arms.

Three months passed; it was now the middle of December.

Amanda, in a crib across the room, woke up a little after 3:00 a.m. and started crying. The sound awoke both Pierre and Molly. Molly went over to the padded chair by the window, and he watched quietly as she sat in the moonlight, breast-feeding his daughter. It was hard to imagine a more beautiful sight.

His left wrist started moving back and forth.

Molly put Amanda back down, kissed her forehead, and returned to their bed. Pierre could soon hear the regular sound of his wife's breathing as she fell back to sleep. Pierre, though, was now wide awake. He tried to steady his left wrist by holding it with his right, but soon that one began to shake, too.

He thought back to the Huntington's support-group meeting in San Francisco. All those people moving, shaking, dancing. All those people, like him. All those poor people ...

We had a guy from your lab give a talk a couple of years ago. Big old bald guy. Can't remember his name, but he won a Nobel Prize.

Burian Klimus had spoken to that group, and—

Holy shit. Holy fucking shit.

Avi Meyer hadn't proven it yet—indeed, might never be able to prove it, after half a century—but Klimus could very well be a Nazi.

Which meant he might very well be involved with the local neo-Nazi movement ...

Neo-Nazis had certainly been responsible for the stabbing attempt on Pierre's life and the shooting of Bryan Proctor, and, given the similarity of weapon, quite possibly for the murder of Joan Dawson.

Klimus had addressed the Huntington's group, had likely met the three members of it who had been murdered.

Klimus worked day in and day out with Joan; surely he'd been aware of her incipient cataracts.

And Klimus knew that Pierre had some genetic disorder; Pierre himself had told him that in explaining why he and Molly wanted to use donated sperm.

Voluntary eugenics, Klimus had said to Pierre. *I approve.*

Could the old man have been trying to improve the gene pool? Weed out some Huntington's sufferers, maybe a diabetic or two?

But no—no, that didn't make sense.

Joan Dawson was way past menopause; although she had a grown daughter, she herself was incapable of making further contributions to the gene pool.

And Klimus knew that Pierre wasn't going to breed.

But if not eugenics, then what?

An image came to his mind from out of the past, from the early 1980s: a drawing on the front page of *Le Devoir.*

Twelve dead babies.

Not eugenics.

Mercy—or, at least, someone's version of it.

After all, the same thought had come to Pierre, too, unbidden, unwelcome, unfair, but there nonetheless: some of those with Huntington's would be better off dead. And the same might be said for an old woman who lived alone and was about to lose her sight.

Pierre lay awake the rest of the night, shaking.

29

Pierre took the elevator up to the third floor of San Francisco police headquarters and walked down to the forensics lab. He knocked on the door, then let himself in. "Hello, Helen."

Helen Kawabata looked up from behind her desk. She was wearing a spruce-green suit today, jade rings, and emerald ear studs. She'd also changed her hair since Pierre had last seen her: it was still frosted blond, but she'd traded the pageboy for a shorter, punkier look. "Oh, hi, Pierre," she said, rapid-fire. "Long time no see. Listen, thanks for that tour of your facilities. I really enjoyed it."

"You're welcome," said Pierre. Every now and then, he tried to respond to a "thank you" with a California "uh-huh," but he had never felt comfortable with it. Still, his smile was a bit sheepish. "I'm afraid I have another favor to ask."

Helen's smile faded just enough to convey that she felt the books were now balanced: she'd done him one favor, and he'd repaid it with lunch and a tour of LBNL. She did not look entirely ready to help him again.

"I went to a Huntington's support-group meeting several months ago, here in San Francisco. They told me three people who belonged to their group had died in the last two years."

"Well," said Helen, gently, "it *is* a fatal condition."

"They didn't die from Huntington's. They were murdered."

"Oh."

"Would the police have done any special investigations of that?"

"Three people belonging to a single group getting killed? Sure, we'd have checked that out."

"I'm the fourth, in a way."

"Because you went to one meeting? What were you doing, giving a talk on genetics?"

"I have Huntington's, Helen."

"Oh." She looked away. "I'm sorry. I'd ..."

"You'd noticed my hands shaking when I gave you the tour of my lab."

She nodded. "I—I'd thought you'd had too much to drink at lunch." A pause. "I'm sorry."

Pierre shrugged. "Me, too."

"So you think somebody has something against Huntington's sufferers?"

"It could be that, or ..."

"Or what?"

"Well, I know this sounds crazy, but the person could actually think they're doing the Huntington's sufferers a favor."

Helen's thin eyebrows rose. "What?"

"There was a famous case in Toronto in the early 1980s. It was everywhere in the Canadian media. You know the Hospital for Sick Children?"

"Sure."

"In 1980 and '81, a dozen babies were murdered in the hospital's cardiac ward. They were all given overdoses of digoxin. A nurse named Susan Nelles was charged in the case, but she was exonerated. The case was never solved, but the most popular theory is that someone on the hospital's staff was killing the babies out of a misguided sense of mercy. They all had congenital heart conditions, and one might have concluded they were going to lead short, agony-filled lives anyway, so someone put them out of their misery."

"And you think that's what's happening to the people in your Huntington's group?"

"It's one possibility."

"But the guy who tried to kill you—what's his name ... ?"

"Hanratty. Chuck Hanratty."

"Right. Wasn't Hanratty a neo-Nazi? Hardly the type known for humanitarian gestures—if you could even call something like this humanitarian."

"No, but he was doing the job on orders from somebody else."

"I don't remember seeing anything about that in the report on the case."

"I—I'm just speculating."

"Mercy killings," said Helen, trying the idea on for size. "It's an interesting angle."

"And, well, I don't think it's just Huntington's sufferers. Joan Dawson—she was the secretary for the Human Genome Center—was murdered, too. The police said the same kind of knife that was used in the attack on me was also used in killing her. She was an elderly diabetic, and she was going blind."

"So you think your angel of mercy is offing anyone who is suffering because of a genetic disorder?"

"Maybe."

"But how would this person find out? Who would know about you and—what's her name?—Joan?"

"Someone we both worked with—and someone who had also spoken to the Huntington's group."

"And is there such a person?"

"Yes."

"Who?"

"I'd rather not say—not until I'm sure."

"But—"

"How long do you keep tissue samples from autopsies?"

"Depends. Years, anyway. You know how court cases drag on. Why?"

"So you'd have samples from various unsolved murders committed in the last couple of years?"

"If an autopsy was ordered—we don't always do one; they're expensive. And if the case is still unsolved. Sure, samples would still be around somewhere."

"Can I get access to them?"

"Whatever for?"

"To see if some of them might have been misguided mercy killings, too."

"Pierre, I don't mean to be harsh, but, well ..."

"What?"

"Well—Huntington's. It does affect the mind, right? Are you sure you're not just being paranoid?"

Pierre started to protest, but then just shrugged. "Maybe. I don't know. But you can help me find out. I only need tiny samples. Just enough to get a complete set of chromosomes."

She thought for a moment. "You ask for the damnedest things, you know."

"Please," said Pierre.

"Well, tell you what: I can get you the ones we've got here. But I'm not going to go calling around to other labs; that would raise too many eyebrows."

"Thank you," said Pierre. "Thank you. Can you make sure that Bryan Proctor is included?"

"Who?"

"That superintendent who was murdered by Chuck Hanratty."

"Oh, yeah." Helen moved over to her computer, tapped some keys. "No can do," she said after a moment. "Says here a tenant heard the gunshot that killed him. That fixed the time of death exactly, so we didn't take any tissue samples."

"Damn. Still, I'll take anything else you can get for me."

"All right—but you owe me big-time. How many samples do you need?"

"As many as I can possibly get." He paused, wondering how much he should take Helen into his confidence. He didn't want to say too much, but, dammit, he *did* need her help. "The person I have in mind is also under investigation by the Department of Justice for being a suspected Nazi war criminal, and—"

"No shit?"

"No—which explains the neo-Nazi connection. And, well, if he murdered thousands fifty years ago, he may very well have ordered a lot more than just the handful we know about murdered today."

Helen thought about it for a moment, then shrugged. "I'll see what I can do. But, look, it's almost Christmas, and that's our busiest time for crime, I'm afraid. You're going to have to be patient."

Pierre knew better than to push. "Thank you," he said.

Helen nodded. "Uh-huh."

Two months later.

Pierre hurried in the back door of the house. He'd given up fighting the steps to the front door a couple of weeks before. It was 5:35 p.m., and he went straight for the couch, scooping up the remote and turning on the TV. "Molly!" he shouted. "Come quickly!"

Molly appeared, holding baby Amanda, who, at eight months, had acquired even more rich brown hair. "What is it?"

"I heard just as I was leaving work that the piece on Felix Sousa is on *Hard Copy* tonight. I thought I'd be home in time, but there was an accident on Cedar."

A commercial for Chrysler minivans was coming to an end. The *Hard Copy* spinning typewriter ball flew out at them, making that annoying *thunk-thunk!* as it did so; then the host, a pretty blonde named Terry Murphy, appeared. "Welcome back," she said. "Are blacks inferior to whites? A new study says yes, and our Wendy Di Maio is on the story. Wendy?"

Molly sat down next to Pierre on the couch, holding Amanda against her shoulder.

The image changed to some historical footage of the UCB courtyard behind Sather Gate, with longhaired flower children strolling by and a bare-chested hippie sitting under a tree, strumming a guitar.

"Thanks, Terry," said a woman's voice over the pictures. "In 1967, the University of California at Berkeley was home to the hippie movement, a movement that preached making love not war, a movement that embraced the family of man."

The image dissolved to modern videotape footage shot from the same angle. "Today, the hippies are gone. Meet the new face of UCB."

Walking toward the camera was a trim, broad-shouldered white man of forty, wearing a black leather pilot's jacket with the collar turned up and mirrored aviator sunglasses. Pierre snorted. "Christ, he's even dressed like a storm trooper."

The reporter's voice-over said, "This is Professor Felix Sousa, a geneticist here. There's no peace in the wake of his research—and no love for him on the part of many of the university's staff and students, who are branding him a racist."

The shot changed to Sousa in one of the chemistry labs in Latimer Hall, beakers and flasks spread out on the counter in front of him. Pierre snorted again; he'd never once actually seen Sousa in any lab. "I've spent years on this research, Miz Di Maio," Sousa said. His voice was crisp and cultured, his enunciation meticulous. "It's hard to reduce it to a few simple statements, but ..."

The picture cut to the reporter, an attractive woman with a wide mouth and mounds of dark hair. She nodded encouragingly, urging Sousa to go on. The picture changed back to Sousa. "In simplest terms, my research demonstrates that the three races of humanity emerged at different times. Blacks appeared as a racially distinct group some two hundred thousand years ago. Whites, on the other hand, first appeared one hundred and ten thousand years ago. And Orientals arrived on the scene forty-one thousand years ago. Well, is it any surprise that the oldest race is the most primitive in terms of brain development?" Sousa spread his hands, palms up, as if asking the audience to use its common sense. "On average, blacks have the smallest brains and the lowest IQs of any of the races. They've also got the highest crime rate and the most promiscuity. Orientals, on the other hand, are the brightest, the least prone to criminal activity, and the most restrained sexually. Whites fall right in the middle between the other two groups."

The picture switched to footage of Sousa lecturing to a class. The students—all white—seemed rapt. "Sousa's theories don't stop there," said the reporter's voice overtop of this. "He's even suggesting that the old locker-room myths are true."

They cut back to the interview tape. "Blacks do have bigger penises than whites, on average," said Sousa. "And whites are better endowed genitally than Orientals. There's an inverse relationship between genital size and intelligence." A pause, and Sousa grinned, showing perfect teeth. "Of course," he said, "there are always exceptions."

Wendy Di Maio's voice-over again: "Much of Sousa's work echoes older, equally controversial studies, such as the research made public in 1989 by Philippe Rushton [still image of Rushton, a surprisingly handsome white man in his mid-forties], a psychologist at the University of Western Ontario in Canada, and the conclusions in the contentious 1994 best-seller *The Bell Curve* [slide of the book's cover]."

An outside shot: Di Maio walking across the campus in the courtyard between Lewis and Hildebrand Halls. "Is it right that such obviously racist research is going on in our publicly funded institutions? We asked the university's president."

The camera panned up to what was presumably supposed to be the president's window, but his office was actually clear across the campus from there. Then it switched to a close-up of the president in an opulent, wood-paneled room. His name and title were superimposed at the bottom of the screen. The elderly man spread his arms. "Professor Sousa has full tenure. That means he has full freedom to pursue any line of intellectual inquiry, without pressure from the administration ..."

Molly and Pierre watched the rest of the report, and then Pierre clicked the OFF button. He shook his head slowly back and forth. "God, that pisses me off," he said. "With all the quality work going on at the university, they pick crap like that to highlight. And you just know there are going to be people who think Sousa must be right ..."

They ate dinner in silence—Stouffer's lasagna done up in the microwave for them (it was Pierre the gourmet's turn), and Gerber apple baby food for Amanda. At eight months, she had acquired a very healthy appetite.

Finally, after Molly had put Amanda to bed, they sat at the dining-room table, sipping coffee. Molly, growing concerned by Pierre's quiet, said, "A penny for your thoughts."

"I thought you could take them for free," said Pierre, a little sharply. His expression showed that he immediately regretted it. "I'm sorry, sweetheart. Forgive me. I'm just angry."

"About ... ?"

"Well, Felix Sousa, of course—which got me to thinking about that paper he and Klimus did a few years ago for *Science* on reproductive technologies. Anyway, thinking about that paper got me thinking about Condor Health Insurance—you know, this business of financially coercing the abortion of imperfect fetuses." He paused. "If I wasn't already manifesting symptoms of Huntington's, I'd cancel my policy in protest."

Molly made a sympathetic face. "I'm sorry."

"And that stupid letter Condor sent me—what patronizing crap, from some flack in the PR department. A complete brush-off."

Molly took a sip of coffee. "Well, there's one way to get a little more attention. Become a stockholder in Condor. Companies are usually more responsive to their stockholders' complaints because they know that if they aren't, the questions might be raised in person at their shareholders' meetings. I took a course in ethics back at UM; that's one of the things the prof said."

"But I don't want to support a company like that."

"Well, you wouldn't invest a lot."

"You mean buy just one share?"

Molly laughed. "I can see you don't play the markets much. Shares are normally bought and sold in multiples of a hundred."

"Oh."

"I take it you don't have a broker, right?"

Pierre shook his head.

"You can call mine: Laurie Lee at Davis Adair. She's great at explaining things."

Pierre looked at her, startled. "You really think I should do this?"

"Sure. It'll increase your clout."

"What would a hundred shares cost?"

"That's a good question," said Molly. She headed down to the den, and Pierre followed her, holding carefully to the banister to help keep his balance on the short flight of stairs. Sitting on a desk was a Dell Pentium computer. Molly booted it up, logged on to CompuServe, scurried down a couple of layers of menus, and pointed to the screen. "Condor closed today at eleven and three-eights per share."

"So a hundred shares would cost—what?—eleven hundred and ... and ..."

"Eleven hundred and thirty-seven dollars and fifty cents, plus commission."

"That's a fair piece of change," said Pierre.

Molly nodded. "I suppose, but it'll all be liquid. You should be able to recover almost all of it, if you decide to sell later on. In fact ..." She tapped some more keys. "Look at that," she said, pointing at the table that appeared on screen. "They've been climbing steadily. They were at just eight and seven-eighths this time last year."

Pierre made an impressed face.

"So we might even end up making money when you eventually sell the stock. But, for the time being at least, Condor will have to take you seriously."

Pierre nodded slowly, thinking it over. "Okay," he said at last. "Let's do it. How do I proceed?"

Molly reached for the phone. "First, we call my broker."

Pierre pointed at the clock. "Surely she won't be in this late."

Molly smiled indulgently. "It may be eight p.m. here, but it's noon in Tokyo. Laurie has a lot of clients who like to play the Nikkei. She could very well still be in." Molly touched a speed-dial key. She was obviously very much into this; she had mentioned her investments in the past, but Pierre had never quite realized just how conversant she was with the field. "Hello," she said into the handset. "Laurie Lee, please." A pause. "Hi, Laurie. It's Molly Bond. Fine, thanks. No, not for me—for my husband. I told him you were the best in the business." Laughter. "That's right; anyway, can you take care of him, please? Thanks. His name is Pierre Tardivel; here he is."

She held the handset out for Pierre. He hesitated for a moment, then brought it to his ear. "Hello, Ms. Lee."

Her voice was high-pitched, but not grating. "Hello, Pierre. What can I do for you?"

"Well, I'd like to set up an account so that I can buy some stock."

"Very good, very good. Let me just get a few personal details ..."

She asked for information about his employer, and for his Social Security number (which Pierre had to consult his wallet to determine, having only recently received it).

"Okay," said Laurie. "You're all set. Was there anything you wanted me to buy for you now?"

Pierre swallowed. "Yes. A hundred shares of Condor Health Insurance, please."

"They're on the California Stock Exchange; I won't be able to place the order until tomorrow. But as soon as the exchange opens, I'll get you one hundred C-H-I Class B." Pierre could hear keyclicks. "You know, that's an excellent choice, Pierre. A very excellent choice. Not only has that stock been doing well on its own—it's very close to its all-time high, which was set just two weeks ago—but it's also done significantly better than its competition in the past year. I'll send you confirmation of the purchase in the mail."

Pierre thanked her and hung up, feeling quite the entrepreneur.

Three weeks later, Pierre was working in his lab. The phone rang. *"Allo?"*

"Hi, Pierre. It's Helen Kawabata at the SFPD."

"Helen, hi! I'd been wondering what had become of you."

"Sorry, but we've been swamped by that serial-killer case. Anyway, I've finally got together some tissue samples for you."

"Thank you! How many did you get?"

"A hundred and seventeen—"

"That's terrific!"

"Well, they're not all from SF; my lab does forensics work on a contract basis for some of the surrounding communities, as well. And some of the samples are several years old."

"But they're all unsolved murders?"

"That's right."

"That's great, Helen. Thanks so much! When can I come and get them?"

"Oh, whenever—"

"I'm on my way."

Pierre picked up the samples, brought them back to LBNL, and turned them over to Shari Cohen and five other grad students; there were always plenty around. Through the polymerase chain reaction, the students would produce copies of each set of DNA, then test the material for thirty-five different major genetic disorders Pierre had specified.

That evening, as he was leaving Building 74, Pierre passed Klimus in a corridor. He responded to Klimus's curt "Good night" with a soft *"Auf Wiedersehen,"* but the old man didn't seem to hear.

30

While he waited for the grad students to report back on the samples Helen Kawabata had provided, Pierre mapped out all the cytosines in the portion of Molly's DNA that contained the code for the telepathy neurotransmitter. He then crunched the numbers backward and forward, looking for a pattern. He'd wanted to crack the hypothesized code that cytosine methylation represented, and he could think of no more interesting stretch of DNA to work on than that part of Molly's chromosome thirteen.

And at last he succeeded.

It was incredible. But if he could verify it, if he could prove it empirically—

It would change everything.

According to his model, cytosine-methylation states provided a checksum—a mathematical test for whether the string of DNA had been copied exactly. It tolerated errors in some parts of the DNA strand (although those errors tended to render the DNA garbled and useless, anyway), but in others—notably right around the telepathy frameshift—it would allow no errors, invoking some sort of enzymatic correction mechanism as soon as copying was initiated. The cytosine-methylation checksum served almost as a *guardian.* The code to synthesize the special neurotransmitter was there, all right, but it was deactivated, and almost any attempt to activate it was reversed the first time the DNA was copied.

Pierre stared out the lab window, contemplating it all.

If a frameshift in a protected region occurred by accident due to a random addition or loss of a base pair from the chromosome, the cytosine-methylation checksum saw to it that any future copies—including those used in eggs or sperm—were corrected, preventing the error in coding from being passed on to the next generation. Molly's parents had not been telepaths, nor was her sister, nor would any of her children be.

Pierre understood what it meant, but was still shocked. The implications were staggering: a built-in mechanism existed to correct frameshifts, a built-in way of keeping certain fully functional bits of the genetic code from becoming active.

Somehow, the enzymatic regulator had failed to work during the development of Molly's own body. Perhaps that had been due to some drug—prescription or illegal—Molly's mother had been using while pregnant with Molly, or to some nutrient missing from Molly's mother's diet. There were so many variables, and it was so long ago, that it would likely be impossible to duplicate the biochemical conditions under which Molly had developed between her conception and birth. But whatever had happened then had allowed the expression of something that was—the anthropomorphic language kept springing to Pierre's mind, despite his efforts to avoid it—that was *designed* to remain hidden.

A Saturday afternoon in June. The doorbell rang.

"Who could that be?" said Pierre to little Amanda, who was sitting in his lap. "Who could that be?" He made his voice high and soft, the exaggerated tones generations of parents have used when talking to their babies. Meanwhile, Molly got up and went to the door. She checked the peephole, then opened the door, revealing Ingrid and Sven Lagerkvist, and their little boy, Erik.

"Look who's here!" said Pierre, still baby-talking to Amanda. "Why, look who's here! It's Erik. See, it's Erik."

Amanda smiled.

Sven was carrying a large wrapped gift. He kissed Molly on the cheek, handed the gift to her, and came into the living room. Molly placed the package on the pine coffee table. She then came over to Pierre and took Amanda from him. Although Pierre loved holding his daughter in his arms while sitting in a chair, he'd given up walking and carrying her after almost dropping her a few weeks before.

Molly carried Amanda into the middle of the room and set her down on the carpet near the coffee table. Sven, holding Erik's chubby little hand, led him across the living room to where Amanda was.

"Manda," said Erik in his soft, slurred way. As was typical of those with Down's syndrome, Erik's tongue stuck partway out of his mouth when he wasn't speaking.

Amanda smiled and made a small sound low in her throat.

Pierre leaned back in his chair. He hated that sound, that little thrumming. Each time Amanda made it, his heart skipped. Maybe this time—maybe at last ...

Molly pointed at the brightly wrapped box and spoke to Amanda. "Look what Erik and Uncle Sven and Aunt Ingrid brought for you," she said. "Look! A present for the birthday girl." She turned to the adult Lagerkvists. "Thanks so much, guys. We really appreciate you coming over."

"Oh, it's our pleasure," said Ingrid. She was wearing her red hair loose about her shoulders. "Erik and Amanda always seem to have such a good time together."

Pierre looked away. Erik was two; Amanda was one. Normally, they wouldn't have made good playmates, but Erik's Down's syndrome had already held up his mental development enough that he really was at much the same stage as Amanda.

"Would either of you care for coffee?" asked Pierre, meticulously rising from his chair, then holding on to its back until he was completely steady.

"Love some," said Sven.

"Please," said Ingrid.

Pierre nodded. They'd gotten past the point, thank God, where Ingrid insisted on offering to help Pierre with every little thing. He could manage making coffee—although he would need someone else to carry the steaming cups back to the living room.

He poured ground coffee into the coffeemaker. Next to the machine sat the cake Molly had bought, a *Flintstones* birthday cake crowned with plastic figures of Fred and Wilma surrounding a baby Pebbles; Molly had said there had been a Barney/Betty/Bamm Bamm version for little boys. Red lettering on the white frosting said, "Happy First Birthday, Amanda." Pierre resisted the urge to sneak a bit of the icing. He added water to the coffeemaker, then headed back into the living room.

The unopened gift had been set aside; they'd wait till after the cake for that. Erik and Amanda were now playing with two of Amanda's favorite plush toys, a pink elephant and a blue rhinoceros.

Molly smiled up at Pierre as he came in. "They're so cute together," she said.

Pierre nodded and tried to return the smile. Erik was a well-behaved little boy; he seemed to be passing calmly through what for a normal child would have been the Terrible Twos. But, then, they knew exactly what was wrong with Erik. It was tearing Pierre up not knowing what was wrong with Amanda. After an entire year of life, she hadn't so much as said "Mama" or "Dada." There was no doubt that Amanda was a bright girl, and no doubt that she seemed to understand spoken language, but she wasn't using it herself. It was both heart-wrenching and puzzling. Of course, many children didn't speak until after their first birthday. But, well, Molly's biological father was a certified genius and her mother was a Ph.D. in psychology; surely she should be on the fast end of the developmental cycle, and—

No, dammit. This was a party—hardly the occasion to be dwelling on such things. Pierre returned to the living room.

Ingrid, on the couch, gestured at Erik and Amanda. "The time goes by so quickly," she said. "Before we know it, they'll be grown."

"We're all getting older," said Sven. He'd been cleaning his Ben Franklin glasses on the hem of his safari shirt. "Of course," he said, replacing them on his nose, "I've felt old ever since the girls in *Playboy* started being younger than me."

Pierre smiled. "What did it for me was *Partridge Family* reruns. When I first encountered that show in the mid-seventies, I thought Susan Dey was the hot one. But I saw a rerun recently, and she's just a skinny kid. Now I can't take my eyes off Shirley Jones."

Laughter.

"I knew that I was getting old," said Molly, "when I found my first gray hair."

Sven waved his arm dismissively. "Gray hair is nothing," he said; there were more than a few in his massive beard. "Now, gray *pubic* hair ..."

The doorbell rang again. Pierre went to open it this time. Burian Klimus stood on the stoop, his ever-present pocket notebook visible in his breast pocket.

"I hope I'm not too late," said the old man.

Pierre smiled without warmth. He had hoped that his boss had been kidding about wanting to come over for the baby's birthday. Klimus kept finding reasons to visit Molly and Pierre at home, kept looking at little Amanda, kept writing things in his notebook. Pierre wanted to tell him to go to hell, but he still wasn't permanently assigned to LBNL. Sighing, he stood aside and let Klimus come in.

Everyone had gone home. The cake had been devoured, but the cardboard tray it had come on still sat on the dining-room table, a ring of frosting and crumbs on its upper surface. Empty wine glasses were perched on various pieces of furniture and on one of the stereo speakers. They'd clean it up later; for now, Pierre just wanted to sit on the couch and relax, his arm around his wife's shoulders. Little Amanda sat in Molly's lap, and with her chubby left hand was holding on to one of her father's fingers.

"You were a good girl today," Pierre said in a high-pitched voice to Amanda. "Yes, you were."

Amanda looked up at him with her big brown eyes.

"A very good girl," said Pierre.

She smiled.

"Da-da," said Pierre. "Say 'Da-da.'"

Amanda's smile faded.

"She's thinking it," said Molly. "I can hear the words. 'Da-da, Da-da.' She can articulate the thought."

Pierre felt his eyes stinging. Amanda could think the thought, and Molly could hear the thought, but for Pierre from his daughter there was only silence.

Time passed.

Pierre had spent a long and mostly fruitless morning trying different computer models for coding schemes in his junk-DNA studies. He leaned back in his desk chair, interlaced his fingers behind his head, and arched his spine in a stretch. His can of Diet Pepsi was empty; he thought about going to the vending machine to get another.

The door opened, and Shari Cohen came in. "I've finally got the last of those reports, Pierre," she said. "Sorry it took so long."

Pierre waved her closer and had her place them on his desk. He thanked her, added the new reports to the pile of other genetic tests of murder victims that had been submitted earlier, squared all the pages off by tapping them on their four sides, then started going through them.

Nothing unusual on the first. Nada on the second. Zip on the third. Oh, here's one—the Alzheimer's gene. *Bupkes* on number five. Diddly on six. Ah, a gene for breast cancer. And here's a poor fellow who had both the Alzheimer's gene and the neurofibromatosis gene. Three more with nothing. Then one with a gene for heart disease, and another with a predisposition to rectal cancer ...

Pierre made notes on a pad of graph paper. When he'd gone through all 117 reports, he leaned back in his chair again, flabbergasted.

Twenty-two of the murder victims had major genetic disorders. That was—he rummaged on his cluttered desk for his calculator—just under 19 percent. Only seven percent of the general population had the genetic disorders Pierre had asked the grad students to test for.

The samples Helen had provided had all been labeled, but Pierre didn't recognize any of the 117 names, let alone the twenty-two of them who had had major genetic disorders. He'd hoped some of them would have been people he knew of from the UCB/LBNL community, or people he'd heard Klimus mention in passing.

And there was still the problem of Bryan Proctor. The only murder conclusively related to the attempt on Pierre's life was Proctor's; Chuck Hanratty had been involved in both. But there was no tissue sample from Proctor, and nothing Proctor's wife had said to Pierre indicated that he'd had any genetic disorder. He'd have to find the time to visit Mrs. Proctor again, but—

Merde! It was already 14:00. Time to leave to pick up Molly. His stomach started churning. The murders could wait; this afternoon, they were going to find out what was wrong with Amanda.

"Hello, Mr. and Mrs. Tardivel," said Dr. Gainsley. He was a short man with a fringe of reddish gray hair around his bald head, and a completely gray mustache. "Thank you for coming in."

Pierre shot a glance at his wife to see if she was going to correct the doctor by pointing out that it was Mr. Tardivel and Ms. Bond, but she didn't say a word. Pierre could tell by her expression that the only thing on her mind was Amanda.

The doctor looked at each of them in turn, a grim expression on his face. "Frankly, I thought your pediatrician was just humoring you when she referred you to me; after all, lots of kids don't speak until they're eighteen months or more. But, well, have a look at this x-ray." He led them over to an illuminated wall panel with a single gray piece of film clipped to it. The picture showed the bottom half of a child's skull, the jaw, and the neck. "This is Amanda," he said. He tapped a small spot high up in the throat. "It's hard to see the soft tissues, but can you see that little U-shaped bone? That's called the hyoid. Unlike most bones in the body, it's not attached directly to any other bone. Rather, the hyoid floats in the throat, serving as an anchor for the muscles that connect the jaw, the larynx, and the tongue. Well, in a normal child Amanda's age, we'd expect to see that bone down around here." He tapped the x-ray farther down in the throat, in a line directly behind the middle of the lower jaw.

"And?" said Molly, her tone perplexed.

Gainsley motioned for them to take the two chairs in front of his wide glass-topped desk. "Let me see if I can explain this simply," he said. "Mrs. Tardivel, did you breast-feed your daughter?"

"Of course."

"Well, you must have noticed that she could suckle continuously without pausing to breathe."

Molly nodded slightly. "Is that abnormal?"

"Not for newborns. In them, the path between the mouth and the throat curves very gently downward. This allows air drawn in by the nose to flow directly into the lungs, bypassing the mouth altogether, making it possible to breathe and eat at the same time."

Molly nodded again.

"Well, as a baby begins to grow up, things change. The larynx migrates down the throat—and with it, the hyoid bone moves down, too. The path between the lips and the voice box becomes a right angle instead of a gentle curve. The downside of this is that a space opens up above the larynx where food can get caught, making it possible to choke to death. The upside, though, is that the repositioning of the larynx allows for a much greater vocal range."

Pierre and Molly looked briefly at each other, but said nothing.

"Well," continued Gainsley, "the migration of the larynx is normally well under way by the first birthday and completed by the time the baby is eighteen months old. But Amanda's larynx isn't migrating at all; it's still up high in her throat. Although she can make some sounds, a lot of other sounds will elude her, especially the vowels *aw, ee,* and *oo*—like in 'hot,' 'heat,' and 'hoot.' She's also going to have trouble with the *guh* and *kuh* sounds of G and K."

"But her larynx will eventually descend, right?" asked Pierre. He had one testicle that hadn't descended until he was five or six—no big deal, supposedly.

Gainsley shook his head. "I doubt it. In most other ways, Amanda is developing like a normal child. In fact, she's even a bit on the large size for her age. But in this particular area, she seems completely arrested."

"Can it be corrected surgically?" asked Pierre.

Gainsley pulled at his mustache. "You're talking about massive restructuring of the throat. It would be extremely risky, and have only minimal chances of success. I would not advise it."

Pierre reached over and took his wife's hand. "What about—what about the other things?"

Gainsley nodded. "Well, lots of children are hairy—there's more than one reason why we sometimes call our kids little monkeys. At puberty, her hormones will change, and she may lose most of it."

"And—and her face?" said Pierre.

"I did the genetic test for Down's syndrome. I didn't think that was her problem, but the test is easy enough to do. She doesn't have that. And her pituitary hormones and thyroid gland seem normal for a child her age." Gainsley looked at the space between the two of them. "Is there, ah, anything I should know?"

Pierre stole a glance at Molly, then made a tight little nod at the doctor. "I'm not Amanda's biological father; we used donated sperm."

Gainsley nodded. "I'd thought as much. Do you know the ethnicity of the father?"

"Ukrainian," said Pierre.

The doctor nodded again. "Lots of Eastern Europeans have stockier builds, heavier faces, and more body hair than do Western Europeans. So, as far as her appearance is concerned, you're probably worrying about nothing. She clearly just takes after her biological father."

31

Pierre drove over to San Francisco, made his way to the dilapidated apartment building, and touched the button labeled SUPER. A few moments later, a familiar female voice said, "Yes?"

"Mrs. Proctor? It's Pierre Tardivel again. I've just got one more quick question, if you don't mind."

"You must get *Columbo* reruns up in Canada."

Pierre winced, getting the joke. "I'm sorry, but if I could just—"

He was cut off by the sound of the door mechanism buzzing. He grabbed the handle and headed through the drab lobby to apartment 101. An elderly Asian man was just getting off the small elevator next to the apartment. He eyed Pierre suspiciously, but went upon his way. Mrs. Proctor opened the door just as Pierre was about to knock.

"Thank you for seeing me again," said Pierre.

"I was just teasing," said the plump woman with the golf-ball chin. She'd had her hair cut since the last time Pierre had been here. "Come in, come in." She stepped aside and motioned Pierre into the living room. The old TV set was on, showing *The Price Is Right.*

"I just wanted to ask you a question about your husband," Pierre said, taking a seat on the couch. "If you—"

"Jesus, man. Are you drunk?"

Pierre felt his face growing flush. "No. I have a neurological disorder, and—"

"Oh. Sorry." She shrugged. "We get a lot of drunks around here. Bad neighborhood."

Pierre took a deep breath and tried to calm himself. "I just have a quick question. This may sound funny, but did your husband have any sort of genetic disorder? You know—anything that his doctor ever said was inherited? High blood pressure, diabetes, anything like that?"

She shook her head. "No."

Pierre pursed his lips, disappointed. Still ... "Do you know what his parents died of? If either of them had died of heart disease, for instance, Bryan could have inherited those bad genes."

She looked at Pierre. "That's a thoughtless remark, young man."

Pierre blinked, confused. "Sorry?"

"Bryan's parents are both still alive. They live in Florida."

"Oh, I'm sorry."

"Sorry they're alive?"

"No, no, no. Sorry for my mistake." Still—still—"Are they in good health? Either of them have Alzheimer's?"

Mrs. Proctor laughed. "Bryan's dad plays eighteen holes a day down there, and his mother is sharp as a tack. No, there's nothing wrong with them."

"How old are they?"

"Let's see. Ted is ... eighty-three or eighty-four. And Paula is two years younger."

Pierre nodded. "Thank you. One final question: did you ever know a man named Burian Klimus?"

"What kind of name is that?"

"Ukrainian. He's an old man, in his eighties, bald, built like a wrestler."

"No, nobody like that."

"He might have used a different name. Did you ever know an Ivan Marchenko?"

She shook her head.

"Or someone named Grozny? Ivan Grozny?"

"Sorry."

Pierre nodded and got up off the couch. Maybe Bryan Proctor was a red herring—maybe Chuck Hanratty *had* just been after his tools or his money. After all, it sounded like the guy had had a fine genetic profile, and—

"Umm, could I use your bathroom before I go?"

She pointed down a short corridor, illuminated by a single bulb inside a frosted white sphere attached to the ceiling.

Pierre nodded and made his way slowly into the room, which had pale blue walls and dark green fixtures. He closed the door behind him, having to push a bit to get it to fit the frame; it had apparently warped from years of exposure to steaming showers. Feeling like an absolute heel, he opened the mirrored door to the medicine cabinet and looked inside. There! A man's Gillette razor. He slipped it into his pocket, made a show of flushing the toilet and running the sink for a few moments, then headed out.

"Thank you very much," said Pierre, wondering if he looked as embarrassed as he felt.

"Why were you asking all this?"

"Oh, nothing," he said. "Just a crazy idea. Sorry."

She shrugged. "Don't worry about it."

"I won't be bothering you again."

"No problem. I've been sleeping a lot easier since you—since that Hanratty guy died. You're welcome here anytime." She smiled. "'Sides, I like *Columbo.*"

Pierre made his way out of the apartment building and headed for San Francisco police headquarters.

Molly had taken a two-year maternity leave from classroom teaching (the maximum the faculty-association agreement allowed without loss of seniority), but still went into the campus for a half day once a week to meet with the students for whom she was thesis adviser and to attend departmental meetings. Since Pierre was off in San Francisco, Mrs. Bailey was looking after Amanda.

After her last student appointment, Molly took advantage of the PC in her office to do some on-line research using Magazine Database Plus, the joys of which Pierre had introduced her to.

She was about to log off when a thought occurred to her. She had tried to digest everything Dr. Gainsley had said, but she still didn't understand it all. She typed in a query on the topic of "speech disorders," but saw that there were over three hundred articles. She cleared that query, and thought. What was it that Gainsley had said? Something about the hyoid bone? Molly wasn't even sure how to spell that word. Still, it was worth a try. She selected "Search for words in article text," then tapped out HYOID. The screen immediately filled with citations for fourteen articles. She stared at the screen, reading and re-reading three of the citations:

> "Quoth the cavemen: nevermore" (laryngeal structures in human ancestors), *Speech Dynamics,* January-February 1997, v6 n2 p24(3). Reference #A19429340. Text: Yes (1551 words); Abstract: Yes.
>
> "Neanderthal neck bone sparks cross talk" (hyoid fossil may indicate capacity for speech), *Science News,* April 24, 1993, v143 n17 p262(1). Reference #A13805017. Text: Yes (557 words); Abstract: Yes.
>
> "Neanderthal language debate: tongues wag anew" (new reconstruction of La Chapelle Neanderthal skull), *Science,* April 3, 1992, v256 n5053 p33(2). Reference #A12180871. Text: Yes (1273 words); Abstract: No.

She selected each of the articles in turn, and read them through.

There'd long been a debate among anthropologists over whether Neanderthals could speak, but it was difficult to resolve the issue since no soft tissues had been preserved. In the 1960s, linguist Philip Lieberman and anatomist Edmund Crelin had made a study of the most famous Neanderthal of all, the La Chapelle-aux-Saints specimen found in 1908. Based on that specimen, they concluded that Neanderthals had a larynx high in their throats, with the air path curving gently down from the back of the mouth, meaning they would have lacked the vocal range of modern humans.

This view was challenged in 1989, when a Neanderthal skeleton dubbed Moshe was discovered near Israel's Mount Carmel. For the first time ever, a Neanderthal hyoid bone had been found. Although somewhat larger than a modern human's hyoid, the proportions were the same. Unfortunately, Moshe's skull was missing, making a complete reconstruction of his vocal tract—including the all-important positioning of the hyoid—impossible.

The *Science* article contained a quote from the University of Pennsylvania's Alan Mann, who said that given the current contradictory evidence, he didn't see "how a dispassionate observer could make a choice" between the pro-Neanderthal-speech and anti-Neanderthal-speech positions. Ian Tattersall of the American Museum of Natural History agreed, saying most anthropologists were in "bystander mode," awaiting some new evidence.

Molly's whole body was shaking by the time she'd finished reading it all. It looked horribly, incredibly, unthinkably as though Burian Klimus had found a way to bring just such new evidence to light.

"Hello, Helen."

Helen Kawabata looked up. "Jesus, Pierre, we should really get you your own parking space."

Pierre smiled sheepishly. "I'm sorry, but—"

"But you've got one more favor to ask."

"One of these days I'm going to stop by just to say hello."

"Yeah, right. What is it this time?"

Pierre fished the razor out of his jacket pocket. "I got this from Mrs. Proctor. It's Bryan Proctor's razor, and I thought maybe you could see if a DNA sample could be lifted from it. I'm no expert at getting samples from dried blood specks or things like that."

Helen walked over to a cupboard, pulled out a plastic specimen bag, came over to Pierre, and held it out with its mouth open. "Drop it in."

Pierre did so.

"It'll be a few days before I get a chance to look at it."

"Thank you, Helen. You're a peach."

She laughed. "A peach? You need a more recent edition of *Berlitz,* Pierre. Nobody talks like that anymore."

Molly, furious at what Klimus had possibly done, was on her way out of the campus, walking by North Gate Hall, when she first heard the argument. She looked around to see where the sounds were coming from. About twenty yards away, she saw a couple of students, one male and one female, both twenty or so. The male had long brown hair gathered into a ponytail. His face was round and full and, just now, rather flushed. He was yelling at a petite woman with frosted blond hair. The woman was wearing stonewashed jeans and a yellow *Simpsons* sweatshirt. The man was wearing black jeans and a corduroy jacket, which was unzipped, showing a white T-shirt beneath. He was shouting at the woman in a language that Molly didn't recognize. As he spoke, he drove home each point by thrusting a finger toward the woman's face.

Molly slowed her walking a little. There was a never-ending problem with female students being harassed, and Molly wanted to ascertain if she should intervene.

But the woman seemed to be holding her own. She shouted back at the man in the same language. The woman's body language was different from the man's, but equally hostile: she held both hands out in front of her, fingers splayed, as if wanting to wrap them around his throat.

Molly only intended to watch long enough to satisfy herself that it wasn't going to become violent, and that the woman was a willing participant in the exchange. A few other passersby had stopped to watch as well, although many more were continuing on after gawking for only a moment or two. The woman pulled a ring off her hand. It wasn't a wedding or engagement ring; it came off the wrong finger. Still, it clearly had been a gift from the man. She threw it at him and stormed away. It bounced off his chest and went flying into the grass.

Molly turned to go, but as the man went to his knees, trying to find the ring, he shouted *"Blyat!"* at the departing woman. Molly froze. Her mind flashed back to that long-ago day in San Francisco: the old geezer tormenting the dying cat. The word she'd just heard was precisely what that horrible man had yelled at Molly then.

Molly took off after the woman, who was marching purposefully toward the doors of the nearest building, her head held defiantly high, ignoring the stares of onlookers. The man was still rooting in the grass for the ring. Molly caught up with the woman just as she was pulling on one of the vertical tubular door handles, polished smooth by the hands of a thousand students each day.

"Are you okay?" asked Molly.

The woman looked at her, face still red with anger, but said nothing.

"I'm Molly Bond. I'm a professor in the psych department. I'm just wondering if you're okay."

The woman looked at her for a moment longer, then gestured with her head toward the man. "Never better," she said in an accented voice.

"That your boyfriend?" asked Molly. As she looked, the man rose to his feet, holding the ring high. He glared across the distance at the two of them.

"Was," said the student. "But I caught him cheating."

"Are you an international student?"

"From Lithuania. Here to study computers."

Molly nodded. That was the natural place for their conversation to end. She knew she should just say, "Well, as long as you're okay ...," and head on her way. But she couldn't resist; she had to know. She tried to make her tone light, offhand. "He called you *'blyat'*" said Molly. "Is that—" and she realized she was about to look like an ignoramus. Was there such a language as Lithuanian? Her Midwestern upbringing had left a few things to be desired. She finished her question, though: "Is that Lithuanian?"

"*Nyet.* It's Russian."

"What's it mean?"

The woman looked at her. "It's not a nice thing to say."

"I'm sorry, but—" What the hell, why not just tell the truth? "Somebody called me that once. I've always wondered what it meant."

"I don't know the English," said the student. "It has to do with the female sex part, you know?" She looked bitterly at the receding figure of the man she'd been arguing with. "Not that he's ever going to see mine again."

Molly looked back at the receding figure. "The jerk," she said.

"Da," said the student. She nodded curtly at Molly and continued on into the building.

Pierre accompanied Molly as she carried Amanda upstairs and put her in the crib at the foot of the king-size bed. They each leaned over in turn and kissed their daughter on the top of the head. Molly had been strangely subdued all evening—something was clearly on her mind.

Amanda looked at her father expectantly. Pierre smiled; he knew he wasn't going to get off that easily. He picked up a copy of *Put Me in the Zoo* from the top of the dresser. Amanda shook her head. Pierre raised his eyebrows, but put the book back down. It had been her favorite five nights in a row. He'd yet to figure out what prompted his daughter to want a change, but since he now knew every word of that book by heart, he was quite ready to comply. He picked up a small square book called *Little Miss Contrary,* but Amanda shook her head again. Pierre tried a third time, picking up a *Sesame Street* book called *Grover's Big Day.* Amanda smiled broadly. Pierre came over, sat on the foot of the bed, and began to read. Molly, meanwhile, went back downstairs. Pierre got all the way through the book—about ten minutes' worth of reading—

before Amanda looked ready to fall asleep. He bent over again, kissed his daughter's head once more, checked to make sure the baby monitor was still on, and slipped quietly out of the bedroom.

When he got down to the living room, Molly was sitting on the couch, one leg tucked up underneath her. She was holding a copy of *The New Yorker,* but didn't seem to really be looking at it. A Shania Twain CD was playing softly in the background. Molly put down the magazine and looked at him. "Is Amanda asleep?" she said.

Pierre nodded. "I think so."

Her tone was serious. "Good. I've been waiting for her to go down. We have to talk."

Pierre came over to the couch and sat next to her. She looked at him briefly, then looked away. "Have I done something wrong?"

She faced him again. "No—no, not you."

"Then what?"

Molly exhaled noisily. "I was worried about Amanda, so I did some research today."

Pierre smiled encouragingly. "And?"

She looked away again. "It's probably crazy, but ..." She folded her hands in her lap and stared down at them. "Some anthropologists contend that Neanderthal man had exactly the same throat structure as Dr. Gainsley said Amanda has."

Pierre felt his eyebrows going up. "So?"

"So your boss, the famous Burian Klimus, has succeeded in extracting DNA from that Israeli Neanderthal specimen."

"Hapless Hannah," said Pierre. "But surely you don't think—"

Molly looked at Pierre. "I love Amanda just as she is, but ..."

"*Tabernac,*" said Pierre. "*Tabernac.*"

He could see it all in his mind. After Molly, Pierre, Dr. Bacon, and Bacon's assistants had left the operating theater, Klimus hadn't proceeded to masturbate into a cup. Instead, he'd maneuvered the first of Molly's eggs onto the end of a glass pipette, holding it there by suction. Working carefully under a microscope, he'd then slit the egg open and, using a smaller pipette, had drawn out Molly's own haploid set of twenty-three chromosomes, and replaced them with a diploid set of Hannah's forty-six chromosomes. The end result: a fertilized egg containing solely Hannah's DNA.

Of course, opening up the egg would have damaged the *zona pellucida,* a jellylike coating on its surface necessary for embryo implantation and development. But ever since Jerry Hall and Sandra Yee had shown in 1991 that a synthetic *zona pellucida* could be coated onto egg cells, human cloning had been theoretically possible. And just two years later, at an American Fertility Society meeting in Montreal, of all places, Hall and his colleagues announced they had actually done it, although the embryos they'd cloned weren't taken beyond the earliest stage. Yes, the technology *did* exist. What Molly was suggesting *was* a real possibility. Klimus could have used the procedure to make several eggs containing copies of Hannah's DNA, cultured them in vitro to the multicellular state, and then Dr. Bacon—presumably unaware of their pedigree—would have inserted the embryos into Molly, hoping that at least one of them would implant.

"If it's true," said Molly, looking up at Pierre, gaze flicking back and forth between his left eye and his right, "if it's true, it wouldn't change the way you feel about Amanda, would it?"

Pierre was quiet for a moment.

Molly's voice took on an urgent tone. "Would it?"

"Well, no. No, I suppose not. It's just that, well, I mean, I knew she wasn't my child—biologically, that is. I knew she wasn't part of me. But I'd always thought she was part of you. But if what you're suggesting is true, then ..." He let the words trail off.

The Shania Twain CD had stopped playing. Pierre got up, made his way slowly over to the stereo, ejected the disc, fumbled to get it back in its jewel case, and turned the power off. He was trying desperately to think. It was a crazy idea—*crazy.* Sure, Amanda had a speech disorder. So what? Lots of kids dealt with things that were much more severe. He thought of little Erik Lagerkvist, who was infinitely worse off than Amanda. He put the CD back in the rack and made his way over to the couch. "I do love her," he said as he sat down. He took his wife's hand in his. "She's our daughter."

Molly nodded, relieved. But after a long moment she said, "Still, we need to know. It affects so much—her schooling, maybe even her susceptibility to disease."

Pierre looked at the clock on the mantel. It was just after 9:00 p.m. "I'm going to the lab."

"What for?"

"Most everyone will have gone home by now. I'm going to steal a sample of Hapless Hannah's DNA."

32

Pierre used his card key to get into the Human Genome Center offices. Hapless Hannah's bones were normally kept at the Institute of Human Origins, and Pierre had no doubt that at least some copies of her DNA were kept there, too. The material was too precious to have it stored in only one facility.

There had to be an emergency set of keys somewhere. He went over to the desk that used to be Joan Dawson's. The top drawer was unlocked. In it was a key ring with perhaps two dozen different keys on it. Pierre picked it up and headed down the corridor.

He looked at the keyhole in Klimus's doorknob, but nothing gave away which key might fit it. He began trying keys one after another, and, in the process, vainly attempted to keep the jostling of the keys from making too much noise. Pierre felt nervous as hell, and—

"Can I help you?" said an accented voice.

Pierre's heart did a flip-flop. He looked up. "Carlos!" he said, seeing the head janitor. "You startled me."

"Sorry, Dr. Tardivel. I didn't realize it was you. You need to get into Dr. Klimus's office?"

"Umm, yes. Yes, I need a reference book he's got."

Carlos reached for his own key ring, which was attached to his belt by a device that let out cord if he pulled on it but wound it back in when he let go. He leaned over and unlocked the door. Then he stepped inside and flicked on the lights, the overhead panels sputtering a bit as they came to life; glare from them reflected off the sheets of glass covering the framed astronomical photos. Carlos motioned for Pierre to follow him in. Pierre made a show of going over to one of the floor-to-ceiling oak bookcases. "See what you need?" asked Carlos.

"No—they're not in alphabetical order. It'll take me a while to find it."

"Well, you go ahead and look. But be sure to lock up when you're through. We've had some trouble lately with break-ins."

"I will," said Pierre. "Thanks."

Carlos left. Pierre listened as the caretaker's footfalls receded into the distance. He went over to the second door. It was locked. He tried all twenty keys; none of them opened it. He walked over to Klimus's desk, opening the top drawer, hoping there'd be another set of keys in there. Nothing. He closed the door and turned around. His arm moved unexpectedly, hitting the Mars globe on the credenza. For one horrible moment, Pierre thought he was going to knock it to the floor, but the red planet just spun on its axis a couple of times, then came to rest.

Pierre took out his wallet, fished out his Macy's card, and tried to jiggle it into the gap between the door and the jamb, just as he'd seen on countless TV shows. Time passed. He was terrified that Carlos would return. But eventually he got the little bolt to slide aside. He opened the door, stepped in, and fumbled for the light switch.

There was a small refrigerator in there, sitting on what looked like a stand for a microwave oven. Taped to the fridge door was a laser-printed sign that said, "Biological specimens. Highly perishable. Do not turn off or unplug this unit."

Pierre opened the refrigerator door. There were three wire shelves inside, each holding sealed glass containers. In the door of the fridge were cans of Dr Pepper. The glass containers were all labeled, and it took Pierre only a few minutes to find the one he wanted. A handwritten sticker on it said, simply, "Hannah."

Pierre took the vial, closed the fridge door, turned off the light in the small room, turned off Klimus's office light, and closed, but did not lock, the main door. He walked down to his own lab, used restriction enzymes to snip out some test fragments of the DNA, then set them up to undergo the polymerase chain reaction to make more duplicates. By the time he returned tomorrow, he'd have millions of copies of the test fragments.

He headed back to Klimus's office, returned the sample container to the fridge, closed the door, locked up the office, and went home, adrenaline flowing.

The next day, as Pierre was coming down the corridor to his lab, he heard his phone ringing. He hurried along (at least it was hurrying for him; anybody else could have outpaced him by walking briskly), opened his lab, and scooped up the phone. "Hello?"

"Hey, Pierre. It's Helen Kawabata."

"Hi, Helen."

"You're in luck. There was actually a fair bit of DNA on Bryan Proctor's razor. The blade was getting dull; he'd obviously been using it for a long time. Anyway, I'm going to be in court this morning, but you can come pick up the samples this afternoon if you like."

"Thanks very much, Helen. I really appreciate it."

"It's the least a peach could do. Bye."

Pierre turned to the work of PCR typing Amanda's and Hannah's DNA—not as complete as full genetic-profile DNA fingerprinting, but it would give results in two days instead of two weeks. When he had the process set up, he got in his car and drove over the Bay Bridge to San Francisco, went to police headquarters, picked up the refrigerated samples of Bryan Proctor's DNA, and drove straight back to LBNL. Shari Cohen happened to be coming down the corridor.

"Shari," said Pierre, "would you have a chance to run that same battery of tests on one more sample for me, please?"

"Sure."

"Thanks. Here it is. Oh, and can you also check to make sure there's a Y chromosome present?" There was always a small chance that Mrs. Proctor used a man's razor on her legs or armpits.

"Will do."

"Thanks. Let me know as soon as you've got the results."

That night, Pierre came home, kissed Molly and Amanda, and sat down on the couch to look at his mail. He was trying to keep his mind off Amanda's DNA; he wouldn't have results until the day after tomorrow.

Pierre's copy of *Maclean's* had shown up, with news that was now two weeks out of date from Canada; his *Solaris* had arrived, as well. He made a point of reading French magazines to keep himself still primarily thinking in that language. There was also his Visa bill, and—

Hey, something from Condor Health Insurance. A big manila envelope.

He opened it up. It was the company's annual report, and a note announcing their next annual general meeting.

Molly sat down on the couch next to him. While Pierre read over the annual-meeting notice, she started flipping through the annual report. It was a thin perfect-bound book with a textured yellow-and-black cover, measuring the same size as a standard piece of typing paper. "'Condor is the Pacific Northwest's leader in progressive health coverage,'" she said, reading from the first interior page. "'With foresight and a commitment to excellence, we provide peace of mind for 1.7 million policyholders in Northern California, Oregon, and Washington State.'"

"Peace of mind my ass," said Pierre. "There's no peace of mind in telling a pregnant mother that she has to either abort her baby or lose her insurance, nor in telling a Huntington's at-risk that he has to take a genetic test." He held up the meeting notice. "Do you think I should go?"

"When is it?"

He peered at it. "Friday, October eighteenth. That's—what?—three months from now."

"Sure. Give them a piece of *your* mind."

It was the first day of August. Pierre got into his lab early, ready to check over the DNA fingerprints for Hapless Hannah and Amanda Tardivel-Bond.

All he had to do was glance at the autorads, and—

God damn it. God fucking damn it.

Every marker was the same.

He found a chair and sat down in it before he fell down.

His daughter, his baby daughter, was a clone of a Neanderthal woman who had lived and died in the Middle East sixty-two thousand years ago. It was all—

"Dr. Tardivel?"

Pierre looked up. It took a moment for his eyes to focus. He covered the autorads he'd been looking at with his hands. "Oh, hi, Shari."

"I've finished testing that last DNA sample."

Pierre's head was still swimming. He almost said, "What DNA sample?" Of course: the Bryan Proctor specimen, the one Helen Kawabata had recovered from his razor. "And?"

Shari Cohen shrugged. "Nothing. He—and it *was* a he—tested negative for every genetic disorder I tried."

"Diabetes? Heart disease? Alzheimer's? Huntington's?"

"Clean as a whistle."

Pierre sighed. "Thanks, Shari. I appreciate your help."

"Is everything all right, Pierre?"

Pierre couldn't meet her eyes. "Fine. Just fine."

Shari looked at him for a moment more, then, with a little lifting of her shoulders, went over to one of the lab counters and began to work. Pierre leaned back in his chair. He was so sure that he was onto something—some vast conspiracy involving mercy killing of those who faced dark genetic futures. But Chuck Hanratty had killed Bryan Proctor, a man without any major genetic disorder. It made no sense.

Pierre glanced again at the autorads of Hannah's and Amanda's DNA, then got to his feet.

"I'm going home," he said to Shari as he passed her.

"Are you sure everything's okay?" asked Shari.

Pierre heard her, but didn't trust himself to respond. He made his way out to the parking lot and found his car.

33

Pierre came in the front door. Molly rushed over to greet him, little Amanda toddling behind.

"Well?" said Molly.

Pierre exhaled, unsure how to break the news. "She's a clone," he said simply.

Even though she'd been the one to originally suspect it, Molly's eyes went wide. "That asshole," she said.

Pierre nodded.

Amanda had made it over to where her daddy was standing. She looked at him with big brown eyes and stretched her arms up at him.

Pierre looked down.

Amanda.

Amanda Hélène Tardivel-Bond.

Or ...

Or Hapless Hannah, Mark II.

Her arms continued reaching up toward him. She looked confused about why he wasn't picking her up.

No, dammit, thought Pierre. No. She *is* Amanda—is my daughter.

He reached down and lifted her off the ground. She put her arms around his neck and squirmed with delight. Pierre was supporting her now with one hand and tousling her brown hair with the other. "How you doin'?" he said to her. "How's Daddy's little girl?"

Amanda smiled at him. He wanted to carry her over to the living-room couch, but that was risky. Instead he set her down, took her tiny hand in his, and together they managed the big walk over to it. He sat down and she clambered into his lap.

Molly came into the living room and took a seat in the easy chair opposite the couch. "So what do we do now?" she said.

"I don't know. I don't know if we should do anything—"

Molly's eyes went wide again. "After what he did?"

Pierre raised a hand. "I know, I know. Don't you think I feel the same way? God, I feel like he's raped my wife—I want to wring his neck, kill him with my bare hands, but ..."

"But what?"

"But there's Amanda to think about." He stroked his daughter's head, smoothing out the hair he'd made disheveled earlier. "If we go after Klimus, the truth about her might come out."

Molly considered this. "We have to get him out of our lives—I won't have him coming over here, making her an object of study. Look, once he realizes we know the truth, he should back down. What he did was unethical—"

"Completely."

"—so he risks losing everything if it's exposed—his position at LBNL, his consulting contracts, everything."

"But what if the truth about Amanda *does* come out?" asked Pierre.

"I don't know. Couldn't we leave here? Go to Canada, and change our names? You can still return to Canada, right?"

Pierre nodded.

"I know you wanted to stay here, but—"

Pierre shook his head. "That's secondary. I'll do anything for my daughter—anything at all." He hugged Amanda to his chest, and she cooed with pleasure.

"Professor Klimus," said Pierre, his voice sharp. He had intended to go in calm and reasonable, but the mere sight of the old man started his blood boiling.

Klimus looked up. His brown eyes flickered between Pierre and Molly. He then tilted his bald head back down and turned the page in the journal that was spread open on his desk. "I'm very busy. If you want to see me, you must make an appointment with my secretary."

Molly closed the door to the office.

"How could you?" said Pierre through clenched teeth.

Klimus reached for the phone on his desk. "I think I'll call security."

Pierre lunged forward, grabbed the handset from Klimus's bony hand, and slammed it down on the cradle. "Don't call anyone," said Pierre, his voice quavering with fury. "I asked you how you could do it."

"Do what?" said Klimus, now trying to feign innocence. He used his left hand to rub the one from which Pierre had wrenched the phone.

"Don't play games," said Pierre. "I got hold of a sample of Hapless Hannah's DNA. It's the same as Amanda's."

Klimus leaned forward. "Yes, it is. But, tell me—what made you suspect?"

"What the fuck difference does that make?"

"It's the heart of the matter, no?" said Klimus, spreading his arms. "Something made you realize that the infant specimen was not *Homo sapiens sapiens.* What gave it away?"

"'Infant specimen,'" repeated Molly, shuddering. "Don't call her that."

"How could you tell she was not your daughter?" asked Klimus.

"God damn it!" said Pierre. "God—" He launched into a string of French profanity, unable to control himself. Then: "Damn you, damn you—you sit there asking *us* questions! I should break you in two, you pathetic old man!"

Klimus shrugged his broad shoulders. "Asking questions is what a scientist does."

"Scientist?" sneered Pierre. "You're not a scientist. You're a monster."

Klimus rose from his chair. "You snot-nosed kid—I am *Burian Klimus."* He said his own name as though uttering a prayer. "Don't *dare* snap at me. I could see to it that you never work in any lab anywhere in the world again."

Molly was red in the face and breathing in snorts. "Burian—we trusted you."

"You wanted a baby. You have a baby. You wanted in vitro fertilization, normally an expensive process. You got that for free."

Pierre's fists were clenching and unclenching. "You bastard. You don't feel any remorse over what you did."

"What I did was *wonderful,"* said Klimus. "There hasn't been a child like the infant specimen since the Stone Age."

"Don't call her 'the infant specimen,' damn it," said Molly. "She's my daughter."

"Say that again," said Klimus.

"Don't try that—don't you fucking dare to try that," said Pierre. "Yes, we love Amanda—that has nothing to do with this."

"It has *everything* to do with it," said Klimus. "And it has to do with why you, Dr. Tardivel, shall now sit down and shut up."

"I'm not going to shut up," said Pierre. "I'm going to LBNL's director, and to the police."

"You shall do neither. You would have to explain the nature of your complaint—and that would mean revealing the nature of the child." He turned to Molly. "Do you really want your *daughter* to be an object of great public attention, Ms. Bond?" Klimus's expression was smug.

"You think that's your ace in the hole, don't you?" snapped Pierre. "Well, you're wrong. We're prepared to tell the truth to anyone who can lock you up."

"We'll get you put in jail," said Molly, "and then we'll go to Canada and take new names—something I'm sure you know all about."

Klimus didn't blink. "I advise against such actions. If you have the best interests of the infant specimen—"

"I've had enough of you, you son of a bitch," said Pierre. He reached for the phone, and pounded out the extension number for the office of LBNL's director.

"That is your choice," said Klimus with a shrug. "Of course, I should have thought you would want to avoid a custody battle—"

"Cust—" Molly's eyes went wide. "You couldn't do that."

"The child is a clone, Dr. Bond. You may have brought the egg to term, but you aren't the child's biological mother; she is in fact not related to either of you by blood."

"Hello?" said a male voice at the other end of the phone.

"Your choice, Tardivel," said Klimus. "I am prepared to fight to the bitter end."

Pierre glared at him, but replaced the handset on its cradle. "You could never win."

"Couldn't I? Amanda's closest relative is Hapless Hannah—and Hannah's remains are in the legal guardianship of the Institute of Human Origins, under an agreement with the government of Israel. Dr. Bond here is nothing but a surrogate—and the courts have traditionally conferred very few rights on such people."

Molly turned to Pierre. "He can't do that, can he? He can't take Amanda away?"

"You bastard," said Pierre to Klimus.

"Not me," said Klimus, with a small shrug. "If anyone's parentage is in question, it is Amanda." He looked at each of them in turn. "Now, I believe I asked you how you knew the child was not yours. I expect an answer." He reached for the phone. "Or perhaps *I* shall call the director. The sooner we start this legal battle, the sooner it will be resolved."

Pierre yanked the phone away again.

"I see you now prefer this matter kept quiet," said Klimus. "Very well; tell me how you discovered Amanda's pedigree."

Pierre's face was flushed, and his fist was closing and opening in spasms. Molly said nothing.

"She is a very ugly child, you know," said Klimus.

"Damn you—you *are* a monster," said Molly. "She's beautiful."

Klimus didn't seem to hear. He spoke in measured tones, looking at Molly, then Pierre. "Yes, we had Neanderthal DNA—but there were still many questions we couldn't answer. Could Neanderthals talk, for instance? There's a huge debate over that in the anthropological community—you should hear Leakey and Johanson go on about it. Well, now we know. They could not speak aloud; they probably had their own very efficient sign language instead. We'll want to see if Amanda picks up Ameslan faster than normal. Perhaps she's hardwired in some way that we aren't to communicate by signing.

"And the biggest question of all: are they the same species as us? That is, was Neanderthal man *Homo sapiens neanderthalensis*—just a subspecies, capable of producing fertile offspring with modern human? Or were they something else entirely—*Homo neanderthalensis,* a different species altogether, perhaps able to have a sterile child with a modern human, just as a horse and a donkey can produce a mule, but incapable of producing offspring that can breed. Well, as soon as Amanda enters puberty we'll be able to find that out."

"Fuck you," said Molly.

Klimus nodded. "That would be one option."

Molly lunged with her arms outstretched, ready to kill. Pierre moved in, grabbing his wife, holding her back. "Not now," he said to her.

"We shall continue the charade that she is your child," said Klimus, not in the least flustered. "But I shall visit her weekly and record details about her growth and intellectual abilities. When it comes time for me to publish that information, I will do so just as you would, Dr. Bond, in a psychological case study—referring to the infant specimen merely as 'Child A.' You will take no action against me; if you do, I will put on a custody fight that will make O. J. Simpson's defense look like a public defender's first case." He swung on Pierre. "And *you,* Dr. Tardivel, will never speak to me in that tone of voice again. Now, do we have an understanding?"

Pierre, furious, said nothing.

Molly looked at her husband. "Don't let him take her away from me. When—"

She stopped short, but sometimes one could read minds without having the benefit of that special genetic quirk. *When you're gone, she'll be all that I have left.*

"All right," said Pierre at last, through clenched teeth. "Come on, Molly."

"But—"

"Come on."

"I'll be over this Saturday," said Klimus. "Oh, and I shall bring equipment to take blood samples. You will not mind, I'm sure."

"You fucking asshole," said Molly.

"Sticks and stones," said Klimus, with a shrug—"but *I* own Amanda's bones."

Molly rose. Her face was completely red.

"Come on," said Pierre. He opened the door to Klimus's office.

They exited the room. Pierre slammed the door behind them, took her hand, and continued down the corridor. They made it into Pierre's lab; Shari was off somewhere else.

"Damn it," said Molly, bursting into tears. "Damn it, damn it, damn it." She looked up at Pierre. "We have to find some way to get rid of him," she said. "If there was ever a justified case of murder—"

"Don't say that," said Pierre.

"Why not? I *know* you're thinking the same thing."

"I wasn't sure before," said Pierre, "but now I am—this kind of experimentation is pure fucking Hitler. Klimus *must* be Marchenko." He took his wife in his arms. "Don't worry—he's going to die, all right. But it won't be us doing it. It will be the Israelis, hanging him for war crimes."

34

"Justice," said the female voice at the other end of the phone.

"Avi Meyer, OSI," said Pierre.

"I'm sorry, Agent Meyer is out of the office today. Would you—"

"His voice mail, then."

"Transferring."

"This is Agent Avi Meyer. I'm at a meeting in Quantico today, and won't be back in the office until tomorrow. Please leave a message at the tone."

Beep!

"Avi, call me as soon as you can. It's Pierre Tardivel—the geneticist at Lawrence Berkeley. Call me right away. It's important." Pierre read out his number, then hung up.

"He's out of town for the day," said Pierre to Molly, who was sitting on a lab stool. "I'll call him again Monday if he doesn't call first." He moved over to her and hugged her. "It'll be all right," he said. "We'll get through this."

Molly's eyes were still bloodshot. "I know," she said, nodding slightly. "I know." She looked at her watch. "Let's go get Amanda from Mrs. Bailey. I want to hold my daughter."

Pierre hugged her again.

Pierre's conscience had been bothering him for days. It wasn't as though he'd taken anything valuable. But, still, a man's razor was a very personal item. It might have meant a lot to Bryan Proctor's widow—an important way of remembering him. And, well, if things did get out of hand with Klimus, and they had to flee to Canada, Pierre didn't want this continuing to prey on his mind. He wasn't sure what pretext he'd use to explain his visit, but if he could get back into the apartment, he could return the razor to the medicine chest, maybe hiding it behind some other items so that its reappearance wouldn't be obvious.

He pulled up to the dilapidated apartment building in San Francisco, walked into the entryway, and pushed the intercom button labeled SUPER.

"Yes?"

"Mrs. Proctor? It's Pierre Tardivel."

Silence for several seconds, then buzzing from the door. Pierre made his way slowly over to apartment 101. Mrs. Proctor was waiting for him in the doorway, hands on hips. "You took my husband's razor," she said flatly.

Pierre felt his face grow flush. "I'm sorry. I didn't mean any disrespect." He pulled a small, clear plastic bag containing the razor out of his pocket. "I'm—I'm a geneticist; I wanted a DNA sample."

"What on earth for?"

"I thought maybe he had a genetic disorder that you didn't know about."

"And?"

"He didn't. At least not a common, easily-tested-for one."

"Which is precisely what I told you. What's this all about, Mr. Tardivel?"

Pierre wanted to be a million kilometers away. "I'm sorry. It's all crazy. I feel terrible."

She kept staring at him, unblinking, golf-ball chin thrust out.

"I just had this crazy theory that maybe your husband's death and the attempt on my life were linked. You know I've got a genetic disorder, and I though maybe he did, too."

"But he didn't."

"No, he was in perfect health."

The woman looked at Pierre, surprise on her face. "Well, I'd hardly say that. He was on a waiting list for a kidney transplant."

Pierre felt his heart skip a beat. "*What?*"

"He had bum kidneys."

Pierre was angry. "But I asked you if he had any inherited disorders—"

"He didn't inherit this problem. It was a result of an injury. His kidneys were damaged in a car accident about ten years ago and had gotten steadily worse."

"God," said Pierre. "Jesus God."

"Justice."

"Avi Meyer, OSI, please."

"Just a sec."

"Meyer."

"Avi, it's Pierre Tardivel."

"Hi, Pierre. Sorry not to get back to you yet. I was out of town. Say, any luck with your complaint against Condor Health?" Pierre had previously called Avi to find out whether the coercing of abortions was legal under federal law; it was.

"No," said Pierre, "but that's not why I'm calling. I'm phoning about Burian Klimus."

"We don't have anything new," said Avi with a sigh.

"Maybe you don't, but I do. You're right about him. He's Ivan Grozny."

Avi's voice was excited, but cautious. "What makes you say that?"

"You know the attempt on my life? The guy who tried to kill me was a neo-Nazi, right? Chuck Hanratty?"

"Uh-huh."

"Well, Hanratty previously killed a guy named Bryan Proctor—and Proctor had bum kidneys."

"So?"

"And Joan Dawson, a diabetic here at LBNL, was murdered, too, by a very similar knife to the one used in the attack on me; it wasn't Hanratty who killed her, of course—he was dead by that point. But it could very well have been someone connected to Hanratty—meaning someone connected to the Millennial Reich."

"Yeah, but—"

"And three Huntington's disease sufferers were murdered recently in San Francisco—and Burian Klimus had met all three of them."

"Really?"

"And I've checked tissue samples from a hundred and seventeen victims of unsolved murders here in the Bay Area—a vastly disproportionate number of them had bad genes."

"So you think—shit, you think Klimus is doing what? Purging society of defectives?"

"Mein Kampf, chapter one, verse one," said Pierre.

"You're sure about all this?" said Avi.

"Positive."

"You better be right," said Avi.

"I am."

"'Cause if this is just some disgruntled-employee shit—if you're just making trouble for your boss—then you're making a huge mistake. OSI's part of the Department of Justice, and you don't fuck with Justice."

Pierre's tone was determined. "Klimus is Ivan the Terrible. I'm convinced of that."

35

Pierre loved his daughter—of that he had no doubts. But, well, he *was* a scientist, and he couldn't help being intrigued by her special heritage. He knew that her DNA would differ from that of a modern human by far less than one percent. Hell, chimpanzee DNA deviated from modern human DNA by only 1.6 percent (chimps and humans having diverged some six million years ago). The differences between Amanda and other children who hadn't bypassed the last sixty thousand years of human evolution were surely very subtle. Still, something—some tiny genetic change—had given the less-physically-robust modern humans some sort of advantage over the Neanderthals, leading to the disappearance of the latter. The attachment areas for Neanderthal pectoral muscles were twice the size of those in modern humans; they would have had Arnold Schwarzenegger's physique without working at it. Yet something tipped the balance in favor of *Homo sapiens sapiens.* Even while reviling Klimus's outrageous experiment, Pierre could understand the fascination with studying Neanderthal DNA.

Using restriction enzymes to break up Amanda's DNA into manageable fragments, he started looking for differences, and was surprised to find some unexpected ones. They weren't in her protein-synthesizing DNA but rather in several long strands of junk DNA.

Intrigued, Pierre decided to visit the San Francisco Zoo. Surely he could cajole an array of primate tissue samples from the curator ...

Pierre and Molly attended another meeting of the Bay Area Huntington's Support Group in San Francisco; by this stage, he really did need the support.

The guest speaker was a loud PR woman from a company that made wheelchairs, walkers, and other aids for the mobility-impaired. Pierre hadn't realized so many high-tech options were available.

After the meeting, he spoke again to white-haired Carl Berringer. "Good meeting," said Pierre. "Interesting speaker."

Carl's whole upper body was shaking. "We've met before, haven't we?"

"Umm, yes. Pierre Tardivel, from Montreal, originally. I came to a meeting about fifteen months ago."

"Forgive me. My memory's not what it used to be."

Pierre nodded. He himself had not yet encountered many mental difficulties, but he knew they were a common part of Huntington's.

"It's a mixed blessing, a speaker like that," said Berringer, nodding in the direction of the woman. She was talking with some people on the other side of the classroom. "For those of us who've got insurance, we think, Great—look at all those neat ideas. But a lot of our members *don't* have any coverage, and couldn't possibly afford any of those gadgets."

Although the California law that went into effect two years earlier let anyone with the Huntington's gene get insurance so long as they weren't yet displaying overt symptoms, those already manifesting the disease were still generally uninsurable. "I tell you," Carl said, "that system you've got up in Canada is the only thing that makes sense in the genetic age—universal coverage, with the population as a whole sharing the risks." He paused. "You got insurance?"

"Yeah."

"Lucky guy," said Berringer. "I'm under my wife's company plan now, but I had to quit my job to get that; it only covers dependent spouses."

Pierre nodded grimly. "Sorry."

"It probably wasn't worth it," said Carl. "She's with Bay Area Health: B-A-H. We call them 'Bah, Humbug.' They've got ridiculously low caps for catastrophic illness." A pause. "Who are you with?"

"Condor."

"Oh, yeah. They turned me down."

"I actually own some Condor stock," said Pierre. "I was thinking of going to their shareholders' meeting this year, raise a bit of a stink about their policies. Is anybody else here with them?"

Berringer steadied himself by holding on to the brushed aluminum molding beneath the classroom greenboard. He looked around the room. "Well, let's see. Peter Mansbridge had been with them."

That name had stuck in Pierre's mind the first time Berringer had said it to him because by coincidence it was the same name as the anchor of *The National,* CBC's nightly newscast. "Peter Mansbridge?" Pierre said. "Wasn't he the fellow you said was shot to death?"

Berringer nodded. "Real shame that. Nicest guy you ever wanted to meet."

"Anybody else?"

Berringer moved his left hand up to scratch the side of his head. His hand made the journey like a fluttering bird. "I used to know all this." He shook his head sadly. "Time was, I had a memory sharp as a tack."

"Don't worry about it," said Pierre. "It's not important."

"No, no, let's see ..." He turned to face the room. "Excuse me!" he said loudly. "Excuse me!"

People turned to look at him; the caregivers in the group stopped moving.

"Excuse me, everybody. This fellow here, um—"

"Pierre."

"—Pierre here is wondering if anyone else has insurance with Condor?"

Pierre was embarrassed that his simple question had been made into a big deal, but he smiled wanly.

"I do," said a stunning black woman of about forty, holding up a manicured hand. She was standing next to a wheelchair; a black man was seated in it, his legs moving about constantly. "Of course, they won't cover Burt."

"Anybody else?" asked Carl.

A white fellow with Huntington's raised his hand, his arm moving like a sapling's trunk in a variable wind. "Wasn't Cathy Jurima with them?" he said.

"That's right," another caregiver said. "She was an orphan—no family-history records. She got in years ago."

"Who's Cathy Jurima?" said Pierre.

Carl frowned. "Another of our members who was murdered."

A crazy thought hit Pierre. "What about the other one who was killed? Who was he insured by?"

Carl raised his voice again. "Anyone remember who covered—oh, what was his name now? Juan Kahlo?"

Heads shaking around the room—some in negation.

Carl shrugged. "Sorry."

"Thanks, anyway," said Pierre, trying to sound calm.

Pierre and Molly left the meeting. Pierre was quiet the whole trip home, thinking. Molly drove. They parked in their driveway, then walked next door to pick up Amanda from Mrs. Bailey. It was 10:40 p.m.; they begged off from the offered coffee and cake.

Amanda had been sleeping, but she woke up when her parents arrived. Molly scooped up her daughter—it wasn't safe for Pierre to carry her when they had to walk down the cement steps that led up to Mrs. Bailey's front door. Molly hugged Amanda close, and as they walked back to their house, she said, "No, sweetheart, that's all right ... Did you, now? Did you really? I bet Mrs. Bailey was surprised at how good you are at drawing!"

Pierre's heart pounded. He loved Amanda with all his soul, but he always felt like there was a wall between him and her, especially when Molly was carrying on what sounded like one-sided conversations, detecting Amanda's thoughts and replying to them.

The three of them came into their house, and Molly moved over to sit on the couch, Amanda perching herself in her mother's lap.

"Would Joan Dawson have been under the same health plan as you?" asked Pierre.

Molly was stroking Amanda's brown hair soothingly. "Not necessarily. I'm on the faculty-association plan; she was support staff. Completely different union."

"Remember Joan's funeral?" said Pierre.

Amanda was apparently thinking something at her mother. "Just a second, dear," said Molly to the girl. She then looked up at Pierre. "Sure, I remember the funeral."

"We met Joan's daughter there. Beth—remember?"

"Slim redhead? Yeah."

"What was her husband's name?"

"Umm—Christopher, wasn't it?"

"Christopher, right. But what was his last name?"

"Good grief, I don't have the foggiest—"

Pierre was insistent. "It was Irish—O'Connor, O'Brien, something like that."

Molly frowned, thinking. "Christopher ... Christopher ... Christopher *O'Malley,* that was it."

"O'Malley, right!" He went into the dining room and got the phone book from a cupboard there.

"It's too late to be calling anyone," said Molly.

Pierre didn't seem to hear her. He was already dialing. "Hello? Hello, is that Beth? Beth, I'm sorry to be calling so late. This is Pierre Tardivel; we met at your mother's funeral, remember? I worked with her at LBNL. That's right. Listen, I need to know who provided your mother's health insurance. No, no—that's a life-insurance company; her *health* insurance. Right, health. Are you sure? Are you positive? Okay, thanks. Thanks very much; sorry to disturb you. What? No, no, nothing like that. Nothing for you to worry about. Just, ah, just some paperwork back at the office. Thanks. Bye."

He put down the phone, his hand shaking.

"Well?" asked Molly.

"Condor," said Pierre, as if it were a swear word.

"Christ," said Molly.

"One more," said Pierre, putting away the Berkeley phone book and pulling out the much-thicker San Francisco one.

"Hello? Hello, Mrs. Proctor. It's Pierre Tardivel. I'm really sorry about calling so late, but—yes, that's right." He did his best Peter Falk. "'Just one more little thing.'" Back to his normal voice. "I'm wondering if you can tell me who provided your husband Bryan's health insurance. No, no, I don't mind holding on." He covered the mouthpiece and looked at Molly. "She's checking."

Molly nodded. Amanda was now fast asleep in her arms.

"Yes, I'm still here. Really? Thanks. Thanks a million. And sorry to have disturbed you. Bye."

"Well?" said Molly.

"Do the words 'the Pacific Northwest's leader in progressive health coverage' mean anything to you?"

"Holy shit," said Molly.

"Where's that Condor annual report?"

"Down in the den, I think. In the magazine rack."

Pierre left the dining room, hurried down the half flight of stairs—and tripped at the bottom, an unexpected movement of his left foot having caught him off guard. Molly appeared at the top of the stairs, holding Amanda, who, having been awoken by the crash, was now crying.

"Are you all right?" Molly called, her face contorted in fear.

Pierre used the banister to haul himself back to his feet. "Fine," he said. He continued on down the short corridor and emerged a moment later holding the annual report. He came up the stairs more carefully and sat down on the living-room couch. Amanda had stopped crying and was now looking around curiously.

Molly sat next to Pierre, who was rubbing his shin. He handed her the report. "Find that part you read aloud when we first got it—the part about how many policies Condor has."

She folded back the yellow-and-black cover, flipped past the first couple of pages, then: "Here it is. 'With foresight and a commitment to excellence, we provide peace of mind for 1.7 million policyholders in Northern California, Oregon, and Washington State.'"

Pierre tasted bile at the back of his throat. "No wonder their stock is doing so well. What a great way to increase profitability: eliminate anyone who is going to make a major claim. Huntington's sufferers, diabetics going blind, a superintendent about to have a kidney transplant ..."

"Eliminate!"

"Eliminate—and for that, read 'kill.'"

"That's crazy, Pierre."

"For me or you, maybe. But for a company that coerces abortions? A company that forces people to take genetic tests that might drive them to suicide?"

"But, look," said Molly, trying to bring a note of reason back to the conversation, "Condor's a big company. Think of how many people they'd have to get rid of to have any real effect on their bottom line."

Pierre thought for a moment. "If they knocked off a thousand policyholders, each of whom were going to make claims averaging one hundred thousand dollars—the cost of a bypass operation, or a couple of years of at-home nursing—they'd increase their profits by one hundred million dollars."

"But a thousand murders? That's crazy, Pierre."

"Is it? Spread them out over three states and several years, and no one would notice."

"But how would they know who to go after? I mean, sure, they knew you were going to come down with Huntington's because you told them, but they wouldn't know in advance in most cases who was going to end up making a big claim."

"They could get genetic reports from the policyholders' doctors."

Molly shook her head. "Not in this state. That's part of the same law that prevents them from doing genetic discrimination: it's illegal for an insurance company to request genetic data from a person's doctor."

Pierre got up and began pacing in a shaky fashion. "The only way to pull it off would be by doing their own genetic tests on all their policyholders, detecting in advance the ones who might file claims. After all, if you wait until the claims are filed before killing the person, someone would surely notice the connection."

"But insurers don't routinely take tissue samples. Lots of medical insurance is granted based on questionnaires, and if a checkup *is* required, it's usually done by the family doctor. But, again, the law says the doctor can't turn over genetic results to the insurer, at least here in California."

"Then they must get tissue samples some other way—some *clandestine* way."

"Oh, come on, Pierre. How could they possibly do that?"

"It would have to be during the initial interview with the customer—that's the only time someone from the insurance company normally is physically close to the policyholder."

"So what about your own interview? Did the salesperson touch you?"

"No. No, we didn't even shake hands."

"Are you sure?"

He nodded. "I don't remember everyone I meet, but, well, I remember her." He shrugged. "She was, ah, quite fetching."

"Well, if she didn't touch you, she couldn't have taken a tissue sample."

"Maybe," said Pierre. "But there's one way to find out for sure."

"Hello, Ms. Jacobs. I'm Tiffany Feng from Condor Health."

"Won't you come in?" said Molly.

"Thank you—my, what a charming place you have."

"Thanks. Can I get you some coffee?"

"No, I'm fine."

"Well, then, please, have a seat."

Tiffany sat down on the living-room couch and removed a few brochures from her attaché case, then placed them on the pine coffee table, next to the blue-and-white transmitter for the baby monitor. Molly sat down next to her, putting Tiffany inside her zone. "Maybe you can tell me a bit about yourself, Ms. Jacobs," said Tiffany.

"Please," said Molly, "call me Karen."

"Karen."

"Well, I'm divorced. And I'm self-employed. I've got a preschooler." Molly gestured at the baby monitor. "But she's with a neighbor right now. Anyway, I got to thinking I should probably have some health insurance."

"Well, you can't go wrong with Condor," said Tiffany. "Let me start by telling you about our Gold Plan. It's our most comprehensive package ..."

Molly listened intently to everything Tiffany said. All of Tiffany's thoughts were benign: How much commission she'd get for landing the policy (Molly was surprised to learn that it was more than an entire year's worth of premiums), the other appointments she had for the rest of the day, and so on.

When Tiffany's spiel was over, Molly said, "Fine, I'll take the Gold policy."

"Oh, you won't be sorry," said Tiffany. "I just need you to fill in a form." She got a legal-size sheet out of her attaché case and placed it on the table. She then opened her jacket, revealing an inside pocket with a row of pens clipped to it. She selected one and handed it to Molly. It was a retractable ballpoint. Molly pressed on the button with her thumb, the tip clicked out, and she began filling in the form.

Suddenly, there was the sound of a door opening upstairs.

Tiffany looked up, startled. "I thought we were alone."

"Oh," said Molly, "that's just my husband."

"Your husband—but I thought ... Oh, my!"

Pierre was staggering down the stairs; for once, he didn't mind the monster-movie sight he made as he did so. His left hand was holding on firmly to the banister, and in his right, which was swinging wildly, he held the receiver for the baby monitor. "Hello, Tiffany," he said. Tiffany's lipsticked mouth was open in shock. "Remember me?"

"You're Pierre Trudeau!" said Tiffany, her eyes wide in recognition.

"Not quite," said Pierre. "It's Tardivel, actually." He turned to his wife. "Molly, I want to have a look at that pen."

Tiffany tried to take the pen from Molly, but Molly jerked it away. Pierre closed the distance, took the pen, sat down on an easy chair, unscrewed the barrel, and spilled the contents out on the coffee table. There was a refill in there, with a spring wrapped around it. But the components of the button at the top of the pen were unusual. Pierre held the chrome-plated button up toward the window. There was a tiny, almost imperceptible spike projecting from its rounded top. He turned it toward his eye and squinted at it. It was hollow.

Pierre made an impressed face. "Nice piece of work," he said, looking over at Tiffany. "When the customer presses down on the button with his thumb, a small core of skin cells is dug out. He wouldn't feel a thing."

Tiffany's eyes were wide, and her voice was full of pleading. "Please, Mr. Tardivel, give me back the pen—I'm going to get in so much trouble!"

"I'll say," said Pierre grimly. "It's against the law in this state to discriminate based on genetic tests—and I bet stealing cells from a body meets the legal definition of assault."

"But we don't discriminate!" said Tiffany. "The tissue samples are just for actuarial purposes."

"What?" said Pierre, startled.

"Look—the new law, it's crippling the insurance companies. We're not allowed to get any genetic information from doctors unless it's stripped of all other personal details about the individuals tested. How can we keep our actuarial tables current? We've got to have our own tissue database, do our own tests."

"But you're doing far more than that," said Pierre. "You're going after the policyholders—"

"What?" said Tiffany.

"The policyholders," repeated Pierre. "If they've got bad genes, you—"

"We don't keep any records relating the tissue samples to specific individuals. I told you, it's just for actuarial studies—just for statistics."

"But you—"

"No," said Molly, still sitting next to Tiffany on the couch. "No, she really believes that."

"It's true," said Tiffany emphatically.

"But then—" Pierre shut up. *Maudit,* she really didn't know.

"Look," said Tiffany, "please don't say anything to anyone about that pen—it'll cost me my job."

"Do all the Condor salespeople use these pens?"

Tiffany shook her head. "No, no—only the top producers, like me. We get paid extra commissions for it, so—"

Pierre nodded grimly. "So no one ever leaves the company." His voice was hard. "You want some advice? Quit your job. Quit today, right now, and start looking for work with another company—before everyone else from Condor is out there pounding the pavement with you."

"Please," said Tiffany, "my secretary doesn't even know who I was seeing this morning. Just don't tell them you got the pen from me, I beg you."

Pierre looked at her for a time. "All right—if you don't let anyone know we've got the pen, I won't reveal where we got it. Deal?"

"Thank you!" said Tiffany. "Thank you!"

Pierre nodded, and pointed with a shaking arm at the front door. "Now get the hell out of my house."

Tiffany rose, grabbed her attaché case, and scurried out the door. Pierre leaned back in the chair and looked at Molly. They were both silent for a very long time. Finally, Molly said, "So what do we do now?"

Pierre looked up at the ceiling, thinking. "Well, a conspiracy like this would have to be at the very highest level of the company, so we need to get in to see the president—what's his name?"

Molly went and got the Condor annual report, and flipped pages in it until she found the officers' listing. "'Craig D. Bullen, M.B.A. (Harvard), President and CEO.'"

"Okay, we get in to see this Craig Bullen, and—"

"How on Earth do we do that?"

"They might not have cared about what I had to say about their coercing abortions, but they will damn sure pay attention to me as a geneticist."

"Huh?"

"I'll send him another letter on Human Genome Center stationery, telling him there's been a breakthrough—something that will revolutionize actuarial science—and that I'm prepared to give him an advance look. Hell, even salespeople like Tiffany know all about the HGP; you can bet the company's president is following it closely and will jump at the chance to get ahead of his competitors."

Molly nodded, impressed. "But even if he does agree to see you, what do we do next?"

Pierre smiled. "We put Wonder Woman to work."

36

Molly and Pierre drove up to the Condor Health Insurance Building in Pierre's Toyota. The building was located on a well-treed thirty-acre lot on the outskirts of San Francisco, not far from the ocean. The tower in the center of it all was a Bauhaus monolith of glass and steel, stretching forty stories above the landscape. It was surrounded by parking lots on all four sides. The whole property was contained by a high chain-link fence.

They pulled up to the gatehouse, told the guard they had an appointment with Craig Bullen, and waited while he confirmed that by telephone. The barricade, painted with black and yellow chevrons, swung up, and they drove in, parked, and made their way to the front door.

The spacious lobby was done in brass and red marble. Two giant American flags stood on poles in the atrium, which also contained a pond with goldfish the length of Pierre's forearm swimming in it. Another guard was sitting behind a wide marble desk. Pierre and Molly presented themselves there and received date-stamped visitors' badges.

"The executive offices are on the thirty-seventh floor," said the guard, pointing to a bank of elevators. The sign above the faux-marble door-skins said "31st to 40th Floors Only."

They entered the cab, which had mirrored walls and pot lights in the ceiling, and headed up. The Muzak was an instrumental version of the old Supremes' song "Reflections."

When they got off the elevator, a sign directed them to the President's office. Pierre placed both his hands in his hip pockets to help control their shaking. As they came to the floor-to-ceiling glass doors, Pierre's eyes went wide. Bullen's brunette receptionist was gorgeous—*Playboy* Playmate of the Year gorgeous. She smiled, her teeth Liquid Paper white.

"Hello," said Pierre. "Drs. Tardivel and Bond, to see Mr. Bullen."

She lifted a telephone handset to her ear. Pierre thought briefly that this must be part of *Silicone* Valley. Molly, picking up the word "silicone," whapped him lightly on the upper arm.

Having gotten the okay, she rose and, hips swaying atop black stiletto heels, escorted Pierre and Molly to the inner sanctum, opening the heavy wooden door and gesturing them inside.

A goodly hunk of Condor Health Insurance's profits had clearly been spent on Craig Bullen's office. It was twenty feet wide and forty feet long, paneled in rich reddish wood—California redwood, Pierre imagined—with intricate carvings of hunting dogs and deer along the frieze. Eight oil paintings of landscapes hung in the room, all doubtless originals. Pierre was astounded to see that the one closest to him, depicting the Scottish moors, was by John Constable, and, like every good Canadian, he immediately recognized the distinctive stylized work of Emily Carr next to it. Her painting included one of her trademark Haida totem poles.

Bullen rose from behind his wide mahogany desk and strode down the length of the room. He was a broad-shouldered, athletic man of about forty, with the lined, dark face of someone who often spent time lying on southern beaches. He had a squarish head, brown eyes, and a hairline that had receded, leaving behind a graying dust bunny at the top of his forehead. His designer suit was dark blue, and he wore intriguing inch-wide cuff links made of gold-plated watch innards.

"Dr. Tardivel," he said in a deep voice as he extended a large hand. "How good of you to come."

"Thank you," said Pierre, quickly taking the proffered hand and shaking vigorously enough to hide his own palsied movements.

Bullen's grip was firm, perhaps overly so—an aggressive, macho display. He turned to Molly, his eyebrows moving up for a conference with his dust bunny. "And this is?"

"My wife, Dr. Molly Bond," said Pierre, returning his hands to his pockets. He stepped on his left foot with his right, trying to keep it from moving.

Bullen shook her hand as well. "You're very beautiful," he said, smiling right at her. "I hadn't realized Dr. Tardivel was bringing anyone with him, but now that I see you, I'm delighted that he did."

Molly blushed slightly. "Thank you."

Bullen started walking. "Please, please, come in."

A long conference table of polished wood filled part of the room; it had seating for fourteen. Bullen walked along its length to a giant antique Earth globe and tilted off the Northern Hemisphere, revealing a stock of liquor bottles within.

"Won't you have a drink?" he said.

Pierre shook his head.

"No, thank you," said Molly.

"Coffee? A soft drink, perhaps? Rosalee will be glad to get you anything you'd like."

Pierre thought for half a second about asking for something, just to get another look at the spectacular secretary. He smiled ruefully to himself. You can't escape your genes. "No, thank you."

"Very well," said Bullen. He closed up the Earth and took a seat at the conference table. "Now, Dr. Tardivel, I understand you've had a breakthrough over at your lab."

Pierre nodded and gestured for Molly to sit down. She took the padded leather seat next to Bullen, then moved the chair slightly, bringing him into her zone; her right knee was now practically touching his. Pierre walked around to the other side of the long table, using the backs of the chairs as supports. He removed his sports jacket—he was wearing a pale blue short-sleeved shirt beneath—and sat opposite both of them. "I think it's safe to say," said Pierre, "that what we've discovered will shock the entire insurance industry."

Bullen nodded, fascinated. "Do go on, sir. I'm all ears." A writing pad bound in calf leather was sitting on the table. Bullen drew it to him, opened it up, and took a gold-and-black fountain pen from his jacket pocket.

"What we've discovered," said Pierre, "is, well, shall we say in the nature of a statistical anomaly." He paused, looking significantly at Bullen.

The man nodded. "Statistics are the lifeblood of insurance, Dr. Tardivel."

"Well said," remarked Pierre, "for blood figures very heavily in all of this." He looked over at Molly and raised his eyebrows a tiny amount, conveying the question of whether she was succeeding at reading Bullen's mind. She nodded slightly. Pierre went on. "What we've discovered, Mr. Bullen, is that your company has a very low rate of major claims payments."

A few vertical creases joined the horizontal ones on Bullen's bronzed forehead as he drew his brows together. "We've been very lucky of late."

"Isn't it more than just luck, Mr. Bullen?"

Bullen was becoming visibly annoyed. "We strive for good management. I don't suppose you've read Milton Friedman, but—"

"As a matter of fact, I have," said Pierre. He was pleased to see Bullen's eyebrows go up—but Friedman had won the 1976 Nobel Prize in economics. "I know he asked the question, 'Do corporate executives, provided they stay within the law, have responsibilities in their business activities other than to make as much money for their stockholders as possible?'"

Bullen nodded. "And Friedman's answer was, No, they do not."

"But staying within the law is the key point, no? And that's very hard to do."

"I thought you had something to tell me about the Human Genome Project," said Bullen, his face reddening. He placed the cap back on his pen.

Pierre's heart was pounding so loudly he suspected Bullen and Molly could both hear it. He was suddenly confused. It had been happening more and more lately, but he'd been denying it to himself. That Huntington's had already robbed him of much of his physical prowess he could accept, but that it also was bound to affect his mind was something he'd been refusing to deal with. He closed his eyes for a moment, and took a deep breath, trying to remember what he was supposed to say next. "Mr. Bullen, I believe your company is illegally taking genetic samples from its policy applicants."

Molly's eyes went wide. As soon as the words were out, Pierre realized he'd said the precise thing they'd decided he would not say. All he'd intended to do was steer the conversation lightly around the issue, letting Molly listen to his thoughts. But now ...

Bullen looked first at Pierre, then at Molly sitting next to him, then back at Pierre. "I don't know what you're talking about," he said slowly.

What to do? Try to backtrack? But the accusation was out, and Bullen was clearly on guard now. "I've seen the pens," said Pierre.

Bullen shrugged. "There's nothing illegal about them."

To press on? Surely that was the only thing to do. "You're collecting tissue samples without permission."

Bullen leaned back in his chair and spread his arms. "Dr. Tardivel, that chair you're sitting in is upholstered in leather, and today is a nice, hot summer's day, even with the air-conditioning. Your forearm is probably sticking to the chair's arm, no? When you lift up your arm, your skin will peel away from it, and you'll leave many hundreds of skin cells behind on the chair. I could freely collect those. If you used my bathroom"—he gestured at an unmarked door set into the redwood paneling—"and left a bowel movement in the toilet bowl, there would be thousands upon thousands of sloughed-off epithelial cells from your intestines coating the feces, and I could collect those, too. If you shed a hair with attached follicle, or spit out some mouthwash in my sink, or blew your nose, or did any of hundreds of other things, I could collect samples of your DNA without you knowing it. My lawyers tell me there's absolutely nothing illegal about picking up material people are dropping all the time anyway."

"But you're not just collecting cells," said Pierre. "You're using the information to determine which policyholders are likely to submit expensive claims."

Bullen raised his hand, palms out. "Only in general terms, so we can plan responsibly. It lets my statisticians forecast the dollar value in claims payouts we'll likely have to make to existing policyholders in the future—and that is to the policyholders' benefit, actually. We were totally unprepared for all the claims related to AIDS, for instance; there was a while there in the late eighties when we thought we might have to file Chapter Eleven."

"Chapter Eleven?"

"Bankruptcy, Dr. Tardivel. It doesn't do a person much good to have a policy with a bankrupt insurer. This way, we're able to responsibly plan for the claims we'll have to pay."

"I don't think it's that at all, Mr. Bullen. I think you're doing it to *avoid* having to pay claims. I think you're doing it to identify in advance and eliminate policyholders who will make substantial claims in the future."

Molly shook her head slightly. Pierre knew he was going too far. Dammit, why couldn't he think straight?

Bullen tipped his head to one side. "What?"

Pierre looked over at Molly, then back at Bullen. He took a deep breath, but it was too late now to stop. "Your company is killing people, isn't it, Mr. Bullen? You arrange the murder of anyone you discover might make a big claim against you."

"Dr. Tardivel—if you *are* a doctor—I think you should leave."

"It's true, isn't it?" said Pierre, wanting to resolve it once and for all. "You killed Joan Dawson. You killed Bryan Proctor. You killed

Peter Mansbridge. You killed Cathy Jurima. And you tried to have me killed, too—and probably would have tried again, except that that would have aroused too much suspicion."

Bullen was on his feet now. "Rosalee!" he shouted. *"Rosalee!"*

The heavy door opened a bit, and the stunning brunette poked her head in. "Sir?"

"Call security! These people are crazy." Bullen was moving quickly back toward his desk. "Get out, you two! Get out of here." Rosalee was already on the phone. Bullen opened the top left drawer of his desk and pulled out a small revolver. "Get out!"

Pierre lifted his rump onto the table, slid across its wide, polished surface, got off on the other side, and quickly interposed himself between Molly and Bullen's line of fire. "We're leaving," said Pierre. "We're leaving. Put that away."

Rosalee reappeared. Her collagen-injected lips opened wide when she saw Bullen's gun. "S-s-security is on its way," she stammered.

Soon four burly guards in gray uniforms appeared. Two of them had large revolvers drawn.

"Eject these two from the premises," snapped Bullen.

"Come along," said one of the guards, gesturing with his gun.

Pierre started walking. Molly soon followed. The guards took them immediately to the elevator lobby. One of the cars was locked off on-service; they were hustled into that one. A guard turned a key in the control panel, and the elevator dropped rapidly down the thirty-seven stories to the ground, Pierre's ears popping as it did so.

"Outside," said the same guard who had spoken before.

Pierre and Molly hightailed it into the parking lot, two guards following them. They got into the Toyota, Molly driving, and sped out of the lot.

Pierre was shaking from head to toe, his chorea aggravated by the adrenaline coursing through his system.

"What happened in there?" said Molly.

"I—I got confused."

"You said far more than you were supposed to."

Pierre closed his eyes. "I know. I know. I'm sorry. It's—damn, I hate this fucking disease."

The road curved to the left. The tires squealed slightly as the car followed the bend.

"What about Bullen?" said Pierre at last.

Molly shook her head. "Nothing."

"What do you mean, 'Nothing'?"

"Bullen just kept thinking things like, 'My God—he's a lunatic,' and 'He's out of his mind,' and ..."

"Yes?"

"And 'Look at the way he's shaking—he must be drunk.'"

"But nothing about the murders?"

She turned down another road. "Nothing."

"No guilt? No sense of shock that he'd been caught?"

"No. Nothing like that. I tell you, Pierre, he honestly didn't have a clue as to what you were talking about."

"But I was so sure. All the evidence ..."

They came to a traffic signal. Molly stopped the car. "Evidence that you've seen," she said softly. She looked at him briefly, then dropped her eyes.

"No," said Pierre sharply. "Dammit, no. What happened in there was a fluke. This isn't a hallucination. I haven't lost my mind."

The light turned green. Molly pressed down on the accelerator.

They drove the rest of the way home in silence.

37

A month later.

Pierre, exhausted, came through the back door and immediately felt his spirits lifting. Their house wasn't expensive, and their IKEA furnishings weren't elaborate. But it was comfortable—the kind of life he never thought he'd have. A wife, a child, the smell of dinner cooking, toys scattered across the living-room floor, a fireplace.

Molly came into the living room, carrying Amanda. "Look who's here!" she said to her daughter. "That's right! It's Daddy! ... I don't know. I'll ask him." Molly looked at her husband. "She wants to know if you liked the cookies we made for you."

Pierre always brought a bagged lunch to work these days; it was easier to eat right in his lab than making his way down Building 74's long corridors to the snack bar. "They were delicious," said Pierre. "Thank you."

Amanda smiled.

Molly gave Pierre a kiss, Pierre sat down on the couch, and Molly transferred Amanda to his waiting arms. He lifted her above his head. She made little gurgling sounds of joy.

"How's my girl?" he said to her. "How's my little girl?"

Molly stepped briefly into the kitchen to stir the stew, then rejoined them. Pierre sat Amanda on his knee and bounced her up and down. *Sesame Street* was on the TV, the sound turned off.

"Were you a good girl today?" asked Pierre. "You didn't give Mommy any trouble did you?"

Amanda was squirming with delight, as if the suggestion that she might be a troublemaker pleased her greatly.

"Dinner will be ready in about twenty minutes," said Molly.

Pierre smiled. "Thanks. Sorry I wasn't home in time to make it. I know it's my turn."

"Oh, don't worry, hon. I'm enjoying this time."

She looked a bit wistful. Neither of them knew exactly what they would do with Amanda when Molly's two-year leave was over. They couldn't put a mute child in a normal day care, and they'd yet to find a special-needs one that seemed suitable. There was one nearby for deaf children, but none for those who could hear but couldn't speak. Molly had talked about not going back to the university at all, but they both knew she couldn't do that. She was on the path toward tenure, and would need to build a solid career for the time when Pierre was no longer with them.

Pierre picked up Amanda again and held her in front of him. He started making goofy faces at her, and she giggled wildly. But after a few moments, she started flapping her hands about, trying to say something. Pierre put her down on his lap, so that she could move her hands freely. *Drink,* she signed.

Pierre looked at her sternly, and signed, *What do you say?*

Please, she signed. *Drink, please.*

Molly smiled. "I'll get it. Apple juice?"

Amanda nodded. For a while, Amanda had resisted learning sign language; it had seemed a needless bother—until she came to understand that although her mother could hear what she was thinking, neither her father nor anyone else could.

Molly reappeared a few moments later with a small plastic glass half-filled with juice. Amanda took it with both hands and drained it in a couple of gulps. She handed the glass back to her mother.

"I've got to make the salad," said Molly.

"Thanks," said Pierre.

She smiled and went away. Pierre lifted Amanda off his lap and placed her on the couch next to him. He knew that sign language was, at best, a poor substitute for spoken language, and an even worse one for having thoughts read directly, but to be able to communicate with her meant the world to him. When they were signing, it was like that wall between them had disappeared. Pierre's hands moved. *What did you do today?*

Played, signed Amanda. *Watched TV. Drew a picture.*

What did you draw?

Amanda looked at him blankly.

What did you draw? Pierre signed again.

Amanda shrugged a little.

Pierre didn't get as much practice as he'd like at signing. He figured he must be making a mistake, so he tried a different way of asking. *You drew a picture of what?*

Amanda's eyes were wide.

Pierre looked down at his hands ... and saw that they were shaking. He hadn't felt it at all. He gripped his right hand with his left, attempting to steady it. He tried to make the signs again, but they weren't coming out properly. He couldn't get his left palm to open correctly for "drew," couldn't get his right index finger to move smoothly across the fingers of his left hand for "what" ...

Amanda's brow was creasing. She could clearly see that Pierre was upset. Pierre tried again, but the gestures looked clawlike, unfriendly. He realized he was scaring his daughter, but, dammit, if he could only *control* his fingers he would—

Amanda began to cry.

"You know, hon, the Condor shareholders' meeting is coming up next month," said Molly that weekend. They were having steak, barbecued in their backyard. Molly had cut Pierre's sirloin into manageable pieces; he had no trouble using knives on soft food, but had difficulty when consecutive slices in the same spot were required.

Pierre nodded. His hands moved constantly now, and his legs moved most of the time. "But they probably won't let us in after what happened when we saw Craig Bullen."

"They can't legally bar you from attending. You're a stockholder."

"Still, it might be easier if we kept a low profile."

"We could go in disguise," said Molly.

"Disguise?" Pierre's tone indicated his surprise.

"Sure. Nothing major, but—well, you could grow a beard. You've got four weeks after all, and ..." She trailed off, but Pierre knew what she was thinking—that his jobs of shaving had been getting worse and worse as his hands had been shaking more and more. A beard would simplify his life anyway.

He nodded. "Okay, I'll grow a beard. What about you?"

"No, I'd have to take testosterone pills for that."

Pierre grinned. "I mean, what are you going to do about a disguise?"

"Well, I know Constance Brinkley over at the Center for Theater Arts pretty well. A lot of her acting students take psych courses. I'm sure she'd let me borrow a brown wig."

Pierre considered. "Real undercover work, eh?"

Molly smiled. "Why not? That's always been one of your strongest points ..."

After a month of growth, Pierre's beard turned out to be much more satisfactory than he'd imagined. Molly had brought home the wig the previous night. Pierre was startled by how different it made his wife look: her skin seemed almost porcelain white by comparison, and her cornflower eyes stood out piercingly. He'd talked her into wearing the wig to bed that night, and it inspired him to new levels of creativity. Molly gently teased him about being her six-foot vibrator.

The next day, Molly drove them to San Francisco; Pierre had quietly given up driving after an uncontrollable arm movement had almost sent them off Highway 1 into the Pacific.

As they approached the Condor Tower, Pierre caught sight of a small helicopter flying overhead. Although he couldn't make out the markings on it, it was painted yellow and black, the Condor corporate colors. He shook his head as he watched it land on the roof of the forty-story building. More premiums well spent.

They parked the car and went inside.

Molly and Pierre got off the elevator in the basement of the Condor Tower. For the last few weeks, Pierre had been walking with the aid of a cane. There were long tables set up for shareholders to register, and he made his way slowly over to them, where he received a copy of the meeting agenda. Hundreds of people were milling about, drinking coffee or mineral water and snacking on canapés served by women in stylish uniforms. Molly and Pierre entered the auditorium, which had about seven hundred seats. They found two chairs together near the middle, one of them on an aisle. Pierre took the aisle seat and held tightly to the handle of his cane, trying to control his shaking. Molly sat down, adjusted the position of her dark wig slightly, and read over the agenda.

On the stage, a line of nine white men and one white woman took seats behind a long mahogany table. Craig Bullen was in the middle. He was wearing a charcoal gray suit with a red carnation pinned to his lapel. He conferred with the men on either side of him, then rose to his feet and moved over to the podium. "Ladies and gentlemen," he said into the mike, "welcome to the Annual General Meeting of Condor Health Insurance. My name is Craig Bullen and I'm the president of the company."

A few latecomers were still in the process of seating themselves, but everyone else broke into applause. Pierre resisted the urge to boo. The applause continued longer than mere manners would have required. The auditorium was three-quarters full. Many of the people were apparently individual stockholders, but Molly had pointed out several suited types who were probably representatives of mutual funds that had invested in the company.

Bullen was grinning from ear to ear. "Thank you," he said as the applause finally died down. "Thank you very much. It *has* been a spectacular year, hasn't it?"

More clapping.

"Our chief financial officer, Garrett Sims, will have a few words to say about that later, but for now, let me take you through our progress of the past year. We'll start by introducing the auditors ..."

All the usual reports were given, and three motions were brought to the floor—although it was clear that the board of directors had enough proxy votes to pass anything it wished. A few members of the audience asked questions. One young guy was all worked up about the fact that the annual report wasn't printed on recycled paper. Pierre smiled. The spirit of California radicalism wasn't dead.

Bullen returned to the podium. "Of course, the biggest impact on our cash flow has been Senator Patrick Johnston's bill 1146, which became law on January first, three years ago. That bill has prevented us from denying policies to those who have genetic tests proving that they have serious disorders, so long as the disorder has not yet manifested itself. California insurance companies had lobbied hard in Sacramento to get that law defeated, and indeed had succeeded in getting Governor Wilson to veto it. But, as you may know, Senator Johnston kept reintroducing it, and Wilson finally signed it." He looked out at the audience. "That's the bad news. The good news is that we continue to lobby in Oregon and Washington State to make sure that no similar bills are introduced there. So far, the California law is still the only one of its kind in the nation—and we intend to keep it that way."

The audience applauded. Pierre was fuming.

At the end of the formal presentations, Bullen—whose deep voice was now noticeably hoarse—asked if there was any new business. Pierre nudged Molly, who raised a hand on his behalf; he didn't want people to see his arm waving wildly like some sixth-grade brownnose.

Two other people were recognized first, and then Bullen pointed at Molly.

She rose briefly. "Actually," she said loudly, "it's my husband who wishes to speak." Slowly, meticulously, Pierre got up, leaning on his cane. He walked over to the microphone set up in the middle of the aisle. His feet were splayed as he moved, and his free arm—the one not holding the cane—was rising and falling at his side. There were gasps from a few people. Someone a few rows back said to his companion that the guy must be drunk. Molly turned around and gave him a withering stare.

Pierre at last reached the microphone stand. It was too low for him, but he knew he didn't have the coordination to loosen the milled sleeve that would have let him raise one of the telescoping sections. Still, he grabbed the stand with his left hand to help steady its movements, and leaned hard on his cane with his right.

"Hello," he said into the microphone. "I'm not just a stockholder; I'm also a geneticist." Bullen sat up straight in his chair, perhaps recognizing Pierre's accent. He motioned to someone offstage. "I heard Mr. Bullen tell you what an evil thing the California anti-genetic-discrimination law is. But it's not—it's a wonderful thing. I come from Canada, where we believe that the right to health care is as inalienable as the right to free speech. Senator Johnston's law recognizes that none of us can control our genetic makeup."

He paused to catch his breath—his diaphragm spasmed occasionally. He noticed two security guards had appeared at the side of the theater; both had gun holsters. "I work on the Human Genome Project. We're sequencing every bit of DNA that makes up a human being. We already know the location of the gene for Huntington's disease—which is what I have—as well as the locations of the genes for some forms of Alzheimer's and breast cancer and heart disease. But eventually we'll know where *every* gene is, what every gene does. We may very well have that knowledge in the lifetime of many people in this room. Today, there's only a handful of things we can test genetically for, but tomorrow, we'll be able to tell who will become obese, who will develop high cholesterol, who will get colon cancer. Then, if it weren't for laws like Senator Johnston's, it could be you or your already-born children or grandchildren who would have the safety net pulled out from beneath them, all in the name of profit." His natural instinct at this moment was to spread his arms imploringly, but he couldn't do that without losing his balance. "We shouldn't be fighting to keep other states from adopting laws like the one here in California. Rather, we should be helping them all adopt such principles. We should—"

Craig Bullen spoke firmly into his own microphone. "Insurance is a business, Dr. Tardivel."

Pierre started at the use of his name. The cat was clearly out of the bag. "Yes, but—"

"And these good people"—he spread his arms, and Pierre wondered for a moment if Bullen was mocking the gesture he'd been unable to make himself—"have rights, too. The right to see their hard-earned money work for them. The right to profit from the sweat of their brows. They invest their money here, in this company, to give themselves financial security—the security to retire comfortably, the security to weather uncertain times. You identified yourself as a geneticist, correct?"

"Yes."

"But why don't you also tell these good people that you're also a policyholder? Why don't you tell them that you applied for insurance on the day *after* Senator Johnston's bill became law? Why don't you tell them about the thousands of dollars in claims you've already submitted to this company, for everything from drugs to help contain your chorea, to the cost of that cane you're holding? You are a burden, sir—a burden on every person in this room. Providing coverage for you represents state-imposed charity on our part."

"But I'm—"

"—And there *is* a place for charity, I certainly agree. Doubtless it would surprise you, Dr. Tardivel, to know that I personally, from my own pocket, donated ten thousand dollars last year to an AIDS hospice here in San Francisco. But our largesse must know reasonable bounds. Medical services cost money. Your vaunted Canadian socialized health-care system may well collapse as costs spiral ever upwards."

"That's not—"

"Now please, sir, you've had your say. Please sit down."

"But you're trying to—"

A deep-voiced man shouted from the rear: "Sit down, Frenchie!"

"Go back home if you don't like it here," yelled a woman.

"Une minute!" said Pierre.

"Cancel your policy!" shouted another man. "Stop sucking us dry!"

"You people don't understand," said Pierre. "It's—"

One fellow began to boo. He was soon joined by several more. Someone tossed a wadded-up copy of the agenda at Pierre. Bullen motioned with two crooked fingers at his security men, who started to move forward. Pierre exhaled noisily and made his slow, painful way back to his seat. Molly patted him on the arm as he sat down.

"You got a lot of nerve, buddy," said a fellow with a comb-over in the row behind them, leaning forward.

Molly, who had been detecting some thoughts from this man and his wife throughout the evening, wheeled around and snapped, "And you're having an affair with your secretary Rebecca."

The man's mouth dropped open and he began to splutter. His wife immediately laid into him.

Molly turned back to Pierre. "Let's go, honey. There's no point in staying any longer."

Pierre nodded and began the slow process of getting to his feet again. Bullen pressed on with the meeting. "My apologies for that unfortunate display. Now, ladies and gentlemen, as we do every year, we'll close with a few words from the company's founder, Mr. Abraham Danielson."

Pierre was halfway out into the aisle now. Onstage, a completely bald octogenarian rose from the long mahogany table and began his own slow journey across the stage to the podium. Molly was gathering up her purse. She looked up, and—

Oh my God!

That face—those cruel, dark eyes ...

He'd been wearing a watch cap when she'd last seen him, his ears pressed flat against his head, his baldness concealed, but that was him, no doubt about it—

"Pierre, wait!" Her husband turned to look at her. Molly's jaw was hanging open.

"I founded this company forty-eight years ago," said Abraham Danielson, his reedy voice tinged by an Eastern European accent. "At that time—"

"It's him," said Molly in a low voice to Pierre, who was now lowering himself back into his seat. "It's him—it's the man I saw torturing the dying cat!"

"Are you sure?" whispered Pierre.

Molly nodded vigorously. "It's him!"

Pierre squinted to see the guy better: thick necked, bald. Sure, all old geezers looked somewhat alike, but this guy bore more than a passing resemblance to Burian Klimus, although Klimus didn't have flapping ears like that. In fact, who he really looked like was—

Jesus, he was the spitting image of John Demjanjuk.

"Holy God," said Pierre. He sagged back in his chair, as if someone had knocked the wind out of him. "Holy God," he said again. "Molly—it's Ivan Marchenko!"

"But—but when I saw him that morning in San Francisco, he swore at me in Russian, not Ukrainian."

"Lots of people speak Russian in the Ukraine," said Pierre. He shook his head back and forth. It all made sense. What better job for an out-of-work Nazi than being an actuary? He'd spent the war years dividing people into good and bad classes—Aryan, Jew; master, slave—and now he'd found a way to continue doing that. And the murders, conducted by neo-Nazis led by a man they called Grozny. How many people needed to be eliminated to ensure Condor's obscene profits? Whatever the figure, it was chump change compared to the number Marchenko had killed half a century before.

If only he had a camera—if only he could show Avi Meyer what this fucking Goddamned son-of-a-bitch asshole looked like—

They got up to leave again, Pierre moving as fast as he possibly could. They made it to the elevator lobby. Molly pressed the call button. As they waited, a large black man in a tweed jacket came out after them. "Wait!" he called. He had a big leather bag hanging from his shoulder.

Molly looked up at the row of illuminated digits above each of the four doors. The closest elevator was still eight floors away.

"Wait!" said the man again, jogging up to close the distance. "Dr. Tardivel, I want to have a word with you."

Molly moved close to her husband. "He said everything he had to say back there."

The black man shook his head. He was in his early forties, with a dusting of snow throughout his close-cropped hair. "I don't think so. I think he's got a hell of a lot more to say." He looked directly at Pierre. "Don't you?"

Pierre's legs were trying to walk out from underneath him. "Well ..."

"What business is it of yours?" said Molly, cutting Pierre off. The elevator had arrived and the doors slid open.

The black man reached into his jacket. For a horrible moment, Pierre thought he was going for a gun. But all he pulled out was a slim, much-worn leather business-card case. He handed a card to Molly. "I'm Barnaby Lincoln," he said. "I'm a business writer for the *San Francisco Chronicle.*"

"What do—?" began Pierre.

"I'm covering the shareholders' meeting. But there's a better story in what you were saying."

"They can't see the future—can't see where it's all going," said Pierre.

"Exactly," said Lincoln. "I've been covering insurance stories for years; all these guys are out of control. There needs to be federal legislation preventing the use of genetic profiles in determining insurance eligibility everywhere."

Pierre was intrigued. Ivan Marchenko had been free for fifty years now; a few minutes more wouldn't matter. *"D'accord,"* said Pierre.

"Can we go somewhere for coffee?"

"All right," said Pierre. "But before we do, I need you to do me a favor. I need a photo of Abraham Danielson."

Lincoln frowned. "The old man doesn't like having his picture taken. We don't even have a file photo of him at the *Chronicle."*

"I'm not surprised," said Pierre. "Do you have a telephoto lens here? Surely you could snap off a shot from the back of the room. I need a good, clean head-and-shoulders picture of him."

"What for?"

Pierre was quiet for a moment. "I can't tell you now, but if you take the photo, and get me some prints of it right away, I promise you'll be the person I call first when"—he knew the appropriate metaphor in French, but had to rack his brain for a moment to come up with the English equivalent"—when the story breaks."

Lincoln shrugged. "Wait here," he said. He went back into the auditorium. As the door opened, Pierre recognized Craig Bullen's voice coming over the speakers. So much the better: Abraham Danielson had clearly sat back down and would hardly be on guard against his picture being taken now. Lincoln returned a few minutes later. "Got it," he said.

"Good," said Pierre. "Let's get out of here."

38

"Avi Meyer," said a familiar Chicago-accented voice.

"Avi, it's Pierre Tardivel at LBNL." He hit the transmit button on his fax machine.

"Hey, Pierre. What's new with Klimus?"

"Nothing, but—"

"We don't have anything new, either. I've got an agent in Kiev, working on digging up records of his time in a displaced-persons camp, but—"

"No, no, no," said Pierre. "Klimus isn't Ivan Marchenko."

"*What?*"

"I was wrong. He's not Marchenko."

"Are you sure?"

"I'm positive."

"Dammit, Pierre, we've spent months following this up on your insistence—"

"I've seen Marchenko. Face-to-face."

"In Berkeley?"

"No, in San Francisco. And Molly saw him on a street wearing a trench coat."

"What is this? The new version of Elvis sightings?" Avi breathed out loudly. His tone conveyed that he was regretting ever getting involved with an amateur sleuth. "Dammit, Pierre, who are you going to finger next? Ross Perot? He's got jug ears, after all. Or Patrick Stewart? *There's* a suspicious-looking bald guy. Or the Pope? Fucking guy's got an Eastern European accent, and—"

"I'm serious, Avi. I've seen him. He's using the name Abraham Danielson now. He was the founder of a company called Condor Health Insurance."

Keyclicks in the background. "We've got no open file on a guy with that name, and—Condor? Aren't those the people who have that abortion policy you don't like? God damn it, Pierre, I told you not to fuck with Justice. I could have you jailed for this. First you sic us on your boss 'cause he's pissed you off somehow; now you try to get us to hound the guy whose company offends your delicate sensibilities—"

"No, I tell you I've got him this time—"

"Sure you have."

"Really, dammit. This guy is a monster—"

"Because he encourages abortions."

"Because he's Ivan Grozny. Because he runs the Millennial Reich. And because he's ordered the executions of thousands of people here in California—"

"Can you prove that? Can you prove one word of that? Because if you can't—"

"Check your fax machine, Avi."

"What? Oh ... Just a sec." Pierre could hear Avi setting down the handset and moving about the office. A moment later the phone was picked back up. "Where'd you get this picture?"

"A reporter for the *San Francisco Chronicle* took it."

"That's—what was the name you said?—Abraham Danielson?"

"That's him."

"Shit, he *does* look like Marchenko."

“Tell me about it,” said Pierre with satisfaction.

“I’ll have my assistant dig up his immigration papers; that could take a couple of weeks. But if this doesn’t pan out, Pierre—”

“I know, I know. Anne Murray time.”

Amanda still hadn’t said anything aloud, although, according to Molly, she could mentally articulate several hundred words—many more than she’d yet to learn in American Sign Language.

Saturday afternoon meant it was time for Klimus’s weekly visit. The old man arrived at 3:00 p.m. He brought no gift for Amanda—he never did—but, as usual, he did have a small notebook in his breast pocket. He sat back on the couch, making notes about Amanda’s behavior and her ability to communicate with her hands. Throughout it all, Molly had to keep Amanda far out of her zone: Amanda understood that unless she was close to her mother, her mother couldn’t hear her thoughts, but she didn’t yet understand that this ability was a secret, and so Molly simply kept her distance, hoping that nothing in Amanda’s behavior would give it away to Klimus.

After two hours of this, Klimus got up to leave, but Molly sat down next to him on the couch.

“Please stay,” she said.

Klimus looked surprised. He’d grown accustomed to Molly and Pierre’s hostility.

“What for?” he asked.

“Just to talk,” said Molly, inching even closer to him.

“About what?”

“Oh, this and that. Stuff. We don’t really know each other that well, and, well, if you *are* going to be part of the family, I figured we should—”

“I’m a very busy man,” said Klimus.

But Pierre sat down as well, in a chair facing the couch. “We’ve got more coffee on. It won’t be a minute.”

Klimus exhaled and spread his arms. “Very well.”

Amanda toddled over to her mother and started to climb into her lap, but Molly blocked Amanda's way. "Go over to your father," she said. Amanda looked at the distance, obviously thinking the lap at hand was just as good, but then seemed to shrug slightly, and made her way across to Pierre, who lifted her up into his lap.

"Tell us a bit about yourself," said Molly.

"For instance?"

"Oh, I don't know. What TV shows do you like?"

"The only one I watch is *60 Minutes*. Everything else is garbage."

Pierre's eyebrows went up. *60 Minutes* had been where the story about Ivan Marchenko first broke; no wonder Klimus had known the name.

"So," said Klimus awkwardly. "How are your friends the Lagerkvists?"

"They're fine," said Molly. "Ingrid's talking about going into private practice."

"Ah," said Klimus. "Would she stay in Berkeley?"

"If the Lagerkvists have any plans to move," said Molly, "they're keeping it a secret." She paused for a beat. "Secrets are always interesting, aren't they?" She looked right at the old man. "I mean, we've all got secrets. I do, Pierre does, even little Amanda does, I'm sure. What about you, Burian? What's your secret?"

What's she on about? thought Klimus.

"You know—something down deep, something hidden ..."

She's crazy if she thinks I'm going to talk about my private life—

"I don't know what you expect me to say, Molly."

"Oh, nothing really. I'm just rambling. Just wondering what makes a man like you tick. You know I'm a psychologist. You've got to forgive me for being intrigued by the mind of a genius."

That's more like it, thought Klimus. *A little respect.*

"I mean," said Molly, "normal people have all kinds of secrets—sexual things ..."

Christ, I can't remember the last time I had sex ...

"Financial secrets—maybe a little cheating on the old income tax ..."

No more than anyone else ...

"Or secrets related to their jobs ..."

Best damned job in the world, university professor. Travel, respect, decent money, power ...

"Secrets related to your research ..."

Not lately ...

"To your earlier research ..."

The prize should have been mine, anyway ...

"To—to your Nobel Prize, maybe?"

Secrets Tottenham took to the grave ...

Molly looked him directly in the eyes. "Who is Tottenham?"

Klimus's parchment skin showed a little color. "Tottenham—"

"Yes, who is he?"

She.

"Or she?"

Christ, what is— "I don't know anyone named—"

Amanda was playing with Pierre's fingers. He spoke up. "Tottenham—not Myra Tottenham?"

Molly looked at her husband. "You know that name?"

Pierre frowned, thinking. Where had he heard it before? "A biochemist at Stanford during the sixties. I read an old paper of hers recently on missense mutations."

Molly's eyes narrowed. She'd gone over Klimus's bio in *Who's Who* in preparation for today. "Weren't you at Stanford in the sixties?" she said. "Whatever happened to Myra Tottenham?"

"Oh, *that* Tottenham," said Klimus. He shrugged. "She died in 1969, I think. Leukemia." *The frigid bitch.*

Molly frowned. "Myra Tottenham. Pretty name. Did you work together?"

Tried to. "No."

"It's sad when somebody dies like that."

Not for me. "People die all the time, Molly." He rose to his feet. "Now, really, I must be going."

"But the coffee—" said Pierre.

"No. No, I'm leaving now." He made his way to the front door. "Good-bye."

Molly followed him to the door. Once he was gone she came back into the living room and clapped her hands together. Still in her father's lap, Amanda turned to look at her, surprised by the sound.

"Well?" said Pierre.

"I know I'll never get you off hockey," she said, "but fishing is my favorite sport."

"How far is Stanford?" asked Pierre.

Molly shrugged. "Not far. Forty miles."

Pierre kissed his daughter on the cheek and spoke to her in a soothing voice: "Soon you won't have to see that mean old man anymore."

Pierre couldn't do the work himself; it required much too steady a hand. But LBNL did have a comprehensive machine shop: there was a wide variety of work done at Lawrence Berkeley, and custom-designed tools and parts had to be built all the time. Pierre had Shari sketch a design for him from his verbal description, and then he took the shuttle bus down to UCB, where he visited Stanley Hall, home of the university's virus lab. He'd guessed right: that lab had the narrowest-gauge syringes he'd ever seen. He got several of them and headed back up to the machine shop.

The shop master, a mechanical engineer named Jesus DiMarco, looked over Pierre's rough sketch and suggested three or four refinements, then went to write up the work order. LBNL was a government lab, and everything generated paperwork—although not nearly as much as a bureaucracy-crazy Canadian facility would have. "What do you call this gizmo?" asked DiMarco.

Pierre frowned, thinking. Then: "A joy-buzzer."

DiMarco chuckled. "Pretty cute," he said.

"Just call me *koo,*" said Pierre.

"What?"

"You know—" He whistled the *James Bond* theme.

DiMarco laughed. "You mean 'Q'." He looked up at the wall clock. "Come back anytime after three. It'll be ready."

"Newsroom," said the male voice.

"Barnaby Lincoln," said Pierre into the phone. "He's a business reporter."

"He's out right now, and—oh, wait. Here he comes." The voice shouted into the phone; Pierre hated people who didn't cover the mouthpiece when shouting. "Barney! Call for you!" The phone was dropped on a hard surface.

A few moments later it was picked up.

"Lincoln," said the voice.

"Barnaby, it's Pierre Tardivel at LBNL."

"Pierre! Good to hear from you. Have you given some thought to what we talked about?"

"I'm intrigued, yes. But that's not why I'm calling. First, though, thanks for the pictures of Danielson. They were terrific."

"That's why they pay me the big bucks," said Lincoln, deadpan.

"I need you to do one more thing for me, though."

"Yeah?"

"Are you going to be interviewing Abraham Danielson soon?"

"Geez, I haven't interviewed the old man for—hell, must be six years now."

"Would he see you if you called?"

"I guess, sure."

"Can you arrange that? Can you get in to see him? Even for five minutes?"

"Sure, but why?"

"Set it up. But come by my lab on the way. I'll explain everything when you get here."

Lincoln thought this over for a moment. "This better be a good story," he said at last.

"Can you say 'Pulitzer'?" said Pierre.

The receptionist escorted Barnaby Lincoln into Abraham Danielson's office.

"Barney," said Abraham, rising from his leather chair.

Lincoln surged forward, hand extended. "Thanks for seeing me on such short notice."

Abraham looked at Lincoln's outstretched hand. Lincoln left it extended. The old man finally took it. They shook firmly.

Pierre had been working in the den at home—it was awkward getting into LBNL these days, since Molly had to drive him. He decided to head up to the living room to replenish his Diet Pepsi. Coffee was too dangerous a way to get his morning caffeine; he overturned his drink at least once a week now, and didn't want to scald himself. And regular Pepsi contained all that sugar—it would ruin his keyboard or computer if he spilled it in there. But aspartame wasn't conductive; it might make a mess, but it wouldn't wreck electronics if spilled on them.

Of course Pierre made a fair bit of noise going up the stairs, but the dishwasher was going, producing enough racket to drown out the sound. As he entered the living room, he saw Molly sitting with Amanda on the couch. Molly was saying something to Amanda that Pierre couldn't quite make out, and Amanda seemed to be concentrating very, very hard.

He watched them for a moment—and was pleased that, to some degree, at least, his jealousy of his wife's closeness to their daughter had passed. Yes, he still ached at not being able to communicate with her the way he'd like to, but he was coming to realize how important that special relationship between Molly and Amanda was. Amanda seemed totally comfortable with Molly's ability to reach into her mind and hear her thoughts; it was almost a relief to the girl that she could communicate without effort with another human being. And Molly's bond with her daughter went beyond even the normal closeness of mother and child; she could touch Amanda's very mind.

Pierre still thought mostly in French, and he knew, given that he virtually always spoke English, that he was doing this on some subconscious level as a defense against having his thoughts read. But Amanda had accepted her mother's ability from the beginning, and she erected no barriers between herself and Molly; they had a closeness that was transcendental—and Pierre was, at last, glad of it. His wife was no longer tortured by her gift; rather, she was now grateful for it. And Pierre knew that after he was gone, Molly and Amanda would need that special closeness to support each other, to go on and face whatever the future might bring them together, almost as one.

"Try again," Molly, her back to Pierre, said to Amanda. "You can do it."

Pierre stepped fully into the room. "What are you two conspiring about?" he said lightly.

Molly looked up, startled. "Nothing," she said, too quickly. "Nothing." She looked embarrassed. Amanda's brown eyes went wide, the way they did when she'd been caught doing something bad.

"You look like the cat who swallowed the canary," Pierre said to Molly, a bemused smile on his face. "What are—"

The phone rang.

Molly leaped to her feet. "I'll get it," she said, bounding into the kitchen. A moment later, she called out, "Pierre! It's for you."

Pierre made his way ponderously into the kitchen. The noise from the dishwasher was irritating, but it would take him several minutes to hobble down to the den or up to the bedroom to use a different phone.

"Hello?" said Pierre after taking the handset from his wife.

"Pierre? It's Avi."

Molly headed back to the living room; Pierre could barely hear her as she went back to talking to Amanda in conspiratorial tones.

"We've dug up Abraham Danielson's immigration records," continued Avi. "You're right that that's not his real name. Nothing unusual about that, though; lots of immigrants changed their names when they came here after the war. According to his visa application, his real name is Avrom Danylchenko. Born 1911, the same year as Ivan Marchenko—but, then again, so was Klimus, so that's hardly compelling evidence. He was living in Rijeka at the time he applied to come to the States."

"Okay."

"We can't find anything prior to 1945 about Avrom Danylchenko. Again, that doesn't prove spit. Lots of records were lost during the war, and there's tons of stuff from the old Soviet Union that no one has sifted through yet. Still, it *is* interesting that the last record we have of Ivan Marchenko is Nikolai Shelaiev's statement that he saw him in Fiume in 1944, and the first record of Avrom Danylchenko is his visa application the following year in Rijeka."

"How far is Rijeka from Fiume?"

"I wondered that myself—couldn't find Fiume in my atlas at first. It turns out—get this—that Fiume and Rijeka are the same place. Fiume is the old Italian name for the city."

"Jesus. So what happens now?"

"I'm going to show the photo to the remaining Treblinka survivors. I'm flying out to New Mexico tomorrow to see one of them, and I'm off to Israel after that."

"Surely you could just fax the photo to the police there," said Pierre.

"No, I want to be on hand. I want to see the witnesses at the moment they first look at the photo. We were fucked over on the Demjanjuk case because the identifications weren't handled properly. Yoram Sheftel—that's Demjanjuk's Israeli lawyer—says in all his years in the business, he's never once seen the Israeli police conduct a proper photo-spread ID. In the Demjanjuk case, they used a photo spread that had Demjanjuk's photo mixed in with seven others. But some of the photos were bigger or clearer than the others, and most of them didn't bear even a passing resemblance to the man the witnesses had described. This time I'm going to supervise it all, every step of the way. There aren't going to be any fuckups." A pause. "Anyway, I've got to get going."

"Wait—one more thing."

"What are you, Columbo?"

Pierre was taken aback. At least it was an improvement over everyone assuming he was a salesman. "When you have somebody in custody, what kind of identification records do you keep?"

"How do you mean?" said Avi.

"I mean you must keep records, right? The whole idea behind Nazi hunting is proving identity. Surely if you have someone in custody, you must take pains to make sure you can identify the same person again years later if need be."

"Sure. We take fingerprints, even some retinal scans—"

"Do you take tissue samples? For DNA fingerprinting?"

"That sort of routine testing is not legal."

"That's not a direct answer. Do you do it? It's easy enough after all. All you need is a few cells. Do you do it?"

"Off the record, yes."

"Were you doing that as far back as the 1980s?"

"Yes."

"Would you have a tissue sample from John Demjanjuk still on file?"

"I imagine so. Why?"

"Get it. Have it sent to my lab by FedEx."

"Why?"

"Just do it. If I'm right—if I'm right, I can clear up the mystery of exactly what went wrong at the Ivan the Terrible trial in Jerusalem all those years ago."

39

The phone rang again the next day. This time Pierre was down in the den, and he got it there. "Hello?"

"Pierre, it's Avi. I'm calling you from O'Hare. I saw Zalmon Chudzik this morning; he's one of the Treblinka survivors who now lives in the States."

"And?"

"And the poor bastard's got Alzheimer's disease."

"Merde."

"Exactly. But, you know—this may sound cruel—but in this one case, maybe it's a blessing."

"Huh?"

"His daughter says he's forgotten everything about Treblinka. For the first time in over fifty years, he's managing to sleep through the night."

Pierre didn't know how to reply. After a few moments, he said, "When do you leave for Israel?"

"About three hours."

"I hope you have better luck there."

Avi's voice was weary. "Me, too. There were only fifty Treblinka survivors, and over thirty-five of them have passed on in the intervening years. There are only four left who hadn't previously misidentified Demjanjuk as Ivan—and Chudzik was one of those four."

"What happens to our case if we don't get a positive ID?"

"It evaporates. Look at all the evidence they had against O. J. Simpson—made no difference to the jury. Without eyewitnesses, we're sunk. And I do mean eyewitnesses, plural. The Israelis aren't going to pay attention unless we get at least two independent IDs."

"Good Christ," said Pierre softly.

"At this stage," said Avi, "I'd even take his help."

Avi Meyer had spent the last few days wrangling back and forth over jurisdictional issues with Izzy Tischler, a plainclothes detective with the Nazi Crimes Investigation Division of the Israeli State Police. They were now ready to attempt their first ID. Tischler, a tall, thin, red-haired fellow of forty, wore a yarmulke; Avi was wearing a large canvas hat, trying to ward off the brutal sun. They walked down the narrow street, beside buildings of yellow brick with narrow balconies, packed one right up against the next. Two Orthodox Jewish men walked down the lane, and an Arab headed up the other way. They didn't look at each other as they passed.

"This is it," said Tischler, checking the number on the house against an address he had written down on a Post-it note in his hand, folded in half so that the adhesive strip was covered over. The door was set back only a meter from the road. Weeds grew out of the cracks in the stone walk, but the beauty of the ceramic *mezuzah* on the doorpost caught Avi's eye. He knocked. After about half a minute, a middle-aged woman appeared.

"*Shalom,* said Avi. "My name is Avi Meyer, and this is Detective Tischler, of the Israeli State Police. Is Casimir Landowski home?"

"He's upstairs. What's this all about?"

"May we speak to him?"

"About what?"

"We just need him to identify some photos."

The middle-aged woman looked from one man to the other. "You've found Ivan Grozny," she said flatly.

Avi cringed. "It's important that the identification not be prejudiced. Is Casimir Landowski your father?"

"Yes. My husband and I have looked after him since his wife died."

"Your father can't know in advance who we're asking him to identify. If he knows, the defense lawyers will be able to get the identification ruled ineligible. Please, don't say a word to him."

"He won't be able to help you."

"Why not?"

"Because he's blind, that's why not. Complications from diabetes."

"Oh," said Avi, his heart sinking. "I'm sorry."

"Even if he could see," said the woman, "I'm not sure I'd let you speak to him."

"Why?"

"We watched the trial of John Demjanjuk on TV. What was that, ten or more years ago? He could see then—and he knew you had the wrong guy. They'd shown him pictures of Demjanjuk, and he'd said it wasn't Ivan."

"I know. That's why he'd have made a great witness this time."

"But it tore him up, watching that trial. All that testimony about Treblinka. He'd never spoken about it—my whole life, he'd never said a word to me. But he sat there, transfixed, day in and day out, listening to the testimony. He knew some of those who were testifying. Hearing them recount the things that butcher did—murder and rape and torture. He thought if he never spoke about it, somehow he could separate it from his life, keep it isolated from everything else. To have to live through it all again, even from the comfort of his living room, almost killed him. To ask him to do that once more—such a thing I'd never do. He's ninety-three; he'd never survive it."

"I'm sorry," said Avi. He looked at the woman, trying to size her up. It occurred to him that perhaps the man wasn't really blind. Maybe she was just trying to shelter him. "I, ah, I'd like to speak to your father anyway, if I may. You know, just to shake his hand. I've come all the way from the United States."

"You don't believe me," she said, in the same blunt tone she'd used before. But then she shrugged. "I'll let you talk to him, but you can't say a word about why you're here. I won't have you upsetting him."

"I promise."

"Come in, then." She headed upstairs, Avi and Tischler following. The man was sitting in a chair in front of a television set. Avi thought he'd caught the woman in a lie, but it soon became apparent that he wasn't watching the TV. Rather, he was just listening to it. A talk show in Hebrew was on. The interviewer, a young woman, was asking her guests about their first sexual experiences. The man was listening intently. In the corner of the room, a white cane leaned against a wall.

"Abba," said the woman, "I'd like you to meet two people. They're just passing through town. Old friends of mine."

The man rose slowly, painfully, to his feet. As soon as he was standing, Avi saw his eyes. They were completely clouded over. "It's a great pleasure to meet you," said Avi, taking the man's gnarled hand. "A great pleasure."

"Your accent—you're American?"

"Yes."

"What brings you to Israel?" asked the man, his voice slow.

"Just the sights," said Avi. "You know—the history."

"Oh, yes," said the old man. "We've got lots of that."

The phone in Pierre's lab rang. He hobbled over to answer it. "Hello?"

"Pierre?"

"Hi, Avi. What's the score?"

"Forces of good, zero. Forces of evil, two."

"No IDs?"

"Not yet. The second guy is blind. Complications of diabetes, his daughter said."

Pierre snorted.

"What's so funny?"

"It's not funny, really. Just ironic. The first guy had Alzheimer's and this one has diabetes. Those are both genetically related. As Danielson, Marchenko discriminated against people who have those same diseases, and now those diseases are saving him."

"Yeah," said Avi. "Well, let's hope things go better. We've only got two shots left."

"Keep me posted."

"Right. Bye."

Pierre went back to the light table, hunching over the two autorads. He kept at it for hours, but when he was done, he leaned back and nodded to himself in satisfaction. It was exactly what he'd expected.

When Avi got back to the States, Pierre would have one hell of a surprise for him.

Avi and Detective Tischler drove down to Jerusalem for their next attempt. All the buildings were made of stone—there was an ordinance that required it; at sunset, the light reflecting from the stone transformed Jerusalem into the fabled City of Gold. They found the ancient house they were looking for and knocked on the door. After a few moments a young man, perhaps thirteen years old, appeared, wearing a yarmulke and a *Melrose Place* T-shirt. Avi shook his head slightly. He was always surprised at how pervasive American pop culture was no matter where he traveled.

"Yes?" said the boy in Hebrew.

Avi smiled. *"Shalom,"* he said. He knew his Hebrew was rough, but he'd told Tischler that he wanted to do all the talking. He couldn't risk the Israeli police officer saying anything that might contaminate the identification. "My name is Avi Meyer. I'm looking for Shlomo Malamud."

"He's my *zayde,*" said the boy. But then his eyes immediately narrowed. "What do you want?"

"Just to speak to him, just for a moment."

"About what?"

Avi sighed. "I'm an American—"

"No shit," said the boy, making it clear that this had been obvious from the first syllable Avi had uttered.

"—and this man is an Israeli police officer. Show him," said Avi, turning to Tischler. Tischler pulled out his ID and held it up for the boy to see.

The boy shook his head. "My *zayde* is very old," he said, "and almost never leaves the house. He hasn't done anything."

"We know that. We just need to talk to him for a moment."

"Maybe you should come back when my father is home," said the boy.

"When will that be?"

"Friday, for Shabbat. He's on business right now, in Haifa."

"What we want will only take a moment." Through the doorway, Avi could see that an ancient man had appeared, oblivious to their presence, hunched over, shuffling toward the kitchen.

"Is that him?" asked Avi.

The boy didn't have to look back. "He's very old," he said.

"Shlomo Malamud!" shouted Avi.

The man slowly turned around, a look of surprise on his deeply wrinkled, sun-battered face.

"*Mar* Malamud!" Avi shouted again. The man began to shuffle toward them.

"It's all right," said the boy, trying to stop his grandfather from coming nearer. "I'm taking care of everything."

"*Mar* Malamud," said Avi, over the boy. "I've come a long way to ask you just one question, sir. I need you to look at some photographs and tell me if you recognize anyone."

The man was moving slowly toward them, but the boy was still blocking the entrance with his body. "You're wasting your time," said the boy. "He's blind."

Avi felt his heart sinking. Not again! Dammit, why hadn't he thought to check on this before leaving the States? How was he going to explain *this* one to his boss? "Yes, sir, that's right, I spent three thousand dollars flying halfway across the world to show some pictures to a bunch of blind old men."

The old fellow was still working his way down the corridor. "I—I'm sorry to have disturbed you," Avi said, turning to go.

"What do you two want?" asked Malamud, his voice as dry as the desert.

"Nothing," said Avi, and then, almost at once, thinking for a second that his Hebrew had failed him, "Did you say 'you two'?" Tischler hadn't uttered a word since they'd arrived.

"Speak up, young man. I can hardly hear you."

Avi wheeled on the teenager. "Is he blind, or isn't he?"

"'Course he is," said the boy. "Well, *legally* blind."

"Mr. Malamud, how much vision do you have left?"

"Not much."

"If I show you a series of photographs, could you tell them apart?"

"Maybe."

"Can we come in?"

The old man thought for a long time. "I guess," he said at last.

The teenager, looking quite miffed at having had an end run done around him, reluctantly moved aside. Avi and Tischler followed Malamud as he moved at a snail's pace down to the kitchen. He found a chair—whether he could actually see it, or simply knew where it would be, Avi couldn't tell. After he'd sat down, he waved for Avi and Tischler to do the same. Avi opened up his briefcase and took out a small cassette recorder, thumbed it on, then placed it on the table near Malamud. He then took out the photo spread, unfolding it at its central masking-tape hinge and placing it in front of Malamud. The spread consisted of three rows of eight photos—twenty-four in all.

"These are modern pictures," said Avi. "They all show men in their eighties or nineties. But we're trying to identify someone you might have known in your youth—someone you would have known in the early 1940s."

The old man looked up, his eyes full of hope. "You've found Saul?"

Avi looked at the teenager. "Who is Saul?"

"His brother," said the boy. "He disappeared in the war. My grandfather was taken to Treblinka; Saul was taken to Chelm."

"I've been looking for him ever since," said Malamud. "And now you've found him!"

Avi knew this was ideal: if Malamud thought he was looking for someone else and still spotted Ivan Grozny, the identification would be very hard to discredit in court. But Avi couldn't bear to use the man like that. "No," he said. "No, I'm so sorry, but this has nothing to do with your brother."

The man's face visibly sank. "Then what?"

"If you can just look at these pictures ..."

Malamud took a moment to compose himself, then fumbled for a pair of glasses in his breast pocket. They had enormously thick lenses. He balanced them on his large, pitted nose, and peered at the pictures for a few moments. "Still can't see them very well," he said.

Avi sighed. But then Malamud continued, "Ezra, go and get my lens."

The boy, now somewhat intrigued by the proceedings, seemed reluctant to leave, but, after a moment's hesitation, he disappeared into another room and then returned brandishing a magnifying glass worthy of Sherlock Holmes. The old man removed his glasses, held out his hand, let Ezra place the lens within it, and then bent over the photo spread again.

"No," he said, looking at the first photo, and "No," again, after peering at the second.

"Remember," said Avi, knowing he should keep quiet, but unable to do so, "you're looking for someone from fifty-odd years ago. Try to imagine them as young men."

The man grunted, as if to say there was no need to remind him of that—he might be old, but he wasn't stupid. He moved from face to face, his own eye only inches above the snapshots. "No. No. Not him, either. No—oh, my! Oh, heaven—oh, heaven." His finger was on the Danielson photo. "It's him! After all these years, you've found him!"

Avi felt his pulse racing. "Who?" he said, trying to keep his voice under control. "Who is it?"

"That monster from Treblinka." The man's face had gone completely white and his hand was shaking so much it looked like he was going to drop the magnifying glass. Ezra reached over and took it gently from his grandfather.

"Who is he?" asked Avi. "What's his name?"

"Ivan," said the old man, practically spitting the word. "Ivan Grozny."

"Are you sure?" said Avi. "Do you have any doubt?"

"Those eyes. That mouth. No—no doubt. It's him, the very devil himself."

Avi closed his eyes. "Thank you," he said. "If we draw up a statement to that effect, will you sign it?"

The old man turned to face Avi. "Where is he? Have you got him?"

"He's in the United States."

"You'll bring him here? To stand trial?"

"Yes."

The old man was silent for a long time, then: "Yes, I'll sign a statement. You're afraid I'll die before the trial, aren't you? Afraid I won't live to identify him in court?"

Avi said nothing.

"I'll live," said the old man, simply. "You've given me something to live for." He reached out, trying to find Avi's hand. They connected, Avi feeling the rough, loose skin. As he reached out, Malamud's sleeve rode up his forearm, revealing his serial-number tattoo. "Thank you," said Malamud. "Thank you for bringing him to justice." He paused. "What did you say your name was again?"

"Meyer, sir. Agent Avi Meyer, of the United States Department of Justice."

"I knew someone named Meyer, at Treblinka. Jubas Meyer. He was my partner in removing bodies."

Avi felt his eyes stinging. "That was my father."

"A good man, Jubas."

"He died before I was born," said Avi. "What—what was he like?"

"Sit down," said Malamud, "and I'll tell you."

Avi looked at Tischler, his eyes asking for the Israeli cop's indulgence. "Go ahead," said Tischler, gently. "Family is important."

Avi took a seat, his heart pounding.

Malamud told him stories about Jubas, and Avi listened, rapt. When the old man had recounted all he could remember, Avi shook his hand again. "Thank you," he said. "Thank you so very much."

Malamud shook his head, "No, son—thank *you*. Thank you for both of us, both me and your father. He'd be very proud of you today."

Avi smiled, blinking away tears.

Pierre had done tests on various types of primate DNA collected from the zoo, determining not just the degree of genetic divergence but also specific ways in which key segments of their chromosome thirteens varied. Pierre and Shari were now immersed in designing a computer simulation. They integrated all the cytosine-methylation data they had, all the patterns they'd detected in the human and nonhuman introns, all the ideas they had about the significance of codon synonyms.

It was a massive project, with a huge database. The simulation was far too complex for them to run in any reasonable amount of time on their lab's PC. But LBNL had a Cray supercomputer, a machine that could crunch all the numbers six ways from Sunday in the blink of an eye. Pierre had long ago put in a request for some CPU time on the Cray, and he'd slowly been moving up the queue. His time was scheduled for two weeks from now.

They'd need every minute of that time to get the simulation ready to run, but, assuming everything worked, they'd at last have the answers they'd been looking for.

"David Solomon?"

"Yes?"

"My name is Avi Meyer of the United States government. This is Detective Izzy Tischler of the Israeli police. We'd like to show you some pictures, and see if you recognize any of the people."

Solomon had a face like a crumpled paper bag, tanned and coarsened from exposure to sun and wind. The only sharp part was his nose, a giant thing, curved and hooked like an eagle's beak, and webbed over its entire surface by tiny exploded blood vessels. His irises were so dark brown that his pupils were all but lost against them, and the rest of his eyeballs were more yellow than white, shot through with veins.

"Why?" asked Solomon.

"I can tell you after you look at the pictures," said Avi.

Solomon shrugged. "Okay."

"May we come in?"

Another shrug. "Sure." The old man shuffled into his living room and sat on the well-worn couch. There was no air-conditioning; the heat was oppressive. Tischler gingerly removed a vase from the coffee table and, finding nowhere else to set it down, simply held it in his hand. Avi placed his tape recorder on the table, then unfolded the photo spread, with its three rows of eight pictures. Solomon took off the pair of glasses he was wearing and replaced them with another pair from his breast pocket. "These are people that—"

"Ivan Marchenko!" said the man at once.

Avi leaned forward anxiously. "Which one?"

"The middle row. The third one."

Avi felt his stomach sink. The third picture in the middle row was indeed a bald-headed moon-faced man, but it was not Marchenko; rather, it was the caretaker at OSI headquarters in Washington. Avi knew that if he asked any leading questions—"Are you sure? Isn't there somebody else who looks more like Ivan?"—the defense attorneys would get the evidence laughed out of court. Instead, unable to keep the disappointment out of his voice, Avi simply said, "Thank you," and reached over to close up the spread.

But Solomon was leaning forward. "I'd know that face anywhere," he said. He reached over with a gnarled finger and tapped the sixth photo in the row of eight.

Avi felt adrenaline pounding. "But you said the third photo—"

"Sure. Third from the right." The man looked at Avi. "That's an American accent, isn't it? Don't you read Hebrew?"

Avi laughed out loud. "Not as much as I should, obviously."

"Pierre, it's Avi Meyer."

"How'd it go?"

"I've got two positive IDs."

"Terrific!"

"I'll be flying back to Washington in a few days; I've still got some work to do with the Israeli police, helping them draft an extradition request."

"No. Get a flight here. Fly into San Francisco. I've got something here you'll want to see."

40

Pierre tried to ignore the way Avi Meyer was looking at him. It had been twenty-six months since they'd last seen each other face-to-face, and although Pierre had told Avi over the phone about his condition, Avi had not until today actually seen Pierre's chorea.

Pierre slowly, carefully, laid two autoradiographs on the light table set into his lab's countertop, and then, with dancing hands, tried to line them up side by side. He seated himself on a lab stool, then motioned for Avi to come over and look at the autorads. "All right," said Pierre, "what do you see?"

Avi shrugged, not knowing what Pierre wanted him to say. "A bunch of black lines?"

"Right—almost like blurry versions of the bar codes you see on food boxes. But these bar codes"—he tapped one of the pieces of film with a trembling finger—"are DNA fingerprints of two different people."

"Who?"

"I'll get to that in a minute. You see that the bar codes are quite different, right?"

Avi nodded his bulldog head.

"There's a thick black line here," said Pierre, pointing with a trembling finger again, "and there's no corresponding black line at the same point on the other one, right?"

Avi nodded again.

"But some of the lines *are* the same, aren't they? Here's a thin line, and—look!—the other person has a thin line at exactly the same point."

Avi sounded impatient. "So he does."

"Now, have a good close look at the two fingerprints, and tell me by how much you think they overlap."

"I don't see what this—"

"Just do it, will you?"

Avi sighed in resignation and squinted his tiny eyes at the film. "I don't know. Twenty or thirty percent."

"About a quarter, in other words."

"I guess."

"A quarter. Now, you must know something about genetics—everybody does. How much DNA do you get from your parents?"

"All of it."

Pierre grinned. "That's not what I meant. I mean, what proportion comes from your mother and what proportion from your father?"

"Oh—it's half and half, isn't it?"

"Exactly. Of all the DNA that makes up a human being, precisely half comes from each parent. Now, tell me this: do you have a brother?"

"Yes," said Avi.

"Okay, good. Now if you've got half of your mother's DNA, so does your brother, right?"

"Sure."

"But is it the same half?"

Avi ran a hand over the stubble on his face. "How do you mean?"

"Is the DNA you got from your mother the same or different from what your brother got?"

"Well, I don't know. I guess if I got a random selection of my mother's genes, and Barry got a random selection, they'd overlap by—what?—fifty percent?"

"That's right," said Pierre, not nodding deliberately, but his head bobbing in a way that looked as though he was. "An average of fifty percent overlap. So, if I put DNA fingerprints for you and your brother side by side, what would you expect to see?"

"Umm—half of my bars at the same places as half of his bars?"

"Exactly! But what have we here?" He pointed to the two pieces of film on the illuminated panel.

"A twenty-five percent overlap."

"So these two people are highly unlikely to be brothers, right?"

Avi nodded.

"But, still, they do seem to be related, don't they?"

"I guess," said Avi.

"Okay. Now there's something I read when I first looked into this case that has stuck in my mind. On his application for refugee status, John Demjanjuk put his mother's maiden name as Marchenko."

"Yeah, but that was wrong. Her maiden name was Tabachuk. Demjanjuk couldn't remember it, he said, so he just put down a common Ukrainian name."

"And that always struck me as strange. I know my mother's maiden name, Ménard—and *her* mother's maiden name, Bergeron. How could someone *not* remember his own mother's maiden name? After all, Demjanjuk filled out that form in the 1940s, while he was still in his twenties. It's not like he was an old man with a failing memory."

Avi shrugged. "Who knows? The point is he couldn't remember it at the time."

"Oh, I think he remembered very well—but rather that he didn't understand the question."

"What?"

"He didn't understand the question. Tell me—what does the term 'maiden name' mean?"

Avi frowned, irritated. "The name a woman was born with."

"Right. But suppose Demjanjuk—who, according to the articles I read, only had a fourth-grade education—suppose he thought it meant simply the name his mother had before she'd married his father."

"That's the same thing."

"Not necessarily. It's only the same thing if his mother had never been married before."

"But—oh, shit. Shit, shit, shit."

"You see? What was Demjanjuk's mother's first name?"

"Olga. She died in 1970."

"If Olga had been born Olga Tabachuk, but had married a man named Marchenko and then later divorced him before marrying John Demjanjuk's father—"

"—Nikolai Demjanjuk—"

"—then when asked his mother's maiden name, and interpreting it as meaning his mother's *previous* name, John Demjanjuk would have answered 'Marchenko.' And if Olga had had one son named Ivan in 1911 by this elder Marchenko, and another son named Ivan nine years later by Nikolai Demjanjuk, then—"

"—Then Ivan Marchenko and Ivan Demjanjuk would be half brothers!" said Avi.

"Exactly! Half brothers, having about twenty-five percent of their DNA in common. In fact, it even makes sense that they're both bald. The gene for male-pattern baldness is inherited from the mother; it resides on the X chromosome. And it explains why they look so much alike—why witness after witness mistook one for the other."

"But wait—wait. That doesn't work. Nikolai and Olga Tabachuk were married January twenty-fourth, 1910, and Ivan Marchenko was born *after* that—on March second, 1911. That means he would have been conceived in the summer of 1910—*after* Olga had already ended up with the legal last name of Demjanjuk."

Pierre frowned for a moment, but then, thinking briefly of his own mother and Henry Spade, he exclaimed, "A triangle!"

Avi looked at him. "What?"

"A triangle—don't you see? Think about John Demjanjuk's own marriage from 1947. I remember reading that he'd been fooling around with another man's wife while that man was away." Pierre paused. "You know, we sometimes sum up the geneticist's creed as 'like father, like son'—but 'like mother, like son' is just as valid for many things. My wife the behaviorist doesn't like to admit it, but particular kinds of infidelity *do* run in families. Let's say Olga Tabachuk married the senior Marchenko, divorced him, and then married Nikolai Demjanjuk."

Avi nodded. "Okay."

"But Nikolai leaves their village and heads out to—what town was Demjanjuk born in?"

"Dub Macharenzi."

"To Dub-whatever. He goes there, looking for work or something like that, saying he'll send for his wife once he's got a place. Well, while the cat's away ... Olga goes back to sleeping with her ex, Marchenko. She gets pregnant and gives birth to Marchenko's child, a child they name Ivan. But then Nikolai sends word for her to come join him in Dub-thingie. Olga abandons baby Ivan, leaving him with the elder Marchenko. In fact—well, here's one my wife *would* like: Ivan Marchenko grew up to have a predilection for slicing off women's nipples. Call that his revenge for having been abandoned by his mother."

Avi was nodding slowly. "You know, it makes sense. If Olga really did abandon the baby Ivan Marchenko, and if her second husband, Nikolai Demjanjuk, never knew about that incident, when she finally had a son of her own by Nikolai, that could explain why she decided to name *him* Ivan, too—so that she could never give herself away by accidentally referring to her legitimate son by the bastard child's name." Avi looked down at the autorads. "So—so one of these was made from the tissue specimen I sent you that we'd taken from John Demjanjuk, right?"

Pierre nodded, and touched the one on the left. "This one, to be precise."

"And the other one—not Abraham Danielson?"

"Yes, indeed."

"How'd you manage to get a tissue sample from him? I thought you'd only seen him from a distance."

"I had a little device built." He slowly got up from his stool and, holding on to the rounded lip of the countertop for support, made his way over to a shelf and picked up a small object from it. He returned to where Avi was sitting and extended his shaking hand so that Avi could see what he was holding. It was impossible to get a good look at it the way Pierre's arm kept moving; Avi reached in and plucked the small device from Pierre's palm. It looked like a tiny beige thumbtack, with a very short, very narrow spike.

"I call it a joy buzzer," said Pierre, sitting down again. "It sticks to the palm of your hand with a minuscule drop of cyanoacrylate glue, and when you shake hands with someone, it takes a sample of a few skin cells. The pressure of the handshake is enough to distract from the minute pricking sensation." He held up a hand. "I can't take full credit for it—I got the idea from a special pen Condor Health uses; it seemed poetic justice to employ a similar device. A fellow I know, a newspaper reporter—same one who took the photo I originally faxed you of Abraham Danielson—wore it going into a meeting with Danielson, and shook his hand in greeting."

Avi nodded, impressed. "Can I have copies of these ... these—what do you call them?"

"Autorads."

"These autorads?"

"Sure. Why?"

"When we're through, I want to send them to Demjanjuk's lawyer in Cleveland. Maybe they'll help him get his U.S. citizenship back." He looked at Pierre, then shrugged a little. "It's the least I can do."

Pierre nodded. "So where do we stand?"

"We've got two eyewitness identifications, both positive. But, well, the witnesses are old, and one of them is legally blind. I wish we had more. Still, this half-brother stuff to some degree rehabilitates the positive identifications made during Demjanjuk's denaturalization and his trial in Israel."

"So have you got enough to move against Marchenko?"

Avi sighed. "I don't know. Danielson wasn't even *suspected* of being a Nazi. He's done a great job of covering his tracks."

"He's doubtless been able to pay off people over the last few years—make any records he wants disappear."

"More than likely." Avi shook his head. "The Israelis are going to be very wary about taking him on, especially after what happened last time."

"So what else would you need to make the case?"

Avi shrugged. "In the best of all possible worlds? A confession."

Pierre frowned. Of course, Molly could confirm Danielson's guilt easily enough, but there was no way Pierre wanted her to have to testify in court. "I could meet with him while wired for sound."

"What makes you think he'll agree to see you?" The way Avi said "you" grated a little—it was almost as if Avi were saying, "What makes you think he'll see someone in your condition?"

Pierre gritted his teeth. "We'll find a way."

"Even if he is willing to see you," said Avi, spreading his arms, "what makes you think he'll confess to you?"

"He doesn't have to confess then and there. He just has to say something incriminating enough to justify you arresting him. Then you can interrogate him properly."

"I suppose. It would take some paperwork."

"Do it. Set it up."

"I don't know, Pierre. You're a civilian, and—"

"I'm a volunteer. You want to see that bastard go free?"

Avi frowned, considering. "All right," he said at last. "Let's give it a try."

41

"Abraham Danielson's office," said a woman's voice.

"May I speak to him, please?"

"Who's calling?"

"Dr. Pierre Tardivel."

"One moment."

Silence.

"I'm sorry, Dr. Tardivel, Mr. Danielson is unable to take your call just now. Would you like to leave a message?"

"Tell him a woman from Poland named Maria Dudek suggested I call him. Give him the message now; I'll hold on."

"He's really quite busy, sir, and—"

"Just give him the message. I'm sure he'll want to take this call."

"I really can't—"

"Do it."

There was quiet for a moment while the secretary mulled this over. "Just a sec."

A click as Pierre was put on hold. Three minutes went by.

Another click.

"Abraham Danielson speaking."

"Hello, Ivan. Maria Dudek sends her regards."

"I don't know what—"

"Meet me in one hour at the Lawrence Berkeley National Laboratory."

"I'm not going anywhere. You're a crazy person—"

"You can talk to me, or I'll start talking to other people. I understand the Department of Justice has a special office devoted to exposing war criminals."

Silence for almost thirty seconds. Then: "If we're going to talk," said Danielson, "it will be here, on my turf."

"But—"

"Take it or leave it."

Pierre looked over at Avi Meyer, who was listening on an extension phone. Avi held up three fingers.

"I'll be there at three o'clock," said Pierre. "Make sure your gate guard knows to let me in."

"Pierre Tardivel," said Pierre. He was standing in front of the secretary's desk in the founder's outer office on the thirty-seventh floor of the forty-story Condor Building. "Here to see Abraham Danielson."

The secretary was two decades older than Rosalee, the knockout who worked elsewhere on this floor for CEO Craig Bullen. She was clearly startled by Pierre's dancing limbs and facial tics, but she quickly recovered her composure. "Have a seat, please. Mr. Danielson will be with you in a few moments."

Pierre understood that he was being put in his place, that Abraham wanted the upper hand psychologically—you don't sleep with a psychologist every night for three years without picking up a thing or two. Still, his palms were sweaty. With the aid of his cane, Pierre made his way slowly over to the lobby couch. Several current magazines were on the glass-topped coffee table, including *Forbes* and *Business Week*; there was also a copy of the yellow-and-black Condor annual report.

Avi Meyer, four other OSI agents, and two officers from the San Francisco Police Department were parked a short distance away, outside the fence around the Condor property. All of them were crowded into a rented van, huddled over the listening equipment.

After a few minutes, the receptionist's phone rang. She picked up the handset. "Yes, sir? Right away." She put the phone down, then looked at Pierre. "Mr. Danielson will see you now."

Pierre struggled to his feet and made his way slowly into the office. It was smaller than Craig Bullen's—it had no conference table—but the furnishings were equally opulent, although Danielson's tastes were ironically more modern than those of the much younger Bullen, running to black leather and chrome, with turquoise and pink accents.

"Mr. Tardivel," said Abraham Danielson, with no warmth in his thin, accented voice. "Now, what's all this nonsense?"

"I see you recognized the name Maria Dudek," said Pierre, slowly taking a seat in front of Danielson's desk.

"That name meant nothing to me."

"Then why did you agree to see me?"

"You're a stockholder; I recognize you from that shameful bit of grandstanding you did at our meeting. Still, I always make time for my stockholders."

"I've been here once before," said Pierre. "Oh, not to this room, but to this floor. I had a meeting a while ago with Craig Bullen. But I had the wrong person then—the puppet instead of the puppeteer."

"I honestly don't know what you're talking about."

"And it's not just being Ivan Marchenko that I've got you on—not that that isn't bad enough. I know you're also the leader of the Millennial Reich. You've done more than just discriminate against people who have genetic disorders. You're increasing your bottom line by killing off those who would otherwise represent expensive payouts for you, the single largest stockholder in this company."

Danielson looked at Pierre, his expression blank. "You're crazy," he said at last.

Pierre said nothing. His hands danced.

Danielson spread his arms. "You suffer from Huntington's chorea, isn't that right? Huntington's is a degenerative nervous disorder that has a profound effect on the faculties. Whatever you think you know is doubtless just a product of your disease."

Pierre frowned. "Is it, now? I've been doing a lot of research, looking at unsolved murders in the last few years. A disproportionate number of those who died had genetic disorders, or were waiting for expensive medical treatments. And most of that subset were insured by Condor. And I know you routinely take secret skin-cell samples from new policyholders. If someone you insured has bad DNA, or applies for an expensive treatment, you have them killed."

"Come, come, Mr. Tardivel. What you're proposing is monstrous, and I assure you I am not a monster."

"No?" said Pierre. "What exactly did you do during World War II?"

"Not that it's any of your business, but I was a minor Red Army soldier in the Ukraine."

"Bullshit," said Pierre. He let the word hang between them for several seconds. "Your real name is Ivan Marchenko. You were trained at Trawniki and then stationed at Treblinka."

"'Ivan Marchenko,'" said Danielson, pronouncing each syllable with care. "Again, that's an unfamiliar name."

"Is it, now? And I suppose you don't know the name Ivan Grozny, either."

"Ivan—Ivan the Terrible that would be, wouldn't it? Wasn't he the first czar of Russia?" Danielson's face was composed.

"Ivan the Terrible was a gas-chamber operator at the Treblinka death camp in Poland where eight hundred and seventy thousand people were killed."

"That has nothing to do with me."

"There are eyewitnesses."

"To events that took place half a century ago? Come now."

"I can prove both charges against you—the insurance-related

murders, and that you are Ivan. The question is, which one do you want to admit to? Do you fancy your chances are better here in a California court, or in Israel in a war-crimes trial?"

"You're crazy."

"You've said that before."

"Any good defense attorney could make mincemeat of someone with a brain disorder on the witness stand."

Pierre shrugged. "Well, if my story doesn't interest you, I'll take it to the newspapers. I know Barnaby Lincoln at the *Chronicle.*" He started the slow process of getting out of his chair.

Danielson's eyes narrowed. "What do you want?"

Pierre lowered himself back down. "Ah, now that's more like it. What I want, Ivan, is five million dollars—enough to look after my wife and daughter after my Huntington's disease finally takes me."

"That's a lot of money."

"It will buy my silence."

"If I'm the monster you believe I am, what makes you think you could possibly get away with blackmailing me? If I've killed as many people as you say, surely I'd not stop at killing you?" He paused and then looked directly at Pierre. "Or your wife and child."

For once, Pierre was glad of his chorea; it masked the fact that he was trembling with fear. "I've taken precautions. The information is in the hands of people I trust, both here in the States and in Canada—people you will never find. If anything happens to me or my family, they have instructions to make it public."

Danielson was quiet for a long time. Finally, he said, "I'm not a man who likes to be cornered."

Pierre said nothing.

The old man was silent a while longer. Then, finally: "Give me a week to get it ready, and—"

Just then, the door to the office burst open. A husky uniformed security guard entered. Danielson rose to his feet. "What is it?"

"Forgive the interruption, sir, but we've detected a transmitter in this room."

Danielson's eyes narrowed. "Search him," he snapped. And then, loudly, as if to make sure it was part of the official record, "I admitted nothing. I merely humored a mentally deficient person."

The guard grabbed Pierre under the left shoulder, hoisted him from the chair, and began roughly patting down his clothes. In a matter of moments, he found the small radio microphone clipped to the inside of Pierre's shirt. He tore it loose and held it up for Danielson to see.

Pierre tried to sound brave. "It doesn't matter. There are seven assorted cops and government agents waiting outside the building to take you in for questioning, and we have two positive IDs of you from Treblinka survivors—"

Danielson thumped his fist on his desktop. At first Pierre thought it was a gesture of frustration, but a small section of the desktop popped up at an angle, revealing a hidden control console within. Danielson tapped a series of buttons, and suddenly a thin metal wall dropped down from the ceiling, slicing right in front of Pierre's kneecaps. If his feet hadn't just then been moving backward because of the chorea, they would have been sheared off.

The guard looked dumbfounded—either he hadn't known about this secret wall or had never expected to see it actually in use. Pierre was agog, too—but Marchenko/Danielson was a multimillionaire fugitive who had been preparing for all eventualities for five decades. Doubtless there was a secret exit in the part of the office he was still in.

"Come along, pal," said the guard, pocketing the microphone and again grabbing Pierre roughly by the arm. He propelled Pierre out of Danielson's office, through the astonished secretary's office, through the antechamber, and out into the elevator lobby. The man stabbed at the elevator call switch, but the little square of plastic didn't light up. He tried again, then cursed. Marchenko must have shut off the elevators to slow down the OSI agents from getting up here. It would take them a while to climb thirty-seven floors, even if they could get into the building past Marchenko's security people.

The beefy guard let go of Pierre, who, without his cane, which was still back in Marchenko's office, promptly crumpled to the ground. The guard looked at him, a sneer of disgust across his face. "Christ, you're a fucking crip, ain't you?" he said. He looked at the closed elevator doors again, as if thinking, then back at Pierre. "Suppose you can't do any harm if I leave you up here." He headed around the corner. Pierre could hear a door opening and the sound of the big man's feet slapping against stairs as he headed down, presumably to the lobby to join in defending the building's entrance.

Pierre was all alone in the elevator lobby. He looked up, though, and could see Marchenko's secretary through the glass doors of the antechamber and the outer office. She was looking at him, as if unsure what to do. He reached out a hand toward her. She got up, turned her back on him, and disappeared into the inner office. Pierre exhaled. He wished he could just lie there without moving, but his legs were dancing incessantly and his head was bobbing left and right.

The woman reappeared—and she was holding Pierre's cane! She came out to him and helped him to his feet. "I don't know what's wrong with you," she said, "but no one should treat a person the way they're treating you."

Pierre took the cane and leaned on it. *"Merci,"* he said.

"What's going on?" she asked. "What happened to Mr. Danielson?"

"Did you know about that emergency wall?"

She shook her head. "I was terrified when I heard it crash down. I thought we were having another quake."

"There may be men with guns coming into the building," said Pierre. "You should get off this floor. Go down a few floors and find someplace to hide."

She looked at him, overwhelmed by it all. "Are you going to be okay?"

He tried to shrug, but the gesture was lost amid the chorea. "This is as good as I get." He flapped an arm toward the stairwell. "Go on, get yourself somewhere safe."

She nodded and disappeared around the corner. Pierre wasn't sure what to do next. He decided to hobble over to the secretary's desk. He picked up the phone, but it, too, was dead.

Pierre tried to imagine the scene below, the agents and cops storming in the front door, badges flashing—surely they would have started in upon hearing that the microphone had been discovered. They'd be trying to make their way past guards who might well have drawn their pistols. Pierre remembered what this building looked like more from when he'd last seen it, at the shareholders' meeting, than from today. He'd been so nervous preparing for this confrontation that he hadn't really looked at it as he'd driven in this time. A tall building, all glass and steel, with a helicopter landing on its roof...

Sweet Jesus—a *helicopter.* Marchenko wasn't working his way down to the ground floor; he'd probably already gone up to the roof, three stories above.

Pierre hobbled around the corner. The door to the stairs was clearly marked, next to the men's and women's bathrooms. He pushed it open and felt cold air rushing over him. The interior of the stairwell was naked concrete, with steps painted flat gray. He began slowly, painfully, making his way up the first flight. Each flight covered a half floor—there would be at least six before he reached the roof.

His cane was unnecessary as he pulled himself up using the banister, but he didn't dare let it go, and so it twirled, Charlie Chaplin-esque, as he held it in his free palsied hand.

He could hear faint echoes of footfalls far, far below. Others were using the stairs to try to climb up. But thirty-seven flights—even for a young man, that was a lot of potential energy. He pulled himself higher and higher, turning around now as one flight of stairs gave way to the next. He hoped Avi would also figure out that Marchenko had gone up, not down.

Pierre continued his ascent. His lungs were pumping and his breath came in shuddering wheezes. His heart jumped at the sound of a gunshot from far, far below.

Pierre was rounding the thirty-ninth floor now—the number had been crudely stenciled in black paint on the back of the gray metal fire door. For a brief moment he cursed his Canadian upbringing: it had never even occurred to him to ask Avi for a gun before going in.

Pierre grabbed the handrail and hauled himself up some more, but suddenly he tripped—his leg had moved left when he'd told it to go forward. His cane pushed out sideways, wedging between two of the vertical metal rods that supported the banister. Pierre fell backward, grabbing onto the cane for support. There was a cracking sound as that one point in the middle of the cane's shaft took all of Pierre's weight for a second, but then Pierre lost his grip and found himself tumbling down to the bottom of the current flight. His left elbow smashed into the concrete floor. The pain was excruciating. He reached his right hand over to touch the elbow, and it came away with freckles of blood on it. His cane had landed about two meters away. He crawled over to it and then fought to bring himself to his feet. He stood, unable to go on, waiting for his lungs to stop gulping in air. Finally, with an enormous effort, he started up the stairs again.

Up one half-flight, around the corner, then up another. He was now opposite the door labeled "40." But—dammit, he wasn't thinking straight—the heliport was on the roof, another two staircases above him. And all his efforts were predicated on the assumption that there was an exit to the roof at the top. If not, he'd have to come back down to the fortieth floor and try to find the correct way up to the helipad.

He yanked himself up, step after agonizing step. The footfalls below sounded closer; the Justice agents had perhaps made it as high as the twentieth floor by now.

Finally Pierre reached the top. There was a door here, painted blue instead of gray, with the word "ROOF" stenciled on it. Pierre turned the knob, then pushed on it, and the door swung outward, revealing the wide concrete top of the Condor Health Insurance Tower. After all that time in the dim stairwell, the late-afternoon sunlight, positioned directly in front of him, pierced his eyes. Pierre held on to the doorjamb for support. High winds whipped by him, their sound masking that of the door opening.

Marchenko was standing about twenty meters away, his back to Pierre, waiting by a small green-and-white metal shed that presumably held tools for helicopter maintenance. There was no helicopter in sight, but the rooftop near Marchenko was painted with a circular yellow landing target, and the old man was impatiently watching the skies.

The wind shrieked as it went down the stairwell. Pierre stepped out. The rooftop was square, with a meter-high lip around its edges. Gulls were perched in a neat row along the southern lip. Nearby were two cement enclosures, presumably housing the elevator equipment. Three small and two large satellite dishes sat at one corner of the roof and a microwave relay jutted up from another. There was a rotating red light mounted on top of one of the elevator houses, and two searchlights, both off, on top of the other.

Marchenko hadn't noticed Pierre's arrival yet. The old man was holding a cellular phone at his side in his left hand—doubtless he'd used that to call for a chopper to come and get him.

Pierre tried to assess his chances. He was thirty-five, for God's sake. Marchenko was eighty-seven. There should be no contest. Pierre should be able to simply walk up to the old geezer and haul him back downstairs into the arms of justice.

But now—now, who could say? Pierre leaned on his cane. There was a good chance that Marchenko could kill him—especially if he was armed. There was no indication that he had a gun, and, indeed, a lead pipe had been Ivan Grozny's favorite weapon half a century ago. But even unarmed, Marchenko might well be able to take Pierre.

Maybe he didn't have to do anything. He looked up, scanned the sky again. There was no sign of an approaching copter. Avi's agents would be up here soon enough, and—

"You!" Marchenko had turned around and spotted Pierre. His shout startled the gulls into flight; their cries were faintly audible above the whipping wind. The old man started moving toward Pierre with a slow and ancient gait. Pierre realized he should move away from the open door leading to the stairwell. All it would take for Marchenko to defeat him would be a good, swift shove down the stairs.

Pierre hobbled to the north. Marchenko changed course and continued to close the distance. Pierre thought of the *Pequod* and Moby Dick, wallowing in high waves, each ponderously maneuvering around the other. Marchenko continued to circle in.

He tasks me, thought Pierre, *and I shall have him.* With an Ahab-like gait, his cane substituting for the peg leg, Pierre moved forward as quickly as he could. He knew that retreating would be stupid. If he allowed himself to be backed up against the meter-high wall around the edge of the roof, Marchenko would have little trouble pushing him over the side to plummet forty stories to a splattering death. Pierre moved toward the center of the roof, wind whipping his hair, cutting through him with fingers of ice.

Marchenko's broad face was contorted in fury—not just at him, Pierre guessed, but also at whomever he had called to come and get him. There was still no sign of an approaching chopper, although several jet contrails crisscrossed the sky, like lash marks on a prisoner's back.

Just five meters separated them now. Marchenko's bald head glistened with a sheen of sweat, looking, in the ruddy late-afternoon light, almost like a film of blood. The climb up the stairs had been hard on him, too; whatever secret exit he'd had from his office had apparently given him access to the stairwell rather than the elevator lobby.

Marchenko stretched his arms out, as if he expected Pierre to try to slip past him. Pierre wanted to lift his cane high enough to use it as a weapon—something he could only do, he realized, if he were backed up for support against the toolshed or elevator houses. He started crabbing sidewise, moving toward the closest of the concrete structures.

Marchenko narrowed the distance between them. He was still holding the phone in his left hand, but swung out with his right. His fist hit Pierre on the shoulder, but it wasn't hard enough to really hurt.

Marchenko apparently realized that; his right hand dug into his hip pocket and came out with a set of keys, which he proceeded to intertwine between his skeletal fingers—just as Pierre had done more than two years before when Marchenko's henchman, Chuck Hanratty, had tried to kill him.

They were now about three meters from the elevator house. Pierre thought he heard another gunshot coming from the still-open door to the stairs. The OSI men were apparently being held at bay by security guards on one of the upper levels. Still, Avi would have doubtless called for reinforcements by now.

Pierre got his back against the elevator house's wall. He lifted his cane high and smashed it down as hard as he could. He'd been aiming for the top of Marchenko's head, but his arm had shaken coming down and the impact had been on Marchenko's right shoulder instead. There was a loud cracking sound. Pierre hoped it was Marchenko's scapula, but it turned out to be the cane. As Pierre pulled it back, he saw that it was partially broken in the middle, at the point that had taken the brunt of his weight during his earlier tumble down the stairs. Still, the impact had knocked the cellular phone from Marchenko's gnarled hand. It hit the concrete and its black battery pack popped loose.

More gunshots in the background. Pierre looked beyond Marchenko and now saw a helicopter on the horizon, but it was impossible to tell if it was coming toward them. Marchenko started to back away. He was unaware of the copter, but apparently realized he was putting himself at a disadvantage by letting Pierre have both hands free.

"Come on, you piece of shit," taunted Marchenko in his reedy, accented voice. "Come and get me, you fucking piece of shit." He swiped his hand out, the keys glinting in the sunlight. "Come on, you—"

"'*Morceau de merde,*'" supplied Pierre, pushing off the elevator house's wall with his left hand and leaning onto his damaged cane, hoping it would continue to support him as long as he only put pressure straight down on it.

Marchenko was dancing backward now, baiting Pierre closer to—to the toolshed, it looked like, where the old man could probably find a better weapon than a set of keys. Pierre hoped Marchenko would trip as he walked backward. Pierre might not be able to club him into submission, but he still outweighed the geriatric by at least ten kilos. Just sitting on him might be enough to subdue him.

Marchenko looked behind him to make sure the way was clear, and saw the helicopter, now only a couple of kilometers away. Pierre stole a glance behind himself, too, but there was no sign of anyone emerging from the stairwell.

They continued creeping across the roof, wind slapping them like invisible hands. Finally, gathering all his strength, Pierre jumped forward. It wasn't much of a jump, but he did succeed in slamming into Marchenko's chest, and the old man tumbled backward onto the hard concrete. Pierre straddled Marchenko. The hand with the keys lashed out, and Pierre felt them biting into his cheek. He arched his back and tried a roundhouse punch aimed at Marchenko's face. It connected, and there was a cracking sound. Marchenko's mouth opened to yowl in pain, and Pierre saw that his top teeth were all off-kilter—Pierre's punch had knocked his upper denture loose.

Pierre tried to swing again, but this time he missed and the movement threw him off-balance, allowing Marchenko to push him off and struggle to his feet. Pierre could see that the back of Marchenko's bald head was scraped raw from where it had hit the concrete.

Marchenko hobbled to the toolshed. It had a padlock on its door, but one of the now bloody keys in his hand unlocked it. Pierre, lying on his back, fought to catch his breath and struggled to bring his legs, which were dancing wildly, under control. Marchenko ducked into the shed and emerged a moment later holding a long black crowbar, presumably used to open crates shipped by helicopter. He came over to stand above Pierre.

"Before you die," said Marchenko, as he raised the crowbar above his head, "I have to know. Are you a Jew?"

Pierre shook his head slightly.

Marchenko sounded sad. "Too bad. It would have made this perfect." He swung the crowbar down. Pierre rolled aside just in time, the crowbar's splayed end taking a divot out of the roof.

The sound of the helicopter was now quite clear above the wind. Pierre glanced at it. It wasn't the same yellow-and-black chopper he'd seen all those months ago. No, this seemed to be a private, civilian bird, all silver and white. Marchenko had probably called for one of his Millennial Reich cronies to come rescue him.

The old man swung the crowbar again. Pierre rolled to the right; the crowbar sparked against the concrete. Pierre rolled onto his back again, and, praying he could maintain a steady grip, lifted his cane high. But Marchenko parried with the crowbar, and the wooden stick split in two, one part pinwheeling high into the sky.

Marchenko brought the crowbar down in a gillooly on Pierre's knees. He screamed as his left kneecap shattered. Marchenko lifted the crowbar again, this time trying to bring it down on Pierre's head. Pierre squirmed on the ground. His arm reached out, undulating like a snake, and locked onto Marchenko's ankle, yanking the old man down, the crowbar landing with a cracking of brittle ribs on Marchenko's side.

Pierre looked up. The copter was now hovering over the scene, preparing to land, its rotor kicking up grit and debris on the rooftop. The man in the right seat, flying the helicopter—Christ, he was even wearing the same aviator's jacket and mirrored shades as on *Hard Copy*. Felix Sousa. The fucking guy wasn't just a Nazi in his thinking; he was an actual card-carrying member of Ivan Marchenko's Millennial Reich.

The copter was descending now, the wind from its rotor slicing into them. Pierre hoped its downward force would keep Marchenko pinned to the ground, but the old man was soon scrabbling to his feet. The copter touched down.

Pierre glanced back. Another helicopter was approaching. It was hard to see anything in all this wind, but—way to go, Avi! The new copter was clearly marked SFPD—San Francisco Police Department.

Marchenko loomed over Pierre, clearly wanting to finish him off, but Sousa was gesturing frantically for him to hurry up and get aboard his copter; the police helicopter would be there within minutes. Marchenko's round head split in a horrible, lopsided grin, his denture still askew, and he spit a contemptuous bloody gob onto Pierre's face. He then hobbled, holding his cracked ribs, toward the copter, bending low to clear its rotor, which was still revolving counterclockwise at a reduced speed.

Suddenly Avi Meyer appeared at the top of the stairs. He was panting horribly and red as a beet after climbing forty stories. He reached into his jacket, pulled out a gun, and tried to shoot at Sousa's copter. But Marchenko was already aboard, pulling the curving door shut, and the copter was lifting up off the roof.

The SFPD helicopter had closed the distance, though, and was now trying to force Marchenko and Sousa to land by flying directly above them, the downward wind sending grit flying everywhere. Sousa pulled his copter to the north, and it moved sideways a few meters above the rooftop, its body tilted to the side, its rotor barely clearing the lip around the edge of the roof. The police helicopter followed.

Pierre squinted, trying to watch but also trying to shield his eyes. Avi moved out of the stairwell entrance, and two of his men appeared behind him, also gulping for breath. One was holding his side and grimacing in agony. After a moment, Avi staggered to the south edge of the roof, as far from the noise of the helicopters as possible, and pulled out his cellular.

Pierre, meanwhile, picked up the crowbar and, using it as a short cane, keeping all weight off his destroyed left knee, hobbled over to the north edge, the pain almost unbearable, fighting nausea and dizziness with every step. When he got to the meter-high lip around the roof, he collapsed against it and brought both hands to his knee. He could hear the pounding of the helicopter blades, out of sight below him, next to the building.

"This is the police," said a female voice from a bullhorn on the second copter; the voice was all but lost in the noise from the dueling rotors. "You are ordered to land."

Pierre forced himself to his feet, using the lip to support himself. He almost blacked out from the pain; his body shook with agony and chorea. Looking down was dizzying: forty stories of sheer glass, leading straight to the asphalt parking lot. Five SFPD squad cars were pulling up outside the building, sirens blaring. A few meters to Pierre's right, and about ten meters below, was the silver copter with Marchenko and Sousa in it. Marchenko could probably see directly into Craig Bullen's office, with its redwood paneling and priceless paintings.

The cockpit was only a short distance away from the side of the tower. The SFPD copter had moved alongside it now, as if trying to get a bead for a shoot-out. Pierre could clearly see the female pilot and her male companion, both uniformed, in the bubblelike cockpit. They seemed to be arguing with each other, and then the police copter started moving away, whichever one of them who felt flying this close to the building was dangerous having won the fight.

The rotor on Sousa's copter was a circular blur below Pierre. The noise was deafening, but it would be only a matter of seconds before Sousa would head away from the building. He could make a beeline out into the Pacific, out over international waters, beyond the SFPD's—or even the DOJ's—jurisdiction, perhaps landing on a boat and sailing down to Mexico or beyond; surely there was more to Marchenko's escape plan than just the helicopter.

Pierre hefted the crowbar, gauging its weight. It probably wouldn't work—probably would just be deflected away. But he wasn't about to stand by and do nothing—

Pierre closed his eyes, summoning all the control and all the strength he had left. And then he threw the crowbar as hard as he could, spinning it vertically end over end, down into the helicopter's twirling blades, aiming for the outer edge of the rotor disk.

He was prepared to stagger back, in case the crowbar was sent flying up toward him.

It hit with a horrible clanging sound. The helicopter began vibrating, tipping toward the building, and—

—the blades touched glass, sending a shower of sparkling shards down toward the ground below—

—and then the blades began slicing through the metal frame of the curtain wall between two windows, dicing the metal into small fragments, sparks flying everywhere as each successive pass brought the blades into contact at a slightly different angle.

The copter was traveling forward now, and the rotor disk hit the wall between adjacent offices, the tips of the blades splintering the redwood paneling with a buzz-saw sound, then digging into the concrete firewall behind. The tips of the rotor were immediately ground off, and more and more of them sheared away with each revolution, the blades shortening, metal bits flying like confetti.

Then the jagged edge of the rotor dug into the concrete, sending powdery chunks of it airborne until, with a shriek of tortured metal, the rotor came to a dead halt.

The copter tipped forward again, the bird itself now rotating slowly clockwise, its tail rotor swinging into the side of the building, more windows shattering and office furniture splintering.

The copter's turbines were screaming; smoke poured from the engine compartment and flames shot from the exhausts. The cockpit tipped forward, and the whole vehicle began to drop, story after story after story. Pierre could see people far below scattering, trying to get out of its way.

Pierre heard footfalls, all but drowned out by the thunder of the police copter. Avi was running across the rooftop.

Sousa's chopper continued to fall, almost as if in slow motion, its foreshortened blades now revolving lamely, providing a small amount of lift. It passed floor after floor, diminishing in apparent size, until—

Hitting the pavement like an egg, metal and glass splashing everywhere—

—and then, like a flower opening, flames expanding outward

from the crash as the copter's fuel exploded. Soon a pillar of black smoke rose up to the fortieth floor and beyond.

The SFPD copter circled around, surveying the scene, then descended for a landing in the far parking lot.

Pierre looked down at the inferno below, ringed by spectators, illuminated by low, red sunlight and roaring flames reflecting off the windows, and by revolving lights on the police cars. At long, long last, Ivan Grozny was dead.

Pierre staggered back a step, turned around, and collapsed in agony against the short wall around the roof's edge.

"Are you okay?" asked Avi, leaning in to look at him after seeing his fill of the carnage below.

Pierre's hands were on his shattered knee again. The pain was incredible, like daggers being jackhammered into his leg. Wincing, he shook his head.

Avi flipped open his cellular phone. "Meyer here. We need medics on the roof right away."

Another OSI agent appeared from the stairwell—but this one wasn't out of breath. He jogged over to Avi and Pierre. "We've got one of the elevators working again," he said. "They were all locked off on the fortieth floor, but with the fireman's key we were able to reactivate one of them once we pried its door open."

"What happened?" asked Avi.

The agent glanced briefly at Pierre, then looked back at Avi. "It seems a crowbar was dropped from up here into the blades of the helicopter. It caused it to crash."

Avi nodded and then waved the agent away. When they were alone, he leaned in to Pierre, holding Pierre's shoulders with his arms. "Did you drop the crowbar?"

Pierre said nothing.

Avi exhaled. "Dammit, Pierre—we don't cut corners in the OSI. Not anymore. Danielson hadn't even been charged yet."

Pierre shrugged slightly. "'Justice,'" he said, his breath coming out raggedly as he quoted another Nobel laureate—at that precise moment, he couldn't remember which one—"'is always delayed and finally done only by mistake.'" He took his right hand off his knee and held it up in the air. Although they were sheltered from the wind here by the low wall, his arm moved back and forth as if blown by a breeze only it could feel. "Blame it," said Pierre, "on my Huntington's."

Avi's eyes narrowed and then he nodded, turned, and leaned back against the wall, exhausted not just by the climb but also by years of chasing Ivans and Adolphs and Heinrichs. He closed his eyes and exhaled slowly, waiting for the medics to arrive.

42

As soon as visiting hours began, Molly came into Pierre's room at San Francisco General Hospital. Pierre looked up at her from the bed. The left side of his face was bandaged, and his legs were in traction.

"Hi, honey," said Molly.

"Hi, sweetheart," said Pierre. He gestured at all the equipment hooked up to him. "After you left yesterday, somebody said my total hospital bill is going to be in the neighborhood of two hundred thousand dollars." He managed a grin. "I'm sure glad Tiffany talked me into the Gold Plan."

"I brought you a newspaper," said Molly, pulling a copy of the *San Francisco Chronicle* out of the canvas bag she was carrying.

"Thanks, but I don't feel much like reading."

Molly said, "Then let me read it to you. There's a front-page story by that man we met, Barnaby Lincoln."

"Really?"

"Uh-huh." She cleared her throat. "'Officials from the California State Insurance Board, escorted by eight state troopers, today seized control of Condor Health Insurance, Inc., of San Francisco, in the wake of startling revelations made last week. "Condor is out of business, as of today," said Clark Finchurst, State Insurance Commissioner. "The industry's emergency fund, which was established to handle such things, will take care of current claims until Condor's policies can be handed over in an orderly fashion to other insurers." '"

"All right!" said Pierre.

"It says there's going to be a full inquiry. Craig Bullen is cooperating with the authorities."

"Good for him."

"Oh, and I picked up that printout you wanted." She took a two-inch-thick pile of fanfold computer paper out of her bag and placed it on the table beside his bed.

"Thanks," said Pierre.

Molly sat down on the edge of the bed and took one of Pierre's dancing hands in hers. "I love you," she said.

"And I love you, too," said Pierre, squeezing her hand. "I love you more than words can say."

Pierre lay in his hospital bed that night. His six minutes of CPU time on LBNL's Cray supercomputer had at last become available, and the simulation he and Shari had coded had finally been run. Pierre started wading through the 384 pages of printout.

When he was done, he operated the hand control that lowered the motorized back of his bed. He stared at the ceiling.

It made sense. It all fit.

The existence of codon synonyms did indeed allow additional information to be superimposed on the standard A, C, G, T genetic code. Yes, AAA and AAG both made lysine, but the AAA form also coded a zero into what Shari had already dubbed, in a note jotted in the margin, "the gatekeeper function," which governed the correction or invocation of frameshift mutations. Meanwhile, the AAG version coded a one.

But that was just the tip of the iceberg. There were four valid codons that made proline: CCA, CCC, CCG, and CCT. For these, the final letter indicated a base-sixteen order of magnitude shift of the splicing cursor, which marked the position where a nucleotide would be added or deleted from the DNA, causing a frameshift. The CCT form moved the cursor sixteen nucleotides; the CCC form moved it 16^2, or 256 nucleotides; the CCA form 16^3, or 4,096 nucleotides; and the CCG form moved it 16^4, or 65,536 nucleotides.

Other synonyms performed different jobs: GAA and GAG both made glutamine, but they also set the direction of the splicing cursor's movement. GAG set it moving to the "left" (in the direction leading from the three-prime carbon to the five-prime carbon in each deoxyribose), and GAA set it moving to the "right" (the five-prime to three-prime direction). Meanwhile, TTT, which made phenylalanine, coded for a nucleotide insertion, while its synonym TTC was the instruction for a nucleotide deletion. And the four codons that made threonine—ACA, ACC, ACG, and ACT—indicated by their final letter which nucleotide would be inserted at the splicing cursor.

The coding based on synonyms moved the cursor, but the timing of when frameshifts would be invoked was governed by certain of the seemingly endless stuttering sequences in the junk DNA. On the smaller scale of the individual, it had already been demonstrated that the number of CAG stutters set the age at which Huntington's would first manifest itself, and, as Pierre had pointed out to Molly, the number of repeats does change from generation to generation in a phenomenon called "anticipation"—an ironically prophetic name given what Pierre and Shari's model showed.

Indeed, the computer simulation suggested promising lines of research into manipulating genetic timers—research that ultimately might cure Huntington's and related ailments. Certainly, no sudden breakthrough was likely, but, at a guess, inside a decade, controlling individual aberrant genetic timers might be possible. It had come full circle: by deliberately choosing not to pursue Huntington's research, Pierre might have, in fact, made the discovery that would eventually lead to a cure for the disease.

If that had been all that his research suggested, he might have been pleased intellectually, but still profoundly sad, crushed by the cruel irony: after all, anything but an immediate cure would be too late to help Pierre Jacques Tardivel.

But Pierre didn't feel sadness. On the contrary, he was elated, for the genetic timers pointed to something beyond his personal problems, beyond the problems—however real, however poignant—of the one in ten thousand people who had Huntington's. The timers pointed to a truth, a fundamental revelation, that affected every one of the five billion human beings now alive, every one of the billions who had come before, and every one of all the untold trillions of humans yet to be born.

According to the simulation, the DNA timers, incrementing generation by generation through genetic anticipation, could go off across whole populations almost simultaneously. The multiregionalists were more right than they'd ever guessed: Pierre's research proved that preprogrammed evolutionary steps could take place across vast groups of beings all at once.

A quote came to Pierre, from—of course—a Nobel laureate. The French philosopher Henri Bergson had written in his 1907 work *Creative Evolution* that "the present contains nothing more than the past, and what is found in the effect was already in the cause." The junk DNA *was* a language, just as that article Shari had found had suggested: the language in which the master plan for life had been written by its designer. Pierre's heart was pounding with excitement, and adrenaline was coursing through his system, but finally he drifted off to sleep, the printout still resting on his chest, dreaming of the hand of God.

Molly pushed the office door open and barged in. "Dr. Klimus, I—"

"Molly, I'm very busy—"

"Too busy to talk about Myra Tottenham?"

Klimus looked up. Somebody else was passing by in the corridor. "Close the door."

Molly did so and sat down. "Shari Cohen and I have just spent a day at Stanford going through Myra's papers; they've got stacks of them in their archives."

Klimus managed a weak grin. "Universities love paper."

"Indeed they do. Myra Tottenham was working on ways to speed up nucleotide sequencing when she died."

"Was she?" said Klimus. "I really don't know what this has to do—"

"It has everything to do with you, Burian. Her technique—involving specialized restriction enzymes—was years ahead of what others were doing."

"What does a psychologist possibly know about DNA research?"

"Not much. But Shari tells me that what she was doing was close to what we now call the Klimus Technique—the very same technique for which you won the Nobel Prize. We looked through your old papers at Stanford, too. You were flailing about in completely the wrong direction, trying to use direct ion-charging of nucleotides as a sorting technique—"

"It would have worked—"

"—Would have worked in a universe where free hydrogen didn't bond to everything in sight. But here it was a blind alley—a blind alley you didn't abandon until just after Myra Tottenham died."

There was a long, long pause. Finally: "The Nobel committee is very reluctant to award prizes posthumously," said Klimus, as if that justified everything.

Molly crossed her arms in front of her chest. "I want your notebooks on Amanda. And I want your word that you will never try to see her again."

"Ms. Bond—"

"Amanda is my daughter—mine and Pierre's. In every way that matters, that's the whole and complete truth. You will never bother us again."

"But—"

"No buts. Give me the notebooks now."

"I—I need some time to get them all together."

"Time to photocopy them, you mean. Not on your life. I'll go with you wherever you want in order to get them, but I'm not letting you out of my sight until I've found and burned them all."

Klimus sat still for several seconds, thinking. The only sound was the soft whir of an electric clock. "You are one hard bitch," he said at last, opening his lower-left desk drawer and pulling out a dozen small spiral-bound notebooks.

"No, I'm not," said Molly, gathering them up. "I'm simply my daughter's mother."

Four months had passed. As she walked slowly across the lab, Shari Cohen looked like she'd rather be anywhere else in the world. Pierre was sitting on a lab stool. "Pierre," she said, "I—I don't know how to tell you this, but your most recent test results are ..." She looked away. "I'm sorry, Pierre, but they're wrong."

Pierre lifted a shaking arm. "Wrong?"

"You botched the fractionation. I'm afraid I'm going to have to redo it."

Pierre nodded. "I'm sorry. I—I get confused sometimes."

Shari nodded as well. Her upper lip was trembling. "I know." She was quiet for a long, long time. Then: "Maybe it's time, Pierre, for you—"

"No." He said it as firmly as he could. He held his trembling hands out in front of him, as if to ward off her words. "No, don't ask me to stop coming into the lab." He exhaled in a long, shuddery sigh. "Maybe you're right—maybe I can't do the complex stuff anymore. But you have to let me help."

"I can carry on our work," Shari said. "I can finish our paper." She smiled. Their paper would blow people's socks off. "They'll remember you, Pierre—not just in the same breath as Crick and Watson, but as Darwin, too. He told us where we came from, and you've told us where we're going."

She paused, contemplating. Pierre's most recent discovery—probably, it was sad to say, his *final* discovery—was the DNA sequence that apparently governed the lowering of the hyoid bone in the throat, a sequence that was shifted out in Hapless Hannah's DNA, but shifted in within that of *Homo sapiens sapiens.* And he'd shown Shari a DNA sample with the telepathic frameshift shifted in, although she didn't know to whom it belonged, and only half believed Pierre's assertions about what it was for.

Pierre looked around the lab helplessly. "There must be something I can do. Wash beakers, sort files—something."

Shari looked over at the garbage pail, where the broken glass from a flask Pierre had dropped earlier in the day was resting. "You've given so much time to the project," she said. "But—well, I know you're the one who is supposed to quote the Nobel laureates, but didn't Woodrow Wilson say, 'I not only use all the brains I have, but all that I can borrow.' You can borrow mine; I'll carry on for both of us. It's time for you to relax. Spend some time with your wife and daughter."

Pierre felt his eyes stinging. He'd known this day would come, but this was too soon—much too soon.

There was an awkward moment between them, and Pierre was reminded of that afternoon three and a half years earlier when he'd ended up holding Shari as she cried over the breakup of her engagement. She perhaps recognized the similarity, too, for, with a small smile, she moved closer and lightly wrapped her arms around him, not squeezing tightly, not constricting his body's rhythmic dance.

"You *will* be remembered, Pierre," she said. "You know that. You'll be remembered forever for what you discovered here."

Pierre nodded, trying to take comfort in the words, but soon tears were rolling down his cheeks.

"Don't cry," said Shari softly. "Don't cry."

He looked up at her and shook his head. "I know we did good work here," he said, "but ..."

She brushed his hair off his forehead. "But what?"

"Bits and pieces," he said. "I can understand bits and pieces of it. But the big picture—the nucleotides, the enzymes, the reactions, the gene sequences ..." He reached up with a trembling hand and wiped his cheek. "I don't remember it all, and what I do remember, I don't understand anymore."

Shari stroked his shoulder.

"It doesn't matter," she said. "You did the work. You made the discoveries. I can finish it up from here."

Pierre looked up at her. "But what am I going to do now? I—I don't know how to do anything except be a geneticist."

Shari spoke softly. "There was another phone message for you from Barnaby Lincoln at the *Chronicle.* Why not give him a call?"

43

Eighteen Months Later

Pierre was busy these days. Barnaby Lincoln was right—lobbying *was* satisfying work. And who knew? Someday it might even bear fruit. Meanwhile, Shari had finished up their jointly authored paper—"An intronic DNA mechanism for invoking frameshift mutations as a driving force in evolution"—and submitted it to *Nature.*

But today was a day off from worrying about what the journal's referees were going to make of the paper, a day off from working the phones and dictating letters.

They couldn't just go to the portrait studio at Sears; taking pictures of the Tardivel-Bond family was a little more complicated than that. Pierre had good moments and bad, and they had to wait more than an hour for him to have enough control to sit reasonably still. And Amanda—well, at three years of age, she was doing better dealing with other people, but it was still easier to keep her away from well-meaning but stupid adults who constantly said the wrong things, thinking that because she didn't talk she also couldn't hear.

Molly had helped Pierre put on his clothes, as she did every day now. At first she'd thought about having him dress up in a suit and tie, all formal and staid, but that wasn't Pierre, and she wanted to remember him the way he really was. Instead, she helped him put on the red Montreal Canadiens hockey jersey he was so fond of.

For her part, Molly did dress a little more fancily than she normally would, wearing a powder blue silk top and a stylish black skirt. She even put on some lipstick and eye shadow.

They'd borrowed the elaborate camera and tripod from the university. Two chairs were set up in front of the fireplace, and Molly carefully framed the shot.

Amanda was in a lovely pink dress with small flowers on it. Molly had toyed with fighting the stereotype, but for today, at least, she wanted her daughter to look just like any other little girl. Sometimes such things *did* matter.

Finally, Pierre said, "I think ... I'm ready."

Molly smiled and helped him into one of the chairs. His right forearm was moving a little bit, but once he was settled in, Pierre moved his left hand over it, holding it steady. Molly sat down, smoothed out her clothes, and signed for Amanda to come and sit in her lap. She did so, enjoying flouncing across the room in her skirt.

Molly kissed her forehead, and Amanda grinned. In her left hand Molly held the remote control for the camera. She pointed a finger at the lens and told Amanda to look into it and smile.

Pierre lifted his left hand from his right arm and he, too, smiled when he saw that it was, at least for the moment, no longer flailing. He managed to slowly raise it up and drape it around his wife's shoulders. Little Amanda reached up with her small hand and grasped three of her father's fingers. Molly squeezed the remote, and first the preflash and then the real flash went off.

Amanda bounced in her mother's lap, startled but excited by the bright lights. Molly waited for her to settle down a bit before trying another exposure and, while she did so, she reflected on what a truly remarkable family portrait they were making. It wasn't just a woman and her husband and their child, a mother, father, and daughter all very much in love. It was also, in a very real sense, a portrait of the human race—of silence, of speech, and of telepathy, of past, present, and future, of where it had come from, where it is, and where it is going.

Molly's telepathy, here, now, at the dawn of the twenty-first century, had been an accident—the result of a single nucleotide having squeezed its way into her DNA. But the genetic code to produce the telepathy neurotransmitter was there, hidden, frameshifted into something else, in the DNA of every man and woman on Earth.

Molly's words came back to her: "Maybe someday far in the future, humanity might be able to handle something like this. But not now; it's not the right time."

Not the right time.

Pierre's discoveries had been astounding: it was all in there. Not just what we had been. Not just codes to make tails and scales and hard-shelled eggs. Not just our fishy and amphibious and reptilian past. Not just the commands that played out the dance of ontogeny apparently recapitulating phylogeny during an embryo's development. Not just leftovers and discards.

Not just *junk.*

Yes, the past was in there. But so was the future. So was the blueprint, the master plan, what we would become.

What was it she had said to Pierre, all those years ago? "God planned out all the broad strokes in advance—the general direction life would take, the general path for the universe—but, after setting everything in motion, he's content to simply watch it all unfold, to let it grow and develop on its own, following the course he laid down."

She squeezed the camera's remote again. Illumination was everywhere.

Amanda looked up at her father and moved her hands. *Why are we doing this?*

"We're doing this," said Pierre, "because we're a family." The words came out slowly but clearly.

Amanda's large brown eyes looked up at him. Her face contorted. She'd been trying for ages, practicing in secret with her mother. They'd even been interrupted one morning when Pierre had come up to the living room without them being aware of his arrival, but she'd never yet managed it. Still, she knew that this was indeed a very special moment, and so she tried again with all her might.

The sound was raw, like the tearing of coarse paper, more aspirated breath than anything else. But it was also unmistakable, at least to someone who had longed to hear it. "I love you," Amanda said, looking at her daddy.

Pierre thought something in French, but then, smiling at his wife and hugging her close, reformulated the same thought in English.

Life, thought Pierre Tardivel, *doesn't get any better than this.*

Epilogue

There are two tragedies in life. One is to lose your heart's desire. The other is to gain it.

—George Bernard Shaw,
winner of the 1925 Nobel Prize in literature

Thirteen Years Later

Valerie Beckett, president of the United States, looked out at the crowd of five hundred on the White House lawn, most of them sitting on the metal folding chairs provided for the occasion but some in wheelchairs. Beyond the wrought-iron fence around the yard, hundreds of additional spectators and tourists watched in wonder. It was a bright, sunny day, the sky a perfect cerulean bowl, the scent of roses in the air. Beckett's husband, First Gentleman Roger Ashton, smiled at her from the front row. Tiny TV cameras—so much smaller than the ones of just a few years before—were set up on thin-legged tripods. Flags rippled slightly in the gentle breeze.

"We are gathered today to honor a great human being," said Beckett, at the wooden podium with the presidential seal on its front. "His name is known to many of us as the co-winner with Shari Cohen-Goldfarb—who is here with us today—of a Nobel Prize for startling discoveries about the secrets locked in our DNA, discoveries that have changed our view of ourselves and our evolution. For some, no higher honor is possible, and I surely wouldn't presume to suggest that any medal that I could bestow is more significant. But it isn't really the medal that matters—it's the selfless work that it represents. For ten years, the man we are honoring led the fight to get a federal law enacted barring insurance companies in all fifty-one states from discriminating against the born and the unborn based on their genetic profiles or family histories. Well, as you all know, during the last session of Congress, that very principle was passed into law, and—"

She paused for the applause, then continued.

"—and so the Tardivel Bill is no more; it is now the Tardivel *Statute,* a new and binding law of the land. And today, we are gathered here to honor the memory of Dr. Pierre Jacques Tardivel, who fought until his dying day for its passage."

Molly, still beautiful at fifty, looked at her sixteen-year-old daughter Amanda. She missed her husband—God, how she missed him—but, still, Molly was grateful beyond words for Amanda, and for the special bond they shared.

Ready? thought Amanda.

Molly nodded.

I wish Dad could have lived to see this.

Molly took her daughter's hand. "He would be so proud of you," she whispered.

President Beckett continued, "I'm now going to ask Dr. Tardivel's widow, Molly Bond, and his daughter Amanda to come up and accept this medal with the thanks of the people of the United States of America."

Molly rose to her feet. She and Amanda—stocky, with bangs that hung down to her eyebrows covering the subtle shelf of bone at the base of her forehead—moved up to stand next to the president, who shook each of their hands in turn. Molly stepped to the microphone. "Thank you," she said. "I know this would have meant a lot to Pierre. Thank you all so much."

Amanda was still within her mother's zone. *I love you,* she thought. Molly smiled. Amanda couldn't really read her mind—but they were so close, so intertwined, the words didn't need to be spoken aloud for Amanda to know that Molly was thinking, *I love you, too.*

Amanda raised her hands and began to sign.

Molly leaned back into the mike, interpreting. "Amanda says she misses her father every day, and loves him very much. And she says she'd like to recite a short speech that was one of Pierre's favorites, a speech first made only a few hundred meters from this very spot half a century ago by another man who went on to win the Nobel Prize."

Amanda paused for a moment, then glanced at her mother, drawing strength from their bond. Then her hands began to move again in an intricate dance.

"'I have a dream,'" said Molly, giving voice to Amanda's gestures, "'that one day this nation will rise up and live out the true meaning of its creed: We hold these truths to be self-evident, that all men are created equal. I have a dream that my children will one day live in a nation where they will not be judged by the color of their skin but by the content of their character. I have a dream today.'"

Amanda paused. Molly wiped tears from her eyes. Then Amanda's hands moved once more. "By passing this law which makes us look beyond our genes," said Molly, interpreting the signs again, "that great dream of a nation in which all its people truly are considered to be created equal has come another step closer to reality."

Amanda lowered her hands and looked at her mother, sharing a special thought just with her. She then turned and looked out at the crowd, which was applauding wildly.

Pierre Tardivel's daughter smiled.

And a beautiful smile it was, too.

About the Author

ROBERT J. SAWYER is a Member of the Order of Canada, the highest honor bestowed by the Canadian government, as well as the Order of Ontario, the highest honor given by his home province. He was also one of the initial inductees into the Canadian Science Fiction and Fantasy Hall of Fame, the first-ever recipient of a Lifetime Achievement Award from the Mississauga Arts Council, and the first-ever recipient of Humanist Canada's Humanism in the Arts Award.

Rob is one of only eight writers ever to win all three of the world's top awards for best science-fiction novel of the year: the Hugo (which he won in 2003 for *Hominids),* the Nebula (which he won in 1996 for *The Terminal Experiment),* and the John W. Campbell Memorial Award (which he won in 2006 for *Mindscan).*

He's also won the Robert A. Heinlein Award, the Edward E. Smith Memorial Award, and the Hal Clement Memorial Award; the top SF awards in China, Japan, France, and Spain; and a record-setting sixteen Canadian Science Fiction and Fantasy Awards ("Auroras"). In addition, he's received the Crime Writers of Canada's Arthur Ellis Award for Best Short Story of the Year.

Rob's novel *FlashForward* was the basis for the ABC TV series of the same name, and he was a scriptwriter for that program. He also scripted the two-part finale for the popular web series *Star Trek Continues.*

A twenty-year resident of Mississauga, Ontario, his website and blog are at **sfwriter.com**, and on Facebook, Patreon, and Twitter he's **RobertJSawyer.**

Printed in Dunstable, United Kingdom

73424874R00211